THREE
PARTS
DEAD

■ ■ ■

THREE
PARTS
DEAD

Max Gladstone

TOR®

A TOM DOHERTY ASSOCIATES BOOK

NEW YORK

THREE PARTS DEAD

A Tor Book
Published by Tom Doherty Associates, LLC
175 Fifth Avenue
New York, NY 10010

www.tor-forge.com

Tor® is a registered trademark of Tom Doherty Associates, LLC.

Library of Congress Cataloging-in-Publication Data

Gladstone, Max.
  Three parts dead / Max Gladstone. — 1st ed.
      p. cm.
  "A Tom Doherty Associates book."
  ISBN 978-0-7653-3310-0 (hardcover)
  ISBN 978-1-4668-0203-2 (e-book)
  I. Title.
  PS3607.L343T47 2012
  813'.6—dc23

                                    2012019876

First Edition: October 2012

Printed in the United States of America

0 9 8 7 6 5 4 3 2 1

THREE
PARTS
DEAD

■   ■   ■

PROLOGUE

God wasn't answering tonight.

"Glory to Thy Flame, Thou Ever-burning, Ever-transforming Majesty," Abelard chanted, kneeling, before the glistening brass and chrome altar. He hated this part, after the call, when he waited for the response—when he waited and tried to tell himself everything was fine. If there were a real problem, warning flags would fall from the ceiling, alarms would sound, and higher-ups of the Crimson Order would rush in through the side doors, angry and officious.

If there were a real problem, plain Novice Technician Abelard, so young he still needed to shave the inside of his tonsure, wouldn't be all alone to deal with it.

Yet this was Abelard's fifth repetition of the prayer in the last hour. Five times he had bowed his head before the glorious Heart-Fire of the Lord, crackling eternally in its metal cage, five times said the words and opened his soul, brimming with devotion. He felt the flickering warmth in his heart, felt the divine heat that flowed from the altar to power the massed, frightful city of Alt Coulumb beyond the Sanctum walls. But the numinous presence of the Lord of Flame . . .

Well, it wasn't there.

It was a painful two thirty in the morning, which was why Abelard was on duty and not some bishop or elder priest. Lord Kos the Everburning had to be praised every moment of every day, of course, but some periods of rapturous worship were considered preferable to others. Abelard was tired, and though he wouldn't admit it, he was starting to worry.

He rose, turned from the altar, and reached into an inside pocket of his robe for a cigarette.

Savoring his first acrid breath of smoke, he walked to the window that dominated the rear wall of the Inner Sanctum, twenty feet tall and forty feet broad. Alt Coulumb spread out beyond the glass in spiderwebs of spun steel and granite blocks. An elevated train wound between the sharp metal spires of the Business District to the north, trailing steam exhaust into the slate-black sky. Invisible to the east beyond the Pleasure Quarters' domes and palaces, the ocean rolled against the freight docks, marking the city's edge with its ceaseless wash. The city of a nation—the city that *was* a nation.

Ordinary Inner Sanctums did not have windows, but then, Kos Everburning was not an ordinary deity. Most gods preferred to have privacy on earth and watch their people from the distant serenity of the heavens. Kos had survived the God Wars in part because He was not the type to wall Himself off from the world. You got a better angle on humanity from down here, He claimed, than from on high.

What Gods thought near was often distant for man, though, and even as Lord Kos took pleasure in His Sanctum's proximity to His people, Abelard was comforted by its remove. From this window he could see the beauty of Alt Coulumb's architecture, while the infinite small uglinesses of its inhabitants, their murders and betrayals, their vices and addictions, were so tiny as to be almost invisible.

He exhaled a plume of smoke and said to the city, "All right. Now let's see if we can't get you fired up."

He turned around.

In the aftermath it seemed to him that everything had gone a little out of order.

First, several doors burst open at once, and a number of bearded men in crimson robes rushed in, toss-haired and bleary-eyed and recently roused from sleep. All were shouting, and a disconcerting plurality of them were staring angrily at Abelard.

Then the alarms went off. All of them.

It is difficult for people who have never tended an Inner Sanctum to comprehend the number of things that can go wrong within one: deific couplings might uncouple or misalign, grace exchangers overheat, prayer wheels spin free of their prayer axles. Every potential problem required a unique alarm to help technicians find and fix whatever needed to be found and fixed with all possible speed. Decades past, some brilliant priest had thought to give each alarm the voice of a different piece of praise music: the keening "Litany of the Burned Dead" for a steam breach, the "Song of Glorious Motion" for extra friction on the hydraulics, and so forth.

The music of a hundred choirs burst from every corner of the Sanctum, and clashed into cacophony.

One of the senior Crimson Priests approached poor Abelard, the butt of whose cigarette still smoldered between his lips.

Abelard saw then what he should have noticed first.

The fire. The Everburning flame, on the altar of the Defiant, caged within its throne.

It was gone.

1

When the Hidden Schools threw Tara Abernathy out, she fell a thousand feet through wisps of cloud and woke to find herself alive, broken and bleeding, beside the Crack in the World.

By the grace of fortune (or something else), she landed three mere miles from what passed for an oasis in the Badlands, a stand of rough grass and brambles clustered around a brackish spring. She couldn't walk, but made the crawl by sunrise. Caked with dirt and dried blood, she dragged herself over sand and thorn to the muddy pool at the oasis's heart. She drank desperately of the water, and to pull herself from death's brink she also drank the life of that desolate place. Grass withered beneath her clutching fingers. Scrub bushes shrank to desiccated husks. The oasis died around her and she crumpled to the arid earth, wracked with wounds and deep illness.

Dream visions tore at one another in her fever, lent strength and form by her proximity to the Crack. She saw other worlds where the God Wars never happened, where iron ruled and men flew without magic.

When Tara regained consciousness the oasis was dead, its spring dry, grass and brambles ground to dust. She lived. She remembered her name. She remembered her Craft. Her last two months in the Hidden Schools seemed like a twisted hallucination, but they were real. The glyphs tattooed on her arms and between her breasts proved she had studied there, above the clouds, and the glyph below her collarbone meant they really did graduate her before they kicked her out.

She fought them, of course, with shadow and lightning—fought and lost. As her professors held her squirming over empty space, she remembered a soft, unexpected touch—a woman's hand sliding into her pocket, an alto whisper before gravity took hold. "If you survive this, I'll find you." Then the fall.

Squinting against the sun, Tara drew from the pocket of her torn slacks an eggshell-white business card that bore the name "Elayne Kevarian" above the triangular logo of Kelethras, Albrecht, and Ao, one of the world's most prestigious Craft firms. Professors and students at the Hidden Schools whispered the woman's name—and the firm's—in fear and awe.

A job offer? Unlikely, considering the circumstances, and even if so, Tara was not inclined to accept. The world of Craft had not been kind to her of late.

Regardless, her priorities were clear. Food, first. Shelter. Regain strength. Then, perhaps, think about the future.

Good plan.

She collapsed.

Silence settled over the Badlands.

A buzzard descended from the dry blue sky in tightening circles, like a wood chip in a draining pool. It landed beside her body, hopped forward. No heartbeat audible; cooling flesh. Convinced, it bent its head and opened its beak.

Tara's hand twitched up fast as a cobra and wrung the bird's neck before it could flee. The other gathering buzzards took the hint and wheeled to safety, but one bird cooked inexpertly over a fire of dry grass and twigs was more than enough to set a half-starved girl on her feet.

Four weeks later she arrived on the outskirts of Edgemont, gaunt and sun-blasted, seeing things that did not precisely exist. Her mother found her collapsed near their cattle fence. A lot of crying followed her discovery, and a lot of shouting, and more crying after the shouting, and then a lot of soup. Edgemont mothers were renowned for their practicality, and Ma Abernathy in particular had iron faith in the restorative powers of chicken broth.

Tara's father was understanding, considering the circumstances.

"Well, you're back," he said, a concerned expression on his broad face. He did not ask where she had been for the last eight years, or what happened there, or how she earned her scars. Tara would have thanked him for that had she known how. There were too many ways he could have said "I told you so."

That evening the Abernathy family sat around their kitchen table and settled on the story they would tell the other residents of Edgemont: When Tara left home at sixteen, she signed on with a traveling merchant, from whom she learned the fundamentals of Craft. The Hidden Schools never opened themselves to her, and at last, tired of dust and long wandering, she returned home. It was a good enough lie, and explained Tara's undeniable skill with contracts and bargains without stirring up any of the local fear of true Craftswomen.

Tara put the business card from her mind. The people of Edgemont needed her, though they would have chased her from town if they knew where she learned to use her talents. Ned Thorpe lost half the profit from his lemon crop every year, due to a bad arbitration clause in his reseller's contract. Ghosts stole dead men's bequests through loopholes in poorly written wills. Tara offered her services tentatively at first, but soon she had to refuse work. She was a productive citizen. Shopkeeps came to her to draft their pacts, farmers for help investing the scraps of soulstuff they eked out of the dry soil.

Over time she picked up the pieces of her childhood, hot cocoa and pitching horseshoes on the front lawn. It was easier than she expected to reacclimate herself to a country life without much Craft. Indoor plumbing was a luxury again. When summer came, she and her parents sat outside in the breeze or inside with windows shut and shades drawn to ward off heat. When cold wind blew they built fires with wood and flint. No elementals of air were summoned to fan the brow, no fiery dancers cavorted to warm cold halls. At school she had condemned such a life as simple, provincial, boring, but words like "simple," "provincial," and "boring" did not seem so pejorative to her now.

Once, she nearly took a lover, after a solstice dance on the village green. Staggering back tipsy and arm-in-arm with a boy she barely remembered from her days in Edgemont's two-room school, who had grown into a young man tending his family's sheep, she stopped to rest on a swell of ground and watch the stars in the fleeting summer night. The young man sat next to her and watched with her, but when he touched her face and the small of her back she pulled away, apologized, and left.

The days were long, and safe, but she felt something wither inside her as she lingered there. The world beyond Edgemont, the world of Craft more profound than a farmer's spring planting and the mending of small cuts and bruises, faded and began to seem unreal. Her memories of the Hidden Schools acquired the cotton haze of dream, and she woke once or twice from nightmares in which she had never left home at all.

The Raiders struck at night, three months after the solstice. Swift and savage, they took little, but at dawn three of Edgemont's watchmen lay on the field of battle, shrunken in death by a clinging curse that corroded anything that drew near. The villagers lifted the bodies on long spears of cold iron and buried them in a blessed grave. The chaplain said a few words, and as Edgemont bowed its collective head Tara watched him weave the town's faith into a net, taking from each man or woman what little soulstuff he or she could afford and binding it close about the loose earth. He was no Craftsman, but his Applied Theology was sound as such things went.

Tara was the last to leave the grave.

"I don't know how we'll manage." Father stood alone by their hearth after the funeral and before the wake, the whiskey in his glass the same color as their small early autumn fire. "They were good boys, and well trained. Held off the Raiders for years. We'll have to hire others, but we can't spare the price."

"I can help."

He looked back at her, and she saw a splinter of fear in his eyes. "You're not a fighter, Tara."

"No," she admitted. "But I can do more than fight."

"We'll manage." His tone left no avenue for appeal. "We've managed before."

She did not challenge him, but she thought: *The chaplain's skills are antiquated. He struggles to keep the village safe. What's the use of all I've learned, if I can't protect the people I care about?*

Her father turned from the fireplace and fixed her with his steady gaze. "Tara, promise me you won't . . . intervene."

Over the last few months Tara had learned that the best lies were lies not told. "Dad. Do you think I'm stupid?"

He frowned, but said no more. This suited Tara, because she would not have promised. Her father was not a Craftsman, but all pledges were dangerous.

That night she leapt from her second-story room, calling upon a bit of Craft to cushion her fall. Shadows clustered around her as she made her way to the fresh grave. Her father's voice echoed in her ears as she unslung the shovel from her back. She ignored him. This dark work would help Edgemont, and her family.

Besides, it would be fun.

She did not use her Craft to open the grave. That was one of the few rules a Craftswoman always obeyed, even at the highest levels of study. The fresher the bodies, the better, and Craft sapped freshness from them. Instead Tara relied on the strength of her arms, and of her back.

She pulled a muscle after the first three feet of digging, and adjourned to a safe distance to rest before attacking the dirt again. The shovel wasn't made for this work, and her hands were months out of practice, their old digging calluses gone soft. She had stolen her father's work gloves, but they were comically large on her and their slipping against her skin caused blisters almost as bad as those she intended to prevent.

It took an hour's work to reach the corpses.

They were buried without coffins, so the soil would reclaim their bodies faster and leech the poison magic from them. Tara hadn't even needed to bring a crowbar. Pulling the corpses out of the hole was harder than she expected, though. Back at school, they had golems for this sort of work, or hirelings.

When she grabbed the first body by its wrists, the Raiders' curse lashed out and spent itself against the wards glyphed into her skin. Harmless to her, the curse still stung, bad as when she chased her dog into stinging nettles as a girl. She swore.

Removing the corpses from the grave made more noise than Tara liked, but she couldn't work inside the pit. A grave's mouth circumscribed the night sky, and she wanted as much starfire as possible for the work at hand. It had been too long since she last stretched her wings.

In retrospect, the whole thing was a really, exceptionally, wonderfully bad idea. Had she expected the Edgemonters' gratitude when their dead comrades stumbled to their posts the next evening, groaning from tongueless mouths? At the same time, though, it was such a *brilliant* idea—simple, and so logical. Battle dead would not return much to the soil, but their corpses had enough strength left to fight for Edgemont. These revenant watchmen might not speak, and would be slower on the uptake than the living variety, but no wound could deter them, and the fiercest Craft would slide through their shambling corpses with no noticeable effect.

Nothing came from nothing, of course. The business of disinternment was strict. A dead body contained a certain amount of order. Locomotion required most of it, simple sensory perception much of the rest, and there wasn't a great deal left over for cognition. Laymen rarely understood. It wasn't like a Craftswoman *could* bring a person back to life unchanged and chose not to.

She drew the bent, sharp moonbeam that was her work knife from its place of concealment within the glyph over her heart, held it up to soak in starlight, and went to work on the twist of spirit and matter most folk still called *man* even after it had been dead for some time.

A revenant didn't require a will of its own, or at least not so robust a will as most humans thought they possessed. Slice! Or complex emotions, though those were more fundamental to the human animal and thus harder to pry free; she made her knife's edge jagged to saw them out, then fine and scalpel-sharp to excise the troublesome bits. Leave a fragment of self-preservation, and the seething rage left over from the last moments of the subject's life. There's almost always rage, Professor Denovo had explained patiently, time and again. Sometimes you have to dig for it, but it's there nonetheless. And buried beneath the detritus of thousands of years of civilization lay that most basic human power of identification: these are *my* people. Those others, well, those are food.

Textbook.

Tara gloried in the work. As her knife sang through dead flesh, she felt years of torment and the waking dream of Edgemont fade away. This was real, the acid-sharp scent of welded nerves, the soulstuff flowing through her hands, the corpses' spasms as she worked her Craft upon them. Forgetting this, she had forgotten a piece of herself. She was complete again.

Which she couldn't exactly explain to the torch-bearing mob.

Her cry when the Raiders' curse struck must have tipped them off, or else the darkness that spread across the village as she twisted starfire and moonlight through the warp and weft of her mind to bring a mockery of life to the dead. Maybe it had been the thunder of reanimation, as of a tombstone falling from a gruesome height.

Also, she had cackled as the corpses woke beneath her: a full-throated belly laugh, a laugh to make the earth shake. Good form required a guffaw at death's expense, though Professor Denovo always recommended his students practice discretion, perhaps for cases like this one.

"Raiders!" cried the front-most Edgemonter, a middle-aged wheat farmer with a round potbelly and the improbably heroic name of Roland DuChamp. Tara had settled his grandfather's will for him a month before. He was mad now with the fury of a man confronting something he cannot understand. "Back for blood!"

It didn't help that shadows still clung to Tara, shielding her from their sight. What the Edgemonters saw across the grave-yard was monster more than woman, wreathed in starfire and night-made-flesh, save where her school glyphs glowed through in purest silver.

The townsfolk raised their weapons and advanced uneasily.

Tara put away her knife and extended her hands, trying to look friendly, or at least less threatening. She didn't banish the shadows, though. Her return had been awkward enough for Mother and Father without bringing a torch-wielding mob down upon them. "I'm not here to hurt anyone."

The corpses, of course, chose that moment to sit up, growl with unearthly voices, and clumsily brandish weapons in their skeletal hands.

The mob screamed. The corpses groaned. And streaking through the darkness came the five remaining watchmen of Edgemont, the power of their office drawn about them. Halos of white light surrounded the watch, granting them spectral armor and the strength of ten men. Tara backed away farther, glancing about for an avenue of escape.

The eldest watchman, Thom Baker, raised his spear and called out, "Stand, Raider!"

Three of his comrades fell upon her revenants and wrestled them down. Tara had done her work well; recognizing their friends, the corpses put up little resistance. The odds stood at two to one against her, and, as her father knew, she was no warrior.

At this stage, dropping her cloak of darkness and trying to explain might not have done any good. They had caught her raising the dead. Perhaps she was not Tara Abernathy after all, but something wearing Tara's skin. They would cut off her head and move on to her family, make sure of the lot of them in one stroke. Justice would be swift, in the name of the Gods, fallen though most of them might be.

Tara was in trouble. The members of this mob were in no mood to discuss the valuable contribution her Craft could make to their lives. In their murmurs of anger and fear, she heard her doom.

A wind blew from the north, bearing cold and death.

Lightning split the clear night sky. Storm clouds boiled up from nothing, and torch-fires flickered and quailed. The glow from the watchmen's armor dimmed, and Tara saw their true forms beneath: Thom Baker's double chin and two-day stubble, Ned Thorpe's freckles.

Thunder rolled and a woman appeared, hovering three feet above the ground, long white scarf flaring in the fierce breeze. She wore a dark, severe suit, with narrow white vertical stripes as if drawn by a fine brush. Her skin was pale, her hair iron gray, her eyes open black pits.

Her smile, on the other hand, was inviting. Even welcoming.

"You are about to attack my assistant," she said in a voice that was soft, but carried, "who is helping your community for no fee but the satisfaction of working for the public good."

Thom Baker tried to say something, but she interrupted him with a look.

"We are required elsewhere. Keep the zombies. You may need them."

This time, Thom managed to form words: "Who are you?"

"Ah," the floating woman said. She held out a hand. Between her first two fingers she clutched a small white rectangle of paper, a business card identical to the one in Tara's pocket. Thom accepted the card gingerly as if it were coated in poison, and examined it with confusion. He had never seen paper before that was not in a schoolbook or a ledger.

"My name," the woman continued, "is Elayne Kevarian. I am a partner in the firm of Kelethras, Albrecht, and Ao." Tara heard the Edgemonters' feet shuffle in the silence that ensued. The corpses moaned again. "Please don't hesitate to contact me if you have any trouble with your new allies."

"Allies?" Thom looked down at the revenants. "What are we supposed to do with them?"

"Keep them away from water," she said. "They melt."

Another gust of wind came, and Tara felt herself borne up on wings of night—up, and away.

They were ten miles outside of Edgemont when Ms. Kevarian addressed Tara for the first time that evening. "That was a nasty bit of incompetence, Ms. Abernathy. If we are to work together, I trust you will be more circumspect in the future."

"You're offering me a job."

"Of course," Ms. Kevarian said with a bemused smile. "Would you rather I return you to your fellow man?"

She looked back at the vanishing village lights, and shook her head. "Whatever you're asking me to do, it has to be better than that."

"You may be surprised." They rose into clouds and thunder. "Our work keeps us a single step ahead of the mob. That's all. If you let your ego rule your reason, you'll find the villagers with pitchforks waiting, no matter how far you've traveled, no matter what you've done on their behalf."

A determined smile spread across Tara's face, despite the rebuke. Let Edgemont shake its torches; let the Hidden Schools rail and Professor Denovo fume. Tara Abernathy would live, and practice the Craft, in spite of them. "Yes, ma'am."

It's hard to read a codex in a storm, ten thousand feet in the air. The rain wasn't a problem; Tara sheltered herself and her books beneath a large umbrella. But the umbrella did not stop the wind, and when one is flying through the sky on a platform of solid nothingness, there is quite a lot of wind.

"In conflicts of deothaumaturgical interest, equity proceeds according to a paradigm originally formalized in the seventeenth century by—"

Just as the sentence was about to mean something, a particularly vicious gust tore the page from her fingers and flipped it, revealing a line of black spindly letters beneath, which read, "Chapter Seven: Personal Default."

She closed the book with a sigh and placed it on top of the stack. Near the bottom of the pile lay basic texts, tersely titled treatises the contents of which she had committed to memory years ago: Contracts, Remedies, Corpse. Atop them teetered more comprehensive works Ms. Kevarian had had borrowed from the library during their midnight pit stop in Chikal. Tara had planned to scan these during the flight, but they were too dense, relying on obscure tricks and arcane turns of theory she haltingly grasped back in school, but hadn't reviewed since.

She glanced up at Elayne Kevarian—Boss, she reminded herself, with the capital letter—and thought better of asking for her help. Ms. Kevarian was busy driving. She hovered fifteen feet in front of Tara, head cocked back, arms outstretched, and gripped bolts of lightning as if they were the reins of the clouds. Gale winds blew her hair about like billowing smoke, and raindrops burst into steam before they could wet the wool of her gray pinstriped suit.

Below them fell the rain, and below that stretched miles and miles of farmland. In the four decades since the God Wars ended, those farms and the villages dotted among them had recovered, prospered, and kept to themselves. Down there lived people who had never flown in their lives, never left their hometown, never seen another nation, let alone another continent. Tara had been one of them, once. No longer.

At that she felt a pang of guilt, and took from her shoulder bag a piece of parchment, a small writing board, and a quill pen. She began the letter:

> *Dear Mother and Father,*
>
> *I received an urgent job offer last night. I am excited by the opportunity, though I am sorry to leave home so soon. I intended to stay longer.*
>
> *It was wonderful to see you both. The garden is coming along well, and the new schoolhouse looks like it will be even bigger and better than the last one.*
>
> *Say good-bye and hello to Edgemont, and if you don't mind, please bake some cookies for the chaplain and say they're from me.* . . .

It was too nice a morning for Al Cabot to die. The storm had passed in the night, leaving shredded clouds to catch red fire as the sun swelled on the horizon. Another bank of thunderheads approached on the western wind, but for the moment the sky was clear. Al stepped out into his rooftop garden, teacup in hand, and took a moment to breathe. According to his doctor he needed to take more of these, or he wouldn't be around to breathe at all for much longer.

Al was a man grown nervously fat during a career of sitting behind a desk and shuffling from one poorly lit room to the next. He never had the time to sweat and acquire the hard-glazed muscles of a common road worker. He told his few friends that he had received the raw end of the deal, but nobody ever asked the road workers.

He savored the morning light, and with it a sip of nightshade tea—toxic to normal humans, but he was hardly normal anymore. Al was no Craftsman, but his occupation left its mark, like the coal miner's dusty cough or the farmer's crop-bent back. For half a century he had stood too close to darkness, and some of it crept into his bones.

It was almost over, though. His debts were nearly paid. Today he felt forty again, young and unburdened. His cares had passed with the storm, and once this last bit of business was complete he could stride into the dawn of his coming retirement.

His butler had left the morning's pertinent mail on the table by the azaleas. Perusing the shallow stack, Al found a few professional notes and a letter from his son, David, who had left years ago to rebuild the world. Whole continents had been shattered in the God Wars, David proclaimed when he set off on his quest. So many nations and cities are less fortunate than we of Alt Coulumb, and we owe them aid.

Al had not approved. Words were said that could not easily be unsaid after one's son shipped off to the Old World. Al tried to track him, making long and involved sacrifices to Kos and calling upon favors from priests and even from the Deathless Kings who frequented his chambers. All his efforts failed. Six months ago, however, David had returned on his own to propose a complex business deal, lucrative and good-hearted but of questionable legality. He remained an idealistic fool, and Al a standard-bearer of the old guard, but years of separation had taught them to avoid most of their habitual arguments. They were father and son, and they talked now. That was enough.

Al tapped the envelope, considered opening it, set it down. Wait. Start the day properly. He took a deep draught of tea, bitter and smoky and strangely sweet.

The azalea bush behind him rustled.

When the butler found his body forty-five minutes later, the strong, ruddy tea had spilled from his broken mug to mix with his blood. Al Cabot's body had contained a great deal of blood indeed, most now spread in a drying, viscous puddle around the shredded remnants of his flesh. The spilled tea barely diluted it at all.

2

Shale recovered his senses soon after sunrise and discovered to his dismay that he was fleeing down a back alley, covered in blood. The sticky red fluid was everywhere—soaked into his clothes, drying in his hair. It dripped from his brow, rolled down his cheek into his mouth. Worst of all, it tasted good.

The blood wasn't his most immediate problem. Glancing over his shoulder, he saw four black shadows with human shape, rough-featured as cave paintings, chasing him.

Blacksuits. Agents of Justice. The perfect police: you, a citizen, surrender your autonomy for one shift a day in exchange for a salary. Don a suit, and your mind is welded into the intricate network of Justice, seeking everywhere for criminals and enemies of the city. Justice patrols the streets and guards the populace. Justice is blind, but Justice sees all.

Justice was chasing him, implacable and tireless. It was only a matter of time before he faltered.

Goddess above, he was covered in blood. The last thing he remembered was climbing the façade of a tall building past immobile graven images of gargoyles toward a rooftop garden, to meet with Judge Cabot, the great fat man.

Another memory dawned out of rage-tinted mists: Cabot's face, contorted in pain, screaming. Bleeding. Fire rolled in to consume Shale, consciousness fled him, and he had opened his eyes here.

If the Blacksuits were after him—omniscient Justice wondering no doubt how this apparently normal human could outlast her agents at a full sprint, ducking down side alleys and weaving between obstacles, there leaping a trash can, here climbing a chain-link fence in two massive pulls—if the Blacksuits were after him. . . . Was it possible he had lost his mind? Surely. Possible. If he had been betrayed.

Had he killed Cabot?

His mind recoiled from this prospect, but he couldn't deny that a tiny part of him quickened in excitement at the thought of death. A tiny, desperate, hungry part.

Shit.

His people, his Flight, would know what to do, but they were hidden, and if he sought them, the Blacksuits would follow.

He needed a place of refuge, the last place they would look.

First, he had to evade pursuit. With stars set and the moon hidden in Hell, it was hard to change, but he had no other options. His heart beat faster, his nostrils flared. He stumbled forward, tripped, nearly face-planted onto the cobblestones. Smells and sounds rushed in to overwhelm him, muck and alley filth and the savory odor of fresh-fried dough from a street-side breakfast stand, the clatter of carriage wheels and the jingle of harness and the pounding of the Blacksuits' feet. Sweet, transcendent power pulped his mind and turned his muscles into mush.

And transformed that mush to living rock.

The bones of his shoulders broke, warped, and became whole again. Wings of stone burst from his smooth granite back and fanned to taste the air. His jawbone swelled to anchor sharp and curved teeth. Frail, fleshy human hands and feet split and opened like tree buds in spring, his great talons flowering from within.

The world slowed.

He bounded forth faster than Blacksuits could follow, now on two legs, now on four, leaping from wall to wall, talons leaving deep grooves in stone. He did not have much strength left, but sweet Mother, he could run. He could fly.

He was bound once more for Al Cabot's penthouse.

Behind him, the four Blacksuits stopped, their unearthly fluid motion transformed in an instant to the dead stillness of statues. They turned smooth, eyeless faces to one another, and if they conferred in some way that human beings could not hear, they gave no outward sign.

"Boss," Tara asked when she woke and saw beneath her a rolling field of blue and green, "why are we over the ocean?"

Ms. Kevarian sat cross-legged in midair, the backs of her hands resting on her thighs, a meditating monk in a pinstriped suit. A corona of starfire clung to her skin, woven by her will into the platform that held them both aloft. Gone were the lightning and gale-force winds she had used to blow them across a continent. The air was clear and crisp, the sky the light purple of imminent dawn. Clouds loomed on the horizon.

"Why do you think?" Ms. Kevarian replied.

Tara opened her mouth to answer, closed it again, then said, "This is a test."

"Of course it's a test. Reasonable people do not answer questions with further questions. I know from your performance at the Hidden Schools that I want to work with you, but I have not seen your logical abilities firsthand. I do not know whether to treat you as an assistant, or an associate. Show me."

A seagull flew beneath them as Tara thought. It looked up, squawked in astonishment, and plunged into a dive toward the water.

"There's only one answer that makes sense," Tara said at last, "but a piece of the evidence doesn't fit."

Ms. Kevarian nodded. "Continue."

"We're not going to another continent. Or to an island. Judging from the books you had me borrow, we've been retained for a more extensive case than you'd get on some Skeld Archipelago god-haven. Definitely on our side of the ocean—the New World, liberated territory. We were traveling east, and now we're traveling west, so we couldn't simply land at our destination. We had to fly past and wheel back around. We must be bound to a place where flying is restricted. In other words, a city still ruled by gods. But . . ."

"Yes?"

"If we're going to Alt Coulumb, why can't I sense it from here?"

Ms. Kevarian waited, and watched the western horizon with black, unblinking eyes. Below, amid the swells and breakers, Tara saw huge ships, tiny as toys from this height. Some sported sails bowed out by captive winds, others spouted thick gouts of smoke. Red-and-black ironwood hulls glowed with wards wrought by diligent Craftsmen. These were no mere bedraggled merchant vessels laden with cut-rate goods. On this coast of the New World, only Alt Coulumb could attract such a fleet. Two-thirds of all cargo from the Old World across the eastern ocean passed through that city's mighty port, from Iskar and Camlaan and the sweltering Gleb, from the regimented realm of King Clock and the icy wastes that bowed to Dread Koschei. Caravans and traders by the thousands bought the ships' wares in their turn, wholesale, and bore them west, up river and over road, to the free cities of Northern Kath.

"Everything else makes sense." Tara squinted at the ribbon of land visible beyond the ocean and beneath the high, threatening clouds, but could not see details from this distance. A few sharp peaks that might be the tips of skyscrapers, that was all. "The defenses to the Alt's west, south, and north are strong enough to keep us out. They're a trading and shipping power, though, so their ports have to be open. But if that's the home of Kos Everburning, the last divine city in the New World, I should be able to feel something, and I'm drawing a blank. No soulstuff, no starshine, no faith, no aura. As if the whole place were dead."

Ms. Kevarian nodded. Tara held her breath. Was that nod a good sign, or a bad one? "Perhaps you require a change of focus, Ms. Abernathy. Close your eyes, and wait."

She did. The world was black, stretching without pause save for Elayne Kevarian's silhouette, a coruscating pattern of lightning whose every facet mirrored its whole. This much Tara expected. Through closed eyes, a Craftswoman could see behind and beneath the world of gross matter. Ms. Kevarian's pattern was smudged, though, as if emptiness overflowed its edges.

Then the emptiness moved, and Tara realized it was not empty at all, but full of dim and pervasive light: a net of power more intricate than any human Craft Tara had ever seen, layer woven beneath layer upon layer, reaching to the heavens, plunging into the earth, arching over the sea. Within that net she felt the echoed, billowing heat of a distant fire.

"My god." Tara's jaw went slack. When she opened her eyes, Ms. Kevarian remained unmoved.

"Quite," she said. "You've never dealt with deities before, have you?"

"Not directly." She counted her breaths, and stilled her racing heart. "Once or twice at school, in a controlled environment. I know the theory, of course, but I've never seen anything like this." Tara closed her eyes again, and sat amazed by the complexity ahead.

Divine Craft was less obvious than the mortal variety, much as the mechanisms of a living creature were less evident to human sight than those of springs and steel gears. Few Craftswomen could see a god's work at first glance. Still, Tara had not expected the wards with which Kos shrouded his city to be so subtle, nor so large that she couldn't find their edge.

The Craft was difficult to master, half art, half science, and an extra half bull-headed determination. Most people could barely light a candle using their own soulstuff, let alone bind and direct the power nascent in the world around them. To bring a single corpse back to a semblance of animation required years of training and rigorous study. That grand construct, with its redoubts and fail-safes, its subtle interdependencies, would have taken a team of human Craftsmen fifty years to plan and shape. It was immense, organic, all-encompassing. Divine.

Looking on Alt Coulumb, Tara experienced for the first time the same emotions which, a century and a half before, had driven a handful of theologians and scholars to take up the Craft and become the first Deathless Kings: the awe at how well divine hands had made a thing, and the insatiable need to improve on that design. The backup filter, for example, which sheltered Alt Coulumb's harbor from ocean beasts, could use some work. And there was something else, some faint, pervasive problem she couldn't quite sum up in words.

"Well," Ms. Kevarian said, "you will soon have firsthand experience with a deity who deserves his title."

"But why," Tara asked, "does it look so cold?"

"What do you mean?"

"The wards are all there, sure. But where's the god inside them? He should shine through the whole system, but the wards are dark as ash. Is that normal?"

Ms. Kevarian opened her mouth to reply.

Before she could speak, however, the solid air upon which they sat lurched, quivered, and became distressingly permeable. Sunlight broke through the morning mist behind them and trapped the moment in liquid amber, sky and sea and distant cloud-covered city, blue waves and ships below.

They fell.

Flying isn't easy, and falling is harder than most people think. Fortunately, Tara had practice at both. The last time she fell, on the occasion of her so-called graduation from the Hidden Schools, she had time to prepare; three days of excruciating confinement preceded her quite literal downfall. On the other hand, her prison cell had weakened her, as did her struggle against her former professors. Perhaps those effects cancelled the advantages of foreknowledge.

Blind, unreasoning terror is the first obstacle to be overcome if one wishes to survive a fall from a great height, but it is by no means the most dangerous. Fear can cloud the mind, but if one is on good terms with fear, as Tara was, it can also aid concentration.

Wind whipped past her face and the ocean accelerated toward her. Tara saw a glint of starshine out of the corner of her eye—Ms. Kevarian, no doubt, saving herself. Was this another test? A potentially fatal one, if so, but Ms. Kevarian did not seem a tender or forgiving person.

Suspicion later, though. Falling now.

The second, and far more insidious, obstacle to surviving such a fall is the pleasant inevitability of death. The brain shuts down, and the soul watches from a distance as the body tumbles at ever-increasing speed toward doom. This is because, though instinct is good at many things, it's stupid about death. The body knows that any monkey falling thousands of feet to a distant sea would be dead in short order, so it starts to relax. There's an enlightenment to be attained in these plummeting moments that men and women spend years in monasteries trying to achieve.

But Tara wasn't a monkey. She wasn't even precisely a human being anymore, and whatever her body's opinion on the matter, she would not give up.

Eight hundred feet. Falling faster.

Ms. Kevarian no doubt knew an elegant solution to this problem, something grand and complicated, involving perilous pacts with demonic entities. Tara had no such resources at her disposal. All but the strongest stars had fled the rising sun, and what little of their light remained was weak. She could only rely upon her own mind. She hoped that would be enough.

Ignoring the chemical acceptance inundating her brain, Tara extended her awareness beyond the limits of her skin and made her soul flat and broad as a geometric plane, infinite in reach. She became aware of Ms. Kevarian's falling body, of a flock of gulls a mile to the south, of flitting wisps of cloud and vapor.

When her senses were broad as the surface of a great lake, she closed them off, made them impenetrable and solid as old wood.

Some people thought matter and spirit were different substances engaged in a delicate dance. The first principle of Craft, which had taken thousands of scholars an embarrassing length of time to comprehend, was that matter and spirit were in truth different aspects of the same substance, and there were tricks for making one act like the other. If a broad piece of cloth, stretched taut by the wind, could slow her fall, so, too, could spirit.

Spirit, of course, is more permeable than matter under normal conditions. If one were foolish enough to rework one's soul completely into matter, one would become a limp sack of flesh, a drooling idiot who might barely qualify as alive for the moment it took her to forget to breathe. There was a fine line to tread: concentrate, but don't destroy, your consciousness. Spread your soul wider than any parachute, and slowly, slowly, *slowly* (but maybe a little faster than that, because now you're only five hundred feet up) congeal your thoughts and feelings until they can affect physical matter, and a few square miles of empty air start to resist the passage of your body and soul.

Few people have felt their soul billow out behind them like a parachute. During Tara's previous fall, she was numb from battle and imprisonment, and hadn't appreciated how much it hurt.

She screamed. Not a normal scream of pain, but a deep and blind cry as reason deserted her. Of all the screams cataloged in the encyclopedic audio library of the Hidden Schools, Tara's bore the closest resemblance to the scream of a man whose abdomen was being devoured by a jagged-clawed insect that wore a child's face.

After the scream came oblivion. She was simultaneously a tiny feather of a body drifting down to a rolling ocean, and a diffuse cloud of soul, one with the sky, one with the wind. A thousand prickling tender touches lit upon her, as if she was caught in a rainstorm and the raindrops were love.

That's new, she thought, before she hit the water.

Abelard sat in the confessional, smoking. He hadn't been able to stop for two days. If he so much as paused between inhalations, the shakes began. He could barely catch a half hour's sleep at a time before he woke, trembling and desperate for a drag from the cigarette that lay, ember somehow still glowing, by his bedside.

He should have been tired. Maybe he was, but the shakes were worse than exhaustion. They manifested first in his fingertips and toes, then crept up the limbs, taking root in his forearms and calves before clutching at his groin and chest. He didn't know what might happen if he let them grip his heart. He didn't want to find out.

"It's normal," the Cardinal's doctor had told him when he reported his tremors the previous evening. "More intense than I expected, but normal. As an initiate of the Discipline of the Eternal Flame, you smoke between three and five packs of cigarettes a day. God's grace has protected you from the ill effects of tobacco addiction, but under the current circumstances, His beneficence has been withdrawn."

The doctor's advice did not make Abelard feel better. Deep nausea clenched his stomach as he listened, and had not left him since. Even here, in God's own confessional, he felt empty, deserted. The doctor warned him to quit, or cut back, but Abelard would not listen. He was dedicated to his Lord, no matter what.

The confessional was cramped and spare, walled to his right by a fine grille. His side was well lit, and the confessor's side dark. He knew his confessor's identity, though. Not strictly permitted, but this was an unprecedented situation.

"Tell me, my son," said Senior Technical Cardinal Gustave, "did you notice anything strange before the alarms sounded?" His deep voice resounded in the confines of their confessional. A Church leader for decades, head of the Council of Cardinals, Gustave was accustomed to addressing great halls and inveighing against injustice. Years of leadership and Church politics had rendered him less deft at supporting a single troubled soul. He was trying, but he was tired.

Abelard's biceps shook, and his thighs. *Hold, dammit,* he told himself. *The Cardinal is watching. The confessing man sits bereft of God's grace, seeking restitution, and does not deserve the taste of flame. You lasted before until the spasms reached your shoulders and the fork of your legs. You can do it again.* "There was nothing out of the ordinary, Father." His lips were still dry. He licked them once more. *The Cardinal remains steadfast. Why can't you?* "Nothing out of the ordinary, on the technical side. All readouts nominal. Steam pressure low, but within tolerance."

"You reported that the Most Holy was reluctant to answer your prayer?"

The heavy scratch of Cardinal Gustave's pen sounded like stone tearing. The confessional walls loomed on all sides. "You know how it goes, Father." Abelard gestured weakly with his cigarette. The ember at its tip danced a trace in the air.

"I know many things, my son," Gustave said, "but there are outsiders approaching to help us, and they will not be familiar with the particulars of serving our God."

"Yes, Father." If only he would turn away for an instant, or blink. "I . . . Ah . . . Um." Gustave's face was barely visible in the darkness of the confessor's compartment. Hollow cheeks, high forehead, bushy eyebrows. That mustache grown a decade and a half ago, which never went out of style because it was never in style. He's here to help, not judge, Abelard told himself. Take comfort in him, because nothing else remains to comfort you. "It sometimes takes a while for me to properly prepare my mind for union with the Everburning Lord. God is great, and I am young, and weak. Sometimes I come before him with my soul unshriven. Sometimes, try as I might, I cannot give my offering with a pure heart." He cursed himself inwardly. He sounded like a pervert, or an apostate. He hurried on. "Sometimes the Consuming Fire of His Grace is simply . . . elsewhere. Gods are always present, but They don't always pay attention. Like in Lehman's parable about the monk guarding the pantry. He can only watch one set of cabinets at a time, and the rats get in."

"Thank you," Cardinal Gustave said when Abelard stopped for breath. "That will be quite sufficient."

Talking had distracted him for a wonderful moment. His chest began to twitch. He felt so cold.

"Tell me, my son, what methods did you undertake to attract the attention of the Most Fierce?"

This part, at least, did not make him feel ashamed. "I intoned the Prayers for the Coming Flame, polished the conduits on the Throne, and recited the first ten stanzas of the Litany of the Burned Dead."

Gustave nodded and made more notes. While the Cardinal's attention was on the paper, Abelard cupped mouth and cigarette with one hand, and sucked in tobacco-stained air. The cigarette flame flared in the confessional darkness, and his quivering muscles stilled. When he looked up, he saw Gustave waiting. The other man's expression was illegible through the grille. He might have been an exquisitely crafted doll with human features.

This is what we have become, Abelard thought. Seemings without souls, cut off from one another by our fear.

"I'm sorry, Father, I'm so sorry, but the experience, the moment, Lord Kos . . ." He gestured vaguely at the cigarette.

Gustave bowed his head. "I understand, my son."

"Are we in trouble, Father?"

"I do not believe so."

"You said there were outsiders coming."

"These problems are more common beyond our walls than within our blessed City. There are firms that resolve such matters with speed, efficiency, and discretion."

"They'll help us?"

"They're the best we could find." Gustave's eyes were gray, fierce, and confident. Iron towers of faith could have been built on the strength of his gaze. "Professionals. We're safe in their hands."

The tips of Abelard's fingers and toes began, once more, to twitch.

Tara floated in a cold womb, wrapped in sunlight. Fragmentary dreams grasped her and loosed her again into unconsciousness. She was six years old, running in the fallow fields of her father's farm beneath the black angry belly of a thunderstorm. Lightning sparked in the clouds, flashed and crackled, bridging earth and heaven. She raised her hands, frail fingers cupped, and caught it.

Something long, narrow, and heavy collided with her ribs, and she remembered that she needed to breathe. She thrashed in the waves with limbs of twigs and paper, and coughed up a lungful of saltwater. She heard a voice.

"Catch the line, woman!"

Line was what sailors called rope, her bedraggled brain recalled. That was what had struck her in the side, like a lead weight: a wet length of corded hemp, a line to salvation. Her hands sought blindly, grasping it before she sank again. The rope grew taut and pulled her halfway out of the water with a heave that almost tore her arms free of their joints. Her body slammed into a slick, smooth surface.

Her warm pink stupor split like an egg from within and opened upon a brilliant day. The right-hand side of the world was sky and ocean, and the left a wall of dark, wet wood: a keel. Tara followed the rope up the side of the ship with her eyes and saw a man leaning over the deck's railing to look down at her. He was silhouetted against the clouds.

Someone on the other end of the rope heaved again. Another wash of pain drew Tara's legs free of the water and left her dangling and dripping against the keel. Black dust and fragments of charcoaled wood stained her clothes and flaked off on her face.

"We've caught a young lady, boys," the silhouette called over his shoulder. "Or a young woman, at any rate."

She gulped in breath and, recovering her voice, shouted, "Stop the torture! Hold the rope, and I'll make my own way up."

"With those skinny arms, and you waterlogged to half again your normal weight? I'll not believe that."

"If your last couple pulls are any indication, I'll make my way up with these skinny arms or without any arms whatsoever."

"Well said! Hold her steady," the silhouette advised his invisible assistants.

She hung dripping until certain the other sailors would heed her interlocutor. Satisfied, she planted her feet against the keel, and, with agonizing slowness, began to walk up the side of the ship.

"Keep climbing this slow and we'll be in port before you reach the deck."

"I prefer to . . ." Pull, step. Breathe. Pull, step. ". . . to take a measured pace!"

"What are you measuring it against?"

Pull. Step. "Not your tongue, certainly." To her left, she saw a rich and massive ship, and a third past that one. In the distance, she made out the green-black ribbon of the horizon, spiked with pinnacles, towers, minarets. The great city approached. Clouds brooded above it and spilled out over the water.

"What's your name, sailor?"

"Raz," the shadow called down. "Raz Pelham, of the *Kell's Bounty*, bound from Iskar to Alt Coulumb by way of Ashmere. What's yours, beauty?"

She laughed harshly. Whatever she looked like, drenched and half-drowned, she doubted it was beautiful. At least bantering with this sailor took her mind off the strain of climbing his ship. "Tara Abernathy, of nowhere in particular." She spat a flake of charcoaled wood out of her mouth. Free of the water, she saw that burn scars tiger-striped the hull of the *Kell's Bounty*, save for a few undamaged spots where new planks marked the site of hasty repairs. "Do you know your ship is falling apart?"

"We're keenly aware," he replied. "A few days ago we ran into a spot of trouble in Kraben's Pillars west of Iskar, but we had little time for repairs before a client hired us for a speedy passenger run to Alt Coulumb. We'll dry-dock here, with luck."

"I should have thought a swift ship like this could outrun any trouble."

"Ah, there's your error. You assume we were running from the trouble, not toward it."

She paused to breathe, and rest her aching arms. "Why not refuse the passenger? Seems dangerous to sail while damaged."

"Does the *Kell's Bounty* look like one of those fat-heeled merchantmen yonder, rich enough to accept and refuse commissions on a whim?" He slumped against the railing. "My arms are open to all who pay, though I do wish I were more my own master and less the client's slave."

"I know that feeling."

"What form of clients would a lady like yourself have?" he said with a leer.

She almost laughed, almost lost her grip on the rope, almost tumbled back into the water. She would not allow such a lapse before this man. "No clients, but my new boss is a bit of a witch."

He didn't respond. Pull, step. Two feet. One.

Raz reached down to take her outstretched hand. Her eyes adjusted. His skin was brown as old, worked mahogany, and he gripped her forearm with fingers just as smooth. He pulled her up one-handed with no more trouble than he might have taken to raise a bottle of beer. The railing brushed her shins. When he set her down on the gently pitching deck, she saw his body. Muscular, yes, but too thin to hold such preternatural strength.

He smiled, and she saw the tips of fangs peek beneath his upper lip. His eyes were the color of a dried scab, and deep as an ocean trench.

She exhaled. "Thank you for the hand, sailor."

Raz laughed. "Well done! Not many meet my gaze and stand on the first try. Especially after almost drowning." He clasped her shoulder and squeezed. "Good to see you're not all tongue."

She measured her breath. Her arms shook. "Thank you. You're a vampire."

"While you're on my vessel," he said, "you might as well call me Captain. For the crew's sake."

Still wobbling on her feet, Tara looked about the broad deck. It was busy with sailors: the three who had held the rope steady for her to climb, and twelve more tying off lines and raising sheets and swabbing decks, preparing the *Kell's Bounty* for arrival in port.

She would have seen more, but her attention was occupied by a single figure, pale, slender, female, holding a steaming mug of coffee. The fall had not wrinkled Ms. Kevarian's suit. Behind her, stacked on the deck neatly as if carried aboard by a conscientious porter, rested Tara's books and their luggage.

"Thank you for rescuing Ms. Abernathy, Captain," Ms. Kevarian said with a quick nod to Raz.

"Always a pleasure to be of service, Lady K. If you don't mind me saying, this one has a nice mouth on her." He winked at Tara, who ignored him. "I have to run below before I get any more of a tan. Captain Davis'll be up in a flash if you need anything."

"Won't you stay and catch some sun?" Ms. Kevarian asked pleasantly.

"Oh, no," Raz replied, already halfway down the ladder into his cabin. "You know me, crazy lady. I don't brown. I burn."

"Perhaps tonight, then."

"I'm for the Pleasure Quarters soon as the sun sets. It's been awhile since my last visit to Alt Coulumb, and I fancy a drink. Come find me if you're interested in sharing one."

When he had slammed and latched the trapdoor behind him, a cool silence settled between Tara and Ms. Kevarian. The older woman sipped her coffee. The younger stood there, dripping.

"A witch?" Ms. Kevarian said, bemused. "I'd think you'd give me more credit than that, Ms. Abernathy. Riding broomsticks, consorting with unholy powers. Who has the time for such pleasantries anymore? Why, I haven't been on a date since the late eighties."

"Do I pass the test?" Tara tried to keep her voice level, but adrenaline stuck its cat claws into her heart, and her voice tightened at the wrong moment.

"I beg your pardon," Ms. Kevarian said.

"You knew we were going to fall, Boss. You had this boat set up to catch us. The whole thing was a test."

"Hardly."

"So it's a coincidence that we crash-land onto a boat captained by your vampire friend?"

A small audience of sailors had gathered. They looked to Ms. Kevarian for her reply, but soon shuddered and looked away. Something about her made the eyes cringe. Maybe it was the way her dark gray suit soaked in the light, maybe it was the way steam from her coffee cup swirled about her like a demon's wreath of flames. Maybe it was the neon yellow smiley face on the cup's side.

"Flight near Alt Coulumb is interdicted by divine wards," Ms. Kevarian said, "but we are more than a thousand feet beyond their edge. I intended for us to land on this ship, and for Raz to bear us into port. I was every bit as surprised as you by our fall."

Confusion blunted Tara's anger. "People do business in Alt Coulumb all the time. There must be a shuttle to get them through the wards. Why bother with Captain Pelham?"

"Water taxis receive most incoming flights. We didn't take one because professionals use them. Mages, vampires, businessmen and businesswomen of all sorts. Someone would recognize me, and guess what I've come to do."

"Why be so secretive about Craftwork? Unless our client is so big that . . ." She recalled the great dim embers of Alt Coulumb's wards, and remembered, too, the tingle against her soul as she fell, before she lost consciousness: the love like fire, or the fire like love. That had been the touch of Kos's power, beautiful but faint—fainter even than the captive Gods she'd studied at school, and those were more ghosts than divine spirits, eviscerated and lonely.

The immensity of what she was about to say choked her off.

Ms. Kevarian drew close. Tara smelled her: coffee, lavender, magic, and something else, strange and unnamable. She whispered into Tara's ear.

"Kos the Everburning is dead. We're here to bring him back to life."

3

The towers of Alt Coulumb dwarfed the gargantuan supply ships moored at the docks below, even as the ships themselves dwarfed the ferries that plied the Edgemont River back home.

Tara stared at those buildings, stunned. They were monuments to power. Every arch, every spire, every massy pillar proclaimed the city's might. Even the Hidden Schools in their airy and metallic splendor hadn't seemed so aware of their own grandiosity, or so proud of it.

It had taken armies to tear rock and metal from the earth to build Alt Coulumb, hosts of priests to beg fire from their god and twist that ore into skeleton frames. Legions broke their backs and arms and fingers piling stone on stone, melted skin and burned hair fusing steel with steel. These buildings remembered the taste of blood sacrifice, and hungered for more.

"Ah," Ms. Kevarian said, joining Tara at the guardrail. "I missed this place. It has such . . . attitude."

"You've worked here before, Boss?"

"Soon after the God Wars. It was less welcoming then. The Church hired us to fix a problem beyond the range of the priests' Applied Theology." She said that term with controlled scorn. "The whole affair was quite secret at the time, as I'm sure you can imagine. Alt Coulumb never entered the war, and Kos remained neutral, but there would have been public outcry had our involvement become known. It was hard to get office attendants, because everyone we interviewed was afraid we'd steal their souls." One corner of her mouth crept up.

"What was the job? If it's not a secret."

"Oh, no. That's been public for a while." People swarmed the docks, dockhands loading and unloading, locals greeting passengers and haggling for the small luxuries that sailors smuggled to pad their meager wages: charms of pear wood, dyed silks, intricately woven rugs, pirate editions of the latest Iskari serial novels. Ms. Kevarian pointed to the crowd's edge, where stood a line of figures dressed in black. No. Not dressed. Enclosed in black. Annihilated by it. Featured like unfinished statues: suggestions of eyes, a swell of nose, a hint of mouth. Hands clasped behind their backs. Mostly men, but a few women, too, each one pierced through head and heart and groin with a strand of lightning Tara doubted anyone here but Ms. Kevarian and herself could see.

"What are those?"

"Justice. They used to be the City Guard, anointed of Seril Green-Eyed, Seril Undying, the goddess upon whom Kos's priesthood relied to keep order in the city."

"But Seril was killed in the fifties, in the God Wars."

"I'm glad to see you know your history. Yes. Seril and her warrior-priests rode off to battle, not caring whether Alt Coulumb followed them. She died at the hands of the King in Red, and left the city without protectors." Ms. Kevarian took another sip of coffee. "Kos's Church hired me, and a senior partner from the firm, to do what we could. The Blacksuits were part of the result. I met Captain Pelham on that first trip. He was still human then. As, I suppose, was I."

They started down the ramp, followed by a pair of deckhands who carried their belongings. Tara looked about, hoping to catch a glimpse of Raz, but he had ensconced himself belowdecks. The sun was far above the horizon, and he needed his rest. Two captains, two crews, one for the night watch, one for the day—no wonder the *Kell's Bounty* flourished in such a cutthroat business, despite being one of the smaller ships currently moored at Alt Coulumb's docks.

How cutthroat was their business, after all? Tara had asked some of the sailors about Captain Pelham's "spot of trouble," but they evaded her questions, and when pressed they paled and drew away. Captain Davis had been no more communicative.

A driverless carriage waited at the bottom of the ramp, drawn by a black monster of a horse so huge that Tara could not imag-

ine anyone daring to fit it to harness. It pawed the ground and
fixed her with an intelligent and malicious eye.

She quickened her step and followed Ms. Kevarian into the
darkness of the carriage, where they sat amid black leather and
velvet curtains as their few pieces of luggage were loaded after
them. When Tara closed the door, the coach rolled forward as
though the crowd were vapor.

Ms. Kevarian set her mug down, steepled her fingers, and said
nothing for some time.

"I'm sorry I called you a witch," Tara said.

It took a moment for Ms. Kevarian to notice she had spoken.
Even then, she did not respond.

"Boss?"

"Ms. Abernathy. I've wrestled with gods and demons. My ego
is hardly so fragile as to be bruised by an associate's poor choice of
words. I'm thinking."

Associate. Pride bloomed inside Tara. "Just thinking?"

"There's never any 'just' about thinking, Ms. Abernathy."

The bloom shriveled. No matter. Pride was dangerous, anyway. "What are you thinking about?"

"Strategy. We have a daunting case before us, and it has grown
more complex in the last two hours."

"You're talking about our crash."

"My Craft does not fail without reason. Something struck us
in the air, overpowering as a god's flight interdict, and swift
enough to shred my Craft without warning. Had either of us been
slow to respond, we might never have made it to shore. We were
meant to die, I think, and our deaths to look like an accident. Pilot
error."

"What do we do?" Tara summoned a fragment of lightning
and set it dancing between her fingertips. "Find the person who's
gunning for us?"

"Unfortunately, no. Pleasant as it would be to hunt our assailant down, I have business to attend to. And," she said as
their carriage took a sharp turn onto a side thoroughfare, "so do
you."

Thirty minutes later Tara stood on a cobblestone sidewalk before the double doors of a huge building. She didn't have much experience with skyscrapers, but this one was rich by any standard, decorated with marble and gold leaf. Gargoyles glowered from its ornately adorned façade.

Deep, old grooves marred the stonework in angular patterns, like rune writing but unfamiliar to Tara. They didn't fit the skyscraper's stark, elegant decor, and she wondered why they had not been patched or repaired.

The brass-flashed double doors swung open when she approached, as Ms. Kevarian had told her they would. The doors were simple constructs. They checked for power, and yielded to it. Before the end of the God Wars, it was rare for a citizen of Alt Coulumb to possess much Craft. This building hadn't changed its locks since. Quaint.

Tara advanced over the floor's marble tiles, her gaze fixed upon the lifts at the far end of the hallway. The walls were lined with mirrors, the building's second line of defense. If she caught her own eye in the glass, she would stand entranced by her reflection until security arrived. If she looked into the mirrors but not at herself, she might simply wander through their surface and never be seen again in the real world, unless the building sent someone to fetch her back.

She reached the lift without incident, stepped inside, turned the dial to the forty-seventh floor, and pressed the GO button. The doors rolled closed, leaving her trapped in a shining brass box. With a lurch, the entire assembly began to rise.

She schooled herself for her encounter with Judge Cabot. This would be her first professional meeting as a full-fledged Craftswoman, and her chance to make a good impression in Alt Coulumb. She ignored the nervous tremor in her chest. "Your Honor," she said to the walls of the empty lift. Good. Lead off strong and with respect. "Elayne Kevarian of the firm Kelethras, Albrecht, and—" No. Not quite. Don't be too arrogant, Ms. Kevarian had said. Step in, pay your respects. Be direct and businesslike. "Elayne Kevarian sent me to tell you she has agreed to represent the

Clergy of Kos Everburning, and wishes to speak with you at your convenience."

She wondered who this Judge was, and how well Ms. Kevarian knew him. A city the size of Alt Coulumb had many lesser Judges, the better to help Craftsmen coordinate the reanimation of people, animals, and great Concerns, but this case . . . This case was beyond any Craft Tara had ever expected to touch.

The thought made her heart race with excitement.

The engine driving this lift ran on steam pressure, steam produced from water by heat. Alt Coulumb's generators derived that heat not from felled trees or the black magic oils of the ancient dead, but from the grace of a god who, ages ago, took the people of this twist of coastline as his own.

If Ms. Kevarian was to be believed, that god was dead. His gifts of fire and heat would persist until the dark of the moon, when debts resolve and prices fall due. Then, they would fade. Tara stood in a metal box dangling by a thin cord over a thirty-story drop, and the other end of that cord was held by the promise of a ghost.

Had Tara not known better, she would have been unnerved.

The lift rocked to a halt, and its doors rolled open.

Three Blacksuits stood in the ornate lobby on the gold-thread Skeldic rug: two male, one female. Light shone through the crystal ceiling off their molten obsidian skin. Tara checked an indrawn breath when she saw them. Justice's minions. That was what Ms. Kevarian had called them, back at the dock.

She told herself to relax. She had done nothing wrong.

Of course, in her experience, this rarely meant one had nothing to fear from the authorities. Forcing a fog of bad memories aside, she stepped into the lobby, chin high and hands clasped primly before her. She had changed on the *Kell's Bounty* from her bedraggled sea-soaked clothes into her second, and far more formal suit, an executioner's black against her nut-brown skin. She was glad of the suit's severity as three blank reflective faces confronted her. She returned their stare.

"I want to speak with Judge Cabot."

Judge Cabot is not available. The figures' lips did not move, but Tara heard three voices nevertheless, or the nightmare echoes of three voices, not-quite-sounds on the edge of hearing. *What business did you have with him?*

"I . . ." Dammit, she would not be quelled by a trio of professional security nightmares. Steel yourself, woman, and get on with it. You're not a farm girl come to beg for favors. You have a purpose here. "I'm a Craftswoman from the firm Kelethras, Albrecht, and Ao, here to speak with Judge Cabot. Do you know when he will return?"

Yes. They raised their faces toward the skylight with a unity even more unsettling than their voices. *He will return when the moon is broken and the land fades, when the waters rise and burn to steam, when the stars fall and the Everburning Lord rises.*

"Ah." She paused, thinking. "He's dead."

As of this morning.

She heard a high-pitched and prolonged scream behind the double doors that led into Cabot's apartment. "Who's that?"

The butler.

She waited.

He discovered the body, and thus is likely to be involved. We are ascertaining the details of the event.

Discovered the body? Involved? "You think Cabot was murdered."

It is likely. Considering the condition of the body.

Another scream. This one broke into deep, powerful sobs.

"Sounds like it hurts, this 'ascertaining.'"

Most do not find it pleasant, but Justice must be served. After we are done, we will ease his memory of the pain.

"Tidy."

Economical. Pain is a valuable resource, and should be used sparingly.

Tara crossed her arms and looked from one to the next to the last. Murder. Because Judge Cabot was involved in a perfectly routine, if large-scale, Craft proceeding?

If she returned to Ms. Kevarian with this scrap of information, she'd be sent right back to learn more. Besides, she was on the scent.

"Listen. My boss wants me to see Judge Cabot. How do I know he's not still alive and telling you to lie to keep me out?"

What purpose would that serve?

"How should I know? I can't go back to my boss empty-handed. She'd use my skin for shadow puppets, and if I was lucky she'd let me die first, and then she'd come looking for whoever stood in my way."

That is unfortunate for you.

"My point is, it will take a lot more than some screams to convince me you've really got a murder scene here."

You believe we would lie?

"I'm new in town. I see a trio of moving statues and I don't know what to expect."

We are Justice. We have rules.

This wasn't working. Change tactic. They like rules, do they? "What are your rules, then?"

The just heart is lighter than a feather. They raised their faces heavenward again. *We weigh hearts.*

"Ah."

The Blacksuits seemed comfortable with silence. The repeated cries from the Judge's apartment did not appear to perturb them, either.

"There are other rules, right?"

The Book of Regulations is twenty pages long.

"Not so bad."

Appendix A is three thousand one hundred twelve. Pause. *We will not repeat them aloud. Copies are on public display at the Temple of Justice as a service to the City.*

She tried to press past them as they spoke, but they moved, more like flowing lava than people, to block her way.

We are not permitted to let you pass. Our examination of the scene is incomplete.

Tara was about to give up and storm off, cursing cities and law enforcement and Elayne Kevarian for good measure. She turned around and raised her foot. Had she set it down, the momentum of that step would have carried her to the street and on with the rest of her life.

She turned back to the sentinels.

"You're examining the body?"

Yes.

"You know how to do that?"

We are waiting for experts.

"I'm an expert."

They said nothing.

"I'm a Craftswoman. A graduate of the Hidden Schools. I'm as competent to judge the state of a corpse as anyone in the City."

You are not approved by the Council of Justice, nor certified as an examiner.

"The examiner isn't here, though, is she? I am. Every minute you spend waiting in the foyer, you lose valuable information. Evidence decays faster than the corpse, and your killer is racing to cover her tracks."

The information of which you speak will be gathered by the proper authorities.

Tara smirked. "What proper authorities?" She extended one arm, palm up, and pulled back her sleeve with the other hand. At first, there was no way to tell if the Blacksuits were looking, their pupils invisible beneath their ebon shells, but they turned toward her when the sunlight began to die. Tara's forearm had been brown and unmarked when she pulled up her sleeve, but as shadows deepened and the world went gray, traces of silver light appeared on her skin.

Her glyphs resembled spiderwebs laid by machine. Precise lines wove around her arm, spirals devouring spirals, hermetic diagrams inscribed with the script of half a dozen languages, most of them dead. A repeated symbol interrupted this pattern along the course of her radial artery: circle, nested within triangle, within circle, the mark of the Hidden Schools. The glyphs' light was strong enough to cast shadows.

The Blacksuits retreated a fraction of a step.

"I've come a long way," Tara said. "I can help. Now, please, let me inside."

———

She nearly threw up when she saw the body, but she wasn't about to give her Blacksuit escort the satisfaction. Blasted thing would probably lock her up for vomiting all over a crime scene.

Judge Cabot had been what an older century would have called a portly man, the kind who hit his second chin at the age of twenty-nine and decided there was no point going back. His figure was—had been—toroidal, narrow shoulders broadening to a wide chest and a wider belly before tapering to inverse—cone thighs, thin, strong calves, and eight-inch feet. Birthmarks dotted his shoulders and arms, and he had a nasty scar on his right hip from some accident or botched attempt at medicine. His body was pallid, and not particularly hairy.

Tara saw all this because Judge Cabot's robe and dressing gown had been torn away, along with much of his flesh. He lay in pieces on the garden floor, in a pool of his own blood. The part of her that was her father's daughter quailed and hid in a far corner of her mind. What remained was a consummate professional. At least, that's what she told herself.

"What do you see?" she asked the Blacksuit.

It is immaterial. We are interested in your observations.

The initial trio of Blacksuits had divided, one to watch the foyer, and two to escort her. The second split off, presumably to help interrogate the butler, as they crossed the oak-paneled sitting room. The third brought Tara through a glass door into a rooftop garden of fluorescent flowers and miniature date palms. Elaborate Craft focused sunlight and trapped humidity to transform the roof into a private rainforest. The effect was not perfect—the air had the proper sticky weight, but there weren't enough flies. In a true jungle, that congealing red puddle would be writhing with vampiric vermin.

Here there was only the blood. And the limbs. And the face.

The Blacksuit stood ten feet back, near the door, watching. It was a woman, when it wasn't working.

What can you tell us?

Tara stepped gingerly around the blood pool. At its edge she saw ceramic fragments, and a discoloration in the deep red tide.

He had been drinking tea. And now he was dead. No. Focus on the details, not the horror. This was just another cadaver, like any of the others she had studied back at the Hidden Schools.

Ms. Kevarian had intended Tara's visit to the Judge as a test, a chance to demonstrate her ability to work alone. It could still fulfill that purpose.

The smaller shards of clay were covered with dried or drying blood; Cabot's head rested atop one piece. This much the Black-suits almost certainly knew: he had been surprised, dropped the cup, and fallen.

There was no bruising, and no foreign blood or dirt or hair beneath Cabot's nails, though his fingers were mangled and broken. He hadn't put up a fight. Whatever happened to him happened fast.

The body had a sharp, hot silver smell beneath the stench of spoiling meat.

"How were you contacted?"

Cabot had special wards to notify Justice in the event of his death, and give us an image of his body. Pause. *Also, the butler summoned us.*

"Does your image show who did this?"

We have suspects.

Tara laced her fingers together. "Someone pulled Cabot's spine out of his back, through the skin. Death should have been instantaneous, but whatever did this wanted him alive." She pointed to the discs of bone arranged in a rough circle around the body, like poker chips strewn on a table. "The corpse has been ritualistically encircled by its spinal vertebrae. Necromancers use a more advanced version of the same technique to bind spirits. Doctors use it, too, to keep the patient alive on the operating table. Bone is a powerful focus, especially if it's your own. With the Judge's own spine, even an amateur Craftsman could have kept him alive and sane for . . . I'd guess a minute. If they only wanted to keep his soul bound to his body, and didn't care about his sanity, it could have lasted longer. Much longer." It would have felt longer still to Cabot. The heart kept time in the human body. Without its beat thoughts elongated, stretched, changed. She had stopped her own heart as an experiment back at school, under close observation, keeping her brain alive the entire time. For Cabot, seconds of agony would have felt like hours.

Stay professional. Keep your breakfast where it should be, and your voice level.

The Blacksuit cocked her head to one side. *Is there any way to call him back?*

Tara continued her slow revolution around the corpse. "The body's a complicated system. Bringing someone back requires the corpse have enough order to build upon, and there's hardly any of Cabot left. Even if we had the proper equipment to sift his memories, we'd need the organs that bear the imprints of sense experience. The eyes have burst. The tongue, here, well. The brain, missing out the back of the skull. The spine you see, and the heart is gone entirely." She looked up at the Blacksuit. "Did you really think it was possible he died of natural causes?"

These are strange days. We have had to widen the definition of the word "natural" six times in the last decade.

"Well, whoever did this was a poor student of the Craft, otherwise she wouldn't have needed the bones—only beginners use such a strong physical focus for something this simple—but she knows enough to keep the dead from talking. Which brings me to another oddity. The body is pristine, or at least no more rotten than it ought to be based on time of death. The Craft used to bind his soul should have accelerated decay." There was that scent again, the urgent tang of hot silver. She breathed it in, and turned from the body to the thick vegetation. "Do you mind if I look around the garden? The murderer could have hidden the missing organs nearby. Keeping them out of our hands for an hour would spoil them. Our killer needn't have run through the city in broad daylight with a bleeding heart clenched in her fist."

I will remain to guard the corpse.

Tara walked off between the looming sunflowers. The garden growth was thick, but not thick enough to dampen all sound. With a shout, she could call the Blacksuit to her.

It was indeed possible that the murderer, whoever, whatever she was, hid Cabot's heart somewhere nearby. She could also have burned the heart to ash and mixed it with the blood as an additional focus for her ritual. But searching for the heart gave Tara a plausible excuse to investigate without supervision.

The burnt silver smell haunted the garden. She traced it to a point near the terrace's corner, between a trellis of ivy and a carefully cultivated orchid. Approaching the edge, Tara reached to her heart and drew her knife.

The odor's source was not hidden behind the trellis, and the orchid provided no cover. Elsewhere in the rooftop garden, vines had been strung overhead to blot out the sky, but here she looked up and saw nothing but clouds. No ambush would come from above.

She leaned over the roof's edge. Far below ran the street, full of tiny people and tiny carriages. Gargoyles leered at the passersby. At ground level, the carvings were common monsters, sharp-nosed and snaggle-toothed, but as the building rose, their complexity grew. The sharp gouges Tara had seen from below marred the intricate artwork.

The gargoyles one floor beneath Cabot's penthouse seemed almost alive. To her right loomed a giant with three eyes and a massive tusked maw, each of his six arms clutching a different weapon. To her left stood a similar statue, and clinging to the ledge beside that another, in a different style. The first two were built from planes and angles, while this last gargoyle's sculptor had carved the curves of its hunched back and powerful torso with an anatomist's devotion. It was limbed as a man, save for two folded leathery wings and a long tail. A snarl contorted its gruesome, hook-beaked face. The creature was bent like a drawn bow, ready to fly.

Statues. The smell was strongest here, burning in her nostrils. Tara tightened her grip on her knife, and pondered.

This building had been built to a careful pattern, architects and artists weighing each decoration against every other. Nothing was accidental or asymmetrical save for the strange rune carvings, which did not seem part of the original design. Yet to her right there was a single gargoyle, and to her left—

As she turned to look, something long and sharp pressed

against her throat, the point dimpling her skin. She swallowed, involuntarily, and her skin almost gave.

"Scream," said a low voice like crushed rock, "and you die."

It was amazing, she thought for the second time that day, how imminent death focused the mind.

She remained still and quiet with the gargoyle's claw at her throat, to show she would not call for help. When he didn't say anything further, she whispered, "There's no need to kill me."

"There is if you scream."

"What would my death accomplish if I did? As soon as they know you're here, they'll be after you, and they move fast."

"So do I."

She had to admit that. He was fast, and quiet. She hadn't heard him climb onto the roof and approach her, for all his bulk. "Killing me will convince them you killed Judge Cabot. No evidence will stand against your murder of an innocent while fleeing the scene of the crime. The Blacksuits will track you to the ends of the earth. They're tireless." His claw twitched against her throat. "And you're tired already."

"Quiet."

"How long have you been hanging off this building? Hiding from them? Hoping they couldn't smell you the way I can?"

"Stop."

"What's your name?"

"I am a Guardian."

She heard the capital letter. "I'm not interested in your title," she said, as conversationally as she could manage. "I asked you to tell me your name. Because if I'm going to help you get out of this alive, we should get to know each other."

His breath should have been hot on the back of her neck, but he did not breathe. One cannot breathe with lungs of stone. She fought to control her pounding heart.

"You need my help," she said. "You're obviously innocent."

"What?"

Keep him talking, Tara thought. If you're wrong, and you're seldom wrong, then you want him to think you're on his side. If you're right, he wants to believe you. Recite the facts. Her throat was dry. Her breath came short. Dammit, be calm. Cool as crystal, as ice. Cool as Ms. Kevarian. "Whoever killed Cabot planned the murder well. Knew how to do it without leaving traces someone like me could follow. The murderer kept Cabot alive, more or less, until you came. You broke that pretty little bone circle, Cabot's spirit left his body, and bam, his wards went off and the Blacksuits had a nice picture of you looming over his corpse, talons out. It won't even matter if they were bloody."

The pressure against her throat eased.

Ms. Abernathy?

The Blacksuits were coming. She had to work fast.

Tara turned around. The claw did not leave her neck. The gargoyle stood before her, seven and a half feet of silver-gray stone bowed forward until his face was level with her own. Furled wings rose like twin mountains from his back. His open eyes were emerald green and large—at least three times as big as hers, eyes the size of billiard balls. She focused on the eyes because otherwise she would focus on his hooked, toothed beak.

"Listen. Is there any way you can make yourself less threatening? More human?"

"They might recognize me. I looked human earlier, when I ran from them."

"Did they see you up close?"

"No."

"Fine. I'll deal with that. Just try to be a little less with the huge and monstrous, please?"

There came a horrid twisting, and an inrush of air. The creature collapsed into himself, passing through a stomach-churning stage where he was emphatically not gargoyle, but not human either. Strands of muscle showed through the broken stone, which melted into yielding, warm flesh.

A young man stood before her, strong, good chin, ripped clothes, ripped chest. His eyes remained green as gems.

Tara's eyebrows floated upward of their own accord.

"What?" the gargoyle said.

"You're . . ."

"A monster?"

"I was going to go for cute."

Ms. Abernathy? Are you well? Again the shout scraped across her soul.

"Thanks?"

"Don't thank me. That makes it harder."

He opened his mouth to ask what she meant, but before he could speak, before he could react with all that mind-numbing speed and strength, she drove her knife deep into his stomach. It entered with a sizzling of seared flesh. His mouth opened in a silent gasp.

As she pulled the knife up and out, his body was already healing. With a swipe of her mind she took that power from him. He started to turn himself to stone, but the glyphs on her left arm sparked silver as she stopped him. The plan relied on him looking human: no swift healing, no claws, no rocky skin. His blood would have stained her clothes, but a wave of heat surrounded her and turned that blood to vapor.

She'd chosen her target well, and her depth. Missed the intestines and vital organs but nicked a few arteries going in, not so bad that he'd bleed out in minutes, but bad enough. He went slack, and fell free of her blade.

She knelt beside him and passed the knife to her left hand. The glyph-rings on her fingers, the spider on her palm, sparked silver as the blade faded into them. Next came the hard part. She framed his face with her fingertips and tightened her grip. Her nails pressed into flesh, and her Craft pressed deeper.

She twisted her wrist and peeled his face away. Eyes, nose, mouth, ears. Behind, she left a smooth, unbroken pane of skin.

Why do this? Why get involved? Save that someone had tried to kill her before breakfast, and someone else apparently succeeded at killing Judge Cabot. Two attacks in one morning, both on people connected with the case. Tara needed to know more, and she had little confidence in these Blacksuits and their Justice.

Holding the face in her left hand, she reached into her purse with her right and produced a black, leather-bound book, cover scrawled with silver. She stuck the face, carefully folded, between pages 110 and 111. Click went the latch, then back in her shoulder bag.

She had little power left. Enough to make a pass over the bleeding, faceless body and wipe away the miniscule traces of her Craft. Add to that a light ward against discovery, strong enough to block normal sight, but weak enough that it would never fool a Craftswoman.

Ms. Abernathy?

She stood, stepped back from the body, brushed a stray lock of hair into place, and squeezed her fists tight. Her nails bit into her palms, and she screamed.

The Blacksuits weren't the individuals Tara would have chosen to comfort a person who had discovered a faceless body. If she had been telling the truth, and indeed stumbled upon a wounded, comatose man while wandering through the garden, their precise questions would have driven her to hysterics. As it was, after she staunched the gargoyle's bleeding and bound his wound Tara felt compelled to hyperventilate, sit down in Cabot's parlor, and ask for a strong cup of tea.

What might have happened to this young man?

"I almost tripped over him, by all the gods. Couldn't have seen him if not for the Craft. I mean . . . Shit. I think . . . Maybe he was here. Talking to Cabot? Maybe whoever killed Cabot didn't notice him at first?"

Why not kill him in the same way?

"Not enough time. Oh. Thank you. Tea. Maybe not enough power. We're dealing with an amateur here—little skill, less soulstuff to work with than a full Craftswoman. Easier this way. Stab him, take his face, run."

What can we do?

"Not much. Steal the face, steal the mind. The wound will recover, but you won't get any testimony from him. On the plus side, once stolen, the face is almost impossible to destroy. Neither half can live without the other, but they can't die, either. Keep his body safe, and you might find the face if you look hard enough.

"Of course I'll be available to answer questions. I don't know where we'll be staying. You can reach my boss or me through the Sanctum of Kos Everburning. I assume you know the—

"Yes. Absolutely."

Heart pounding, she reached the street, hand in the air and a gargoyle's face in her shoulder bag. It had been an odd couple of hours, and she had a feeling that, before the week was out, her life would grow stranger still.

But she could deal with strange. She was starting to like the big city.

"Taxi!"

4

At Alt Coulumb's heart, the press of humanity and architecture yielded to a green circle half a mile in diameter: the Holy Precinct, with the towering Sanctum of Kos at its heart. To the north it bordered the business district, where skeletal mages in flowing robes bargained with creatures from beyond the mortal world in towers of black glass that scraped the sky. To the south lay the university campuses, gentrified, upper-class, and comfortably distant from the machinations of Northtown. East and west spread the no-man's land between the poles, home to residential zones, slums, dives, and vice.

The most notorious of these regions, the Pleasure Quarters, actually abutted the Holy Precinct, a holdover from centuries past when some saint decreed that the fire in the blood and loins belonged to Kos Everburning as much as the fire of hearth and furnace.

"Problem being," Tara's taxi driver said as he swung the goad halfheartedly at the flanks of his slow-moving nag, "that Kos is great and wise"—he pointed to the holy symbol suspended from the buggy's rearview mirror, a stylized three-tongued flame within a diamond—"but not as practiced as a fertility deity in managing diseases. I love our Lord with all my soul, but the Church did well to give up on sex and focus on the burning. Stick to what you know, I say."

"So the priests got out of the business, but the brothels remained?"

"Well. I wouldn't say the priests got out of the business. They're still, ah, joined to it, at the hip as it were. The Church got out, though, and well done, too. Man goes to pray to leave that kind of stuff behind. Nowadays, if the girls and their boys go wild and roll onto the temple grounds, the priests tromp over, round them up, and cart them off."

Their buggy rattled along, and the basalt tower grew ever larger before them. Tara watched the buildings that flanked their taxi. The closer they drew to the Holy Precinct, the more grooved scars she saw in the towers' stone, always several stories above street level. "What about those marks on the buildings? Did the priests take up decorating, too?"

Harness jangled and leather creaked. When the driver spoke again his voice was low and strained. "Ah. Those."

"I'm sorry. If it's a sensitive subject, I can . . ."

"No trouble, miss. They're war scars, is all."

"I thought Alt Coulumb wasn't damaged in the God Wars."

He snorted. "Weren't any Craftsmen, but it was damaged all the same."

Tara was confused, but her driver seemed uneasy with the subject. She chose her next words with care. "Shouldn't someone have fixed them by now? It's been fifty years."

"Can't be fixed."

"What do you mean?"

"The Stone Men made 'em, didn't they?" He spit onto the street. "Can't cover up their claw marks. The building remembers. Put in new stones and a minute later they're scarred again."

Tara's breath caught, but she tried to keep her tone conversational. "Stone Men. You mean gargoyles?"

He didn't respond, but it was an affirmative silence.

"Some of the . . . scars . . . look like writing."

"Some are. Marking territory. Blasphemous prayers written by mad beasts. The rest are battle scars."

"Are the gargoyles still around?"

The man glanced back at her and she saw that his face had closed like a door. "No Stone Men here." He said those words as if they were a curse. "Not since my father's time."

"What happened?"

"They left."

He turned the cab down a broad road leading into the temple compound. Seen from above, the path they traced over white gravel would follow the outer curves of a massive binding circle, large as the Holy Precinct. Tara wondered if the design served a purpose beyond decoration. Without an army of Craftsmen to manage it, not even a circle this size could contain a god as strong as Kos.

"Why'd they leave? Religious differences?"

He didn't answer, and Tara didn't ask for further clarification. Arguing war-era politics with a fanatic in a god-benighted city could be trouble. She wasn't concerned for her own safety, but arriving on her client's doorstep in a burning taxi with an injured driver would make a horrible first impression.

They approached the black tower of the Sanctum of Kos, tall and polished, an abstract vision of flame trapped in dark and un-scarred stone. The same echoed warmth she had felt while falling washed over her again. Was it always like this here? And if the divine radiance was this strong when Kos was dead, what must it have been like when he was alive?

Their road dead-ended in a broad semicircle of white gravel where a double handful of other vehicles lingered, awaiting their masters: a couple ordinary taxis like Tara's own, five or six fancier models, and even a few driverless carriages.

A young man in brown and orange robes sat at the base of the steps leading into the Sanctum. He was tonsured, smoking a ciga-rette, and represented the only non-carriage-related life in the vicinity.

"That's funny," her driver said.

"There's usually a crowd?"

"Place is generally packed with folks, you know, come to pray for this or that or the other thing. Monsters from Northtown come when they've got business. If you dream about fire, you visit to pay your respects." The cabbie frowned. "Fewer than usual to-day."

She slid from the cab to the ground, fished a small metal disc out of her purse, and passed it to the driver. A piece of Tara's soul flowed from her to him through the token. The soulstuff mat-tered, not the token; metals were just an easy focus. Soon after she paid him, all traces of her would fade from the payment, and only raw power remain, for the driver to trade with others in exchange for food or shelter, goods or services, or pleasure. If he were a Craftsman, and gained enough of this power from others, from the stars, or from the earth, he could use it to resurrect the dead and rain doom upon a nation. If the power remained in Alt Coulumb, on the other hand, some faithful citizen would inevitably sacrifice it to Kos, who kept the city protected and commerce secure and the whole damn system functioning.

Until, that is, a few days ago.

"Be well," she said to the cabbie, but his frown deepened. With a flick of the reins and a swipe of the crop he goaded his horse into a sloppy canter and left Tara alone in the shadow of the fire god's tower.

The Sanctum of Kos was a surprisingly modern building, she thought as she approached the broad, black steps. A few architectural peculiarities marked it as a product of a prior era: unnecessary columns around the base, and structurally superfluous buttresses added no doubt by nervous designers when the Sanctum was first conceived, back when twenty-story buildings had been the precinct of the ambitious, and eighty-story plans the product of fevered imaginations.

"Beautiful, isn't it?"

The speaker's voice cracked and wavered, and he drew in a ragged breath as he paused for the comma. Tara looked down from the staggering heights and saw the same young acolyte who had been waiting on the stairs when she pulled into the lot. He was seated, bent forward over his knees. A cigarette dangled from his mouth. Voluminous robes hung from his thin body, and his upturned eyes were set deep in a pale face.

"It is," she acknowledged.

"I know what you're thinking."

She arched an eyebrow at him.

The young man plucked the cigarette from his mouth and exhaled a long, narrow stream of smoke. "Or, I know what you were thinking."

"Try me."

"You were thinking that the columns, the buttresses, are unnecessary. That we added them for show, or out of fear."

Her eyes widened a tick, and she nodded. "How did you know?"

"You're sharp enough to get fooled." His attempt at a laugh crumbled into a hacking cough.

"Are you all right?" She reached for him, but he waved her off hastily. The coughing fit persisted, long and ugly and wet. The fingers of his extended hand curled slowly into a fist, and he struck himself in the chest, hard. The cough stopped with a low rattle and he kept talking as though nothing had happened.

"See how the columns are broader than they should be? Same with the buttresses?"

She nodded, though she didn't, in fact, see.

"Not structural. A disguise. Building the Sanctum, they thought, no sense having big fat steam pipes coming off the central tower. Too ugly, too vulnerable. Hide 'em. Every other building has columns, so we might as well use these."

"Good idea."

"Stupid idea," the young man said, pointing. "Fancy stonework makes it hard to access the pipe joints there, and there. Whenever anything goes wrong, we need to redo all the masonry, and at night, too, to keep people from seeing."

"Do you tell this to everyone who stops by?"

He drew in another breath. "Only if they're wearing a suit." His ragged smile looked out of place, too broad and sincere for his tonsure and his robes and his slender frame.

"Well, I hope you never get attacked by someone in a suit."

"Hasn't happened yet." He returned the cigarette to his mouth and lurched forward. Tara was afraid he would fall on his face, but he recovered his balance and stood, unsteadily. "You're Tara Abernathy." He stuck out a thin hand, which trembled in hers as she shook it. Beneath the smile and the rambling mode of speech, he was afraid. "I'm Novice Technician Abelard. They told me to wait for you. Outside."

"You say that like it's a bad thing."

"The air out here feels too cold, and I haven't been . . . healthy. Lately."

"You might try quitting." She nodded at his cigarette.

He let his head loll back to the sky, and his eyes drifted closed, as if he was waiting for rain. None fell, and he opened his eyes again. "I started when I joined the priesthood. A sign of my devotion. I won't stop now."

"You're talking about—"

He shot her a look, but she'd already checked her tongue.

"How many people know about our problem?" she asked instead.

"As few as possible. Technical staff, mostly. The higher-ups. We've put it about that the Holy One is contemplating His own perfection, and must not be bothered by mortal concerns."

"How long will that hold?"

He started up the stairs. "We've wasted too much time already."

The tower's twenty-foot-tall main doors were opened on feast days alone, Abelard explained as he led Tara to a smaller side entrance. "Takes too much time. You know, to move these monsters you need about fifty monks hauling on each door." He patted one of his branch-thin arms. "We're not the heartiest people around."

"You can't get Kos to give a push?"

"Of course not. It'd be disrespectful on a feast day. Plus, we wouldn't get to see the Cardinals fall over when the doors finally budge. I think Kos finds it as funny as the rest of us." He looked as if he was about to say more, but pain contorted his features, and he fell silent.

The Sanctum's foyer loomed over them in the shadows. Somehow the single room, with its vaulted ceilings and tall windows, seemed vaster from within than the whole tower appeared from without. Flames of stained glass rose on all sides, and a hundred yards away the golden fires of the nave flickered in the half-light. A pair of initiates in bright red robes swept the otherwise empty hall.

"Nobody comes here during the workday." Abelard indicated the whole room by swinging one forefinger in a quick circle through the air. The hem of his robe flared out around his bony ankles. "Bread and circuses, strictly."

"Expensive bread."

"You have no idea."

A sharp left brought them up against a metal lattice worked to resemble a thick growth of ivy. Abelard placed his hand upon the lattice, and the vines parted with a slow clank of gears. He ducked his head low to pass through. Tara just walked.

More abrupt turns, more shadowy doors, and a rap on a carefully chosen brick in what appeared to be a solid wall, which swung open on a hidden hinge to reveal a long winding stair. As they climbed, occasional shafts of light broke the darkness, concealed peepholes peering into meeting rooms and conference chambers: here a break room where tired priests stood waiting for a tea kettle to boil, there a chamber at least the size of the Sanctum's front worship hall and crowded with pipes, cams, pistons, and gears upon gears, here a tiny room half-glimpsed, where Craft circles glowing blue surrounded a modest wooden altar. She saw these things in eye blinks, shadows on a cave wall as they climbed.

"You said you were a novice Technician. Which means you, what, clean the steam pipes?"

His barking laugh echoed through the stairwell. "We have cleaners for that. Repairmen and machinists. A Technician oversees the Divine Throne, the heart of the city. We design, improve, optimize the devices that keep this place running. Not me, yet, though. I was only promoted to Technician a few months back."

"You're low on the totem pole?"

"As low as a Technician gets. The king of the backed-up burners, that's me, archdeacon of scut work. I'm learning, though. Or, I was learning." He paused, searching the featureless wall for something, and in that pause Tara caught up with him.

"Did they bring you in on this for training? So you'll know what to do if there's ever a problem like this in the future, when you're in charge?"

Abelard faced her. His eyes were dead as a charred forest. "I was the one watching the Throne when God died."

He pressed a hidden catch, and the wall opened smoothly on hidden gears.

After her steady climb through darkness, the well-lit office was blinding. Pale wood panels everywhere, a couple leather chairs, and a large desk of polished oak. A glass bookcase stood against one wall, though few of its shelves contained actual books or codices, the lion's share of space reserved instead for sacred icons, trophies, ceremonial plaques. An aerial picture of Alt Coulumb hung beside it, for comparison, Tara supposed, with the view from the floor-to-ceiling windows.

The city stretched there, a teeming metropolis beneath slate-gray skies, beating heart of commerce, bridge between the god-benighted Old World and the Deathless Kingdoms of the West. Millions breathed, worked, prayed, copulated in those palaces, parks, and tenements, sure in the knowledge that Kos Everburning watched over them. If their faith was strong, they could feel the constant presence of his love, sustaining and aiding them in a thousand ways, breaking fevers and checking accidents and powering their city.

Millions of people, unaware that Kos's ever-beating heart had been still for days.

Ms. Kevarian stood by the window, engaged in low, earnest conversation with a senior priest Tara assumed to be their client. He sat behind the oak desk, clad in deep red robes and his own authority. Physically, he was unremarkable, silver-haired and thin with age, but his posture suggested that he often spoke while others listened. Never before had Tara seen someone with such presence who was not a Craftsman.

But Kos's death must have strained him beyond endurance. His shoulders bent as if they bore a heavy weight, and his face looked drawn and robbed of sleep. Accustomed to power, he was scrambling for purchase on events beyond his control.

Abelard announced her. "Technical Cardinal Gustave, Lady Kevarian, this is Tara Abernathy." He closed his eyes, opened them again, shifted his feet. "I, uh, assume. She never showed me any identification."

Ms. Kevarian's expression darkened, but before she said anything Cardinal Gustave extended a firm, reassuring hand. He had a preacher's deep voice, quiet at the moment, though Tara did not doubt it could fill a cathedral. "Novice Abelard must have recognized Ms. Abernathy from your description. He's usually prudent, but the current . . . situation has shaken him, as it has shaken us all."

"I'm sorry." Abelard bowed his head, and with shaking fingers raised his cigarette to his lips. Finding it nearly exhausted, he dug frantically into the pockets of his robe for a fresh pack. "I'm sorry. I wasn't thinking. It won't happen again."

"See that it does not," Ms. Kevarian said. "If we are to succeed in this case, we must control the flow of information. The future of your faith depends on your ability to keep secrets."

Abelard froze, and Tara felt a spark of pity for him. He was terrified to the brink of endurance by his god's death, and neither Ms. Kevarian nor his own boss were being much help.

So she lied. "He checked my name. I should have remembered to show him some ID. Security only works if both sides are on board, after all."

Gratitude beamed from Abelard's face as he produced a new cigarette and lit it from the embers of the old. Ms. Kevarian's gaze flicked from Abelard, to the cigarette, and back. She watched and weighed him for a silent moment before continuing the introductions. "Tara, meet His Excellency Cardinal Gustave. He contacted Kelethras, Albrecht, and Ao via nightmare courier two days ago."

"A pleasure, Your Excellency," Tara said with a slight bow. "Happy to serve."

"You may," Cardinal Gustave said, "address me as Cardinal, or Father. Anything more presumes that, at the end of this process, I will still have a Church to lead." He laughed without a trace of humor. "Have Lady Kevarian and Novice Abelard told you the basics?"

"The basics." *Judge Cabot is dead*, she wanted to shout at Ms.

Kevarian across the room. Someone's trying to kill us. Business can wait.

But of course it couldn't.

Cardinal Gustave stood in a creaking of leather. He was a battered edifice, deep lines on his face and dark circles under his eyes. She recognized the look; the events of the few days had worn joy and certainty from him, like a flood scouring away topsoil to reveal the bedrock beneath. "What do you know, Ms. Abernathy," he said, "about the death of gods?"

Tara knew quite a lot, actually. Her grasp of the underlying theory was probably more profound than Cardinal Gustave's, but she did not interrupt the lecture that followed. The Cardinal looked to have frayed without the fire of his Lord to shelter him. He was desperate, and lecturing Lady Kevarian's junior associate (and whence that title "Lady" anyway?) was a chance to establish his knowledge and authority.

"Gods, like humans," he said, "are order imposed on chaos. With humans, the imposition is easy to see. Millions of cells, long twisted chains of atoms, so much bone and blood and *juice*, every piece performing its function. When one of those numberless pumps refuses to beat, when one of those infinitesimal pipes gets blocked, all the pent-up chaos springs forward like a bent sword, and the soul is lost to the physical world unless something catches it first.

"So, too, with gods. Gods live and reproduce much like humans, and, like humans, their higher functions (language, pact-making, careful exercise of power, sentience) developed quite recently on the timescale of eons. In the unrecorded mists of prehistory, when mankind prowled the savannah and the swamps, their gods hunted with them, little more than shadows on a cave wall, the gleam in a hunter's eye, a mammoth's death roar, primitive as the men they ruled. As men grew in size, complexity, and might, the gods grew with them.

"Gods, like men, can die. They just die harder, and smite the earth with their passing."

This was basic stuff. It had formed the theoretical foundation for Maestre Gerhardt's famous (or infamous, depending on which circles you ran in) treatise *Das Thaumas*, the work that first theorized, a century and a half ago, that human beings could stop begging for miracles, take the power of the gods into their own hands, and shape the course of destiny.

Gerhardt's work spread like wildfire through academies and lecture halls around the world; in ten years the shuddering and imprecise research of the former masters of Applied Theology, who became the first adepts of the Craft, laid waste to hundreds of miles of verdant countryside and sparked the jealous gods to war. Cardinal Gustave had been born during the century-long conflict that followed, and raised by an order that cleaved to the old ways and the old gods. Tara's parents were teenagers during the Siege of Skeld and the Battle of Kath near the God Wars' end, and fled to the edge of the Badlands to escape the convulsions of their dying nation. Ms. Kevarian, who had lived through most of the story, stood by the window, read her scroll as the Cardinal spoke, and kept her thoughts to herself.

The key difference between gods and men in the manner of their dying was that men possessed only two deep obligations: to the earth, from which came their flesh, and to the stars, from which came their soul. Neither earth nor stars were particularly concerned about the return on their investment. Humans were very good at adding order to the earth, and enlivening the world of the stars with ideas and myth. When a human being died, nobody had a vested interest in keeping her around.

Gods, however, made deals. It was the essence of their power. They accepted a tribe's sacrifice and in turn protected its hunters from wolves and wild beasts. They received the devotion of their people, and gave back grace. A successful god arranged to receive more than he returned to the world. Thus your power and your people grew together, slowly, from family to tribe, from tribe to city, from city to nation, and so on to infinity.

Nice strategy, but slow. Theologians centuries back had developed a faster method. One god gave of his power to another, or to a group of worshipers, on a promise of repayment in kind, and of more soulstuff than had been initially lent. Gods grew knit to gods, pantheons to pantheons, expecting, and indeed requiring, their services to be returned. Power flowed, and divine might increased beyond measure. There were risks, though. If a goddess owed more than she could support, she might die as easily as a human who shed too much blood.

When a goddess neared death, the needs of her faithful, and of those to whom she was bound in contract, stuck like hooks in her soul. She could not desert her obligations, nor honor them and remain intact. The tension tore her mind to shreds of ectoplasm, leaving behind a body of inchoate divine power that a competent Craftswoman could reassemble into something that looked and functioned like the old goddess. But . . .

Well. Much like Tara's revenants back at Edgemont, a being once resurrected was never quite the same.

"How did he die?" Tara asked.

Cardinal Gustave frowned. "I defer to Lady Kevarian's judgment here."

"It appears," Ms. Kevarian said, setting down her scroll, "that as Novice Abelard undertook his routine prostrations two days ago, a complex set of agreements fell due. Kos"—Abelard flinched at the casual tone with which she said his deity's name—"was unable to satisfy these agreements, and unable to back out of his pacts. The strain seems to have killed him."

"Seems?" Cardinal Gustave asked.

"Seems."

"What else could have happened?"

Ms. Kevarian clasped her hands behind her back. "Ms. Abernathy, please list some of the other possibilities for our friends."

"Kos's willing abandonment of his responsibilities. Some fundamental inconsistency in his pacts with the city. A mass crisis of faith." She took a breath there, and searched Ms. Kevarian's face for some sign of approval, no matter how vanishingly swift. Nothing.

"Not to mention," Ms. Kevarian said, "death in battle. As happened with Seril."

The Cardinal's face was firm, fixed, and ashen.

"We must rule out other options in the early stages of the process and assemble our case before the adversary asserts his claim."

"Adversary?" Poor Abelard. He sounded like he wanted nothing more than to return to his engines and pipes and altars.

Ms. Kevarian let the question hang. Cardinal Gustave stared out the window into the overcast sky. Tara's turn, apparently. "The Church is not the only group interested in Kos's revivification. Your god was one of the last in the New World, and his influence extended around the globe. The pantheons of Iskar draw power from him. His flame drives oceangoing vessels, heats the sprawling metropolises in Koschei's realm, lights the caverns of King Clock. Gods who wish to deal with Deathless Kings pass their power through Kos to do so, and Deathless Kings who deal with gods do the same. People around the world are invested in his survival. When these groups realize Kos is no longer alive to honor his agreements, they will choose a representative and send him here, to ensure Kos's pacts are fulfilled. If the representative discovers something we didn't know, some sign, say, that the Church made unwise bargains in Kos's name, he'll use that to gain more control over your god's resurrection."

Abelard's expression clouded as she spoke. Cardinal Gustave stood with his back to her, and it was impossible to see his face. His shoulders were squared off ready to resist a terrible wind.

"We should begin work as soon as possible," Ms. Kevarian said. "Ms. Abernathy and I require a staff, until the rest of our firm's complement arrives."

"Whatever you need," Gustave replied.

"Security is of the essence. We must keep the number of people involved to a minimum. Perhaps you could loan us Abelard?"

Gustave glanced over his shoulder at Ms. Kevarian, as if he were about to argue. At last he decided against it, and addressed the young priest. "Abelard?"

"Yes, Cardinal?"

"Will you serve Lady Kevarian?"

Tara hoped he would refuse. The Craft involved would be hard enough without Abelard scuttling along scattering ash in her wake. Sure, he understood his faith better than Tara did, but the Craft was the Craft. What use had she for local mysticism?

Besides, the death of his god seemed to have struck the young priest deeply. Working with the divine corpse might be too much for him to bear.

He looked at Ms. Kevarian, and she looked back. He did not quail, or turn away.

"Yes, Father."

After that, the meeting dissolved into logistics. Ms. Kevarian waved her hand through the air and produced a long list of components they required: candles made from blood wax, a box of bone chalk, various thaumaturgic implements of sterling silver and copper and ironwood. They were to room within the Sanctum, on a floor reserved for guests. Tara asked for a wig stand for her room, and pointedly ignored Ms. Kevarian's questioning glance. She'd explain later.

Cardinal Gustave had things to do. "You are here to save our Church, but in the meantime I must prepare for its demise." Abelard led them upstairs to their rooms, which were surprisingly posh when compared with the Gothic complexity of the worship halls below, and with the bright, spacious offices. Tara's chambers would have satisfied a merchant prince. Pale walls and plush carpet set off the luxurious red leather upholstery of her armchair and the clawed golden feet of her vanity table. The bed was a four-poster, complete with gossamer curtains, like something out of an old novel.

Someone had even found her a wig stand.

Abelard produced a wrench out of a hidden pocket in his robe, opened a panel concealed behind one of the room's full-length mirrors, and did something that involved a lot of swearing and banging. Minutes later, he announced he had connected her bell-pull to the call box in his quarters, in case she needed anything. He then retired, tripping over the hem of his robe on the way out. Ms. Kevarian remained with Tara to drink a cup of tea and discuss business.

Tara sat on her divan, watching the gas burner's flame lick

the belly of the small iron kettle, and counted to ten before Ms. Kevarian said, "How is Judge Cabot?"

"Dead," Tara replied. "Murdered."

Ms. Kevarian blinked, once.

"You don't seem surprised," Tara said.

"I won't say I was expecting his murder, but it was a possibility."

"You think it has something to do with the case? With Kos?"

"Cabot was one of my oldest contacts in the Craft in this city. If someone tried and failed to kill me, it stands to reason he might be in danger as well." She stood, and began to pace. Her shadow and her mood sucked light from the room. "He was destroyed, I take it?"

"No hope of raising him. Most of the organs gone. I couldn't have pulled his memories even if the Blacksuits had left me alone with the body."

Ms. Kevarian said nothing. The darkness around her deepened.

"You said you knew the man?" Tara asked.

"He worked on the Seril case. Fair judge. That was forty years ago, and he wanted to get out of the game even then." She stopped pacing and stood, eyes closed, hands at her side, for a moment that stretched. "Tell me the circumstances."

She told her everything. The butler's screams, talking her way in to see the body, its condition. Ms. Kevarian asked Tara for exceptional detail there, and she described the corpse, its expression, its disposition, and especially its vertebrae. But the gargoyle interested Ms. Kevarian most.

"Here?"

"Hand to any god you want to name."

"You're sure?"

"One minute, seven and a half feet tall, big beak, wings and talons and teeth." She raised one arm to its fullest extent over her head. "The next he turns inside out and becomes a six-one kind of handsome guy. Dark hair, green eyes. Definitely not a golem. I've never seen anything like it before."

"Is he alone? His Flight—his group—have they returned?"

That question came a little fast. "Is there something I should know?"

"Answer me."

Her tone chilled the air in Tara's lungs. She took another breath. "He didn't say much."

"He's in Blacksuit custody?"

"His body is."

Ms. Kevarian stopped her pacing. Something welled within her chest, a cracking, burbling sound that Tara realized with shock was laughter. "His body. You brilliant girl."

Tara felt a fierce rush of pride, but by now she knew better than to stop and bask in her boss's praise.

She opened her purse and reached for the book within. Before she could produce it, Ms. Kevarian laid an iron-cold hand on her wrist. "You've done well, but I must be able to answer truthfully when Justice asks me about this."

"Got it." She released the book and withdrew her hand. "I was just looking for a pen."

"Under no circumstances are you to attempt to ascertain whether Cabot's death was connected with our business here."

"Of course not," Tara replied with a knowing nod.

"You are certainly not to pursue this line of inquiry on your own. It seems unlikely that his death has any bearing on our case. Cabot's death, and our own troubles, and Kos's demise, are clearly related by no more than coincidence."

"Clearly." The kettle screamed. Tara poured some tea into her mug. "And I'm not supposed to start at once?"

"Actually, no," Ms. Kevarian said. "I need you and Abelard to begin document review. Go through everything we have, and see how complete a picture you can assemble of what happened to Kos. Get a report to me by tomorrow morning."

"Boss . . ." That book with its silver-traced binding felt like a lead weight in her purse. Every minute it sat there, the trail grew colder. "Don't we have more important things to worry about?"

"Extracurricular matters do compete for our attention, but we are obliged to serve our clients." Ms. Kevarian ran her thumbs down the lapels of her jacket. "In your case, the obligation is personal, as well as professional."

Tara frowned. "What do you mean?"

"I have a great deal of influence and seniority within our firm, but I am not all-powerful." Ms. Kevarian paused. Tara waited, and at last her boss found the words she sought. "The circumstances surrounding your graduation from the Hidden Schools convinced me that you had a place with Kelethras, Albrecht, and Ao. However, those same circumstances disturbed some senior partners at the firm."

Striking at her teachers and masters with fire, with lightning, with shadow and thorn. Laughing as they threw her from Elder Hall into the void above the Crack in the World. Tara swallowed. "I didn't have much choice in the matter."

"So I said, when Belladonna Albrecht challenged my recommendation. Nevertheless, my colleagues' reservations prevailed. For months I advocated on your behalf, without success." Ms. Kevarian glanced back at Tara, her face composed. "At last, this case came across my desk, and with it my chance. The firm chose me for this assignment, and due to the sensitive nature of the case, they gave me staffing authority. I chose you."

Tara counted back the days, the hours, since Kos died. Hiring a new associate took time. Ms. Kevarian couldn't have left for Edgemont more than a day after word of the god's death reached her, hardly enough time to ink the complex contracts and pacts binding Tara to the firm. "This isn't settled, is it? You have me for the moment, but they haven't decided whether to let you keep me." The language rankled: keep, give, as if she were a possession, or a prize.

"You are on a, shall we say, performance plan. If you perform to my expectations, your position with the firm is assured. If you fail, or compromise our clients, then our time together will be cut short." She shook her head. "I do not appreciate working under such conditions. I do not wish to threaten you into obedience. I would not have told you, but that I want you to understand the risks you face, and the gravity of the task we were called here to perform."

Tara's tea tasted of bergamot and ash. Ms. Kevarian didn't need to say any of this. She could have waited and watched to see if her new associate flew or failed. Her admission was a gift—a confession of respect, an invitation into confidence—but also a curse. In addition to gargoyles and assassins, now Tara had to fear her own superiors. From their distant stronghold, the senior partners of Kelethras, Albrecht, and Ao settled their fiery gaze upon her, weighing, probing, seeking every flaw and imperfection. She felt like a tightrope walker forced to gaze into the yawning gulf beneath her feet.

The drop made little difference, Tara told herself. She did not intend to fall. Then again, few women fell on purpose. "So, what are we supposed to do?"

"Our jobs," Ms. Kevarian said, "with care, professionalism, and speed. Time is of the essence." She turned to the window. The sky, though pale in the morning, had darkened in the intervening hours and drawn closer to earth, as if to crush the city. "I don't like the look of those clouds."

"Tea?" Tara offered.

"Later. Work now. For both of us."

Before she left for her own chambers, Ms. Kevarian grabbed the long red tongue of Tara's bell-pull and tugged. It produced a hiss of steam.

5

Fifteen minutes, give or take, was all Tara could allow herself before Abelard arrived in answer to the bell. Not much time, but there was no sense wasting this opportunity.

If she failed the Church, her career was over. No one would take a chance on her if Kelethras, Albrecht, and Ao fired her once this probation ended. She would eke out some sort of living in obscurity, or else . . . back to the mob. The thought chilled her.

But there were many ways to fail a client. If Cabot's murder was related to the case somehow, she would be neglecting her duties not to investigate.

Thus bolstered by flimsy logic, Tara brought her mug of tea to the vanity table. The wig stand stared at her with empty wooden eyes. Rooting in her purse, she produced the black leather book, a black marker, a tiny silver mallet, and a small black velvet bag with a sapphire clasp, the contents of which jangled as she set it down.

Face-stealing had been perfect for her purposes at Cabot's penthouse, but was far from ideal on this end. The face required a mount. This wig stand was the right shape, at least, but poorly prepared, and she could only do so much with the marker, scribing elaborate designs on the smooth undifferentiated features, to improve upon it. Fortunately, she had brought her own silver nails.

She unfolded the face from the book, removed the first nail from the velvet bag, and drove it through the gargoyle's forehead into the wig stand with the mallet. She fastened the remaining eight nails at the temples, ears, the base of the jaw, the chin, and the bridge of the nose, whispering as she did so a simple binding formula.

Don't look at him as you do this, she told herself. *Don't even think of him as a him. That makes it easier.*

At least it was easier until she drove in the final nail and the deep green eyes opened. Before she could speak, he bared his teeth and said, in a voice void of all emotion, "Who the hell are you? What did you do to me? I'll kill you."

His brow wrinkled in confusion, a strange effect when compounded with the creases and furrows produced by Tara's hasty nail work. Tara knew what to expect, but watching still churned her stomach.

"I'm going to tear your throat out with my teeth." This said with all the inflection of a bored lector at Sunday chapel. "I'll drink your blood and splinter your bones." Comprehension dawned, slower than the sun. "Why do I sound like this?"

"Disinterested? Surprisingly calm given your situation?"

"I should be furious. You tried to kill me."

"I didn't try to kill you. I got you off that roof without hurting anyone. Or," she amended, "without hurting anyone in the long term. This is hardly a permanent arrangement."

"Why aren't I angry?" His nostrils flared. His eyes flicked left, right. "Why can't I move?"

"Two related questions with a related answer." She turned the wig stand to face the vanity table's mirror.

His eyes widened, and his mouth fell open. No sound came out.

"You can't move because you don't have a body. You're not feeling anything because, well, you'd be surprised how much of what we call emotion is really chemistry. A few extra grams of this or that hormone in your blood, and you're angry, or sad, or in love. You have no blood at present, though, or whatever it is a gargoyle has for blood. Lava, maybe? Your personality exists in a self-sustaining matrix I Crafted for it. Your face is the locus, and your own body's chemical energy powers the whole thing from a distance. A nice piece of work, if I do say so myself."

"I'm going to kill you."

"No, no, no!" She shook her head. "That's not how we get anywhere. You start by telling me your name."

"I can't feel pain. You can't torture me."

Neither statement was precisely true, but it would not be politic to tell him that. "I'm not trying to hurt you. All I want to know is what happened to Judge Cabot."

"You want a confession."

"I don't!" She raised her right hand to the mirror so he could see it. "Honest. I think you're innocent."

"Why stab me in the stomach and steal my face?"

"I said *I* think you're innocent. The Blacksuits don't. You said they were chasing you down, and if you thought a gargoyle could get a fair trial in this city, I doubt you'd have run from them."

The face said nothing.

"Am I right?"

"Stone Men don't deserve a fair trial," he said at last, his tone dry and grating. "We tear the city apart. We thirst for blood—or haven't you heard? You couldn't assemble a jury to acquit me, whatever evidence you showed them. Not that Justice would bother with a jury."

"Look," she said, "I'm sorry. We've started off on the wrong . . ." She checked herself. He didn't have feet at the moment, and it would be rude to remind him of that. "I'm Tara. I'm trying to help you."

His eyes locked with hers in the mirror, and she took an involuntary breath. They were more than green: the color of emeralds, the color of the sea. "Shale," he said.

"That's it? Shale?"

"Why do you people always think we need more names than everyone else?"

"I've never met a gargoyle personally. . . ."

"So you assume we go around painting ourselves with pitch and swooping from rooftops to devour innocents, and call ourselves things like Shale Swiftwing, Beloved of the Goddess, Scout-in-Shadows."

"You were a lot less sarcastic when we first met."

"When I was hiding from the Blacksuits?"

"And threatening to kill me."

"Well, I had a body then."

The tea was well steeped, and Abelard was no doubt ascending the last flight of stairs to the guest level. She might not have enough time alone to try this again for days, and she'd learned nothing useful so far. Expulsion from the firm weighed on her left shoulder, and death by a murderer's hand on her right. She drummed her fingers on the vanity table and tried to clear her head. "Is that your actual name?"

"What?"

"You know, Swiftwing and all the rest?"

He rolled his eyes.

"If I am to help you, I need to know who you are. Where you come from. What you were doing in Cabot's penthouse."

He pursed his lips, but finally allowed, "Swiftwing I made up. The rest are honorifics."

"What were you doing in the penthouse?"

"I don't know."

She clenched her fist in frustration. "Oh, come on!"

"Do you think it makes me happy, being kept in the dark? Cabot was supposed to give me a package. That's all I know."

"Shale, you're cute, but you're frustrating."

"You think I'm cute now, you should see me when I have a real body."

"How could you possibly not know what you were doing there?"

"I was told the Judge would give me something to bring back to my Flight."

"Who told you?"

"Aev. Our leader."

"She didn't say what the package was? Why she needed to speak with a Judge? Anything like that?"

"I don't know."

If she pressed him, he might stop talking entirely, and she needed more information. *Move on.* "You were supposed to return to your, ah, Flight, after you retrieved this package. Where are they?"

At first she thought he was being reticent, but she realized, from the twitches in his cheeks, that he was trying to shake his head. "I know where my Flight rested yesterday, but they're long gone by now. We know this city better than anyone. We were born of its stone, and it bears our mark. On the rare occasions when we return, we keep moving from hiding spot to hiding spot so the Blacksuits can't find us."

Dammit. "How were you planning to bring them the package?"

"Wasn't." His voice was fading. A limitation of face-stealing: the consciousness tired easily when free of the body. "They'll find me, or I'll find them. By smell."

A knock on the door. Tara swore under her breath.

"Ms. Abernathy?"

Factors in this case multiplied too swiftly for her taste. Gargoyles. Abelard. Blacksuits. Foolishness.

"Ms. Abernathy, you rang." Abelard started to turn the doorknob.

"Wait! Hold on a second. I'm not decent."

The door paused, already open a crack. "But you rang."

"Hold on!"

"Trying to keep me a secret?" Shale sneered.

"Shut up," she whispered.

"What if I call for help?"

"Ms. Abernathy, is there someone else there?"

"Talking to myself," she said as she raised the hammer.

Fortunately, the setup took less time to dismantle than to assemble. A few pulls with the prying end of the hammer, a slow peel from the wig stand, and Shale's face was safely back in the book by the time Abelard opened her bedroom door. The young priest stood on the threshold peering into the room as if afraid something within might leap out to dismember him. A fresh cigarette drooped from his lips, and he appeared, if possible, more disheveled than a half hour before.

"Ms. Abernathy?"

"Sorry," she said, slinging her purse back over her shoulder. "Female troubles. Shall we go?"

The Sanctum had been built in the optimistic era before the God Wars reached the New World, when the Church of Kos saw the future as an endless sequence of bright vistas, one opening upon the next. Mad with expansionist dreams, the Church planned its new Sanctum with enough empty space to accommodate a century of growth. Then the war came, and the bright vistas crumbled. To this day, great tracts of the Sanctum remained unoccupied and unknown to the world. Which was to the best, really, because sometimes the Church required spaces that were large, unoccupied, and unknown.

This was the explanation Abelard gave Tara when, after climbing another winding stair three stories up from the guest chambers, they arrived at an otherwise unassuming door, which opened, once Abelard found the proper key, into the largest room she had ever seen. The Hidden Schools' main quadrangle would have fit inside, easily, along with the east wing of Elder Hall.

The entire room was filled with paper.

Loose sheets of foolscap lay piled by the ream in boxes around the chamber's edge. Near the center, the boxes gave way to thick piles of scrolls, some in racks, some loose. The dry, comforting aroma of scribe's ink and parchment filled the dead air.

"It's a lot of paper," Abelard admitted. "Lots of scribes, and lots of Craft supporting the scribes. Every deal the Church of Kos ever made, every contract with deity or Deathless King. The founding covenant of Alt Coulumb is here somewhere. Not the original, of course."

Tara couldn't resist a low whistle at the sheer quantity of information. She'd seen larger libraries in the Hidden Schools and in the fortresses of Deathless Kings, but most of those held the same sets of dusky tomes. This archive was unique in the world. A bare handful of people knew even a fraction of what was written here, and her job was to learn it all. Her mouth went dry from desire and a little fear.

Abelard preceded her down a narrow alley between piles of paperwork. "It's crazy that we keep all this stuff, but the Church's Craftsmen insist. They don't know anything about engines or steam or fire but to hear them talk you'd think they knew the Church better than Kos's own priests."

"It's beautiful." The words slipped from her mouth, but once they were out she couldn't find fault with them. Abelard fixed her with a confused expression.

"Beautiful?"

"There's so much. You really kept everything." Spreading her arms wide, she walked down the alley, running her fingers over dusty boxes and the polished wood rollers of professional-grade scrolls. Secrets pulsed within, eager to escape.

"Impressive, sure. I don't know about beautiful." Abelard followed her. "You want to see beautiful, I'll take you down to the furnaces sometime. Not an ounce of steel wasted. Kos's glory runs through every pipe, shines from each bearing and gauge. They are the heart of the city, and the center of the Church."

"Sounds like fun," she said, unable to think of anything nice to say about a furnace however efficient it might be. "But furnaces aren't relevant to this case. Everything we need to know about Kos is here."

"These are just glorified receipts. Lists of goods bought and sold." From his mouth those words sounded small and petty. "Shouldn't you try to understand who He was before you look at His accounts?"

Tara let the archive's silence swallow his words, and wished that the Hidden Schools had taught her how to work with clients. Her textbooks mentioned the subject in a sidebar, if at all, before they moved on to important technical concerns like the Rule Against Perpetuities or the seven orthodox uses of the spleen. "These papers," she said at last, "will show us how Kos died, and what we need to do to bring him back. That's my main concern. Faith and glory are more your line of work."

Abelard did not reply, and Tara walked on, knowing she hadn't said the right thing, and mystified as to what the right thing would have been. She almost sagged with relief when Abelard spoke again, however tentatively. "Your boss, Lady Kevarian, said that the, ah, problem, happened because of an imbalance."

Had Tara been a god-worshiper, she would have given thanks for a chance to return their conversation to technical matters. "She's making an educated guess based on what your Cardinal told her, but it's too general to be much use."

"What do you think happened?" Abelard gazed up at the vaulted ceiling.

"Me?" She shrugged. "I don't know more than Ms. Kevarian does. Some kind of imbalance almost has to happen for a god as big as Kos to die. If he expends much more energy than he reaps from his believers' faith and supplication, poof. We're here to learn specifics: what drew Kos's power away, and why."

"That's how you kill gods?" Abelard's voice had gone hollow, but she didn't notice.

"Sort of. That's how gods kill themselves. If you want to kill one, you need to make it expend itself trying to destroy you, or trick it somehow. . . ." She trailed off, hearing his silence. "I'm sorry. I didn't think. I know this is a sensitive subject."

"It's fine." Tara knew from his tone of voice that "it" was not fine, but Abelard didn't press the issue. They walked on between walls of dead words. "You seem very . . . confident around all this stuff for someone so young."

She pondered that as she scanned the labeled stacks of scrolls. Old World contracts, A through Adelmo. Good. The in-house Craftsmen followed standard filing practices. "I studied hard at school. If I ever take you up on your invitation to the furnaces, I'll probably feel the same way when you talk about them."

"I don't know. There's a lot less death and war in furnaces."

"Ironically, right?" No response. "I mean, because of all the fire, and the flame, and the pressure." She stopped trying. They were close.

"How many times," he asked, "have you raised a god from the dead?"

"Ms. Kevarian has been a partner with Kelethras, Albrecht, and Ao for thirty years. She's handled a dozen cases this large, and at least a hundred smaller ones."

"Not her. You."

She let out a breath, closed her eyes, and yearned for the day when she could answer this question without feeling inadequate. "This is my first."

The hall dead-ended in a circular clearing, from which seven more paths branched out into the stacks. By twisting and turning through the maze of those paths, one could reach any scroll in the archives. A shallow bowl of cold iron rested on the stone floor, precisely in the clearing's center. "We're here."

Abelard drew up short. He looked from shelved scrolls, to Tara, to the bowl, and back to the shelves. Tara waited, and wished she could peek inside his mind without damaging it.

At last, his thoughts resolved into language. He cleared his throat, the ugly human sound echoing amid the books. "I was hoping for, you know, a . . ." He glanced back at the bowl, and made some vague gestures with his hands. "A desk. Or a chair, at least."

Tara blinked. "Whatever for?"

"Reading?"

"That's why we have the bowl."

"So we put the books . . . in . . . the bowl?"

Comprehension dawned. She tried to keep a straight face, because Abelard didn't deserve further ridicule, but in the end she had to physically stifle a laugh.

"This is some Craft thing, isn't it?"

"You thought we were going to read this entire room? Tonight?" She walked over to the bowl and tapped it with the toe of her boot. It rang a deeper note than its size and thickness suggested. "Seriously?"

"I didn't know," Abelard said, defensive, "that there was another option."

"Look." She extended one hand and a scroll floated from the nearest shelf to her palm. Unrolling it, she revealed a carefully drawn list of abbreviated names, dates, figures, and arcane symbols, divided in neat rows and columns and simplified to the third normal form. "Your Craftsmen and Craftswomen told you to format your records this way, right?"

He nodded.

"They also set up the archive? Told your scribes and monks where to store everything, and in what order?"

Another nod.

"Why do you think that was?"

"I don't know. Someone had to do it."

Come on, Tara thought. *New kid, monastery kid, churchgoer, and engineer. You've lived in the dark so long you've forgotten that everything has a reason.* She beckoned him toward the center of the clearing. "I'm going to show you a trick."

He hesitated, suddenly aware that he was alone with a woman he barely trusted, a woman who, had they met only a few decades before, would have tried to kill him and destroy the god he served. Tara hated propaganda for this reason. Stories always outlasted their usefulness.

"Give me your arm," she said.

He shot a terrified glance at the iron bowl. "Hell no."

"It's absolutely safe." *Yokel.* "Look, I'll go first, but you need to promise me that after I show you, you'll do as I tell you immediately."

"Okay," he said, uncomprehending.

"Great." Tara reached beneath her jacket, to the neckline of her blouse, and opened her heart. The shadows about them deepened; her nerves tingled, half as though she were holding something and half as though her palm had gone to sleep. Cold blue light sparked between her fingers. Because she was doing this slowly for his benefit, she felt the aftershock of her knife's detachment, a tremor in her soul like a caress from everyone who had ever wronged her.

Her expression must have betrayed some hint of pain or grief, but if it had, Abelard was too busy recoiling with fear to notice. The hairs on his arm stood at unquestioning attention.

"Never seen a knife before?" She held the blade before her face. It crackled.

It took him a few tries to find his voice. "I've never seen Craft so close."

"You've seen Applied Theology, miracle work, right? This is the same principle, only instead of telling a god what I want, receiving power from him, vaguely directing it and letting him do all the hard parts, I do everything myself."

"How is that the same? A god is supposed to have that power. You—"

"I'm a Craftswoman." She knelt by the iron bowl and held out her left arm. "Come closer." He did. "This will look like it hurts, but it doesn't really." Slowly, again for his benefit, she lowered the tip of the knife to her forearm. She chose a nice small capillary flowing near the skin and pricked herself with the blade of moonlight and lightning, cleanly as an old woman ripping open a seam in a worn-out dress.

A scarlet drop of blood swelled from the wound and fell to splash in the iron bowl. She shivered from the pate of her skull to the soles of her feet, as if she had plunged into a lake of metal.

Did Abelard feel the change as her blood sank into the iron, the turning and falling like tumblers in a lock, the sudden tension in the air? Could this boy who spent his life following gods tell when dormant Craft swung into action around him? Or had the color drained from his face merely at the sight of her blood?

When she reached for him, he pulled back.

"You promised," she said. "It's only a drop."

"Your blood is still on that knife!" he shouted over the rush of wind that rose about them without ruffling the slightest leaf of paper. "You're going to make me sick!"

Of all the things for him to know . . . "We make the knife out of lightning for a reason." A sharp tug of building Craft almost pulled Tara from her body, but she resisted with dogged force of will. If Abelard were to help in his god's resurrection, he needed to see. "You think we'd use the Craft where a pocketknife would manage if we weren't worried about infection? Give me your damn arm!"

Thin blue lines had spread from her drop of blood up the sides of the iron bowl, and out, like cracks across thin ice. The cracks widened, and through them, Tara saw a fractal mosaic of spheres, big and small. Each held a design in its center: circles, toroids, slits, stars and spirals, and stranger patterns. Eyes, thousands of them, watched her through the cracks.

"Abelard!"

He lurched forward, arm out, as the archives trembled. His cigarette tumbled from his lips toward one of the hungry, ever-widening cracks, but he caught it before it fell through. Tara's knife flashed, numberless eyes surged against the membrane of the world, and—

Silence.

All she saw was silence. All she heard was a faint, dead scent like fallen leaves in autumn. She tasted night, smelled smooth black marble, and felt ice melting on her tongue.

She had done this sort of thing before, and knew to wait as her senses twisted round again to normal. Abelard was not so fortunate. She would have warned him, she thought as she walked to where he lay collapsed in the dark, if he hadn't been such a pansy about the blood.

He shook. Tara felt empty and a little ashamed.

"Hey." She knelt beside him and squeezed his arm. He didn't look up, and kept shaking. "It's easier when you realize you *can't* throw up, and stop trying." A bedraggled sound, like the whimper of a drowning dog, rose from the vicinity of his mouth. She assumed it was a question. "You don't really have a stomach here, is why. It's not a biological kind of place."

His shivers stilled. Her hand lingered awkwardly on his shoulder.

The new world lightened around them. Finally, he stirred and sat up, blinking, eyes raw and unfocused. He raised the cigarette to his mouth with a trembling hand.

"It felt . . ." He shook his head. "I'm sorry."

"Nothing to be ashamed of. It happens." She stood slowly so as not to startle him, and extended her hand. He regarded her palm as if it might be a trap, but finally let her pull him to his feet. He swayed like a tree about to topple, yet he did not fall.

In the dim light, he looked past her and saw what lay before him, beneath him, all around him. They were standing on an immense body.

The god's flesh was black and deep as night. The curvature of his limbs was the subtle and paradoxical curvature of deep space. He swelled in the dark, a pregnancy of form in nothingness.

The body had the usual four limbs, two eyes the size of small moons, a mouth that could swallow a fleet of ships—features that for all their immensity were beautiful, and because of their immensity were terrifying. It was a great and hoary thing ancient of days, a clutch of power that would shatter any mind that tried to grasp it all at once. It was more than man evolved to comprehend, and Tara's job was to comprehend it.

She bared her teeth in a hungry smile.

"I know Him," Abelard said, quietly.

"Yes."

Kos Everburning, Lord of Flame.

His chest was not moving.

6

Elayne Kevarian meditated on the rooftop of the Sanctum of Kos as the sun declined behind its mask of thick clouds. Before her and beneath her, Alt Coulumb hungered for the coming night.

She was levitating two inches above the ground, and would have reprimanded herself had she noticed. Levitation was a reflex of immature Craftsmen. Students floated in air to feel in tune with the universe, but like any other unnatural posture, hovering caused more tension than it relieved—especially in this city, where Kos's interdict prevented any flight higher than a fist's breadth above the ground.

Thoughts wandered through the corridors of her mind like phantoms in an old house. Judge Cabot, her best contact in Alt Coulumb, was dead. Murdered with crude Craft designed to throw suspicion onto a third party. Had the gargoyle—the Guardian?—been purposefully framed, or did the killer simply set a trap for whoever might stumble by?

This case lay at the bottom of it all, like a fat and voracious catfish in a muddy river: the Church of Kos, the greatest divine institution left in the West, hub of thaumaturgic trade on this continent, wilting with its divine patron. Elayne didn't believe incompetence was at fault. Cardinal Gustave made the right noises, and the documents seemed in order. Nor did it seem likely that Kos died of natural causes. Perhaps one of the Church's far-ranging plans had gone awry. Or else . . . Treachery.

She tasted that word in her mind, exhaled it with her breath.

If it had been treachery, then the traitors were every bit as aware as the Church that Kos had failed, had fallen. Somewhere, they marshaled their forces.

Tara was a good kid. Smart. She would wrestle something

like truth from the archives—truth, that strange monster often pursued but rarely captured. Meanwhile, Elayne watched, laid deep strategy, and prepared.

Soon her opposing number would arrive, a Craftsman chosen to represent the powers to whom Kos was bound by contract and debt. The creditors would select someone respected for age and strength, who had stood trial in dark matters and emerged strong and sure. Someone familiar with Alt Coulumb.

A handful of Craftsmen and Craftswomen in the world fit that description. She knew most of them.

Winds circled within clouds of slate, and the sun was setting. She and Tara had brought the storm with them to the city. Tomorrow, there would be work to do.

Abelard paled, and Tara feared he might collapse again. "God?"

She bit her lower lip and tried to think how to explain. "It's not Kos. Not precisely. What you think of as your god is a manifold of power and information and relationships, deals and bargains and compromises congealed over millennia. For the last century at least, your scribes recorded the Church's contracts and compromises in this archive. Our blood in the iron bowl triggered dormant Craft that combined information from those thousands upon thousands of scrolls into a three-dimensional image we can navigate, manipulate, and come to understand." With a gesture she indicated the landscape of the divine corpse.

"He looks dead."

"He is dead. How did you expect him to look?" She started walking. Abelard followed her, footsteps tender on the god's marble flesh. "You're familiar with what's called a convenient fiction?"

Abelard answered with the flat tone of rote recitation. Good. Retreating to familiar concepts might help him cope. "A convenient fiction is a model used to approximate the behavior of a system. Like engines. Often, a mechanic doesn't need to worry about compression chambers and heat exchange. He only needs to know that the engine transforms fuel into mechanical force.

That description of an engine as a box that turns fuel to movement is a convenient fiction."

"I've never heard that example before," Tara admitted.

"What example do you use?"

"Reality."

They skirted the enormous pit of Kos's navel, broken and lifeless like the landscape of a distant planet.

"You're saying that this," Abelard said tentatively, "is not my Lord's body at all, but a convenient fiction. You think of him as a giant corpse because . . . because it helps you evaluate him in the context of your black arts."

"More or less," she replied. "I'm sure the blueprints and daily logs of your furnaces tell you all sorts of things about your god. This is like a giant blueprint for another facet of him. It's easier for me to understand than furnaces." She saw a discoloration in the distance to her left: ichor welling up from within Kos's body to form a river on his vastness.

When they reached the slick shelf of the god's ribs, Abelard scampered up like a monkey, moving with a deceptive, jerky grace in his long brown and orange robes. Tara removed her heels and threw them overhand up the slope, pulled off her stockings, and attacked the ledge with fingers and toes. When she reached the top, she was slick with sweat and breathing hard. She couldn't quite climb the last swell of protruding bone and muscle, and Abelard helped her up, nearly falling himself in the process.

"Where did you learn to climb?" she asked after she recovered her breath and patted her hair back into place.

"The boiler room," he said with a nostalgic smile. "Thousands of pipes, all shapes and sizes, and ladder after ladder. There's no better place than the Sanctum of Kos to be eleven years old. Though maybe there are better places to be sixteen," he conceded.

Instead of donning her shoes again, she stuffed her stockings inside them and put them in her purse. The divine flesh was cool beneath her feet. "The Hidden Schools are not a good place to be either eleven or sixteen. Fine place to be twenty-one, though, if twenty-one is something you wanted to be."

"Nothing fun for kids?"

"Plenty of fun things for kids, but most would kill you if you did them wrong."

They walked on. Abelard at last surrendered and tapped cigarette ash onto his god's skin, no doubt repeating to himself that this was a model, not the actual divine corpse.

"Does all this walking serve a purpose?" he asked after a while.

"I'm inspecting the body," she replied. "God-meat decays like the human variety. Small dark things, neither god nor man, sneak in and chew at it. Spiritual lampreys: ghosts, half-formed concepts that might become the seeds of new deities. We can tell from the damage they inflict on the flesh how long a god has been dead. Other signs indicate the cause of death."

"What do you see?"

"Some confusing things."

"For example?"

"For example." She let out a rush of breath that fell over the quiet corpse-scape like a heavy robe on a cold floor. "We've passed pools of ichor—divine blood, divine power. Little ones, consistent with a god who died recently. The maggots have dined, but not much. There are more wounds than there should be, though, and they're distributed, where they should cluster. Scavengers are drawn to weak points in the body's defenses. Then there's the flesh itself. Perhaps you've noticed."

"It's cold, and hard."

"Where it should be warm, yes?"

"If He were alive." Abelard shuddered when he said the last word.

Poor kid. "The heat of gods fades slowly. He should still feel lukewarm, at least. Also, there's not enough blood."

"What?"

"A body with much blood in it doesn't remain firm for long. The blood—the power—attracts pests that accelerate decay. This has not happened with Kos. Your deity had much of his blood removed before he died. The drain wasn't sudden, or the skin would be more discolored. His power faded slowly, over time." She looked up. "Do you know what might have caused this?"

Abelard shook his head, mute.

"Has there been anything strange about Kos's behavior in the last few months?"

"Not really. He's been strong as ever." He faltered, as if wondering whether to continue. She didn't wait for him to make up his mind.

"Save for what?"

"Save . . . He has been slow to respond to my prayers for the last few weeks. He always came, but it sometimes took half an hour or longer to attract His attention." Abelard's gaze fell to the ground beneath his feet. "On the night He died, I thought he was ignoring me. Perhaps He found me unworthy. Perhaps I was."

"Did other people have this problem?"

He shifted from foot to foot, unwilling to face her. "The Everburning Lord doesn't often respond directly to prayer. Even the most faithful may receive little more than a moment of His grace. Once in a while, maybe a couple words from Him."

"Don't priests get a direct line?"

"There's a range of faith in the priesthood, as in the laity, but the Technicians of the Divine Throne, who oversee the patch between the Everburning and the city grid, we meet God whenever we come to our post. Or we should."

"If you had a problem, others might have as well. Did you mention it to anyone?"

"To Cardinal Gustave, when we spoke this morning."

"You didn't report anything before his . . . before two nights ago? Didn't ask for help?"

"No." Abelard exhaled smoke. His eyes were red.

"Why not?"

"Would you run to Lady Kevarian at the first sign of trouble, if this investigation grew difficult?"

She didn't answer.

"I'm the youngest Technician in the office," Abelard said. His voice was quiet, and his quietness cut her. "Positions open up once every few years. I barely made it this time around. If I let on I had trouble speaking with our Lord, what do you think would happen? There are scores of people hungry for my place." His narrow shoulders slumped, as if he was melting beneath the folds of his robe.

"The others might have kept silent as well."

"I heard them talking. Maybe they hid their problems, as I did, but Cardinal Gustave sounded surprised when I told him. It was just me."

She reached out and gripped his frail, thin arm. He didn't pull away.

No wind blew in this space beyond the world. Not even the sound of their heartbeats intruded on the silence. "I thought," he said at last, "that if I helped you, I might be able to deal with His death. Find some meaning in it."

"My boss and I aren't in the meaning business," Tara replied. "I'm sorry."

"I know." Abelard did not look up from the god at his feet. "But what am I supposed to do? My faith was weak before. Without my Lord, what's left?"

Millions of people live without gods, she wanted to say. They live good lives. They love, and they laugh, and they don't miss churches and bells and sacrifice. She weighed all the words that leapt to mind, and found them wanting. "I don't know."

He nodded.

"I'd still like your help." Silence. "What would he want you to do?" She pointed to the body at their feet.

Abelard sagged. "He'd want me to help—help Him, help the city, help the world. I want to. Helping is the only way I have left to honor Him. But I don't know how."

"That's what we're trying to do."

"We're like insects here. Less than insects. How can we make a difference?"

"Maybe the problem isn't as big as you think. Maybe we're trying to see it from too close. Want to get a better view?"

He rubbed the back of his hand across his eyes. When he looked up, they were dry. "What do you mean?"

She glanced up. He followed her gaze into the black.

"You can fly?"

"Not outside. It takes too much power for me, even if flight weren't interdicted in your city. But this is a shared hallucination. We can do anything here, as long as it doesn't change the truth behind the picture."

She raised her hand.

There was no sensation of movement, because they were not truly flying. Gravity broke, and they ascended.

As they rose, Kos shrank. At first, the slopes and valleys of his ribs and the swells of his oblique muscles filled Tara's field of vision. Then she saw his whole chest at once, sculpted and magnificent. The stomach she saw next, and for the first time she detected edges to the universe of him, an endless gulf separating the peninsulas of his arms from the plateau of his mighty chest. His face glowed softly, its features almost but not quite those of a man. They shifted as she watched, now blurred and unfocused, now clear and distant as the tiny upside-down image in a magnifying glass. A single detail remained constant: the corners of his mouth quirked into a knowing smile, the smile of one who had seen the earth as a distant blue marble, one who swam in the liquid flames of the sun.

I've seen the world from a distance, too, Tara thought, full of awe and ambition. *Someday I'll match you stroke for stroke.*

"Those wounds," Abelard said, pointing down. "Those are from the creatures you mentioned earlier? The maggots, the ghosts?"

"Yes." Though they had been large as lakes when Tara and Abelard walked beside them, they were barely visible from this height. Little gouges, as if someone had taken a chisel to Kos's flesh. "But those . . ." She indicated large round gaps in the god's arm and leg and throat and chest, punctures from which no blood issued. "Those aren't wounds."

"They look awfully woundlike," Abelard said.

"A defect of the system. You see there's no blood around their edges, no sign of forced entry." He blanched and wavered, but seemed to be handling this part well enough. "They're patch points. When a god makes deals with other people, deities, or Craftsmen, they borrow his power, his blood, through those holes. Out when it's paid out, and in when it returns, increased by the terms of the contract." She frowned. "Here, it's easier to see this way."

She turned her hand, and glowing conduits of power coalesced about the gaping patch points. Blood coursed up half of them, tinted red, sluggish and reluctant, drawn by contracts stronger than iron now that it was no longer sent forth in a free rush by the ceaseless pulse of Kos's divine will. Down the other conduits, blue-tinted blood returned, swift and pure.

"The red tubes send his power out into the world, and the blue tubes bring it back. More blood is going out than returning. You can see, even maintaining the current contracts costs your Church by draining away the little innate power that would defend Kos's body against the maggots."

"And you'll what, fix it so Kos brings in more than He sends out? Restart His heart? Make Him live again?"

She considered lying. Abelard hadn't asked for any of this. He wanted to be reassured, wanted to hear that yes, within a few weeks the madness would be over and Kos whole.

She considered it.

"The Craft doesn't work that way," she said.

He didn't respond.

"We can make something from this body that will honor Kos's obligations, but we will have to cut out other parts of him. Alt Coulumb will be warm this winter, and the trains will run on time. Gods and Craftsmen throughout the world will continue to draw on the power of Alt Coulumb's fire-god, but the entity you call Kos is gone."

"What will be different?"

She tried to think of something encouraging to tell him, but failed. "It sounds like Kos was a hands-on deity. Knew the people of Alt Coulumb by name. That will change. He used to visit your dreams, in the long nights of your soul. I imagine the faithful felt his radiance throughout the city. No more. Even his voice won't be the same."

"But we'll have heat, and trains."

"Yes." Don't sneer at heat and power and transportation, she wanted to say. Hundreds of thousands in this city would die without them even before the winter, from riots and looting, pestilence and war.

She kept silent.

"There's no other way?"

"What would you propose?" she asked.

"Surely some of my Lord's people loved Him more than they needed His gifts. Couldn't that love call Him back to life?"

"Maybe." She chose her words carefully. "He could take refuge in their love to escape his obligations. Consciousness is a higher order function, though. A god requires the faith of around a thousand followers before displaying rudimentary intelligence, and that's if those followers ask nothing in return for their love. If a heavily contracted god, like Kos, tried to do what you describe, he would be barely alive, and in constant, excruciating pain from the contracts that tore at him. If you asked him, he would probably rather die."

"It sounds horrible."

"It is."

He said nothing for a while, and neither did she. There was no sound but their breath.

"He loved this city, you know. Loved His people, and the world."

"Yes," Tara said. She didn't know if this was true, but she didn't care. Abelard did.

He tapped ash from his cigarette and it floated down the miles below. "How do I help?"

She removed a pad of paper and a quill pen with a silver nib from her purse, and handed them to him. "Start by taking notes."

Somewhere, there was a bright room in a high tower, with windows that opened on a field of mist. Other towers rose from the mist, too, forming a forest in the sky beneath a moon that burnt the world silver.

The sun had set, and night was come. Within the bright

room, people were hard at work. A young woman bent over a laboratory bench, making careful incisions in a cadaver. Next to her, a jowly older man scanned tables of densely written figures. At a chalkboard in the corner, two students reviewed an equation from an obscure branch of thaumaturgy. Conversation, when it occurred, was hushed. Each individual diligently pursued their portion of the project at hand. It was a laboratory among laboratories, a perfect, organized system.

As the pretty young vivisectionist inhaled so, too, did the thaumaturgy scholars at the blackboard; when she exhaled, so did the man with his tables. Chalk left white lines on slate as the scalpel parted skin and fat. Sluggish blood flowed. The supervising student at the window sipped his tea and swallowed. A foot came down in one corner of the room and a hand was raised in another. Whispered questions received muted answers. Students relinquished equipment precisely when their successors required it.

The Professor strode through the laboratory, breathing in time with the rest—or they breathed in time with him. His light steps on the worn checkerboard floor were the taps of the primum mobile on a wheel that moved their world. The beats of his heart drove blood in their veins.

He held a clipboard and a pencil. Once in a while, in his ceaseless circuit, he made a note, erased an older mark, modified a sum, or sliced out a sentence. The work of ages lingered on that clipboard, and many were the men and women who would have killed for its contents.

His eyes lingered on the vivisectionist's legs as he passed her table. They were well curved beneath the hem of her lab coat. Supple. And her work was exact.

Pleasures of the flesh, pleasures of the flesh. Unimportant compared with the keen joy of the mind.

He moved to the window where the supervising student waited. The Professor tilted his head back to regard his own image in the window glass: round, high brow, bushy brown beard, pince-nez glasses perched on a broad nose. Reflected in his orbit was the world of his lab.

He closed his eyes, and saw the ties that bound.

He knew the student next to him was about to say something, and prepared his answer as he waited for the words. "You received a letter, Professor. They want you in Alt Coulumb."

He listened to the music of his world, to gentle footfalls, to the murmured symphony of conversation and the slick passage of blade and needle through dead human meat, to the splash of fluid in glass bowls and the flow of blood. Always, he listened to the flow of blood. He thought about the vivisectionist's legs.

He accepted the letter, examined the lead seal, and broke it with a narrowing of his eyes that cut through the dull metal like a hot razor. Removing the folded creamy paper within the envelope, he held it up to the light and read.

"Well," he said at the proper moment. "Tomorrow morning I descend."

The clouds beneath them were a field of black, and the moon shone down.

Tara approached the last of the blue-tinted conduits, and measured its girth with a piece of knotted string. As the string drew taut, glyphs appeared on the conduit's surface in silver spiderweb script. "This is the return from the Iskari Defense Ministry's Naval Division, which amounts to principal plus ten percent guaranteed over rate of inflation, accounted monthly, priority secured, drawn off the stomach chakra."

"That's not usual, right?" Abelard had mostly filled Tara's notepad with sketches and figures. He possessed an excellent draftsman's hand, far more exact than Tara's own. As they worked, he had asked a slow but constant stream of questions, trying to learn enough about their task to help rather than merely assist. The questions kept Tara focused, at least. Document review, even for so momentous a case as this, even with your career on the line, was always a chore. "Most of the patches so far have drawn off the arms, or the legs, not the chakras themselves."

"It's not usual. Nor is it especially unusual." She double-checked the glyphs to ensure she had read them correctly. "Different circumstances call for different contracts. The Is'De'Min is a grotesque, many-tentacled entity ruling over a population of millions, challenged to the south by Deathless Kings, to the north by Camlaan, and to the east by Koschei. This contract is earmarked for use in their own defense. If they rely on Kos for firepower, they have to be able to call upon it at a moment's notice, no matter what. The contract is dangerous for Kos because the power leaves him at such a fundamental level, but it nets him a high rate of return, absolutely guaranteed."

"I see. This is a likely culprit, then." He made a check mark.

"What do you mean by that?"

Abelard hesitated, but at last he answered, in a determined voice without stammer or flinch: "It was probably what killed Him. You said the chakras move up from basic life functions to the most advanced—tailbone, groin, stomach, heart, throat, forehead, crown. This is the farthest south any of the deals have gone. If there was a draw here at the wrong time, it might have taken too much power, and the rest of Him shut down."

"Couldn't have happened. It's too small a contract."

Abelard regarded the blue conduit and its red mate skeptically. Each was thick around as an old redwood tree.

"Too small to do that kind of damage, I mean," Tara said. "It looks large to us, but compared with the rest of the body? Have some respect for your god and your Church. They would never let anyone patch in this far down if there was a chance they might kill the system."

"Kos."

"Excuse me?"

"At least call Him Kos, please. When you say it like that, 'your god,' 'the system' . . ."

"Sorry. But my point stands."

"I thought you said Kos was weak."

"Weaker than he should have been, yes, but not that weak."

Abelard made a note. Even the angle of the cigarette in his mouth suggested doubt.

"You don't believe me?"

"I didn't say that."

"I'll show you." She untied her string from the conduit and

pulled back, skidding and turning on nothingness until she drew
even with Abelard.

"What now?" he asked.

"I'm going to turn back time."

She began before he could protest or ask for clarification.

It was an illusion, of course, but an impressive one. Every record in the Sanctum's archive bore a date and a time stamp. Tara
could manipulate the Craft that modeled dead Kos to show his
body from minutes, hours, weeks ago. When she raised her hand,
time flowed backward.

Blood and ichor rushed in reverse down the conduits that
pierced Abelard's god. The festering sores and decayed pits on his
skin shrank and closed without scabbing over; horrible hungry
things writhed in the darkness, their inverted drones taunting and
tearing at the strings of Tara's mind. The body swelled beneath
them, grew supple. Light streamed from the flesh, and especially
from the heart, an unconscious, vital flow of grace from the god to
his mortal servants. When time wound back to the third day, Tara
felt rather than heard a great pounding, like distant explosions
echoing over a desert. The backbeat of the universe.

His heartbeat.

It battered her soul, demanding worship. Awe quickened at
the base of her spine.

You, she thought to it, *are an echo. A spirit grown fat trading on its own majesty. I'll be damned if I let you see me yield.*

She summoned ice to her mind, endless fields of it, cool starlight and the black between the stars that human minds stitched
together into meaning and Craft. *There is no difference between
us,* she shouted into the vortex of that heartbeat. *I cast you out,
and stand unassisted.*

Her knees wanted to bend.

She closed her fingers, and the whirl of time ceased. "We're
close to the night of your watch, moving forward at thirty times
normal speed."

Abelard had clapped his hands to his ears. Rapture shone
from his face. Useless, but at least he was watching.

"See how smoothly the blood flows? And the light, of course, and the heartbeat."

"What?" he shouted over the noise.

"The heartbeat!"

"What?"

She was about to try again, when the conduits that tied Kos to the shambling horror of the Iskari Defense Ministry erupted with brilliant light. Enough power flowed through those contracts to collapse the walls of a city, to sink a fleet or tear a dragon limb from limb in flight. The light rendered Kos's body in harsh monochrome, and faded as fast as it had burst upon the dark.

When it faded, the heartbeat was gone.

"Amazing," Abelard said, his voice faint and reverent. Then, "It looks like the Iskari contract was a factor to me."

Tara's cheeks flushed. She took a deep breath, and another.

"That can't be it," she said at last.

"Sudden burst of light, and nothing. What more do you need?"

She rolled time back again, to the peak of the Iskari contract's brilliance. Her calculations had been perfect. Well, not perfect perhaps, but good enough. The contract was too small to destroy Kos, yet there it shone, glorious, and seconds later, the god died.

"That's strange." She rolled back time at one-twentieth speed. The Iskari contract flared, faded, died, alone. "Very strange."

"An 'I'm sorry I shot down your idea' would be nice."

"No other contract even flickers. And the Iskari didn't draw any more than their pact allowed."

Abelard looked from Tara, to his God, and back. "So?"

"I'm sorry I shot down your idea. It looks like you were right—the Iskari pact dealt Kos his dying blow. There was no other significant draw on Kos at that time. But I was right, too; the Iskari didn't drain enough power to hurt your god if he was as strong as the Church records show. He must have been weaker. Much weaker. To die from the Iskari pact, Kos must have been half the strength your people thought, maybe less."

Abelard shook his head. "How is that possible?"

"I don't know yet, but it's great for us. The Church didn't

know Kos was weak, so the Iskari pact wasn't negligent, which means we keep more control over Kos's resurrection. Now, all we need to do is figure out what happened in Iskar."

"Aren't we going to look for the source of His weakness?"

"Of course, but that information isn't here. The problem's deeper than your Church. Tomorrow, we'll dive into raw Craft, and find where Kos's power went. For now, Iskar is our best lead."

"We know what they drew, and when. What more do we need?"

"We need to know why. The Iskari made that pact for self-defense, but I haven't heard any news of war from Iskar or the Old World. If your god died because the Iskari abused their pact, we gain ground on his creditors, and even more control over the case. We might be able to bring some of the old Kos back after all."

She released her grip on the visualization. The world around her blurred, cracked, inverted. This time, at least, Abelard didn't scream.

When the cosmos righted itself, they stood flanking the iron bowl in the center of the archives, surrounded by scrolls. A faint odor of iron and salt lingered in the air, the smell of steam from boiled blood. The room was darker than before, but more familiar, too. Abelard clasped the notebook to his chest. His skin was slick with sweat and his eyes were wide from the transition, but he'd get used to this stuff in time. Already he looked more confident than when he had met her on the Sanctum's front steps.

She pulled her watch from her jacket pocket and checked its skeleton hands. Eight in the evening. Not bad.

"Where can I find a newspaper in this town?"

Abelard's expression was blank. "A what?"

7

Shale floated in a pit of night, encircled by cords of lightning. He sought within himself for the fire of rage and found nothing, sought too for the quickened shivering breath of fear and was no more successful. It was as if he had reached down to the fork of his legs and felt there undifferentiated flesh, smooth and polished as a wood floor.

Of course, he had no hands with which to reach down, no legs, nor anything at their fork. The girl had taken all that from him and left him in this prison, where a thousand blankets piled atop his mind and every thought came with slow deliberation or not at all.

Tara claimed she was on his side, and indeed she had pulled him from the jaws of death. The Blacksuits, blasphemers, wasted no love on Seril's children. She did not seem perturbed by his suffering, though, or eager to return him to his body. She needed his information, and who knew what black arts she could practice on him to force compliance? Could she bend him to betray his Flight?

Shale could not break Tara's hold over him, but one act of protest remained to him that not even sorcery could bar.

He had no mouth to open, nor throat through which to draw breath; neither lungs to hold that breath nor diaphragm to propel it out. Yet he howled.

A gargoyle's howl is only in part a sound carried on air like other sounds. A gargoyle's howl, like a poet's, resounds from spirit to spirit within the walls of a city.

Shale's howl shook the darkness beyond his prison.

He let the blankets press him down, and he began to wait.

———

"Let me get this straight," Abelard said as he chased Tara down the Sanctum's spiral staircase. "You can buy a sheet of paper that tells you what's happening on the other side of the world?"

"Yes," Tara replied, focusing on her steps rather than the conversation. Why weren't these stairwells better lit?

"How does it know?"

"Every evening, reporters in the Old World write down what happened that day, and tell the Concerns that print the paper."

"How can they get the information across the ocean so fast?"

"It's like a semaphore, with Craft instead of a flag, and the message moves through nightmares instead of air."

"What?"

"Look," she shouted over the clattering of their feet, "it works. Trust me."

"Then they print the news on paper, and make so many copies that anyone who wants can read one?"

"Exactly."

"Where do they get the paper?"

"The same way you get it for your archives, I imagine."

"The Church makes its own paper," Abelard said, panting with the speed of their descent, "and it's very expensive. We couldn't sell paper for what people could afford to pay."

"Which is why it's so expensive."

"What?"

"If you bought the paper from other Concerns instead of making it yourself, you could have them compete against one another for your business. Each Concern would try to make paper better and cheaper than its competitors, and you'd pay less."

"That doesn't make any sense. Why would the Concerns try to sell paper cheaper than one another? That hurts them all in the end."

Exasperated, she dropped that line of discussion. She would have time to explain the problems of a command economy to Abelard after Kos's return. "How do you get news in this city, if you don't have newspapers?"

"The Crier's Guild. Their news about the Old World lags a

Dispatches come on the big, slow ships, because the ⸻ re too expensive."

⸻ ell silent. As they clattered down endless winding stairs ⸻ ought about ships—about Kos's contract with the Iskari ⸻ nse Ministry's Naval Division, and about the damage to the *Kell's Bounty*'s hull, long and narrow wounds as if someone had raked the ship with claws of flame. Two days ago, Raz Pelham said, we had a bit of nasty business south of Iskar. Running toward trouble, not away.

Pelham's crew had been closemouthed when she pressed them. Unlikely that they'd warm to her now. Pelham himself, on the other hand, had seemed less reticent, and more knowledgeable.

"Abelard." She paused on the steps and turned back to face him. "Where would a vampire go for a drink in this city?"

He smiled. This worried her.

As night sunk its claws into the world, Cardinal Gustave reached a caesura in his paperwork. He handed a stack of documents to his assistant, returned his pen to his desk drawer, stood, and, gathering his crimson robes about him and leaning on his staff, descended to walk the grounds of the Holy Precinct.

Dark thoughts prowled his mind as he searched the empty evening sky. The lights of Alt Coulumb rendered the stars dim and faint, but usually the strongest burned through. Their light invited quiet remembrance of things past, and contemplation of the future. Tonight, though, the heavens were a blank slate.

He wandered, wondering.

His steps took him down the long roads that bisected and trisected the Holy Precinct, along this paved arc section, that curving path. The tip of his staff dug pits in the white gravel as he walked. Occasionally he stopped and stood swaying, and his lips moved without sound. Long fingers gripped the staff as if it were a living thing that might betray him. His face in those moments was made from slabs of rock.

During one such pause, he looked up from his prayer to see a pale figure in a deep lavender dress approaching on the narrow path that led from the Sanctum. Elayne Kevarian. No one else would advance on the Technical Cardinal with such determination as he prayed. He did not want to speak with the Craftswoman, but neither could he avoid her.

She stopped a few paces from him, short-nailed fingers tapping at her slender hips. "Praying, Cardinal?"

"As is my custom," he admitted with a nod. "Not every night, but as many nights as I can manage, I walk the grounds. Pray the prayers. See to the wards."

"I wondered about that," she said. With her toe she carved a small trench in the gravel before her. "I understand the basic protective circles, the purifying patterns, but containment . . . Wards to keep Kos in? Doesn't seem very respectful."

"They were built years ago, in the depths of the God Wars. Seril's death hit this city hard."

"I arrived shortly afterward to work on Justice. I remember."

He shuddered, and searched the empty sky for words. "Some of the Church fathers worried Kos would try to leave his people, run to the front and perish with his lover at the hands of the Deathless Kings."

She said nothing.

"They made this circle in vainglorious hope of keeping him here, safe, with us. All were punished for their presumption, but the circle remains to remind us of the cost of hubris."

Ms. Kevarian looked back at the tower, rising black and thin above the precinct. "War," she said. "It sounds so normal, doesn't it? So pretty." That last word blighted the air as it left her throat. "A few bodies impaled on a few swords, some bright young boys skewered by arrows, and done. What we did, what was done to us, was not war. The sky opened and the earth rose. Water burned and fire flowed. The dead became weapons. The weapons came alive." A gleam appeared at the Sanctum's pinnacle as a novice set lanterns for the evening. Their light reflected off Ms. Kevarian's flat eyes. "Had Kos joined Seril at the front, she might not have died. We might not have won. If you can call anything that happened in that . . . war . . . winning."

It took effort to find his voice. "Why are you telling me this?"

"Because," she said, quietly, "whatever you think of me and

my kind, whatever you blame us for, know this: Kos was a good Lord. I will not let the same thing that happened to his lover happen to him."

Gustave let out a harsh bark that could not have been called a laugh. "Was that what you told Seril's priests before you blinded their goddess and made her crawl? Before you blackened their silver and tarnished their faith?"

The distant lights of Alt Coulumb cast a thousand shadows at their feet.

"I was a junior partner last time," she replied after a long silence. "I did not have much control over the case. This will be different."

A tide of anger swelled within the Cardinal, and he mastered the urge to snap back: I hope so, for your sake and mine. I have fought to defend my Church and my God, and I will fight for them again, until the seas boil and the stars fall. He took a slow breath, and rode that tide until it subsided. This woman was his ally, or so she claimed. She deserved a chance. He turned his face studiously downward.

"If you say so, Lady."

The two left wheels of Tara and Abelard's carriage lurched off the ground as the driver swung them into the narrow gap between a large driverless wagon and a mounted courier. Tara scrambled to the elevated side of the passenger cabin, eyes wide, and shot an angry look at Abelard when he chortled.

The airborne wheels returned to the cobblestones with a bone-jarring thud. Tara's teeth clapped together so hard her jaw ached. "Is our driver insane?"

He brought one finger to his lips. "Don't let him hear you. Cabbies in Alt Coulumb are touchy, with reason. The Guild has zero tolerance for accidents."

"They fire you if you have a wreck?"

"It involves fire, yes. Trust me, there's no safer place on the road in Alt Coulumb than in a cab."

"Especially when there are cabs on the road," she noted as

they cut off a one-horse hatchback, which careened out of control into a delivery wagon.

On the carriage floor lay a canvas sack Abelard had retrieved from his cell. From within, he produced a shiny black mass that unfolded into a pair of leather trousers. Kicking off his sandals, he slid the trousers on beneath his robe. When he saw her curious expression, he said, "Everyone keeps a few personal items. For special occasions, nights off, you know."

"Those look pretty tight." This wasn't because Abelard had extra fat on his bones. His legs were rails, and the leather accentuated their meagerness. She watched him lever the pants into place with some concern for what would happen to his anatomy when they were ultimately fastened.

"What did your boss have to say?" He pulled a shirt from his bag.

"Nothing."

"She knows what we're doing?"

"I told her we were going to find Raz, the captain who brought us here."

"The vampire."

"Right. I told her some Iskari naval claims will influence how we proceed, and, judging from the condition of Raz's ship, I thought he might have inside information. I gave her your notebook."

"You didn't say anything about the Iskari contracts and Kos's death?"

"No." The carriage lurched, and she gripped the inner railing to steady herself. Abelard had unlaced the front of his robe, and was unfolding a white muslin shirt with narrow sleeves.

"Isn't it worth mentioning?" As he lifted the robe over his head, he passed her his cigarette. It was lighter than she expected, and warm to the touch. She had smoked before, but something about the way he handled his cigarettes made them look heavier than normal.

"Of course it is." She studied the glowing orange ember. "You were right, back in the archives. This is my first big assignment, and I don't want to run to Ms. Kevarian whenever something important comes up. I want to have a complete story for her when she asks about the Iskari contract." *I can't risk looking weak,* she thought but did not say. *There are people waiting to see me fail.*

The ember faded as she watched, starved for air. No sense letting it die. As she lifted the cigarette to her mouth, though, she heard a rustle of fabric; her fingers stung and were suddenly empty, and Abelard had his cigarette again. He stuck it into his mouth with a possessive glare, took a long drag, and exhaled smoke. "Which means we need to track down a vampire in the middle of the Pleasure Quarters at night."

He had extricated himself from his brown robes, and the change was shocking. Where a novice once sat, young, eager, earnest, now rested a young man of Alt Coulumb, slick and polished in a rake's tight clothes. The tonsure spoiled the effect so adroitly that Tara had to suppress a laugh before she spoke. "You said you knew someone who could help."

"I've been studying for the priesthood since I was a boy, but I have a friend who spends a lot of time in low places. She knows the undercity." His gaze trailed out the small window into the gathering night. "The question is whether she'll be in any shape to help us."

Catherine Elle arched her back and let out a scream of iridescent pleasure. Her world was bright colors and ecstasy, an explosion of light that shattered the shadows of the bar and broke the pounding music's rhythm. Each second was beautiful and forever, a torrent of lava in her blood, melting her then cooling and compressing, tightening.

Until it was over. Then, the music seemed only repetitive, high strings slicing out a basic melody over punctilious bass. The room was small and dark, clogged with smoke and the sour stench of stale sweat. The strobing dance-hall lights cut her into slices bereft of movement, picture after picture of a small woman in a private booth in a disgusting bar.

The vampire raised his face from her wrist. Blood ran down

his chin in rivulets. His eyes were wide in shock or fear, and the wound in her wrist was already closing.

"What the hell," she said. "What the hell."

Awareness returned slowly as the whiplash subsided. She knew where she was: a little booth off the Undercroft's main dance floor, one of the myriad nooks Walsh set aside for clients who needed a little privacy. A translucent damask curtain separated the booth from the gyrating bodies on the dance floor, a smoky meld of flesh tones and black leather.

She rounded on the vampire. "You let go. You dropped me right when it was getting good."

"Cat." His fangs hadn't retracted all the way, and there was still blood on his lips, so he spit a little as he tried to say her name. "You were way gone, you were great, I didn't want to hurt you, that's all."

"Didn't want to hurt me." He reached for her arm again but she pulled away and he stumbled off the couch, colliding with the far wall. "You think I'm a damn cup? You drink up and put me down?"

Falling, the vampire cut his forehead on the corner of a picture frame—some pale-skinned human chick, mostly naked and wrapped in roses and thorns. The artist thought blood was the same color as roses, but neither the roses nor the blood in his painting was the same color as the blood—Cat's blood—drying on the leech's chin and shirt.

His excuses sickened her. She reached for the curtain.

"I took you as far down as you could go," the leech stammered. At least he could talk now without spitting everywhere. "Farther than I've ever taken anyone. No human could have survived so much."

"You saying I'm not human?" Her voice went low, menacing.

"You should be lying on the floor! You should be limp. You should be . . ." He stopped. Knew what was good for him.

For a moment she felt a little soft. "When did you get to the city, kid?"

"I'm fifty years old."

"When?"

He snarled, and looked into her with a gaze that drunk life. He met something in her eyes that fell on him like a wall, and he flinched and recoiled.

"When?"

"A month back," he said after a while.

"Living rough?"

He staggered under her question. "I heard the city was a good place to find work."

"Last month. Hell. You've spent fifty years jumping farmers' daughters and scaring livestock." She wore a belt of braided black chain around her tight black skirt, with twenty gold coins woven into it. She worked two free, sunk a fraction of her soul into each, and tossed them on the booth seat. "There. Buy yourself someone who's not looking for pleasure out of the deal. But for the love of Kos, don't go around claiming you'll be able to take a girl somewhere she's never been before."

He leapt for her, teeth bared and sharp, hands clutched into claws.

She dodged his grasping arms and brought her elbow down hard on his neck as he sailed past. He dropped to the floor and lay there.

"What are you," he said, panting. "A Stone Woman?"

"A Stone Woman?" She spat on him. "A woman wants more than you have and she's a godsdamn abomination. I was going to let you go easy." She put the toe of her boot into the small of his back and pressed.

He screamed.

Before she did anything more, the curtain ripped back to reveal a man so large he eclipsed the dance floor entirely: Walsh, the bar's owner and minder.

"Ms. Elle," he said. "Is there a problem?"

She shook her head, and the world shook with her. Somewhere behind the mass of Walsh, the party continued. "He called me a Stone Woman, Walsh." She heard the plaintive, angry whine in her voice and hated herself for it. "Can't hold his blood, and he attacks me and calls me a Stone Woman."

The vampire writhed on the floor. She had removed her boot from his back when Walsh arrived.

"This woman hurting you, buddy?"

The vampire muttered something in the negative, and pushed himself onto his hands and knees. It took him a moment to stand.

"Don't forget your tip," Cat said, not breaking eye contact with Walsh. The vampire cursed her in what sounded like Kathic and scuttled out. He took the coins.

"You can't keep doing this." Walsh's voice was so deep it competed with the bass. "I run a clean place."

"Guy was a cheat. A hungry cheat."

"Being hungry's not a crime."

"Used to be good vamps in this city, Walsh. One sip and I was gone. What happened?" The bad comedown was getting to her, haze clouding the edges of her vision like spectators at a crime scene. She staggered forward, put out a hand, leaned on him for support. He hesitated before resting one ham-hock arm around her shoulders.

"You ever think the problem isn't the vamps?"

"Whatchyou mean," she murmured into his chest as he guided her out of the booth.

"I mean you're in here every night, here or Claude's or one of a half-dozen other places. You started with the kiddie leeches, and you've been moving up. Before too long, it'll be you and the real old ones, and they can drain you in seconds. You won't be able to give them lip or beat them up if they mess with you, either."

"I c'n beat up anyone."

"Sure you can, Ms. Elle."

They made their way back to the bar, skirting the edge of the crowd. Somewhere in that dancing mass a young kid was getting her first taste. A quick bite and she'd be flying.

The bar was sparsely peopled. Walsh pulled a glass and a bottle of gin from the middle shelf and poured the glass half full for her. "Look, Ms. Elle. Do me a favor. Drink this, go somewhere, clean yourself up. Read a book or something. Don't hurt any more of my customers."

She downed half the gin with her first pull, the other half

with her second. "You shouldn't let that trash in anyway. Gives you a bad name."

"Will you go? Please? One night, clean and mostly sober, no sticking anything into any veins?"

She looked at him incredulously. "You're kicking me out."

"Better to drink and run away and live to drink another day, kiddo." He motioned to one of the bouncers, a tall, square-shouldered chick with bright orange hair and a blouse cut off at the sleeves to expose daunting musculature. She escorted Cat to the front door, pushed her outside, and shut the door behind her.

The dark alley stank of stagnant water. Two gas lamps shed pale light on the cobblestones, and a large metal dumpster a few yards away swelled with trash. Halfhearted graffiti overlaid deep old scars left by the talons of Stone Men.

A score of back doors led into this alley, but only the Undercroft had an entrance here.

Bums and hobos lay against bare brick walls, hats out to catch change from the passing night scum and the Northtown nobs who drifted east to the Pleasure Quarters after nightfall for their fun. The beggars kept their hands to themselves. If they chased away custom, Walsh would have them cleared out overnight.

Cat staggered upstream against the intermittent current of customers, ignoring the outstretched hands and needy faces and the smiles of the pushers near the corner. She'd tried their drugs before, their Old World poppy milk and their pills stuffed with ground herbs from the Shining Kingdom. A vampire's fang made them all seem frail, flabby jokes. She had less patience for the pimps, and promised herself she would return some night soon when she was on duty.

The alley opened onto a broad and crowded street lit by ghostlight. You could tell the priests from the other reprobates by the hooded cloaks they wore to hide their tonsures.

The world grayed out and her veins ached for something sharp to spread poison through them. Her sweat was cold. Her legs twitched under her and her back hit the brick wall. She slid down until she was sitting on her heels, shoulders bowed forward and hands resting on the sharp toes of her boots. Some Blacksuit would be along soon, to sweep her off the main street and set her on her way home.

It was barely nine o'clock. It had been an early morning at work, with the murder and all. She was okay. Right?

Breathe in, breathe out. Don't look up, because the light hurts your eyes.

A pair of black-clad legs trespassed on the upper edge of her field of vision. That hadn't taken long. She prepared herself for the Blacksuit's words to rake across her mind.

They never came.

Instead, a voice she hadn't heard in far too long said, "Cat, is that you?" It wasn't the most gallant one-liner with which to re-enter her life, but Abelard had never been a gallant type.

"Abe!" She reached out and grabbed his legs, using his body as a prop with which to lever herself, slowly, to her feet. "What the hell, man! What are you doing here?"

He was wearing a black felt hat, she noticed when she climbed her way to his shoulders. The hat covered the tonsure, which was about all you could say for it.

There was a woman with him. Age hard to place; smooth tea-and-milk skin dusted with brown freckles, and her snake-hazel eyes were smooth as well, the way eyes got when they saw too much. She was dressed oddly for a night out, in a black skirt and a blouse with a neckline that barely showed the hollow of her collarbones. Too simple for eveningwear and too severe to be casual.

"Abe, are you *working*?" Cat put all the scorn she could muster into that word.

His eyes searched the graffiti on the wall behind her for an answer, and in his pause the woman extended her hand. "I'm Tara Abernathy. Abe"—she said it with an amused glance at Abelard—"said you might be able to help us."

"Sure," Cat replied. Her head spun from gin and blood loss. "Soon as I finish being sick. Excuse me."

8

Ms. Kevarian received the letter at the door of the small suite that served as her office and quarters. Her features tightened when she saw the seal, as if it were a vicious insect that she couldn't decide whether to crush or fling away. Quietly, she closed the door.

She laid the letter in the center of her desk and sat in an armchair across the room. Light filtered through the narrow windows from the city and cast a long shadow off the rolled parchment. Her elbows pressed against her knees, and she clasped her hands in front of her face, one atop the other. Night deepened, and still she sat, pondering.

At last she moved to the table and held one hand above the letter, palm flat and fingers splayed as though testing a skillet's heat. Starfire glimmered faintly between her hand and the scroll. The seal sparked, hissed, and emitted a line of sick black smoke. She caught the smoke and crushed it into a tiny crystal, pea-sized and jagged-edged, which she tucked into her jacket pocket.

She opened the letter.

It was written in the flowing, watery hand of a person who normally used small, rapid letters but on rare occasions allowed himself a calligrapher's flourish. As she read, the corners of her lips curled downward and fire crept into her eyes.

Dearest Elayne,
If you're reading this, you noticed my little joke.
If not, then I remind you once again, as you cough up
your lungs and breathe your last, to move slowly and
be careful. I would send flowers to your employers and
seek out what remnants of a family you no doubt
possess were I not certain you had contingencies in

*place to resuscitate you in the event of your demise. An
apprentice, perhaps?*

*It has been a pleasure to watch you grow, though of
course from a distance. Partner now, and in Kelethras,
Albrecht, and Ao no less! How it would warm old
Mikhailov's heart to see.*

*I know you don't welcome advice from me, dearest,
but please understand. This is a complex case. Many
twists and turns here, many shadowy corners where
unsavory secrets hide.*

*Be careful. Watch the Cardinal. My roots in Alt
Coulumb run more deeply than your own, and I know
him as an untrustworthy and backward devotee of an
untrustworthy and backward faith. I say this not as
your friend but as your colleague, and one who, if the
letters I have received today are true, is every bit as
interested as yourself in the development of this case.*

*We should speak. I will arrive in Alt Coulumb
tomorrow morning, but look for me tonight in dreams.*

Your adversary of the moment, but always,

Your friend,

Alexander Denovo

A jaunty line from that last "o" jagged off the scroll's edge.

There was no one in the room to see the momentary slouch of
Elayne's shoulders, the bow of her head. No one saw her set the
scroll down and lean against the desk. Of the four million souls
in the artificially brilliant city beyond her window, not one saw
her bend.

Nor did they see her head rise and starlight bloom from her
eyes and from the numberless, fractally dense glyphs upon her
flesh, shining through her body and garments as if they were fog.
The room darkened, and smoke rose from the parchment where
she touched it.

Her wrath broke, and she shrank within her skin and was
nearly human again. Breath moved back and forth over her lips.
She lifted her hand from the scroll, and saw that her thumb had

burned a small dark spot on the velvety surface, over the trailing line of Denovo's signature.

Alexander's signature.

She rolled up the scroll, placed it in a desk drawer, and wove a curse around the drawer so that none who looked within save her would see anything of note. She paused, considered, and amended the curse to exclude Tara Abernathy. Succession planning. You never could be too careful.

A wicker box lay on the desk, stacked with contracts to sign, bindings and wards against invasion and the client's further decay. On top of that stack she placed the book containing the notes of Ms. Abernathy's accomplice. What was his name again? She frowned, and gripped the memory as in her youth she gripped the trout that swam close to the riverbank near her house. Abelard.

Ms. Kevarian had taught herself how to tickle trout an age of the world ago, to hold her hand in the brook and entice with her fingers, to soothe with the light brush of skin against scale, and then, fluid and fast, to grip and lift. She had been five when she gained the knack. Her parents had noticed. Everyone noticed when the word got around, including a young scholar, a boy of nearly twelve whose family was passing through on horseback, bearing him away for study at the Academies, those faltering predecessors of the Hidden Schools. That young boy had asked her how she learned, and she said it seemed natural to her, and he said things that seemed natural seldom were.

Alexander.

He would be here tomorrow, as creditors' counsel, representative of the gods and men and Deathless Kings to whom Kos Everburning made promises that could not now be repaid.

She had expected this. She always hoped for the best, and expected the worst.

She looked through the window upon the starless city, and though she did not pray, she hoped that Ms. Abernathy could protect herself for one evening. When she returned, there would be a great deal to do.

Elayne sat down at the desk, removed the first few hundred

pages of documents, prepared her black candle and her phial of red ink, her quill pen and her thin steel knife and her polished silver bowl, and began to read.

"You're sure you know where you're going?" Tara asked.

Cat did not respond. She held pace five steps ahead, heels clicking on the paving stones.

"I mean," Tara said, "no disrespect, but we've been walking for almost an hour."

Click, click. Click, click.

Abelard, to Tara's right, walked stiffly and said nothing that might break the tension. Tara wished she could ask him questions with her eyes, questions like, "I thought you said this woman was your friend," and, "We've been to six bars already, how many vamp hangouts can there be in one city," and, "Was she born with that attitude or did it accrete on her with irritation, like an irascible pearl?"

The Pleasure Quarters convulsed with sick life like a corpse on a novice Craftsman's table. Dancers in second-story windows shook their hips in time with music barely audible above the crowd's din. An ermine-robed man vomited in a gutter while his friends laughed; a candy seller blew tiny elegant animals out of molten sugar and breathed a touch of Craft into them so they glowed from inside out. An old man with a distended, hairy belly ate fire on a clapboard stage, while next to him a girl in a pink leotard, no older than twelve and painted like a china doll, swallowed the broad blade of a scimitar.

"You haven't given me much to go on," Cat said, and from her tone Tara knew she, too, was frustrated by their difficulty locating Raz Pelham. "Iskari sailor, vampire. Do you have any idea how many of those there are in this city?"

"No," Tara replied, feeling testy. "I don't. This is my first time in Alt Coulumb."

Cat whirled on her. "Kos!" Had her eyes been less bloodshot and her complexion not as pale, she would have been quite pretty. As it was, the word that came to mind was "striking." "Do you want to get jumped? Your first time. Might as well put on a schoolgirl's dress and walk about complaining you can't get the buttons in the back done."

Already a few slick erstwhile tour guides had proffered their services. Abelard fended them off with no effect; Cat shot them a deadly glance and they fled.

Tara bristled. "I was trying to thank you for helping us."

"I'm helping because Abelard's a friend even if he hasn't dropped by in months, and because maybe your Iskari sailor can find someone to get me high." She took a deep breath. "Look. I'm sorry. There are thousands of bars and dance halls and dives and whorehouses in the Pleasure Quarters. Some are clean, good places, most aren't. We can't cover them all in one night. I've been hitting big vamp lairs, but who knows if that's this guy's idea of a good time? We need more information."

"Well," Tara said, "I've told you most of what I know about him. Iskari, pirate, sailor, vampire. Five-nine, maybe five-ten, broad shoulders, red eyes, black hair. Owns his own ship."

"Do you know how he became a vampire?"

"What difference would it make?"

"Some asked for the change, some didn't. Some are into the terror-that-flaps-in-the-night thing, some aren't. Some mope around all night, some want to dance from dusk till dawn."

"I only met this guy for a minute or two." An excuse. You could learn much in a minute. She remembered standing by his ship's ramp, about to descend into the milling dockside crowd. "He was . . . made about forty years ago. After Seril's death. He doesn't come here often."

Cat pulled back when she mentioned Seril, and made a brief hooking sign with her left hand. Superstition? She didn't seem the type, but Alt Coulumb had long been a city of gods and secrets. "Forty years ago." Cat tasted the words. "The Pleasure Quarters weren't so friendly to vampires and their ilk back then."

"Why not?"

"Because of the Guardians," Abelard whispered from her side. "The, ah, gargoyles. They were still around."

"Ah," Tara said without understanding.

Cat lowered her head in thought, and crossed her arms beneath her breasts. The Pleasure Quarters surged around them. Then, with startling speed, she looked up, and said, "He'll be at the Xiltanda."

She set off through the crowd with a purposeful stride. Tara and Abelard exchanged quick, nervous glances, and followed her.

The rooftops of a great city present a panorama unlike anything in the world. A range of giant gumdrop karst formations may impress, a deep canyon awe, and a jungle canopy stun into silence, but cities alone are the product of human hands and human tools, human blood and human will. They come into being through worship, or not at all.

Too few see a metropolis from its peak. Those who do are a strange mix of the city's angels and its demons, those who hold the strings and those who never rose far enough to have strings tied around them. A penthouse apartment has much the same view as a cardboard box on a tenement roof. The resident of each drinks his wine and calls the other a fool, and seldom is either certain in his laughter.

Both the skeleton in the black suit and the round bedraggled man with his paper-wrapped bottle of rotgut watch the city, and they do not change it as much as it changes them.

Something moved across the rooftops. It had many bodies but one heart, many mouths but one breath, many names but one truth. It leapt in shadow from building to building, gliding on spread granite wings. Dim lights from the distant street illuminated the sculptures of its form.

The Flight returned in glory to the rooftops of its birth, which it once ruled until cast out by traitors and blasphemers. Its talons marked passing buildings with harsh, glorious poems of praise, exhortations to the moon that fools below thought dead.

The Flight's teeth were sharp, its backs strong, and its movements swift.

The Flight heard its brother's howl of pain and captivity. It heard, and answered:

We are coming.

The Xiltanda, Cat explained on the way, was a nightclub that took its name from a Quechal word for hell. Not any hell, either: Xiltanda was one of the old-fashioned hells, a hell of many chambers and many punishments, of rings and layers and ranks and files. Before the end of the God Wars, when the night culture in Alt Coulumb—vampires, Craftsmen, and the like—had been underground, they built the Xiltanda as their first great foray into respectability. And as hell had many levels, so, too, did this club, from the ground floor of black marble and chandeliers to the higher realms where there were chains and straps and hooks and padded walls to deaden screams.

There were lower levels, too. Few knew what transpired there. Rumors told of deep mysteries of Craft and thaumaturgy, of human sacrifices and infernal pacts made while smoking cigars in rooms upholstered in green leather.

"It's gone members-only in the last decade," Cat said over her shoulder. "But if your friend was in town forty years ago, he's probably a member. It's classy, comfortable. Exactly where I'd want to spend time after a long ocean trip."

"I don't know." Tara couldn't imagine Raz among cool marble and shining lamps. "It doesn't sound like his type of place."

"Even if it's not usually, it's one of the few clubs he'd remember," Abelard put in. "The city's changed a lot in forty years. Even the gods were different back then."

They found Club Xiltanda on the main drag, an imposing building in mock Quechal style. Giant sculpted faces leered from the stonework at passersby. Most structures in the Pleasure Quarters were horribly talon-scarred, but if there were any gargoyle marks on the Xiltanda's artfully crumbling, faux-ancient walls, Tara could not see them.

Two waterfalls flowed from the roof to flank the entrance, which was guarded by a large, bare-chested man. Torches everywhere cast smoky light and shadows. Music emanated from within the building, a swing band playing something brassy in four-four time.

Tara sought among the crowd, and to her surprise identified a familiar figure approaching the front gate: Raz Pelham, still wearing his white uniform, sleeves rolled up, cap pushed back on his head. He produced something small from his sleeve, a membership card maybe, and the bouncer stood aside to let him pass.

"Raz!" she shouted, but her voice was lost in the din. She rushed through the crowd, plowing past a clucking coterie of parasol-twirling society girls and nearly overturning a cigarette vendor. "Raz!" He didn't pause. Weren't vampires supposed to have exceptional hearing? "Captain Pelham!"

The crowd near the entrance was thick and sluggish, sporting bad leathers and worse attitudes. Tara shouldered her way to the front of the line as the doors closed behind Raz. From all sides she felt the harsh stares of the drunk and disdainful, but it was easier to press on than fight her way out. A thrashing moment later, she stood before the bouncer, who regarded her and the disgruntled crowd in her wake with detached amusement.

"You got a card?" he asked.

"I'm looking for Captain Pelham. The man that just went in there."

"Wasn't any man just passed through this door."

"Vampire. Whatever you want to call him. I'm a friend of his."

He held out his hand for her card.

The club had been built forty years ago, about the time of the Seril case. Ms. Kevarian was almost certainly a member. Her name could gain Tara access, but also lift the veil of secrecy around their presence in Alt Coulumb. There were other ways into a club. She might as well try them.

"Look, I'm not a member. I just want to talk to him."

"No card, no entrance. That's the rule." He crossed his formidable arms over his chest.

There was an added weight behind that word "rule," and when she blinked she saw its source. Someone had woven Craft through this man's body and brain, granting him strength and speed and protection from simple weapons so long as he obeyed the terms of his contract. To admit a nonmember would weaken him, and cause considerable pain.

She could break that Craft with her own power, or modify it to render the bouncer a kitten in her hand. A mere activation of the glyphs woven into her fingertips, a stroke on the side of his neck. She thought back to her fall from the school, and her throat tightened. No. She would not do those things. There had to be another way.

She was still thinking when she heard Cat's relentless drawl behind her. "Open the door, Bill."

Tara swung her head about. Cat waded through the press of the crowd. Her black leather skirt and her thin sheen of sweat glistened in the torchlight. Tara's eyes flicked to the scars at her throat, camouflaged but not quite concealed by her black silk scarf.

"Ms. Elle," Bill said. "You haven't been by in a while."

She placed her hands on her hips. Tara stepped aside to let her work. "I haven't had a reason to come. You've been glad of that, haven't you, Bill?"

Bill glanced left, right, looking for someone to tell him what to do. Cat had power here, apparently. Tara looked to Abelard for an explanation, but he was still forcing himself through the crowd. "You're always welcome, Cat."

"Don't give me any crap." Her voice was smooth and dangerous. "I've two kids looking for a quick nip, and a hungry old man inside who wants a meal with personality. If you don't get out of my way I'll make sure the Xiltanda doesn't stay open a full night for weeks."

Whatever hold Cat had over the club, this threat was enough for the bouncer. He was wired to serve the institution first and guard the door second. He cast a warning glance back at the crowd, sought once more for a supervisor to consult, then stood aside, opened the door, and bowed his head. "Ms. Elle."

"That's what I thought, Bill." Cat produced a coin from her belt, feathered it down the side of his neck, and rested it in the hollow of his collarbone. He swallowed. "Be well. Say hi to your kids."

She flowed past him through the open door, Tara on her heels. Abelard stumbled out of the clutching crowd and followed.

The club's foyer eschewed the Quechal style for brass, marble, and polished wood, illuminated by a hovering crystal sphere within which glowed a creature tiny, winged, and almost human, trapped by twisting tines of Craft. An imprisoned sprite—but no. Tara's eyes narrowed. Not imprisoned. A ward filled the creature with pain and rapture, yes, but it was temporary, and mutually beneficial. She allowed herself to be captured here every evening, and at dawn a portion of the club's power passed to her. Was this, in truth, slavery? Ask the managers of the club and they would deny it, and the sprite trembling inside the globe would say the same. Tara was uncertain either of them could be believed.

A few patrons lingered in the foyer, checking their coats or smoking or waiting, but Raz Pelham was not among them. A thick, beaded curtain led to the dance hall. Tara strode toward it, and through.

The Xiltanda's main hall was more to Tara's taste than any of the crowded, sweaty dives she had seen in Alt Coulumb thus far. Trapped sprites shone within the crystal chandelier–cage above the oak dance floor, and a swing band twirled a lively tune. Patrons sat at deep booths along the walls, drinking, watching, and waiting. An iron skeleton with a heart of cold fire danced with a bronze-skinned woman whose hair trailed down the plunging back of her dress in long slender braids. The skeleton dipped her and she threw her head back and her teeth flashed. In a corner booth an ancient Iskari Craftsman played an Old World game Tara didn't recognize—a board game with no pieces save stones the size of a thumbnail, some black and some white—against a long thin boy with long thin fingers and golden hair. By the bar, something that might once have been human, but now resembled a winged reptile, was losing an argument against a plump, smiling Crafts-woman who munched on peanuts and nursed a tall glass of stout.

The club reminded Tara of pleasant evenings at the Hidden Schools, but this was not time to join the party. Across from the stage rose a broad iron spiral staircase, winding down into shadow and up through the vaulted ceiling to unknown chambers. Raz Pelham was three quarters of the way to the Xiltanda's second story, and moving fast.

Rather than skirt the dance floor's edge, Tara cut through. She dodged the spinning skeleton and his partner, and nearly tripped over the black dress train of a tall, pale woman dancing with a mustachioed gentleman in a pinstriped suit. A lumbering green-skinned man who looked to have been reanimated many times over nearly crushed Tara with a flailing limb, but she ducked. Behind, Cat shoved dancers out of her way as Abelard apologized in broken sentences. "Very sorry, I mean— My apologies, she— Well that's hardly—"

"Come on," Tara called over her shoulder as she sprinted for the stairs. "Captain Pelham!" she shouted over the music, but the retreating vampire didn't break stride. He must have heard her.

Cat and Abelard started up the stairs behind her. The swift percussion of their footsteps clashed with the tripping rhythm of the band below.

This stairway connected all floors of the Xiltanda, but a veil of opaque shadow divided each level from its neighbors. Tara passed through the shadow between the gleaming first story and the second, a chamber drunk on red velvet and echoing with screams and sighs and repetitive, bass-heavy music. Raz's feet were already disappearing through the shadow above, between the second story and the third.

Tara ran after him. When she reached the third floor (a bare monastic scene, altars and stone walls and the distant crack of whips), Raz had not yet reached the next shadow. He redoubled his speed without a backward glance.

Raz had to know that fleeing would make her pursue. She had already seen him. Even if she didn't catch him, he couldn't hide from her forever, or from Ms. Kevarian for that matter. If he was afraid of being identified, he should try to attack and silence her, not escape. There was no reason to run, if the decision was his to make.

Comprehension congealed in her gut. The next time she closed her eyes, she let herself truly see.

Vampires were creatures of Craft, their life in daylight traded for strength at night, their death for hunger, their satiety for senses more acute than mortal imagination. Folk in Edgemont feared vampires because they looked like people until it was too late, but to Tara's eyes, their twisted souls shone.

Which was why she hadn't previously noticed the hooks of Craft that speared Raz's head and heart. Something was riding Captain Pelham, pulling him upstairs under his power but not of his own will.

"Someone's got his mind!" she shouted back to Abelard and Cat. Whatever gripped Raz must have heard her, because the vampire ran faster still. She reached out with threads of Craft to lock his limbs in place, but the threads melted against his flesh. No surprises there. Craft was difficult to use against a person neither dead nor alive.

Someone had snared Raz's mind all the same.

The fourth floor was white-walled and smelled sickeningly sterile, the fifth dark as pitch and so silent Tara did not hear her own footfalls. She closed her eyes and saw Raz outlined in blue and receding above. Motionless human figures floated in the darkness around her, curled into fetal balls and warded with Craft that banished all sensation. She shivered as she ran, and almost fell.

The sixth floor smelled of sulfur, the seventh of ice. Tara's legs were made of melted metal, and something hot and sticky lodged in her lungs in place of air. Raz disappeared through the shadow ceiling above, to the eighth floor. Tara ran after him and found herself at the top of the stairs, her path blocked by a latched steel door.

With a backhand wave she shattered the deadbolt, crashed the door off its hinges, and burst onto the chill rooftop. Neither moon nor stars relieved the darkness of the cloud-clogged sky. The only light rose from the street below.

"Raz!" she called again. He did not break stride or slow as he neared the roof's edge.

Vampires were difficult to catch with the Craft, but not impossible. She couldn't touch his body nor his soul, but the dense contract that knit his spirit to his dead flesh, that she could hold. Threads of starfire spanned the distance between Raz and Tara; his muscles and mind locked up and he skidded to a halt five feet from the edge of the roof.

He pulled against her Craft. Sweat beaded on her forehead.

This was harder than it should have been. Clouds robbed Tara of the stars' power and left her to bind Raz with her own meager reserves of soulstuff. She needed to get that hook out of his mind quickly, or her strength would fail.

Footsteps on the rooftop gravel behind her. She recognized Cat and Abelard by their breath, hers even and steady, his wheezing.

"Tara," Abelard said when he could form words. "What the hell?"

"Hook in his mind." Raz pitched and strained like a fish against her line and she almost fell. Her unseen opponent didn't seem to care whether the Captain escaped or plummeted to his death, so long as Tara didn't hold him. "Controlling him."

"What?"

She took a step toward Raz, two, the strain increasing with every foot. Her arms ached, her hands shook. She had never been one for raw displays of power. Hers was the clever solution, the quick step, but now she matched might with an old vampire who had been strong even in life.

She bound her feet to the rooftop with Craft to prevent them from sliding, and in that moment of diverted attention he began to pull away.

Someone called her name, but she could not answer. Dark shapes moved around her and she paid them no mind because she had no mind anymore. Raz was four feet from the edge of the roof, three. If he fell with Tara's power hooked through him, so would she.

He would have pulled her off the roof already had she not bound herself to the ground. At that thought, an idea came to her. She knelt, and as he surged against her bonds, fangs bared, she connected the cords of Craft that held him with those that anchored her to the rooftop. One line knit Raz, body and soul, to the solid stone of the Xiltanda. His tether went taut and he bounced back, crumpling on the building's edge like a netted animal.

Tara stumbled forward and fell a few feet from the vampire. The Craft hooked through his soul blazed, and he spasmed in pain as it burned his memories.

"Tara!"

"No," she shouted, not in answer. "No, dammit!"

"There's something you should see."

"They're taking his mind!"

The hook would burn him clean if she let it, without leaving a scar. The mind was good at healing. Breaches in memory it wallpapered with ignorance or echoes of routine. She had to stop the process, but she was weak without starlight. She reached for her purse and the implements within. Silver forceps for drawing the Craft from Raz's mind, and black wax for warding him against its return. There, and there. Rosemary, for remembrance, and fennel, for . . . for something. . . .

Abelard had stopped talking. She glanced back to call for his help. Another pair of hands could make a difference.

Then she saw the gargoyles, in the dark.

There were six of them, and they were large, spread out in a loose semicircle on the roof to cordon Tara, Abelard, and Cat off from the stairwell and escape. Shale had been small and sleek by comparison. Each of these creatures was at least eight feet tall, wings flaring higher behind them. Deep scars crisscrossed their bodies. Six pairs of emerald eyes gleamed in six broad, contorted faces, some beaked, some fanged, some tusked like elephants. Light from the street below illuminated the hungry interior of six large stone mouths.

Tara had only defeated Shale with surprise on her side, when he was in human form. His brethren were ready for battle. There would be no reasoning with them, or, no tricking them through reason. They understood force, and Tara didn't have force on her side.

Cat's eyes were fixed on the tallest gargoyle—immense, female, and blunt-faced like a lion, with long, wicked talons and muscles tight as steel cords. Cat barely breathed. Abelard looked from Tara to the gargoyles and back. An inch of ash shivered at the end of his cigarette. "Tara?" he said, tentatively.

"Abelard, I can't." Raz's brain was being fried from the inside out, and she was almost spent. She could save whatever this unknown Craftsman wished to wipe from the captain's mind, or else try to protect Abelard and his junkie friend and maybe herself.

If Raz knew something about the case, Ms. Kevarian needed to know it, too.

Tara's grip shook on the silver forceps.

"You shouldn't be here," Cat said to the gargoyle.

Stupid addict, Tara thought. Hopped up and ready to fight the world. They'd chew through her first, and save Tara to clean their teeth.

But the gargoyle answered. Her voice rumbled like an avalanche.

"We come to reclaim our brother."

Cat was not fazed. "You violate the law by setting foot within the city."

"This was our city once."

Cat turned to Tara, unperturbed by the several tons of killing machine arrayed before her, and said, "Take care of the vampire." There was authority in her tone and bearing. Tara did not quarrel. Returning her attention to Raz, she gripped the end of that red-hot hook of Craft with her forceps and pulled, evenly and with every fiber of her being. Raz twitched. A soft whine escaped his lips.

Pull harder. If you die here, leave Ms. Kevarian with everything she needs. Otherwise you've failed her, which means you left your home and your family to die on a rooftop in a city your kinfolk abandoned generations ago, all for nothing.

The world turned black and white around her as she pulled. Starfire caught and burned in her eyes. The blacks and whites faded to gray and the gray itself began to blur. Breath came heavy in her ears.

She heard a scream.

Abelard saw the Guardians, their presence staining the air, and he saw Cat rebuke them like an empress, head back, chin up, the scars at her throat wild and red and raw. Tara collapsed over Raz Pelham's body, unconscious. His cigarette smoke tasted of sour, copper panic.

Cat glanced from Tara back to the Guardians and said, "It was your city. Now it's mine."

She raised a hand to her chest, grasped a small statue that hung from a steel chain around her neck, and began to change.

Black ice flowed through Cat's mind as her hand closed around the badge. It chilled and crushed her fear of these six heretic killing machines, and her fury at their presence. The burning tower of her need stood alone against the rushing cold: the need for a fix, the need for a high, the need to be something better than she was.

Catherine Elle was fallible. Afraid. Angry. Desperate. What remained after the black ice washed over her was strong, clear, hard, slick, patient, hungry. Her mind froze as a shallow, clear pond freezes, trapping fish in midflow. The jumping chaos of her thoughts resolved into stillness, and the stillness came alive with whispers.

These Stone Men were members of a Flight that infiltrated the city days before and had thus far eluded capture. Judge Cabot's killer was not among this group, but he had been seen in their company.

Idolaters, Cat would have called them. Wild creatures, barely human.

Cat wasn't here anymore, though. Justice was.

She examined the large Stone Woman with eyes of liquid black. This was the leader of the group, old but still strong. They had not attacked—a good sign.

Your presence is in violation of City law, Justice said through Cat.

"We want our brother," the leader snarled. "Stand aside." The Stone Woman darted left faster than a normal human could have seen. Cat moved faster, and blocked her path.

Justice does not stand aside. But if you leave, I promise to let you go.

"Even if you defeat me, my children will eat your heathen heart. There's one of you, and six of us."

Not one, she said, *but thousands. Fifteen can reach this rooftop before you chew through me.*

"You'll still be dead."

Doesn't matter.

The Stone Woman drew herself to her full height, and her wings unfurled. "You're bluffing."

Try me.

Wind whispered between them. Cat's muscles tensed, ready to spring—but the Stone Men were gone. All six, scattered like dry leaves before an autumn breeze. One landed on the roof of a dance hall to the north, wings flared to catch the night wind; three others glided to the peaked gables of a neighboring bordello. Cat couldn't see the remaining two.

The Suit released her, the oil-slick coating receding reluctantly from her skin. To Cat, it felt like peeling off a scab that was her whole mind. Power left her body, swiftness her thoughts, clarity her soul, and the many voices of Justice died in her ear. Nothing took their place. No, not nothing. The void, an absence strong as any truth.

She sagged to her knees, shaking and cold and in desperate need of a fix. Slender arms encircled her. Abelard. She saw his face as if from the bottom of a pool of water, hazy, naïve, concerned. Her friend.

Poor son of a bitch.

She was lucky, she thought as he held her, that the vampire was unconscious. There was no telling what she would have done for a bite, for a rush to fill the empty space Justice left behind. She would have sold her soul. Maybe she'd done that already. It was hard to remember.

9

Tara fled down dream corridors from a great and terrible fate. Or was she indeed fleeing *from* a great and terrible fate, and not *toward* one?

Demons and gargoyles hounded her, talons gleaming with her blood. In terror she turned and struck, and soon her knife gleamed with theirs, but there were more of them, endless and brutal, and she ran. A turn in the strobe-lit hallway confronted her with an old wooden door, painted white with a brass knob. A sign was pinned to the wood, a child's scrawl: gone.

Whatever she fled, or sought, it was beyond that door, nameless and writhing.

She turned the knob and pushed. Shadows scrabbled around the doorjamb, long and slender and hooked like spider's legs. The howling, clawed things neared behind her. She steeled herself and leapt through.

Blackness melted and ran like wax. She heard a voice.

"Quite to the contrary, Professor. I wasn't surprised to get your letter. Though I admit the curse was a shock."

Ms. Kevarian reclined in an ornate armchair the color of fresh blood, and sipped the dregs of a vodka tonic. Her lips were more full and red than in waking life, and her skin, while not precisely flush with youth, possessed a pleasant rosy hue. Her hair, too, was darker. She seemed a woman still innocent of the years of sleepless nights and deep Craft that would sculpt her into Elayne Kevarian. Only her eyes betrayed the illusion. "I thought we were beyond such games."

With a practiced slump of her wrist, she held out her drink to be refilled, and Tara plucked it from her. The hand that took the glass did not belong to Tara, though. It was too pale, skin alabaster against the black cotton of what appeared to be a waitress's uniform shirt, and its nails were painted red. Tara would have dropped the glass in shock had she been in control of her body, but that hand, hers and not hers, carried out its duty automatically.

She set the glass on the table in front of Ms. Kevarian, removed a tiny bottle of vodka and a tonic spritzer from the tray she carried, set the tray on the table, and mixed the drink. Tara experimented, trying to set aside the vodka bottle or push the glass away, but could not control her movements. Odd. This was her dream, wasn't it?

It was fortunate Tara had no control over her dream body, or she would have spilled the drink when Ms. Kevarian's companion spoke. "You know, we used to enjoy our jokes, you and I."

"Jokes?"

The bearded, barrel-chested man in the sport coat looked no younger in this dream than when Tara had last seen him in the Hidden Schools, leading the faculty to cast her out, flame and starlight shining like a crown about his brow. Professor Denovo.

She handed the vodka tonic to Ms. Kevarian and straightened, reclaiming her tray. Professor Denovo paid her no mind. She was hired help, beneath notice. He held a tall glass of beer and gestured vaguely with his free hand as he spoke. Tara remembered the cadence of his voice from lecture halls long distant.

"Please don't take it poorly, Elayne. We will, regrettably, be working against each other in the coming months, but that hardly requires us to be uncivil."

"We will," Ms. Kevarian corrected, "be working together."

"Exactly," he said with a smile that showed the tips of his upper teeth. "You working for the Church, I for its creditors. It's in neither of our best interest for Kos's demise to last longer than necessary."

"This won't be another Seril case, Alex."

"Of course not." He dismissed the idea with a wave of a hand and a contemptuous expression, as if scooting away a student's distasteful paper. "But you needn't be so vindictive. We were in

THREE PARTS DEAD · 133

the creditors' employ during the Seril case. Naturally we strove for their advantage."

"This is necromancy," Ms. Kevarian said. "There is no winning, and no losing. Death is our enemy. We're both trying to overcome her."

Denovo laughed like a river. "A remarkably traditional paradigm considering your own work's influence on the field. I think I will hold a conference on the subject once my schedule clears. Adversarial Relationships in Necromantic Transaction, that sort of thing. There's been a metric ton of Iskari theory on the subject in recent years, to say nothing about what's come out of the Shining Empire. Camlaan's always half a decade behind the times, of course." He waited for her to comment or interrupt, but when she did neither he returned his attention to his beer.

"What does your party want out of this?"

"Oh, you know clients. Never agree on anything. The radicals want the Church destroyed, or transformed as in the Seril case. There's a conservative faction, content to leave matters largely as they lie. And the Iskari, of course."

"Of course." Ms. Kevarian cradled her glass in both hands, as if it were a slender neck that she was about to wring. "Where do you stand?"

"With my employers. What about you, my dear?"

In the ensuing pause, Tara experienced a moment of terrifying frisson. The interlocutors' dream bodies and the elaborate illusion of time and space fell away, and seated across that table from each other were two forces, irreconcilable and profound and not altogether human, locked in a duel so intricate their conscious minds were barely aware of its complexity. The vision endured for an instant, then broke, and left them old colleagues sharing a drink once more.

One corner of Elayne Kevarian's mouth turned up. "On the side of Kos Everburning."

"I never took you for a sentimentalist." He said that word as if it referred to a form of parasite.

She sipped her drink, and looked up at him. Now she was

smiling indeed. Tara thought she preferred Ms. Kevarian's previous expression. This one chilled.

Tara opened her eyes in a bare room with pale blue walls and an unfamiliar ceiling. Through the gap between the curtains she saw the raw gray of what might have been twilight, but exhaustion told her was the first hint of dawn. Cloth scratched her bare skin: a hospital gown.

Ms. Kevarian stood at the foot of the bed, waiting, arms crossed.

"How long was I out?" Tara croaked.

"Not long. Abelard contacted me soon after your collapse. We've no proper facilities for a Craftswoman's recovery, but the Infirmary of Justice is the best in the city. I added some of my soulstuff to your own, to bring you around faster. I thought you might not wish me to trouble the firm's insurance policy by requesting their aid."

"Thank you." Tara recoiled from the thought of asking Kelethras, Albrecht, and Ao for help. The firm would not approve of her nearly dying after two days on the job.

"You were acting in our interest, and I want to ensure you continue to do so. Besides, this is a learning experience. I expect that in the future you will be more careful than to engage an adversary of unknown power without preparation or backup."

She nodded, and the world shook around her. "Raz. Did I save him?"

"Hard to tell. Captain Pelham seems whole, but I haven't picked his brain in decades. Any damage will be more apparent to you than me."

"I'll . . ." A dew-slick glass of water rested next to a tin pitcher on the bedside table. She almost dropped the glass twice as she worked it to her mouth. Her throat absorbed the liquid like a dry sponge. "I'll see him after I get dressed. Where is he?"

"A few rooms away, angrily maintaining that there's nothing wrong with him and he's fit to return to his ship."

She poured herself another glass of water. "I'll move quickly. I imagine he still sleeps most of the day?"

"Yes. He's spent years training himself to endure the sun. Pain, burning, exhaustion. Some kind of macho thing, but he still goes to bed every morning. Talk to him, learn whatever you can, and come to the Court of Craft. We have to contest a preliminary motion before the judge at eleven."

Her mouth went dry. Standing before a judge after one day on site was borderline insane. They didn't even know why Kos had died. How were they supposed to hold a preliminary hearing? "If you don't mind my saying so, boss, I think that's premature."

She nodded. "As do I. Unfortunately, we are not the only parties at play."

"I saw . . ." She broke off. There was no easy way to say this. "I thought I saw you in a dream. Talking with Professor"— Shivers caught at her voice, and she stilled them by force of will. "Professor Denovo."

"He's the lead Craftsman for the creditors," Ms. Kevarian said with a curt nod.

"It wasn't a dream?"

"It was certainly a dream. It was not, however, your dream. Denovo contacted me last night, proposing a meeting to discuss the case. As he would not arrive in town until this morning, we met beyond the Gates of Horn, through which true dreams flow. It was not a productive meeting, but given your history together I tacitly included you to prepare you for working with him. Or against him, as he would put it."

"You pulled me into a dream without my consent, and kept me there," she said. "I didn't know that was possible."

"You are my employee and my apprentice, Ms. Abernathy. You'll find there is little I cannot do to you, your notions of the possible notwithstanding."

"How did you do it?"

"You came to a choice within your dream. A door, it often looks like, if Dr. Kroen's research is to be believed. I twisted the dream so your choice led to an end of my choosing. This is not a robust strategy—you'll be more cautious of dream doors now that you know it, for example—but it works."

"Yes, ma'am."

Neither of them spoke. Ms. Kevarian doubtless had negotiations to perform, individuals to interview, paperwork to complete, but she remained. Perhaps she smelled a question in the air.

At last Tara gave it voice. "Boss, last night, in the dream. It seemed like you and Professor Denovo had a history together . . ."

"I was his partner," she said after Tara trailed off. "During the Seril case. We were both young, and he was my supervisor. We had a professional relationship." She uncrossed her arms and rested her hands on the railing at the foot of Tara's bed. "I hired you because you're brilliant, and because of the way you stood up to him. I didn't expect you would need to face him again so soon." She paused. "What would you have done, out of curiosity? Had you encountered him without warning?"

Tara considered. "Killed him. Or tried to."

Ms. Kevarian nodded. "Crisis averted. Get your clothes on, and interview Captain Pelham. I expect to see you in court by ten thirty."

"Yes, ma'am." She swung her legs over the edge of the bed and reached for her pants.

Abelard paced the bare waiting room, lost in smoke and thought, taking little notice of his surroundings: a few plants in cheap earthenware pots, beige tables and beige chairs. A drunk slept on a couch in the corner, covered with a flimsy beige blanket.

An orderly approached and Abelard palmed his cigarette. She sniffed for the source of the tobacco stench; her eyes met Abelard's, wide and watery with the pain of the cigarette ember against his skin. He offered her an uneasy smile as she passed, her mouth tight with suspicion and disapproval.

When she was gone, he returned the cigarette to his lips with a gentle sigh. The first puff came as biting, painful relief.

"They'll catch you, you know," Cat said from her perch on a low table. She was browsing a report on the night's events, which a Blacksuit had delivered to her in the hours before dawn.

"Eh." Abelard shrugged. "I'm only hurting myself, right?"

She shot him an odd look.

"What?"

"Don't they teach you priests public health?"

"They didn't teach us anything public. It would defeat the purpose of being an arcane order."

"I thought that just meant you didn't get Saturdays off."

That had been a joke only in part. He heard the anger beneath it. "Cat, I would have sneaked out, but the advancement exams were coming up, and after I became a Technician there was so much to learn. . . ."

"Yeah," she said, distantly. "There was so much to learn for two and a half years?"

He stopped. "Was it really that long?"

"I've gotten two rounds of bonuses. At least that long."

"Kos," he swore, and the tip of his cigarette flared with the exhalation. "Two years, and I show up on your night off, no reason, with this strange woman."

"Who's nice, don't get me wrong."

"I show up, asking for your help, with no more than a hello."

"If I hadn't thought I would get a fang out of the deal, I probably would have told you to stick it."

He rolled his eyes. "And you tell me these are bad for my health."

"They are."

"So's getting some . . . *creature* to chew on you." His mouth hung open after he said the words, as if he could breathe them back in. He tried to say something else, anything else, but all that came out was a slow "Ah."

"You're right," she said. When he did not respond, she raised her eyes from the scroll. There was a flatness to her features. Color had not returned to her face or limbs, hours after she removed the Blacksuit. She shook her head. "Shit, maybe it was better back when Seril was here. Before Justice, the Blacksuits, all of it. I don't know. When I work, I'm Justice. Then it ends, and all that's left is this pit." She lingered on that pause, tasting the sentence in her mouth like stale breath. "You know the feeling now, I guess."

"You heard."

"Justice told me. She thought I should know why you were working with a Craftswoman."

"Do all the Blacksuits know?"

"No. She wants to keep this secret. People will panic when they hear."

"And you won't?"

She shook her head. "He was more your god than mine. I'm sorry."

"I saw His body," Abelard said at last. "Laid out against the dark. Tara showed me. But . . ."

"What?"

"There was something missing." He flicked ash into a potted plant. "I don't know. It must be worse for you. The parts of Kos I cared about, heat, steam, flame, passion, they don't die. Since I knew Him, and since I loved Him, I'll still see Him in everything I love. Seril died long before our time. You never knew her."

"Justice."

"Excuse me?"

"Her name is Justice now." Cat rolled up the scroll and held it before her. Had it been a sword, she would have been staring at its tip. "You're right. It's not the same thing at all."

"Cat . . ."

"I said don't worry about it. You have your own problems. You . . ." Something choked her off.

He approached her slowly, as if she were a cornered and wounded animal. She had always been able to retreat beyond her body to places he couldn't follow, ever since they had ceased being children together and started to grow up. He wished he could follow her into that space behind her skin.

He hadn't made a noise, but when he crossed some invisible border around her she raised her head like a startled drinking bird, and fixed him with a bird's alien eyes. He wanted to say something.

He certainly didn't want Tara to interrupt, from behind, with a "hello."

He turned, but not nearly as fast as Cat rose to her feet.

Tara looked fine. Precisely fine, not well nor so shrunken as she had seemed hours before. Pallor lingered beneath her brown skin, but her eyes were bright. She wore dark pants and a dark shirt and flats, and a flower print hospital gown over the ensemble, open down the front.

"Nice coat," Abelard said. She cocked an eyebrow at him.

Cat stepped forward, and snapped to attention. "Ma'am."

Cat's newfound formality gave Tara pause, but she continued: "Thank you both for bringing me in. Cat, especially, for . . ." Her brow furrowed. "You scared off the gargoyles. You're a Blacksuit? Or did I dream that?"

"No, ma'am." She bowed her head, a sharp, mechanical movement. "Lieutenant Catherine Elle, bound to the service of Justice." She proffered the scroll. "Yesterday Alt Coulumb saw its first Flight of Stone Men in nearly forty years. We're working to ensure they will be the last."

"You don't need to be this formal."

"I do, ma'am." Cat tapped the scroll in her left hand. "I've been assigned to protect you. We can't let you go unshielded with Stone Men in the area."

Tara stiffened. "Protect me? Against what?"

"Against the Stone Men, for one. And against whatever danger you may encounter in our city."

"I don't need protection."

"I have my orders."

"What if I refuse?"

She blinked, slowly, considering. "This is Alt Coulumb. Justice's will is paramount."

"Shouldn't they assign someone else? You have a personal relationship with my assistant." She indicated Abelard with a nod. "No offense."

"I've known Abelard since I was a girl. He won't stand in my way. Also, I think you overestimate the individual prerogative officers of Justice have in their work."

"Individual prerogative. You mean free will?"

"Ah." Cat frowned at that question. "Yes, ma'am."

"Interesting." Tara's expression remained clouded. "Welcome to the team. We'll discuss specifics later, but we're on a tight schedule. Can you lead me to Captain Pelham?"

Tara's eyes adjusted slowly to the dark room. The vampire lay spread out on the bed, long, slender, and naked from the waist up, sheets pooled around his hips, a fallen mast surrounded by twisted sails. Scars webbed his torso, earned from blade and fire before his death. One was a long, wicked, narrow burn that had not been caused by natural flame.

His chest neither rose nor fell.

"Your line," she said, "is, Thank you for saving me."

He laughed. "As I reckon things, we're even. One rescue from drowning and one from, well . . ." His red eyes flicked left, to Abelard and Cat standing against the wall behind her. She had warned them to keep their distance. The stress of last night, combined with her hasty mental surgery, might have damaged Raz's self-control. A Craftswoman's blood was unappealing to most vampires, as a shot of rubbing alcohol was unappealing to most alcoholics. Theirs, though . . .

"What is the last thing you remember?"

"I was going to meet a client," he replied. "Get paid."

"At Club Xiltanda?"

His eyebrows rose. "Xiltanda. Huh."

"Is that a surprise?"

A pause followed, about the length of a breath. Rhetorical habits died hard. "I," he said, "am cursed by peculiar clients. There are not many owner-operators of my . . . persuasion. Clients with needs beyond the natural often choose the *Kell's Bounty* over larger and better-equipped vessels because they know we'll serve their needs and ask few questions. Understand?"

Tara nodded.

"For this reason, we have a reputation that makes it hard to get normal work." His eyes narrowed. "Don't look at me like that. It's not as if I chose this."

"You did," she noted. "Vampiric infection won't work unless you accept it."

"Better unlife than death, as your boss said when she gave me the option." His anger spent itself on her silence. "I suppose you're right, though. I made the choice, even if it didn't seem like a choice at the time, and its consequences have leapt in and out of my wake ever since. Like dolphins." He made an arcing motion with one hand, and Tara saw nine feet of silver-blue glittering wet in moonlight above a silent sea.

"You were hired by a Craftsman."

"I was hired south of Iskar in the Northern Gleb, in a port about thirty miles from the border of King Clock's land. A man sought me out. Six feet tall, maybe, with thin, sallow features. Narrow mustache, long nails. Moved like a snake. Fringe of white hair." He wiggled his fingers in a vague semicircle around the edge of his scalp. "Wore a silver skullcap. He . . ." Raz's features twisted in confusion. "He wanted us to deliver a package. A chest of magesterium wood, with little silver runes. Told us to bring it east, to the Golden Horde . . ." He frowned. "No. Not to the Horde. We delivered it to Iskar. I can't remember which city." The words came out strangled. Had he been human, his forehead would have been beaded with sweat.

"When we first met, you said the *Bounty* came to Alt Coulumb from Iskar via Ashmere. Why stop there?"

"We needed repairs, fast ones. Most of the ship had to be replaced. Burned sails and a broken mast. Demon scars on the hull, a hundred small holes in the keel. It would have taken weeks had there not been a good Craftswoman at the docks."

"I thought sailors didn't like Craftswomen touching your ships."

Raz bared his fangs. "Your boss robbed me of the luxury of such superstition a long time ago."

Tara considered her next words. Raz was in a delicate mental state. Beyond the blackout curtains, orange light threatened the horizon. Morning weakened him, but if she pushed too far too fast he might break. In his rage he could cross the room and tear out her throat before the sun caught him, whether he liked the taste of her blood or not.

"Raz, when was your ship damaged?"

He looked at her as if she'd spoken nonsense. "In the battle."

"Which battle?"

"With the Iskari treasure fleet. Three days ago."

Good, she said to herself. Play dumb a while longer. Bolster his confidence. He likes telling stories. Ask him for one. "Treasure fleet?"

His grin turned rakish. "The Iskari still have colonies in the Skeld Archipelago and on Southern Kath. Diamond mines, silver. Oil. Magesterium wood. Every year, the navy brings treasure home in ships so big it seems wrong to call them ships anymore. Hulls of mystic wood worked by Craftsmen and reinforced with silver and cold iron. Sheets of steel, sails preserved by demonic pact. Charms and wards calm the waves about them, keep the winds loyal and turn attacks away. The Iskari treasure fleet." His voice rose in rapture, and sank to a sigh. "Beautiful sight on a blue morning. Impossible to take."

"Impossible?" she asked in her most curious voice.

"That's what everyone said." He turned to the window, his gaze passing beyond the curtains, beyond the city, to the sea. "They were right, but we came close. Night hid our vessels from enemy eyes and curses. The Craftsman called dead ships from the depths to aid us, crewed by lumbering monsters that once were men. Without him, we would have broken on their defenses. Without us, his clumsy dead things would have been too slow to cordon off the fleet. The Iskari called sea serpents to rake our hull and breathe lightning on us, but we pressed the attack until the fire came."

This part Tara knew. The fire struck near dawn, Iskari time, around two in the morning in Alt Coulumb. Walls of flame and billowing columns of steam erupted from the suddenly boiling ocean as the treasure fleet's admiral invoked the Defense Ministry's contract with Kos Everburning. The pirates scattered, dead ships sinking again beneath the waves. Kos's wrath scorched the *Kell's Bounty*, burnt her sails and shattered her mast and raked her hull. The crew clustered on deck and prayed desperately to whatever gods might hear them—one or two Kosites begging for His mercy—until the fire died with its Lord.

"The treasure fleet escaped in the flames," Raz explained. "We seized what we could from the wreckage of the ships we burned, and made for Ashmere."

"Was that," she said, like a girl taken in by a fantastical bed-time tale, "before or after you delivered the package in Iskar?"

The question brought Raz up short. "What?"

"Did you deliver the package before or after the battle?"

"Package . . ." He shook his head. "What package?"

"The one the old Craftsman asked you to deliver. Did you deliver it and then have this battle, or have the battle and then deliver it?"

"What battle? We dropped off the chest and went straight from Iskar to Ashmere. That's it." Raz's words hung in the air. He heard them, and understood them, and his expression grew dark. "I . . ." His eyes were wide and red. He looked the way Tara herself must have the morning before, drowning until he threw her the line.

She sat on the edge of the bed and laid her hand on his bare arm. His skin was cold, of course. "You're not crazy. You made a stupid deal with what sounds like a desperate man, or maybe a desperate woman, but you're not crazy."

"What do you mean?"

"When I found you at the Xiltanda, someone was trying to burn out your mind. That kind of thing is incredibly hard to do, even standing right next to a person. To do it from a distance, he must have had your permission." She waited for him to respond, but he said nothing. "You met a Craftsman who needed your expertise and wanted anonymity. He proposed a trade. A large share of the treasure, for your memories of the event. The attack failed, but last night he took his part of the bargain anyway. He tried to burn out your mind, and I don't think he intended to stop with your memories of the attack."

His tongue shot out to wet lips that did not need to be moistened with saliva he no longer possessed. Another tic. Tara wondered how many little human mannerisms survived in him. "I don't remember a deal."

"That would have been the first thing burned out. I'm sorry."

"I remember the wizard with the skullcap. The magesterium wood box."

"Raz," she said slowly, and she hoped kindly. "Memories are stories the mind tells itself, based on what it believes happened. Can you think of a Craftsman you know who'd wear skullcaps and robes? Might as well expect me to flounce about in a skull bikini. The secret mission with the mystery box is straight out of a De-Gassant adventure serial. When those memories were burned out of you, your mind tried to bridge the gaps with half-remembered snatches of story. Cliché mystery-play villains. Plots that have bored a thousand readers. Be glad I stepped in when I did. The mind's awfully inventive. A few more minutes and it would have been impossible to convince you there was a difference between your story and the truth."

Raz slumped back into the pillow. "Will these memories go away?"

Lying would be too easy. "No."

"Ah."

"If you're careful, and honest with yourself, you'll be able to reconstruct what you did in those days. You won't forget the other story, with the wooden box. Your memories will lead you back there once in a while, and you'll catch yourself recalling things you know aren't real."

Beyond the drawn blinds, the first errant rays of sunlight peeked through the deep urban canyons of Alt Coulumb. "This city," he said. "Nothing here ever quite works out for me."

"You're a strong guy. You can handle it." She gave him a moment before asking her last question. "Do you remember anything about the person who really hired you?"

"No."

"Thank you, Captain Pelham."

She began to rise, but his hand settled around her arm like an iron cuff. His nails, sharp and hard as diamonds, dug into her skin. If he squeezed a little her flesh would tear.

She counted the length of her breath.

"I'm not going to hurt you," he said. This is not something people often say if they are not about to hurt you, but Tara believed him.

"I know."

"You seem like a good kid, Tara."

"Thanks."

"Is this what you want?"

She wanted her arm back. "What do you mean?"

"Working for a big firm. Ripping my brain open on a rooftop at midnight. Is this what you want?"

There were a lot of answers to that question, but only one came to mind. "Yes."

His grip slackened. Her arm slid free.

"Can you close the curtains the rest of the way before you leave?"

"Sure."

10

A young man with a hollow face stood on a street corner North-side, overshadowed by steel towers and the tracks of an elevated train. He wore a jacket of rough orange cloth and cradled a lute in his thin arms. One by one he plucked its strings, tuning each to match notes that reverberated in his mind.

Pedestrians ignored him, the rich in their cloth-of-gold robes or sleek jackets, the idle ladies in layered confections of lace and cotton and silk, the workers dressed stark and severe. His fingers hovered fearfully above the lute's fretboard, then descended.

He strummed and sang of a four-carriage pileup on Sandesky Street, Northside, sang of a critical low in the three-week barley reserves, sang of the slaughter by knife of a family of three in a Westside tenement, of the killer at large and Justice on the hunt. He sang a rumor leaked by off-duty Blacksuits too much in their cups and too loose in their tongues: the Stone Men had returned to the city. Once more their talons marked the innocent buildings of Alt Coulumb. Justice suspected them of one murder already, and citizens were warned to be watchful, lest this outbreak spell the end of forty years of freedom from heretical fanaticism. Stone Men could be anywhere, disguised as anyone.

This last point wasn't precisely true, but it attracted attention and earned the young Crier tips. The protestations of his professional honor were overcome by the hunger pangs of his not-entirely-professional stomach.

Across Alt Coulumb, men and women of the Crier's Guild sang this dawn song, the morning edition, until sweat slicked their faces and deep impressions of lute strings marred their calloused fingers.

A drop of sweat rolled into the young Crier's eye, and he

blinked. When he opened his eyes again, the world looked much as before.

Had he been more attentive, he would have noticed a new arrival, a man watching him from across the street through the shifting maze of pedestrians and carts and carriages. A mane of dark hair and a bushy brown beard framed his face; his shoulders were wide and his eyes round. He wore a tweed jacket, and his hands were thrust firmly in the pockets of his pleated wool slacks. His angular mouth had trapped an approving smile and did not relinquish it no matter how it struggled.

The man in the tweed jacket listened to the song. The Crier did not mention Kos, nor the death of Gods. A smart analyst could parse the endless thaumaturgy section *("For Alphan Holdings riseth in price / Two and a quarter to four and six tenths, / And Lester McLuhan and Sons doth decrease . . .")* and note a twitch in the energy market, but Church security held. The salient facts of Kos's death remained unknown.

Good. Once that news leaked, chaos would burn through the city, and chaos was bad for business.

Alexander Denovo pulled out his pocket watch. It gleamed silver against the hard, cracked skin of his blunt-fingered hand. His family owned many watches, but he had built this one himself early in his study of the Craft, laboring for long hours with delicate tools, reveling in the exquisite predictability of its clockwork motion. Gears turned within its slender shell, and its face bore many dials, some marked with the usual numbers, some with mystic sigils, some with phases of the moon. One bore every letter of the alphabet. Little knobs and buttons rounded the top edge.

It was nearly time for court.

He fished a silver coin from his jacket pocket, crossed the road, and dropped it in the bowl at the Crier's feet. The young man bowed his head in thanks and continued to sing. When he looked up, Denovo was gone.

"So the Iskari murdered Kos," Cat said as she led Tara and Abelard down the halls of the infirmary, walking backward.

Abelard shook his head. "This isn't a criminal investigation."

"Isn't it? Someone's dead."

He looked at her as though she had suggested an obscenity.

"You said the Iskari could access Kos's power at a very basic level. He didn't have a choice about whether he gave it to them or not, right? Even if the Iskari didn't murder him themselves, someone could have planned that attack on the treasure fleet to kill him."

Abelard looked to Tara for support, and she hesitated. Tara barely trusted Cat, and didn't trust Justice at all, whatever protestations it made of its impartiality. Cat was here in part to protect her, of this Tara had no doubt, but also to watch and report back. Anything she said here, she said to Justice. Then again, the more Tara shared, the less Justice would suspect she was hiding. "It's an interesting idea," she said at last, "but the treasure fleet is a rich target, and this might be a case of simple bad timing. Anyone who wanted to use the pact as a weapon had to know about it first. The Church holds its archives sacred, and the Iskari Defense Ministry is a blood-mad cult that doesn't share knowledge with outsiders. Also, the Iskari contract only hurt Kos because he was low on power already, which not even the Church seems to have known. If this was a murder, our murderer is absurdly well informed."

Abelard, who had grown more agitated as the conversation progressed, stopped and threw up his hands. "Could we please not talk about God as if He were a corpse on the floor?"

Both women fixed him with curious expressions. He lowered his arms, but remained defiant.

"There has to be a connection," Cat continued.

Tara frowned. "There are too many pieces to this puzzle. We've got a murder, an attempted assassination, a divine death, and a case of piracy that may or may not be linked to any of the above."

"Assassination?" Cat asked.

Tara cursed herself silently for letting that slip. "Someone tried to kill my boss and me as we flew toward Alt Coulumb yesterday. Outside of the city's jurisdiction."

"You should have reported it."

"I've been busy. My point is, there are so many puzzles it's hard to keep them straight."

"Don't forget the Guardians," Abelard interrupted, petulant.

"The Stone Men. Shit." Cat looked as though she were about to spit in disgust. "They're crows before the storm. They don't need an excuse to go where they're not wanted."

"Hard for me to believe they aren't tied in somehow," Tara said, "considering that they showed up for the first time in forty years in the thick of this mess."

"They're drawn to doom."

They reached a juncture in the branching hallway, and Tara stopped short. "Wait. Where are we going?"

Abelard glanced from one hall to the next. "I thought you knew."

She rolled her eyes. "I need to get to court. Does anyone know how to reach the street?"

The carriage they hailed was a tiny, driverless two-seater. Cat knew a quick route to the courthouse, and sat up front to direct the horse, which left Abelard in the back with Tara.

This was not an accident. The first carriage that tried to pick them up had been large enough for four, but its right wheel locked on the axle and the two-seater beat it to the curb. Tara felt bad for the first cab's owner, but she wanted to talk with Abelard in private and this was the easiest way to arrange it.

"Do you think Cat's right?" he asked as she glanced back to undo the Craft with which she had bound the first carriage's wheel.

"About what?"

He watched the pedestrians outside their window, garbed in business blacks and blues and grays save for the occasional burst of a Crier's orange. "She thinks God was murdered."

"Cat's a policewoman. She knows one thing, and she knows it well. There are problems with the murder theory, as I said."

"But it's possible."

"Yes," she admitted, rather than lying.

He fell into silent contemplation. She framed a question in her mind, but before she opened her mouth, he spoke again. "What got you into this business?"

"What do you mean by that?"

He looked hurt, and she relented.

"Sorry. I'm tired. I shouldn't have snapped." The risen sun hung invisible behind low clouds. Skyscrapers converged into the haze.

"I was thinking about what you said to the v— to Captain Pelham."

"Vampire," she corrected. "You can say it."

"Back there. About your choices. I can't imagine being happy in the life you lead."

"It's not normally this hectic." Which wasn't an answer. Their carriage proceeded slowly through traffic. She remembered long stretches of empty dirt road winding through Edgemont fields. "I come from the country. My folks were teachers, my friends farmers. I wanted more." It was a question she'd asked and answered a hundred times at the Hidden Schools: Who are you, and why are you here? None of the answers she had given then seemed right now. "And here I am."

"It's a weird kind of more. Necromancy. Black arts."

"That was part of why I chose to study the Craft. It was different from anything I knew. I thought, whatever I get out of this life, it won't be what I would have had in Edgemont."

At age six, Tara had first recognized the divide between her family, refugees who fled west during the Wars, and the native clans of Edgemont with their deep roots in the land. She remembered feeling, as a child, a need to prove something to her classmates. What right had they to look down on her family for hailing from beyond their postage-stamp town? But that memory was likely false. Six years old, she probably felt only confusion: Why don't their parents like mine? Why don't they like me?

Abelard did not reply, and she seized the opportunity to change the topic. "What about Cat? Why does she give half her life to Justice?"

"I don't know." He flicked cigarette ash out the window. "We grew up on the same street. A simple neighborhood, poor enough that the people there struggled to keep up the illusion they weren't poor. Cat wanted to serve the city, but in a different way from me. Gears, pulleys, pistons, theology didn't interest her no matter how I tried. She saw people getting hurt, and other people doing the hurting, and thought she could make a difference through Justice."

"Does Justice make a difference?"

He shot her an odd look. "You should know. Your boss helped create her."

"Ms. Kevarian doesn't really talk about her last visit to Alt Coulumb." This was why she had gone to the trouble of getting the two of them alone. "I hoped you could give me a history lesson."

"About what?"

"Seril. Justice. The gargoyles. They fit together, don't they?"

Abelard's face looked thinner than yesterday morning, as if something inside him were melting flesh and fat and muscle away. "They fit," he said.

"Tell me."

He squirmed, but her silence was unrelenting and at last he surrendered. "Seril was night and moon and rock, everything cold and proud and untouchable. Maybe that was why Kos loved her. She wouldn't burn."

"Kos loved her?" Tara hadn't known that. A pair of gods ruling together, one for day, the other for night, one creating, another ordering. Bonds of love between opposites were powerful, stable yet dynamic. No wonder Alt Coulumb had stood for so long and grown so vast.

"They loved each other," Abelard acknowledged. "But the God Wars were like the opening of a dam for her. She rushed to the front lines, with her priests and soldiers."

"The old City Guard. Who became the Blacksuits."

Abelard shot her a sidelong glance, uncertain what he should say next. As if afraid she was testing him.

A dozen disparate facts fell into place. "The gargoyles." She couldn't keep an edge of shock from her voice. Stupid. Why hadn't she seen it before?

"The Guardians of Seril. The goddess created them. Moonlight and night air sank into stone and the stone came to life." Abelard looked uncomfortable with the idea. "I wasn't alive to know them, but my father was, and my grandfather. They say the Guardians roamed the rooftops in small bands, marking territory with their talons, writing poems to Seril that could only be understood when seen from the air. They hunted the night. If a crime occurred, they swooped down, claws out. Criminals feared them because they were implacable. They had no families, no friends, so you couldn't threaten them. The city was safer in those days. The Blacksuits may be effective, but the Guardians were terrifying."

"What happened?"

"When Seril went to war, they followed her. A few remained in Alt Coulumb. Not enough to keep the peace. At least, not enough to keep the peace, ah, peaceably."

"There were deaths," she said.

"Yeah." He didn't look at her. "I mean, there were always deaths, but now there were more. Criminals, mostly."

"And a few Craftsmen."

He looked up. "I didn't think you knew."

It wasn't hard to guess. The God Wars had not been a pleasant time for Craftsmen and Craftswomen around the world. One day, you're a simple thaumaturge, idly meddling in matters man was not meant to comprehend. The next, a collection of beings as old as humanity, with legions of followers, declare war on your "kind," and neighbors who once thought you a harmless eccentric with a fondness for mystic sigils and foul unguents see you as an affront to Creation.

All the usual things had happened. Riots, pogroms, lynch mobs. Many of the victims had not been Craftsmen at all but mathematicians and philosophers, anatomists and chemists and scholars of ancient languages. Universities around the world were razed. True Craftsmen and Craftswomen protected what and who they could from the riots, sheltering scholars with their might, ripping towers and libraries and great cathedrals from the earth and spiriting them away into the deep sky; in time these stolen buildings congregated and grew into the Hidden Schools and the other great Academies. But there had been too many to save. The great and powerful and angry, like Ambrose Kelethras and Belladonna Albrecht, struggled on the front lines against the gods, while around the world their less militant and more trusting brethren fell to murder and to the madness of crowds.

It was a dangerous era for those who used their minds.

This wasn't the time to say any of these things, so she shrugged, and said, "It happened." And, "Seril died on the front lines."

"She died in battle. The Guardians in Alt Coulumb went mad with fear and fury and grief. They saw rebellion everywhere. Grandpa says the city went to war with itself. Most of the buildings that stand unscarred today were razed in the struggle and rebuilt from the foundations up. Swords can't cut stone, so we defended ourselves with hammers. Priests called down Kos's fire against Seril's children. The old clergymen say God wept." Abelard would not look at her, and she couldn't read his voice. "When the rest of the Guardians returned from the war, they attacked the city walls and we thrust them back. It was a bad time." He broke off. "Have you ever seen a gargoyle enraged?"

"No," she said, pondering what the cute young man trapped within her purse would do to her if—when—freed from her binding spell. It wasn't a pleasant thought. In his native shape he had been large and swift, his talons sharp.

"Neither have I," Abelard admitted. "They attacked the city again and again from the forests and were thrown back each time. It was a long, hard fight. People started to believe Seril's children were monsters all along. Personally, I think the Cardinals were relieved. They mistrusted Seril and her faithful. She was, they were, too dark, too strong, too in love with the old city to belong in the bright world Alt Coulumb was trying to join. We remade their goddess into Justice, and instead of Guardians we made Blacksuits. When the Blacksuits first joined battle, the Guardians fled to the forest, and weren't seen again." They hit a harsh bump in the road. Abelard grabbed the side of the carriage for support. "Until last night."

"And Cat," she ventured, "hates the gargoyles because they betrayed the city she tries to protect?"

"Maybe. Sometimes I think she hates them because they had a goddess, and she doesn't."

The carriage jolted again, but this time to a stop.

"Courthouse" was the wrong name for this building. Courthouse suggested nobility, distance, a polite remove from the world. There was nothing noble or distant or polite about Alt Coulumb's Third Court of Craft. It did not stand at a remove from this world so much as inhabit another one altogether.

It was a soaring pyramid of black, pinnacle lost in low-hanging cloud. Runes covered its face, dense as crosshatching, invisible to the untrained eye though they burned in Tara's mind. This building warped the world around it, purified it, made it real. The skyline near the pyramid's edge flexed concave to convex as in a magician's mirror. Tara's heart sank. Abelard and Cat, by contrast, seemed nonplussed.

"It doesn't look strange to you?"

Abelard didn't say anything. Cat shook her head. "I mean, there's always been something funny about the Court of Craft, but . . ."

"How many sides does it have?" Tara asked.

"Four," Cat replied confidently.

"Five," Abelard said at the same moment with the same self-assurance. They exchanged a brief, frustrated glance.

"Fair enough." Tara squared her shoulders and strode forward.

There was no door in the pyramid's front face, but as they approached the black stone, the runes flowed and rearranged into a familiar pattern. A translation would have begun, "By crossing this barrier you do undertake to bring no harm by Craft or blade to those within. Definitions of 'harm' include, but are not limited to, death, personal injury, injury to the will or to the memory, injury to one's ability to pursue the interests of one's client, acts of God, and all other forms of harm. 'Craft' indicates . . ." and so on, a protracted list of definitions and special cases. The standard contract was full of loopholes and exemptions, but it usually held, a minor miracle for which Tara was glad. There would be blood enough before the Judge today without extracurricular violence.

She walked through the runes and the stone upon which they were printed, and the contract settled against her skin like an old cobweb. Her companions did not follow at first, likely deterred by the prospect of walking into what seemed to them a blank wall. Abelard's loyalty, or perhaps curiosity, got the better of him and he entered after Tara, brushing at his face as the contract took hold. Cat followed a moment later.

"It looks smaller on the inside," Abelard observed.

They stood in a long and narrow hallway, well-lit and carpeted in deep red, its walls paneled with rowan wood. There were no doors to the left or right, and Tara knew that if she looked back she would not see an entrance, only the four edges of wall and ceiling and floor proceeding until perspective crushed them to a point. Far ahead stood a door of wood and smoked glass. As they approached, she read spidery letters in black upon it: KOREL ROOM.

"This," Cat said in a hushed whisper, "doesn't look like any court I've been to before."

"What," Abelard shot back, "they don't usually have disappearing walls and endless hallways?"

"And there's usually more than one courtroom in a building."

"There's more than one courtroom," Tara said. "The hall only takes us where we need to go."

"For privacy reasons?" Cat ventured.

"Privacy, and safety."

"Theirs?"

"Ours. Courts of Craft are dangerous if you don't belong."

"We do, though, right?"

Rather than answering the question, Tara opened the door.

The courtroom was over a hundred yards across, circular, and walled in black. Ghostlight shone from jewels set into the domed ebon ceiling. A massive Craft circle had been acid-etched into the floor and the acid grooves filled with silver. Within the circle's silver arc, at the far end of the room, rose the Judge's empty dais.

Near the entrance sat an array of benches, upon which slouched their audience: a pudgy trailing-whiskered man in an orange Crier's jacket, a few elder Craftsmen come out of curiosity, and a student with lines under her eyes, who glanced nervously at the empty benches around her, hoping more people would arrive so she could doze off without anyone noticing.

Tara felt sorry for the girl. There would be no eager masses today. Tomorrow, after rumors of Kos's death spread, would have provided a better opportunity for a nap. The chamber would be so crowded then that nobody would notice a kid catching some sleep.

Cardinal Gustave sat at a low table to the left of the silver circle, and Ms. Kevarian stood near him, her face a professional mask. She twirled a dry quill pen between her fingers. A squad of Church personnel stood behind the Cardinal, backs pressed against the chamber's rounded wall. They wore a range of expressions, but most were some degree of terrified.

None of the contract holders with claims against Kos Everburning had come in person, unsurprising considering that they were Deathless Kings and other gods. They would send envoys in the coming weeks to observe negotiations, but for now they merely hung immanent in the air about the desk to the right of the circle, where Alexander Denovo sat alone in his tweed jacket. His attention was bent on a yellowed scroll, and he didn't seem to notice Tara's arrival.

She had expected to feel more upon encountering him for the first time since her graduation: a dryness in her mouth, anger curling like a fire in her breast, a sour taste at the back of her throat, the bright purple pulse of fear behind her eyeballs. When she saw him, though, she just felt dead.

Dead. Adrift on currents of air, falling toward the Crack in the World, bloody and bruised, broken, her mind aching. His laughter echoing in her soul.

"Tara?" Abelard's voice. Focus on it.

"What?"

"You looked funny for a second there."

"Funny?"

"Scared, almost."

"Not scared." She wasn't sure what she was feeling, but it wasn't fear. Fear was weakness, and if she had been weak, she would have died a long time ago. "But almost."

"You know that guy?" He pointed to Denovo, but she slapped his arm down. "What?" he asked, cradling his wrist.

"It's rude to point."

She brushed past Abelard toward Ms. Kevarian, who acknowledged her presence with a nod while continuing her conversation with the Cardinal. "Whatever else happens, you must be confident. Don't break faith for a moment. Any weakness can be used against you in an engagement like this." The Cardinal nodded, features stern, and Ms. Kevarian turned from him to Tara. "You've collected another friend."

"Cat is a servant of Justice." She indicated the other woman without turning around. "My watchdog. Says she's supposed to keep me from getting into trouble."

"Well." Something about the way Ms. Kevarian said that word, long and drawn out, made Tara glance back to be certain Cat was still there. "She'll have her hands full soon."

"What do you mean?"

She consulted a codex splayed on the table. "Denovo will open by proposing that our defense contracts with Iskar were negligent, made with the knowledge they could lead to Kos's death."

"Logical." There were two or three acceptable first moves in a complex case of Craft like this, but all involved breaking down the walls that preserved the divine client's dead body against alteration. Tara might have chosen the Iskari contract as the first issue herself, had she been in Denovo's place. Why was Ms. Kevarian reviewing the basics? "The truth will work as a counterargument, for once. The Iskari pact was too small to kill Kos under any conditions that could have been anticipated when it was drawn. Whatever drained Kos's power was at fault, not the Church's deal with Iskar."

"Good." She scratched a sharp black line of ink across the cream of the scroll. "Then you shouldn't have any trouble maintaining that within the circle."

"You're not serious." The stone beneath Tara's feet felt spongy, unstable, soaked with panic.

"This will be a good learning experiene, and an excellent chance to demonstrate your value to the firm. Do either of these goals seem humorous to you for some reason that escapes me?"

"You don't . . ." Tara wanted to steady herself, but the table kept shifting as she tried to rest her hands on it. She focused on her breath. "I assumed I'd have more warning, boss."

"You do know what they say about assumptions, Ms. Abernathy."

Before Tara could answer, a peal of thunder broke the hush of the dark stone room, and a wash of blackness obscured the light. When it passed, a man stood on the Judge's dais. He would have been tall if he had straightened. His back arced forward like the blade of a sickle, and his sallow skin seemed ready to slough off at any moment to reveal the flesh and bone beneath. "I am Judge Cathbad, son of Norbad," he announced in a voice deep and resonant enough to shake stone. "I call from chaos to order. I stand to witness the verities and falsehoods of Kos Everburning and his creditors. I invite counsel to approach."

As he completed the formula, a stream of fierce blue fire rushed from his dais along the silver lines set into the floor, caught there, and burned.

Tara looked to Ms. Kevarian for reassurance, but in her eyes found only quiet expectation.

When Tara practiced for this moment at the schools, she had spent days, weeks memorizing every facet of the cases before her. There wasn't time for that now. Maybe later, after the initial challenges were defeated.

It was this, she thought, or back to Edgemont.

She steeled herself and stepped across the line of blue flame.

11

Summers back home began hot and grew hotter. The sunbaked fields into pale dead yellow clay, and steam collected in toiling farmers' lungs. Every child enduring daily chores yearned to finish her tasks and sprint off, limbs flailing, to the quarry.

It had never been much of a quarry, but for a brief period at the beginning of the last century it supplied rocks for Edgemont's houses and fences. After idle decades the blasting powder and equipment were gone and only its sharp rock face remained, plummeting twenty feet to a deep pool of cold, murky water that seeped from unknown fissures in the earth. An enterprising priest a generation back had erected a prayer pavilion near the edge of the highest cliff, but this was rarely used in recent years save by the children who leapt from the pulpit over the quarry's edge, down, down, screaming through sweltering air, to strike the surface of the pool with a loud splash and sink into chill darkness.

Every time Tara made that jump as a girl, she felt a moment of panic as the water closed about her and the cold of it, the cold of the world's belly, struck her in the chest and seared her muscles and shocked her brain. If you lost yourself and opened your mouth in a desperate bid for air, the cold would reach down your throat, grasp your heart, and stop it with a squeeze.

She felt that same cold when she crossed the line of blue flame in the Third Court of Craft, thousands of miles from Edgemont. Circumstances, however, were different. In Edgemont, she only had to wait for the pool to open its mouth and vomit her out into air and light and heat. Today, she would have to earn her relief.

The world beyond the edges of the circle faded away. The diamonds set in the black canopy above were stars, the canopy itself the endless reach of space. The audience no longer existed.

Abelard, Cat, the Cardinal, all were motes of dust insignificant in the emptiness.

She still felt Ms. Kevarian's eyes upon her, though maybe that was her own imagination.

There were three people left in the universe. Tara. The Judge, grown vast by a trick of the circle's Craft, twisted and dark, eyes shining in the expanse. And, striding into the circle with no twitch of discomfort, because of course the cold held no threat for him, veteran of a thousand battles, tweed-jacketed, his white shirt bright as a cloudless midnight's moon, Alexander Denovo. Professor.

"Tara," he said. "It's good to see you again."

His voice almost undid her. It was exactly as she remembered from school, casual, familiar, polite. Not arrogant, because arrogance implied one had to establish one's superiority. Denovo's voice assumed it.

"Professor," she said at last. "Good to see you've joined us in the real world."

"Tara." He linked his thumbs through his belt loops, a picture of a country Craftsman. That was all it was, a picture. Denovo liked to seem simple, to disarm others with the bumpkin's mask and strike once they were lulled into a false sense of his civility. "I thought you would have realized by now that one world's as good as another. The schools reach everywhere, and everywhere reaches into them." Even his grin was casual. She felt her back stiffen. "How's the family? Still in that little town—Edgewood? Borderhill?"

He didn't need her to tell him the name. She wanted to snap his neck for mentioning her family. "What have you done to them?"

"Nothing!" He laughed. "I'm simply asking a friendly question to an old student. An old student who repaid my kind tutelage with blood and fire." His tone was perfectly urbane.

"You aren't at least surprised to see me alive?"

"You broke the rules, dear Tara, and you were punished, but I was confident you would survive. Have you found the freedom you valued, working for Kelethras, Albrecht, and Ao,

one of the biggest partnerships in the world? Are you truly
your own woman?"

"More than I was in your lab," she said. "Are you going to
make your case, or talk shop all day?"

"Certainly." Denovo bowed, turned to the Judge, and raised
one hand. "Your Honor, Kos Everburning is dead."

The silver-blue flame roared around him, drowning out gasps
from the invisible audience. The Judge knew already, from reading
his Court brief that morning, but even his starlit eyes widened.

Tara raised her right hand. "Your Honor, the Church of Kos
proclaims likewise. Kos is dead, and we come to grant him life."

Great wheels of Craft revolved in the walls of the chamber
around them. Gears ground against gears, and hidden silver needles automatically scribed sacred names upon circles of protection
and of summoning. Abelard had been right. The Court chambers
were smaller than the immensity of the black pyramid led one to
believe. Most of the extra space was packed with the machines required to support human beings who dared meddle in the affairs
of gods.

The Judge threw his head back, and a spiked hook of blue-
white light swung out of the darkness to skewer him on his dais.
His every muscle went rigid as the Craft pierced his body and
mind. He was no longer precisely himself, but an interface between Tara, Denovo, and the Third Court of Craft.

Tara felt the heartbeat of the world weaken and fade as the
machines and magic around her suppressed the universe's back-
ground energy, the subtle butterfly-wing flutter every novice
Craftsman could sense. It was uncanny, exhilarating. She had a
stable place to stand, and from here she could move the world.

"I call upon," she continued, "the powers of stars and of earth.
I call upon the massed divine union, and I call upon the faith of
the people of Alt Coulumb. Kos died honestly and through no
fault of his own, and will not languish in death, but serve his
people still. I invoke the first, third, and seventh protections, to
secure his body against predation and decay as we do our work."
In Craft of smaller scale, like her pro bono zombies back in Edgemont, she would have done this part silently, and in a fraction of a

second. This case was larger, and far more delicate. She needed to be careful and explicit, lest she tread too far too fast and leave herself undefended.

Denovo spoke next. "The lady calls for the protection of the world, of men, and of gods, to preserve her client. My clients challenge her claim that Kos died honestly and through no fault of his own. I will establish that, in point of fact, the Church of Kos bound itself to contracts that would result in its patron's demise, specifically defense pacts with the Pantheon of Iskar. We cannot rely upon the current Church bureaucracy to maintain a functioning god."

"It is noted." The Judge's mouth did not open, but his voice resounded from the chamber walls.

Tara took a deep breath. "The Iskari pacts to which Mister Denovo refers were undertaken with full knowledge of their potential consequences. The Church rightly determined they could cause no long-term damage to Kos."

The flames on her side of the room danced.

The Judge regarded the web of fire on the courtroom floor with unseeing eyes. "Mr. Denovo presents."

Denovo faced Tara directly. She saw what lurked beneath his pleasant, confident exterior: a network of thorns in the shape of a man, a thing that wore him like a suit. He called upon his Craft.

The space about them was charged with lines of starfire, a tapestry woven around and through itself in infinite variety, time its warp and space its weft. His will, cool and smooth as snakeskin, insinuated itself against hers, and she saw the world as he saw it, or as he wanted her to see it: a network of wire and wheels.

His Craft plunged through the bedrock of reality. The world shuddered, shivered, and began to crack, and they no longer stood within the courtroom, but on empty space, several hundred feet above the mile-sprawled corpse of Kos, pierced with contracts that tied him to gods, to governments, to Deathless Kings, to the bureaucracy of his Church Militant. He lay in the center of a globe of stars unlike any visible from earth. In death he radiated something akin to light, but deeper and more profound.

In the archives, Tara's vision of the god had struck her full of awe, but that vision only approximated the being that lay below. This was the reality, or as close to reality as her still mostly mortal brain could come without shattering into a million shards of glass.

Across from her stood Alexander Denovo, no longer playing the country Craftsman's role. His form had grown longer, and thorns peeked through his skin. His pupils were completely white, the white at the center of a forge fire, the white of molten metal. He stretched out his arms over the void, and fire leapt into being beneath him, scouring down like a rain of brilliant talons to rend the god's body flesh from flesh.

The room went black save for the outlines of the mystic circle. Abelard's eyes adjusted swiftly, accustomed as they were to moving in and out of the ill-lit depths of the Sanctum's boiler room, so he was nearly blinded when lightning split the darkness without warning. Tara rose in the air wreathed by tongues of fire, and the opposing Craftsman, too, their bodies rigid. In the crackle and flash he thought he saw Tara's skeleton through her skin.

"What the hell," Cat said next to him. She was a monochrome statue, lit intermittently by clashing brilliant light from the circle. "What are they doing?"

"I thought you'd been to court before," Abelard hissed back.

"I've been to normal court. Where they have witnesses, and evidence, and, you know, light."

"There's light," he observed.

"Light, I said. Not lightning."

As he watched the clash and roar, he noticed something else disturbing.

"She's not breathing."

"She's what?"

"Tara. Not breathing."

Cat held up a hand to shield her eyes. "Hard to see."

"You can see her skeleton," he pointed out. "When it sparks. Her chest doesn't move."

"You *would* look at her chest."

"Novice Abelard." Lady Kevarian had spoken, from her seat to his left. In the dark, the lightning glow suffused her skin.

"Yes, ma'am?"

"This may take a while. You won't be of any help here. Take your friend and sit with the rest of the audience."

"Shouldn't we stay, to support Tara?"

She turned from the action within the circle to him. Her face was smooth, ancient and unforgiving as water-worn rock. He glanced back at Tara, levitating in the circle, and it occurred to him that everything Cardinal Gustave was to him in engineering and theology, Lady Kevarian was to Tara in Craft.

Abelard touched Cat's shoulder. "We should find a seat."

Cardinal Gustave watched them go. His eyes followed the dancing ember tip of Abelard's cigarette, before returning to the tableaux within the circle.

Ms. Kevarian saw it all.

As the fire scorched toward its target, Tara pulled her knife from the glyph above her heart. It gleamed, and her physical form dissolved. She became a creature of shadow and starlight, and wrapped her will about Denovo's fire, stilling, smothering.

She knew his goal from the shape of his Craft. He was trying to force open the conduit forged by the Iskari pact and prove that enough power could flow through it to destroy Kos, even when the god was at full power. He was wrong, but this didn't mean he would fail. Truth and falsehood were flexible, and Denovo a hardened warrior. He would distort the contract, warp it, force it open in ways the original designers never intended. When he was done, it wouldn't matter that the Iskari had never drawn more than they explicitly bargained for, or that neither party ever believed their contract vulnerable to such exploitation.

Unless Tara stopped him. She swooped down toward Kos's mountainous corpse and hovered above the gaping pit where the Iskari pact connected to the god. Her goal was to maintain the pact against distortion, as Kos would have done were he still alive, and to do it without being destroyed herself.

Denovo's quenched flame writhed against her will, within her mind. She had read once of worms that laid eggs beneath human skin, larvae festering into adulthood on a diet of blood and living meat. He would do the same if she let him, consuming her strength and twisting it to his own ends.

She released his fire from her grip, and he struck with it again, in a narrow controlled stream of hungry, probing light. Standing inside the Iskari pact, she could exploit its structure in her defense. Breathing out, she woke the sleeping contract around her, and Denovo's assault broke on an invisible wall.

So far, so good.

Vines of light descended from the black sky, coiling about the pact. Tara sliced them with her knife, flying in a tight spiral upward, but where she cut, the vines grew back together. She had never seen such Craft before. With her every wasted slash, the vines tightened around the pact wall, weaving through one another into a constricting lattice.

No. She looked again, and saw her mistake. Not constricting. Nor were the vines truly woven through one another. Rather, they twined through tiny holes in the pact, linking it with Denovo's mind. The two were one. As she watched, the weave started, slowly, to expand.

Tara strangled a scream in her throat. She was within the pact; her will granted it power. Without realizing, she had let Denovo inside her defenses. When he pulled, when he stretched, it was her mind he pulled against, her soul he was stretching.

It hurt. Not as badly as when she had been cast down from the schools, but badly enough. Her eyes grew wide with the pain, her shadow shocked through with crimson light.

For the first hour the light show was fun to watch. Once or twice Abelard thought he spied repeated patterns in the lightning's dance, but the shape of the conflict remained a mystery to him. He didn't even know who was winning.

"Think Tara's having fun?" Cat asked, bored.

"Doesn't look like it," he replied. Her face was twisted in a mask of agony.

"She never has much fun, that one. You can tell by looking at her."

"She's trying to help Lord Kos." Why was he being defensive? "Even though she doesn't believe in Him. Give her a little respect."

A fierce, brilliant spark burst between Tara and the short, bearded man—Denovo.

"I'm sorry."

"It's fine. I . . . It's been a long week." He exhaled smoke and breathed in more smoke. This cigarette was nearly burnt down to the filter. He searched within his robe for his pack. "Kos, and, well." Anything to change the subject. "How have you been recently?"

She didn't answer. As he tapped the pack, he thought about this woman next to him, his childhood friend, her nights spent chasing through narrow streets for a fix. He held the tip of his new cigarette to the ember of his old and inhaled, passing flame from one to the other.

"You'll find your way through," she said.

He wanted to reply that she didn't know what it was like, living without a god. That she didn't know what it was like to feel nothing where there should be warmth, companionship, love. The surviving echoes of Kos in the world, in sunlight and hearthfire and glory, were a poor sop to the ache of His absence. She did know, of course. That was what being a Blacksuit meant. All the responsibility of a divine servant, and none of the joy.

"Her boss seems relaxed, at least," Cat observed.

Abelard wouldn't have used the word "relaxed." Lady Kevarian looked impassive. Once in a while, she jotted a note on the scroll in front of her. "Her boss has been doing this longer than Tara has."

"Yeah?"

"She was here when Seril died."

Cat tightened beside him, and drew into herself. He laid his hand on the back of hers, as Tara hung in the burning darkness. She did not shake him off.

———

Denovo was almost unrecognizable, his features a black mask slit by alabaster eyes. He touched the quivering barrier between them, the meld of her Craft and his own, and it was the touch of a razor against her skin. "Tara." His voice had not changed. "It's been a long time."

Don't let him distract you, she told herself. Fight through it.

"You're good at this," he said. "Your defense is precise, and you have talent. If you hadn't gotten yourself kicked out of school, we could have made a true Craftswoman out of you. Someone before whom the world would quake in fear." He wandered lackadaisically around the edge of the expanding pact, here applying pressure, there easing it. His knife glistened sickle-silver in his hand as he sliced apart Tara's defenses where they threatened his vines. "You have a frustrating tendency to make the wrong choices."

"Like choosing to fight you?" The words came out strangled with exertion. Somewhere, her physical form was sweating.

"That's one of them," he admitted. "But only one."

The vines woven through her mind began to burn.

She had expected an attack, and deadened her senses against it, but pain wracked her nevertheless. He was fast. *Too* fast. Craft moved at the speed of thought, and there was a limit to how fast human beings could think. Denovo pried at her defenses from all sides, artlessly but without apparent strain. He could not be spinning Craft this swiftly, unless . . .

"You still have them," she said. "Your . . . lab."

He cocked his head to one side, as if shocked that she found this a revelation. "My dear Tara, did you think your tantrum back at school would have any effect on my plans? You burned my laboratory, but you did not burn my students. Put not your trust in things, but in men. And women," he amended. "I put my trust in you once, Tara."

There was no Craft in that statement beyond a simple turn of phrase, but it made her want to vomit.

Now that she knew to look, she saw the seams in the vines of Craft coiled around the Iskari pact. Some bore Denovo's signature style, smooth and polished and full of flare. Some were rough apprentice work, and others wrought with an unerring, boring precision the flashy Professor could never match. He was drawing on other Craftsmen. In his lab in the Hidden Schools sat a hundred students in dutiful trance, their Craft directed by his mind to his ends.

It worked. That was the most horrible part. Tara couldn't match Denovo and his hundred students. Nobody could. Any Craft she used against them, one of their number would grasp its intricacies and counter it. Their every strike pierced her like a serpent's fang, rushing poison through her veins. She wrestled against not one mind, but a multitude.

Her confidence shuddered, and Denovo seized the opportunity to force another opening in her defenses. Some of his light seeped in through the curved walls of the Iskari pact.

She couldn't fight Denovo's entire lab. But his tyrannic, directing mind, that she could fight.

Miles away, her dried blood rested at the bottom of the iron bowl in the Church Archives. Blackened into ash, yes, potency all but consumed, it was still a bond between her and those stacks of scrolls. As her attention split, and more of the pact fell to Denovo, Tara called out with starlight, called out with blood, and called up the endless numbers written on the scrolls of Kos's Sanctum.

Denovo wanted to prove the Iskari contract was negligent, so she gave him the Iskari contract data, without the intricate visualization Craft that had allowed her to comprehend it all without going mad. Endless tables of figures written in rust-red ink passed into Denovo's mind at blinding speed, a sea of paper that would take a team of Craftsmen years to decipher.

Denovo's shadowy eyes went blank, and his spirit form stiffened as a tidal wave of data rushed from her mind to his. Overflow. Neither he nor his students could comprehend the flood, yet they could not ignore it, in case it contained some trap or stratagem. Denovo's Craft became rigid for a second, and that was all it took. Tara sliced through the golden vines, and this time they did not heal. She struck with her knife, and struck again, sharpening its edge with each blow. Denovo tried to stop her, but she moved too fast. She was free. She laughed, and flew.

The world broke open around her with a sound like cracking tinder.

The laws of physics reasserted themselves in a jumble. She had weight again, and physical extension in three dimensions. Time moved swiftly, then slowed as her mind adjusted to the confines of her body. It was a comfortable feeling, like slipping her feet into a pair of old, well-worn boots that had lain years forgotten in the back of her closet.

In the expanse of prehistory, mind and flesh evolved to complement each other. Craft could transport the soul to wage war on strange planes above the corpses of dead gods, but ultimately there were few places more pleasant than the bag of dancing meat and bones that was a living body. It was warmer here.

Tottering in her flats, eyes stung by the dim court lights, Tara wanted nothing more than an iced tea and maybe an afternoon to sit on a front porch somewhere and watch the sun decline.

The Judge was watching, and she couldn't let herself fall. Professor Denovo stood next to her, and of course he did not have the decency to look more than discombobulated. His hair was mussed, at least, and there was a hint of tension in his face.

Tara felt stiff, too, in her back and in the backs of her legs. How long had their battle lasted, in real time?

"Sir," Denovo said with a bow to the Judge. "I ask for a rest to consider the new information Ms. Abernathy has provided. Will you permit us to meet again tomorrow?"

"Indeed."

When she heard Denovo's proposal, she felt a weight settle on her stomach. It was reasonable. She had indeed given him the information, after a fashion, and he was obliged to review it.

"We meet again tomorrow," the Judge said. "Come fire and rain, come ice and the world's end. The court adjourns."

As he said the final word, the hooks of Craft decoupled from his flesh, and the flame in the circle died. The Judge crumpled, hands groping for support. Attendants approached to steady the man (and he was a man once more, not the mouthpiece of the machine, as Tara was once more a woman and Denovo was once more . . . whatever he was), and conduct him gently from the dais. As he walked, he twitched and groaned.

Was that what Judge Cabot had been at the end of his career, a broken thing, too tainted with darkness to live well? Was that what Tara herself would be in twenty years, or forty?

Denovo extended his hand for the customary handshake, but she turned her back on him and staggered away.

"Well done," Ms. Kevarian said when she met Tara at the circle's edge.

Tara crossed the line, sinking into the familiar unsteadiness of the normal as if into a hot bath. The feeling, however wonderful, did not improve her mood. "I gave him," she replied with an angry toss of her head, "exactly what he wanted. I surrendered the Church Archives to win a minor point. I am such an idiot." She glanced around the courtroom for Abelard and Cat, and saw them shouldering through the milling audience toward her.

Denovo had left the circle, too, and was gathering his papers. Ms. Kevarian leaned in, her voice low. "We would have given him that information sooner or later. Now he has it—unexpectedly, he thinks. He'll hope you gave him more than you intended, and will analyze it himself rather than request our help, to keep us from knowing how much he has. You won, for now. Feel the victory."

Tara tried, but the flush of triumph would not come. The floor rested uneasily beneath her feet. "This won't set him back for long. He's rebuilt his lab. They'll reconstruct the visualization Craft from scratch."

"The lab." Her expression darkened. "You didn't expect you had destroyed it for good, did you?"

"Hope springs eternal." Tara grimaced. "I thought I was thorough enough that it would take him longer to recover."

Ms. Kevarian looked as though she were about to respond, but Abelard was there, hands outstretched, complimenting Tara and full of questions, and they had no more privacy.

Across the circle, Denovo looked up from his briefcase to

Tara. His eyes in the real world were pits of tar. She had drowned in them once.

He wanted her to drown in them again.

She turned to answer Abelard's questions.

12

After Tara, Abelard, and Cat left the courtroom, the audience lingered to discuss the proceedings in hushed, frenetic tones. They had not understood much of the battle, due to their unfamiliarity with Craft of such magnitude, but this they knew: Kos was dead.

The student watched the silver circle and said nothing. Her bleary eyes had flown open at the first lightning flash, and down the hours as Tara fought Denovo, she had crept forward until she sat perched on her chair's edge, vibrating with the energy of a person who had seen something beautiful but lacked the words to describe it.

That one, Ms. Kevarian thought, will make a good Craftswoman some day, if the madmen who run this city don't warp her into a priest of something or other. Perhaps the girl was safe, though. It was difficult to be a priest in a city whose gods are dead. Cardinal Gustave, silent beside her, his face a stone mask carved with stone wrinkles, would attest to that.

She was about to say something to the Cardinal when Alexander Denovo's smooth, familiar voice interrupted her. "Fifty years ago, we never expected that someday we would take Alt Coulumb."

She had seen Denovo approach, skirting the edge of the circle; had felt him on the perimeter of her mind. Until he spoke, she did not acknowledge his presence.

"No one had ever managed it. This city's gods were tied to every major civilization in the world. Nothing could touch them. Half a century later," he mused, "they're both dead."

"History is full of reversals." She rolled up one scroll, stacked it atop two others, and placed all three in her bag. "Alexander, I think you've met Cardinal Gustave?"

"Last time you and I were in Alt Coulumb. Forty years back, maybe?"

"Yes," the Cardinal replied, his words heavy with rage. "I was Technician Gustave when you first came to this city. Wiser and more innocent than the years have left me." He stood and extended his hand, rigid as a mannequin.

Alexander was much better than the old priest at faking politeness. He gave Gustave a polo player's handshake, and when their palms touched, his smile widened. "I remember! You helped us in the Seril case. It's been far too long. How have you been?"

A flicker of pain crossed the Cardinal's features when Alexander mentioned Seril. His fingers tightened on his staff, as if its haft were Denovo's throat. "I am as you see me."

"Well." Alexander slapped the Cardinal's shoulder. "Don't worry. Elayne and I are the best there is at this kind of thing. We'll have Kos up and smiting the unbelievers in a flash. Just like last time."

"No," the Cardinal said. "Not like last time."

Ms. Kevarian hoisted her bag to her shoulder. "Might you excuse us, Cardinal?" The old man nodded. She shot Alexander a significant look. "Professor, accompany me to the street?"

He fell into step with her automatically. Her legs were long, but he had a broad stride. She reached the door out of the courtroom first, held it open for him, and closed it behind them. They walked alone down the long hall to the exit.

"What is it, Elayne?"

"What did you plan to accomplish back there?"

"I think the Church knowingly pledged too much to the Iskari, and as such does not deserve the first and third degrees of protection. I'm acting in my clients' best interest."

"I wasn't talking about that."

"What, then?"

"You think Gustave doesn't see right through you? The man spends his days in a confessional. He knows you don't want to bring back the Kos he knew. You're rubbing salt in his wound."

"The Kos he knew, the Kos I knew, what does it matter?" He was keeping his contempt in check at least. "We're going to make something that works. It'll do everything old Kos did, but better. This is an opportunity."

"Let him grieve for his god. He has little enough trust in this process without your snide comments setting him off."

"A man can't say what he feels anymore?"

"You never say what you feel," she observed. "You say what you calculate will have the desired effect."

"As if you cared about all these gods and their worshipers. Hell, I remember when we were starting out, you were more bloodthirsty than I'd ever been."

"Forty years ago. I've seen a lot in that time, and become much better at serving my clients."

"As have I," Alexander said with a grin. "Though I always have been more certain of who my ultimate client was."

"Yourself?"

"None other." He bowed, sweeping one arm out behind him. "Come with me to dinner tonight."

"So forward."

"That's not a no."

"You're here to no good purpose. You took this case because you thought you could turn it to your advantage, and if you can betray a few people at the same time, so much the better."

"That," he said, "is not a no either."

She quickened her pace.

"I'll be at the Xiltanda at seven," he called after her. "Fifth floor, in the dark. You'll come?"

The hallway ended in a blank wall of gray mist. She strode through it without farewell or backward glance.

"Great!" he called after her as she escaped into the day.

After the darkness of the Court of Craft and of astral space, Alt Coulumb's panoply was overwhelming: towers of chrome and silver against the empty white sky, a street full of deadlocked carriages, a boy in an orange jacket singing the noon news on the corner. Tara found no joy in the light and noise. She felt Denovo's smile like a splinter in her mind. Your family, he had said. What was the name of that little town?

Damn him.

"I don't understand," Abelard said. "Why did you give him the archives?"

She needed a drink and a square meal, not questions. Cat, small mercies, stood apart, scanning the street, the sky, the sidewalk for signs of danger. One conversationalist was bad enough.

She fought to produce an answer despite the throbbing pain in her skull. "I needed the archives to distract him long enough for me to win." And soon he would use those archives against her. Tara's victory had been well earned, even Ms. Kevarian said that, but it would not last.

"Why was he winning in the first place?"

"He's the best Craftsman I've ever known. But that's not why." A man sold water in glass bottles from a stand near the court gates. She threw him a small coin. He tossed her back a bottle, which she caught with a tendril of Craft, opened, and drank. Cold clear water chilled her throat and calmed her heart, but the headache did not recede. "He cheats." She took another swig. Had he done something to her, in the circle? No, not likely. The court wards would have kept her safe from his tricks.

"Are you okay?"

"I'm fine," she shot back. "Sorry. Shaken, that's all."

"I understand," he said, and placed a hand on her arm. He didn't understand. Denovo had every advantage. Tara would lose this case if she didn't find a way to assure her victory. She would lose, and be lost to history, shut off from the world of Craft and consequence.

Breath came short to her lungs, and deep thoughts spiraled within her, but she was not afraid. When you were afraid, you ran from the object of your fear, and Tara did not intend to run.

Ms. Kevarian emerged from the court, saving Tara from further introspection. Her heels sounded staccato on the stone sidewalk. "Tara. Thank you for waiting. I needed to attend to affairs inside."

Cat, sensing business, drew back farther to preserve their privacy.

"No problem." Was it Tara's imagination, or did Ms. Kevarian look flustered? "Boss, if you don't need me for something else, I'd like to spend the rest of the day in the court library." She pointed to the pinnacle of the black pyramid behind them. "Denovo has the Church archive data. He'll decode it soon, and learn that Kos was low on power. I want to find out where that power went before he starts asking. Abelard and I should be able to make a good start before sundown."

"No."

"I'm sorry?"

"You will scour the library next—that's the correct move. However, I need Abelard for my own work."

"I'm right here," Abelard observed.

Ms. Kevarian turned to him. "You will accompany me this afternoon to visit the local representatives of several Deathless Kings. They have a stake in Kos's resurrection, and we need to be on good terms with them if your Church is to survive unchanged."

"How can I help?"

"For the most part, by standing in their offices looking like a good young cleric."

He frowned, but did not reply.

"We need to stay ahead of Denovo," Tara said. "Abelard knows the Church inside and out. He's invaluable to my work."

"Your little bodyguard," Ms. Kevarian said, pointing at Cat, "should be able to navigate the bureaucracy at least as well. She's an officer of Justice, after all."

"Abelard would be better, and you know it."

"Yesterday you chafed when I asked him to assist you, and today you don't want to be separated from him. I need his—and your—help. Though our task may sound frivolous, trust me, it is every bit as important as your research."

Abelard lit a fresh cigarette with the tip of the previous one. "Do I get a choice?"

"No," Ms. Kevarian said before Tara could respond.

He gave Tara a reluctant look. She tried to return it. For a god-worshipper, he was a decent human being. More decent than most.

"Will the Deathless Kings mind if I smoke?" Abelard asked.

"Not in this instance."

He shrugged. "Fair enough."

A group of suited men strode out of the court, lesser toadies and plump advisors huddled around an elder Craftsman: a robed skeleton with diamond eyes who sipped coffee from an over-sized black mug. Ms. Kevarian drew close to Tara, and her voice dropped to an urgent whisper. "Beware of Alexander Denovo. I've known the man for half a century. I haven't trusted him so far, and I don't know any reason to start now."

As Tara listened, her tumbling emotions fell into place. She recognized the rapid rhythm of her heart, and the rhythm's name was wrath: wrath at Denovo's smile, at his bumpkin's charade, at his cheerful threats and the lives he chose to break. Her fear of the firm, of failure, crumbled before the sweet, consuming flame of rage. "I will do more than beware him," she said. "I'm going to beat him."

"Good." Ms. Kevarian's words were sharp and quiet, like foot-steps in a distant passage. "But remember, your first duty is to our client, not revenge."

"If I have to raise a god from the dead to defeat Alexander Denovo," she replied, "I will raise a hundred. I'll bring Kos back ten times greater than he was."

"Well said." Ms. Kevarian withdrew, and raised her voice. "You can return, Catherine. We're done talking shop."

"Thank you, ma'am."

"Good luck to both of you. Be careful."

"Be careful, she says." Cat sounded as if she wanted to spit.

Tara's legs ached. Upon re-entering the Court of Craft, they had found the hallway replaced by a long, narrow flight of stairs. Tara welcomed the first hundred steps as a meditative exercise, a chance to master her emotions and prepare for the long afternoon ahead. Anger was a useful tool, but it would not help her track down inconsistencies in cryptic scrolls. The next few hundred steps served no purpose but to embarrass her. After half an hour's ceaseless climb, she was slick with sweat, while Cat's breath re-mained even and assured. Tara's ordeal in the circle, and the pre-vious night's adventure, weighed on her bones like meat on a hanger. She hadn't expected a career in the Craft to involve being beaten up so much.

Tara did not answer Cat, but the other woman continued regardless. "Be careful. As if something's going to jump us in a library."

"You might be surprised."

"What do you mean?"

"You know how people say a book is really gripping?"

"Don't tell me . . ." Cat trailed off.

"Libraries can be dangerous." They reached one of the brief landings that interrupted the stairs every thirty steps or so, a few square feet of flat floor hosting a teak table and a fern—either a flimsy attempt to relieve their tedium or a cunning mockery of the same. Flipping over a frond, Tara found its underside purple. "You'd still probably rather be on the prowl. Hunting down miscreants."

Cat laughed bitterly. "Not until you're gone. I have my orders."

"From whom?"

"Justice."

That word, that name, made Tara shiver despite the heat of her exertion. "Directly? You don't have a superior officer?"

"Justice is always in charge. It's easier that way."

"Easier how?"

"Power corrupts people. Justice isn't people."

Tara let that sentence pass without comment, and cataloged in her mind the retorts she wanted to give.

Of the pair of them, Cat was the least comfortable with silence, and soon she spoke again: "I want to be where the action is, but I'm more likely to run into Stone Men with you than on the street. They came hunting for you last night, and you survived. Stands to reason they'll try again. Maybe they'll send the one that killed Cabot next time."

"You still think a gargoyle was responsible for that?" Tara asked, feeling as though she were carrying an entire gargoyle in her handbag, rather than only his face.

"Justice does."

"And you don't ask questions once Justice has done the thinking?"

"Questions are way above my pay grade."

"What if I asked for your personal opinion?"

"When Cabot died, his security wards took an engram of the scene." She saw Tara's confusion, and made a vague gesture in the air. "Mental picture thing. Like a painting in your head. If you need to know something, Justice flashes an engram into your mind when you put on the Blacksuit. Better than getting news from a Crier. The engram's never off pitch."

"At least the Crier stays out of your head."

"I guess. Cabot's engram shows a Stone Man standing over his body, talons red with blood."

"Couldn't a Craftsman or Craftswoman have killed him, and faked that picture?"

"You know more about that sort of thing than I do, but Justice doesn't think so. Cabot's wards would have alerted us if someone used Craft to break them, or to hurt him for that matter."

"The wards didn't tell you about the bone circle," Tara said, though she was being unfair. She could think of a handful of answers to that objection herself, and was not surprised when Cat gave one of them.

"The circle was a standard piece of medical Craft. Cabot died because his spine was removed in the first place, along with his brain and eyes and everything. The circle just kept him alive a little longer. Besides, why would a Craftsman want Cabot dead? There aren't many students of the Craft in Alt Coulumb, and Cabot was well liked by those that knew him."

They climbed the rest of the way without speaking. Tara considered the other woman's words, and indexed them for the future.

Cat reached the door at the top of the stairway first. It was made of thick, heavy wood, finished with a lattice of ash and rowan designed to ward off harmful Craft.

"Cat?"

"Hm?" Her hand hesitated on the doorknob.

"Why do you think the Guardians attacked Cabot? What was their motive?"

"They don't need a motive for murder. Bloodthirsty creatures. They live for death and destruction. You really should stop calling them Guardians, by the way. People will think you're on their side."

"Gargoyles, then. Justice doesn't think they killed him because of the case?"

"What case?"

"This case. Wasn't Cabot slated to judge Kos before he died?"
Cat looked taken aback. "I don't think so."

"Young man," Lady Kevarian said as the glass lift passed the thirtieth floor and continued its ascent, "you're about to meet the senior representative of the Deathless Kings of the Northern Gleb in Alt Coulumb. His name is James, and you are to be on your best behavior."

Through the transparent walls, Abelard saw the Sanctum of Kos rising like a black needle over the skyline. In ordinary times God's radiance would have shone from its tip, but these were not ordinary times. "His name is James?"

"Honestly, Abelard, I spout a string of long and dangerous-sounding words at you, and you ask me about the most familiar one of the group?"

"James doesn't sound like a Deathless King–type name to me."

"Nor does Elayne, I imagine. Or Tara." Somewhere during Lady Kevarian's long life, she had learned to smile in cold amusement without moving a single muscle on her face.

"You're not a Deathless King, Lady Kevarian."

"Oh," she said. "Am I not?"

"You're a Craftswoman. Deathless Kings are bony, ancient . . ." She was looking at him. Her lips had joined in the smile, but her eyes remained untouched. "Skeleton things," he finished lamely.

"How old do you think I look, Abelard? Be honest."

"Early fifties?"

"I'm seventy-nine years and three months of age," she said as if reading a tally. Abelard almost dropped his cigarette. "Let me show you something. Take my hand."

She held it out, palm up. He touched her and felt a spark—but it wasn't a spark, not a normal spark of electric charge, anyway—leap from her skin to his, or was it the other way around? His world faded, breath stilled in his lungs, and he thought he heard his heartbeat skip.

Before him stood Lady Kevarian, surrounded by empty space. Her skin opened like a hideous flower along invisible fissures and within he saw not a wet, fragile collection of human organs but the will, implacable and cold as steel, that animated the puppet of her flesh. In terror he recoiled and fell away from her, into the black. Time was long, and the world behind his eyes so dark, save for a flicker of deep red at the edge of his vision.

He couldn't tell if she released him or he released her, but when he returned to himself he was plastered against the glass wall of the lift, Alt Coulumb and open air to his back and Lady Kevarian before him, in human guise once more. Had the lift's wall shattered, he wasn't certain whether he would have chosen to leap toward her to safety, or out into the abyss.

She waved dismissively. "Oh, stop looking at me like that. You're fine." She brushed a piece of lint off the sleeve of her jacket. "Don't baby yourself. It wasn't that bad."

Come on, he told himself. *Say something.* "You're so cold."

"The Craft, young Abelard, is the art and science of using power as the gods do. But gods and men are different. Gods draw power from worship and sacrifice, and are shaped by that worship, that sacrifice. Craftsmen draw power from the stars and the earth, and are shaped by them in turn. We can also use human soulstuff for our ends, of course, but the stars are more reliable than men. Over the years a Craftswoman comes to have more in common with sky and stone than with the race to which she was born. Life seeps from her body, replaced with something else."

"What?"

"Power." Her teeth were narrow. "We soak in starlight or bury ourselves in the soil or apply preservative unguents to ward against time, but eventually the flesh gives way. We become, as you put it"—she counted the words on her fingers—"bony, ancient, skeleton things."

Her monologue had given him time to breathe. "And Tara?"

"Is on the path to immortality. A cold and lonely immortality, to be sure, and not one a hedonist would find rewarding, but immortality nevertheless."

He tried to imagine Tara's dark skin paling and her flesh fading away, tried to imagine what she would look like as a walking, brilliant skeleton. That was almost worse than Lady Kevarian's touch had been. Almost. "James?"

"One of the first generation of Craftsmen. His people were colonists of the Northern Gleb for Camlaan, and remained through the Wars to found one of the first true Deathless King nations. He's big, he's old, and though he's mostly polite he'd rip your heart from your chest and devour it if he thought you were trifling with him. Hasn't done that in a while, though. Partly because he no longer has an esophagus." She looked Abelard over, considering. "Perhaps you should remain in the lobby until I introduce you."

"Yes, ma'am."

The doors dinged, and opened.

"Why don't I get to do anything fun?" Cat whispered as she paced the reading room of the Third Court of Craft, regarding the long shelves of books and magazines with evident suspicion.

This was Tara's idea of how a library should look, not the dusty cave of the Church Archives: a spacious chamber at the pinnacle of the Court of Craft, where the four, or was it five, sides of the pyramid came to a point of transparent crystal that would have skewered any pigeon stupid enough to perch upon it. The crystal caught and funneled starlight into the depths of the building. Normally, no doubt, the sky shone blue as sapphire and deeper through that roof, but today the clouds above were the color of milk.

There were no giant heaps of scrolls here, no quaint tome piles or densely packed shelves. The Court of Craft's storage facilities were below, tight well-dusted stacks where only Court servants tread. The main reading room was spacious and quiet. Green carpet and wooden tables devoured any sound that dared trespass on their solemnity.

A young man with short, spiked hair and a stud of jet in each ear attended the reference desk, while an older woman, solid and unshakable as a butte, trundled around the room, checking that periodicals remained in their proper places and casting severe glances at the few patrons who dared speak above a whisper. Cat had already received three of those withering looks, and seemed to be angling for a fourth.

When Tara had requested books from the collection, the young man at the reference desk scrawled the titles on a slip of palimpsest with a quill pen and inserted the slip into a pneumatic slot. Minutes later, a wooden wall panel swung open soundlessly and a book-laden cart rolled out of the darkness, bearing her order. A small glass and silver tank welded to the cart's underside played host to the guiding rat brain. By a trick of Craft, the brain thought it was still a rat, seeking always a trace of food that happened to be one room over, one level up, just around the next turn of the shelf. When Tara claimed her books, the rat brain received its illusory reward and wheeled off in search of the next morsel.

"I'm having fun," Tara replied in a whisper.

"I mean," Cat said, "Abelard said that yesterday you walked on a dead god. Why am I watching you shuffle through books? When do I get to take a vision quest?"

"No vision quests here. The Church Archives and the court have different storage philosophies."

Cat stopped and looked at her as though she had grown an extra head. "What?"

"Every piece of information stored in the Church Archives was about Kos. The Church made careful note of how everything related to him. They described contracts, for example, as drawing from a particular vessel of his power, which in turn drew from a major chakra, which in turn . . . you get the idea. If I wanted to describe you in the same way, I would say that you have an iris that is a part of your eye that is a part of your face, which is a part of your head and so on. That kind of system is hard for people to interpret, but easy for the Craft."

Cat looked frustrated, but willing to follow along. "What about this library?"

"These books are all works of Craft, but the Craft is a less unified subject than Kos. This library contains millions of deals between hundreds of thousands of people, gods, and Deathless Kings. I could try to interpret them all with Craft, but the complexity of that vision would split my mind like an overripe fruit, and horrible things would crawl into it from Outside. Nobody wants that. When the subject is too complicated to represent hierarchically, we use normal paper libraries, and read with our own eyes." She laid one hand on a book spine. "I like this way better." Cracking the book open, she inhaled the bouquet of its pages. "I can smell the paper."

"You're insane," Cat said.

"Knowledge," Tara replied, turning a page as quietly as she could manage, "is power. I need all the power I can get."

"You sound less confident than you did this morning."

"I'm confident, but I also have, let's say, renewed faith in my adversary's strength. I need to be more than right, if I'm going to help the Church. I need to be right, and smart about it."

"So, what kind of power can all this knowledge give you?"

The green leather-bound ledger before her, which was thicker than the holy writ of most religions, contained all of Kos's registered deals and contracts for the last few months. A notebook lay open beside the ledger—a normal notebook, not the black book of shadows in which she had caught Shale's soul. With her quill pen, she wrote a list of contracts that might have been responsible for Kos's weakness. Progress was slow. The archivist's handwriting was cramped and angular, and most of the ledger written in code. A prolonged search had revealed a table of abbreviations hidden within an illuminated invocation of the eternally transient flame on the flyleaf. With this she could interpret most of the entries, but not all.

She crooked a finger, and Cat bent close. Tara underlined an entry with the feathered end of her quill. "That's the date of the contract. This line is the first part of the title."

"What about the number? It's not even a real number. There are letters in it and everything."

"Filing reference. The full contract is somewhere in this

building. If we tell the reference librarian that number, he can find it for us."

"Why not use the contract's name?"

Tara resisted the urge to roll her eyes. It was a valid question from a woman who had never spent an afternoon in a library before. "You see these three entries?"

"They're all the same." Cat spelled the abbreviations out. "C-F-S-R Alt C.-KE to R.I.N."

"Contract for Services Rendered, Alt Coulumb Kos Everburning to Royal Iskari Navy," she translated. "Since the common names are all the same, each contract needs a unique reference so we can tell which one we're talking about."

"What about those names, there to the right?"

"These are the Craftsmen who sealed the contract, and this is the name of the hiring party, on each side."

"So COK is the Church of Kos, and Roskar Blackheart was working for them. R.I.N. is Royal Iskari Navy, represented by . . ." Her forehead wrinkled. "Isn't that the guy you fought this morning?"

"Yes," Tara said. "Alexander Denovo."

"Seemed like the two of you had met before."

Tara tried to return her attention to the ledger, but Cat's question hovered between her eyes and the page. "He was one of the best professors in the Hidden Schools. Taught me much of what I know."

"You ever sleep with him?"

"What?" That squawk earned Tara an angry glance from the librarian. She did her best to look chastened.

"When you saw him in the court, you went all stiff and shivery. There's history between you, and it's not pleasant."

"We did not sleep together."

"But you had a falling out."

"Sort of." Her tone brooked no further discussion.

Cat gave her an odd look, and changed the subject. "This makes sense, anyway. He was working for the Iskari then, and he's working for them now."

"More or less. People take all sides in this business, because there aren't enough good Craftsmen to go around. Last time Ms. Kevarian worked in Alt Coulumb, she represented the creditors, the people Seril's church struck bargains with. Now, she's on Kos's side." The nib of Tara's quill pen scratched a black jagged string of letters in her notebook. "The problem, though, starts in Judge Cabot's ledger."

Tara pulled a fat book covered in marbled paper from the pile. "Here's where he adjudicated Seril's death, and that's the formation of Justice." The earlier pages were dark with age and ink, but whole lines near the ledger's end were blank save for the word "redacted." "Now, look." She pointed to a line near the beginning of the redacted sections.

Cat squinted to decipher the handwriting. "CFA Alt C. New.A. by A. Cabot, J-, A. Cabot, J.- PS, New.A by S. Caplan."

"Below that, too."

"CFA Alt C. C.S. by A. Cabot, J-, A. Cabot, J.- PS, C.S. by S. Schwartz." Cat grimaced. "Doesn't mean anything to me."

"CFA is Contract for Acquisition. PS means *pro se*, 'for himself.' It's an old Telomiri Empire term, don't ask why we still use it. Judge Cabot purchased these two Concerns, Coulumb Securities and Newland Acquisitions."

"A Concern is what, exactly?"

By now, Tara knew better than to be surprised at Cat's ignorance. "It's a system Craftsmen create to magnify their power. Kind of like a church, where everyone's combined faith makes things happen, only with Craft, not religion. Craftsmen pool their powers to a particular end, say summoning a demon or razing a forest or ripping ore from the earth. If they manage the Concern well, they get more power out of it—from the demon, from the life essence of the forest, or the sale of the ore—than they put in."

Cat still seemed lost, but nodded.

"Do the Concerns themselves have ledgers?"

"Yes, but they're not much help." The next two volumes off the pile were more folios than full books, maybe a hundred sheets each for all their gold binding and shiny leather. Initially, they looked like less-crowded versions of the Church's ledger, or

Cabot's, but after three pages the descriptions of contracts signed and acquisitions made, enemies dispatched and victories won, gave way to empty space. The last note in each book was simple. "Acq. A. Cabot, J-, Rec. Red."

"Records Redacted," Tara translated. "These two acquisitions are the last works of public Craft Judge Cabot performed before he died, and they took place four months ago. At about the same time"—she turned back to Kos's ledger—"we see the number of sealed records in Kos's ledger rise dramatically. And if we count the number of sealed records in Kos's ledger, and compare it with those in Judge Cabot's, they're the same." Repeated lines marched across the page, "redacted" over and over again in elegant black letters. "I think Kos and the Judge were working together on something big, and secret, before they died. But I need to see their sealed records to learn more."

"They're restricted. You can't read them."

"I can't, maybe. You can't. But what about Justice?"

Abelard smoked by the window of the Deathless King's foyer. Four plush red chairs squatted on the hardwood floor around a low table upon which lay a few old scrolls and a ceramic vase of dandelions. A fat red stripe climbed the white wall opposite the windows and ended at the ceiling for no discernable reason.

Had he expected a torture chamber? A lake of fire topped with a throne of skulls, upon which the ambassador of the Northern Gleb sat in grim judgment over demonic servitors?

Maybe. Certainly he hadn't expected the waiting room to be this cheerful.

Dandelions, for Kos's sake. They weren't even in season.

He exhaled and waited, and wished Tara was here.

In the past, when sleep would not come, and he lay awake in bed unwilling to rise and check the clock because he knew dawn was still hours off, Abelard had comforted himself in prayer, and the contemplation of God. Fire touched his soul, and would not desert him.

For the last three days, he had been alone, with only his

188 ■ Max Gladstone ■

cigarette flame for a companion. Tara relieved his isolation, strange though she was, but she was gone and here he sat, smoking in silence again. With a sigh, he began to pray.

A quarter of an hour passed, enough time to chant through the Litany of the Unquenchable Flame, complete with colophon and optional sections. No inner warmth came, no communion. Smoke lingered in his lungs longer than usual. That was something, at least.

What did Lady Kevarian want with him? Hardly the pleasure of his company.

Forced idleness was a torment in itself. His hands itched. He could be helping Tara, fixing boilers, serving his dead Lord. Instead, he watched shadows on the wall, and contemplated dandelions.

Not for the first time did his eyes flick to the frosted glass door of the Ambassador's office. The door wasn't thick, and its lower half was silvered. If he drew close, crouched down, and pressed his ear to the glass, his silhouette would be invisible from the other side.

He tipped some ash into the dandelion vase, bent low, and approached the door. He heard Lady Kevarian's voice, and another, deep and rolling like distant thunder.

He pressed his ear to the cool, silvered glass.

". . . place me in a complicated position," said the thunderstorm. "There's much to your story I don't understand."

"Much I don't understand as well, Ambassador, but everything I've told you is true. I can confirm it."

The storm rumbled, but said nothing.

"I would not, of course, ask you to accept my word with no evidence."

"Certainly not."

Her voice sank to a whisper. Abelard leaned against the door as if to press his ear through it. Then the latch gave way, and the door swung in onto nothingness.

Abelard tumbled into a shadowy pit, like night without stars, the way the universe had looked before man opened his eyes, before the gods breathed life into the void. This darkness was deeper even than the darkness into which Ms. Kevarian had thrust him, had flashed with red. Falling, he felt an unexpected warmth at his back.

He gulped reflexively for air but found none to breathe, and would have perished had the dark not broken and reformed around him. Or had his overtaxed mind simply recast the scene into something it could comprehend?

He flailed to find his balance on the carpet. Cool, soothing air rushed back into starved lungs, and sunlight startled his eyes.

He stood in an office, more richly furnished than Cardinal Gustave's. Chairs of soft leather with silver studs, oak bookshelves. Ms. Kevarian stood to his left.

At the far end of the room, behind a polished desk of what looked to be pure magesterium wood, sat a towering skeleton. Standing, it would have been over seven feet tall; seated in a broad chair of leather and iron, it was nearly Abelard's height. A hooked silver tab protruded from the hole where its nose had once been, supporting a pair of half-moon spectacles. Sparks like distant stars glittered in the eyeholes of the blanched skull. Two arms rested on the skeleton's lap, and two more, smaller and grafted below the first pair, were busily taking notes on a yellow pad of paper with a silver-nibbed pen.

"Lord James Regulum, Ambassador Plenipotentiary of the Deathless Kings of the Northern Gleb," said Lady Kevarian with a slight touch of humor, "may I present Novice Technician Abelard of the Church of Kos Everburning."

"So," the skeleton said, and from its voice Abelard realized it was not an it, but a he, "you're the little monk Elayne has brought us."

"Priest, actually," Abelard said. "And engineer." The skeleton—Lord James whatever—did not reply, nor did Ms. Kevarian. Both regarded him with a strange intensity. "Ah. May I ask a question?"

"You have asked one already, Engineer-priest, and you may ask another."

"You, um. Don't have any lips. Or lungs. How are you . . . talking?"

Lord James grinned. He did not need to expend any particular effort to do so. "Good question."

Before he could say anything else, Abelard fainted.

13

The reference librarian looked up from his paperwork and saw a living statue of a woman sandblasted from black glass. He swallowed, and slid the papers into a drawer.

Good afternoon, the Blacksuit said with a voice soft as distant surf. *I am looking for a book.*

"Ah." After this initial exhalation, the librarian took the better part of a minute to realize he hadn't said anything further. "Of course you are." A moment ago he had been waiting through the pleasant, slow half hour before the end of the afternoon shift, answering patrons' easy questions to relieve the boredom. Blacksuits never had easy questions. "What do you need?"

Justice requires the following redacted materials, the Blacksuit said, and slid a scrap of paper across the counter.

The librarian, whose name was Owen, tried to slip the paper out from under the Blacksuit's fingertips. It ripped a little, but did not move.

These materials are to be provided without notifying any parties that have placed requests or holds upon them.

"I don't think I'm allowed to . . ." The protest died on Owen's tongue.

Speed is a priority. All is in the service of Justice.

The Blacksuit released the paper into Owen's grip.

"Yes, ma'am."

In three hours, Abelard had met more Craftsmen and dignitaries than he expected, or desired, to see ever again. Lord James the skeleton had been the most striking, but not the most unnerving. "What happened to that last one?" he asked Lady Kevarian when they returned to her waiting carriage.

"Dame Alban has spent the last half-century experimenting with alternatives to the skeletal phase of a Craftswoman's late life."

"So she's turned herself into a statue?"

"Inhabited a statue, more precisely. A brilliant idea: stone has its own soul, and an artist's skill invests it with more. Not enough to sustain human consciousness indefinitely, but if you have competent artisans and you're willing to pay, you can have any body you wish, until it crumbles."

"All of those statues, on the walls and everything . . ."

"Any one could host her."

"They weren't all women."

"What made you think Dame Alban was?"

"Or human."

Lady Kevarian shrugged.

"She's a ghost? Moving from statue to statue?"

"Hardly. One keeps one's body around, even if one doesn't spend much time inside it. It is the greatest gift of order and power humans receive from the universe."

"You still consider yourself human, then."

"Somewhat."

He wasn't sure how to respond to that statement, so he ignored it. "Dame Alban, or Sir Alban, or whatever. Where is her body?"

"You remember the remarkable sculpture we saw upon first entering her chambers?"

"The thinking skeleton?" His eyes widened. "No."

"Yes."

"It was lacquered black."

"And you're wearing clothes." Their carriage slowed to navigate around an accident ahead. "Abelard, these people have lived in Alt Coulumb for forty years—longer, in some cases. They're no more strangers to this city than you and your Blacksuit friend. Before the events of the last few days, did you not feel the slightest interest in them?"

"It all seems . . . unnatural."

"Whereas using the love of your god as a heat source for steam power is perfectly normal."

"Yes," he said, confused.

"Before this case is over, Abelard, you may have to choose between the city you believe you inhabit, and Alt Coulumb as it exists in truth. What choice will you make?"

Abelard opened his mouth, intending to say, *the Lord will guide me.* He caught himself, and settled instead for, "The right one, I hope."

"So do I."

A Blacksuit left the library carrying a stack of scrolls, and Catherine Elle returned a few minutes later through the same door, rumpled, trembling like a dry leaf in a high wind, and bearing a parcel in her jacket.

"Are you okay?" Tara asked after they retired to a corner out of the reference librarian's line of sight. Here, she could peruse the redacted scrolls without risk of discovery or interruption.

"I'm fine."

"You don't look fine."

"The suit plays hell with clothes." With a shaking hand she indicated her rumpled linen shirt and loose cotton pants. "Wrinkles them beyond all reason, and if you're wearing anything with a bit of slink the blackness rips right through it."

Tara bent close to the first scroll, squinting to read the scribe's cramped calligraphy. "I wasn't talking about your clothes. You're paler than usual, and shivering. Your eyes are bloodshot."

"Nah. I mean, it's part of the job." She gripped her upper arm, which Tara supposed was lean and well-muscled, not that she cared. "The suit gets you kind of high when you use it, and the comedown hurts. That's all."

"That," Tara observed, "doesn't seem like a good idea."

"Not a judgment-impairing high. An I can do anything, nothing can hurt me kind of high." Cat's fingernails dug into her arm, so deep that Tara was surprised they did not draw blood.

"How does that not impair your judgment?"

Cat let out a dry laugh. "With the suit on, you can do pretty much anything, and nothing can hurt you. Most folks see a sword coming at their face, they duck or flinch. The sword would bounce off the suit. I wouldn't even feel it. Justice makes sure I know that, so I can do my job."

"What if you meet something the suit can't handle?"

"It changes the high, makes me cautious."

"And there are no ill effects?" Tara studiously avoided looking at Cat's white-knuckled grip on her own arm, or at the scars on her neck. "No withdrawal?"

"We handle it." Her tone sharpened to an arrow point.

"I see." Tara fell silent, and turned her attention from Cat to the parchment. The tension between them subsided into silence. After a while, Tara frowned, and tapped a line of figures with the feather of her pen. "That's funny."

"More sealed files?"

"Not quite." She translated from the abbreviations: "These contracts give another party joint control of Newland Acquisitions and Coulumb Securities, the two Concerns Judge Cabot purchased."

"Who's the other party?"

"Kos Everburning. The god himself, not his Church."

Cat blinked.

"Cabot purchased these two failing Concerns. Then"—she pointed to one of the contract scrolls—"he gave Kos part control of them. Didn't take any payment. That way, the Church couldn't detect the deal, since no power left Kos at first." Back to the ledger with Kos's redacted records. "Kos combined the two Concerns to make a single, larger one, and filled that one with his power. Lots of power, and the Church didn't know anything about it. This could be the reason Kos was so much weaker than the Archives show."

"If he was still in control of this Concern, why did he die?"

"Soulstuff inside a Concern isn't your own anymore, even if you technically control it. Maybe Kos didn't have time to reclaim his power before he died."

"This shell game was a stupid idea, then."

"It didn't work out well for him," Tara admitted.

"So why would Kos want to give so much power to the Judge?"

"I don't think he did. Cabot withdrew a standard agent's

fee, then tried to transfer his stake in the Concern to someone else."

"Who?"

"That's the funny thing. Look here." Beneath her finger, the last line of the ledger was barely legible after the date. Tara read the abbreviation "ToO" for "Transfer of Ownership," and Cabot's name, but beyond that the paper was burned black as if someone had painted over it with a fiery brush. "Here." Another scroll, the same effect. "And here." A third. "Cabot's ledger, Newland's, Coulumb Security's, all have that mark. The burn is too controlled for a candle or a match. Someone found these scrolls and destroyed the last line in each one."

"Kos could have done it, right? With fire? To cover his tracks? It's not like you people need things written down for them to be real. You just wave your hands and speak some words, and they happen."

"And when they happen, they happen in a sloppy, inefficient, and slipshod manner that's open to attack from all fronts," Tara replied. "For great Craftwork like this, the more precise and explicit your movements, the more secure you are. You want there to be a written contract on file so nobody can lie about it afterward. If the agreement is secret, fine, but it needs to be held somewhere safe and impartial. That's why the court library exists: if there's trouble, the court's might enforces the agreement." Her brow furrowed. "Destroying the receiving party's name would wreck the purpose of reporting this deal in the first place. With the name burned off, the Concern is open to attack. But who could do something like this? A priest wouldn't have been able to burn off the name without Kos knowing. Nor is it a Craftsman's work: Craft would have decayed or yellowed the paper, but there's no sign of either."

"Why use fire, anyway?" Cat asked. "He could have blotted the entries with ink, or stolen the whole thing."

"This isn't a normal scroll. Blot it and the ink will shine through. As for stealing it, do you think the court would build a library without a way to keep people from walking off with their books?" She was talking to fill space, her thoughts rushed ahead

of her words. Burned-out entries. Judge Cabot, lying disembow-
eled beside his azaleas, tea mixed with blood, his dead body un-
tainted by Craft. Kos's corpse, more decayed than it should have
been after three days of death. Shale's reply to her questions yesterday morning: he was a messenger, but didn't know what message he was to have carried.

"We need," she whispered, "to visit the infirmary."

The lonely Sanctum tower rose above the crowd gathered in the
white gravel parking lot. Word of Kos's death had spread from the
Third Court of Craft across the city like a ripple over a still pool,
through scraps of overheard conversation and whispers in quiet
rooms, rumors mixed with truth. Most of Alt Coulumb's four
million citizens remained ignorant. Some heard and disbelieved.
Some heard and hid within their work or their homes or their false
hopes. But a few heard, and grew angry, and came to the Holy
Precinct, bearing with them frenzy and fear and crude signs made
from paint and planks of rough wood. This fraction numbered in
the thousands, and they cried out and pounded against Abelard
and Lady Kevarian's carriage as it shouldered toward the Sanctum.

Abelard stared out the window at the mass. "What are they
doing?"

"They're afraid," Lady Kevarian said. "They want guidance."

He sought in those wild faces the men and women of Alt
Coulumb that he knew, their reason and their compassion, their
faith. He found none of these things. He saw a thin ice-shell of
anger, and beneath that, fear.

"What will they do?"

"If your Church does not respond to their complaints? Perhaps
storm the Tower, though I doubt the Blacksuits will allow it." Justice's servants stood in a loose cordon between the crowd and the
Sanctum steps. The crowd had not yet dared approach them. "Perhaps they will linger. Perhaps loot some stores or set a building or
two in the Pleasure Quarters on fire before they are stopped."

"They wouldn't be so angry if Kos were here." *Of course
they wouldn't*, Abelard thought. *Foolish thing to say.* "Are you
going to do something?"

Ms. Kevarian shook her head. "I am a Craftswoman. Public relations are my client's responsibility."

They rolled through the Blacksuit cordon and stopped at the foot of the Sanctum steps. Ms. Kevarian paid the horse as Abelard stumbled out. The crowd's cries intensified when they saw his robes. He took a deep drag on his cigarette. "We need to tell Cardinal Gustave," he said.

"I will speak with the Cardinal. You should return to your cell and rest."

The crowd screamed behind him—the voice of his city in pain. "I don't want rest. I want to do something. I want to help."

She hesitated halfway up the broad front steps. "You're a Technician, correct?"

"Yes, ma'am."

"Check the Church's generators. We've reached a delicate stage of the case. The Iskari question came out in our favor, but if the Church has been wasting power, we will lose ground. While Tara seeks weapons, you can tend our armor."

When he didn't respond, she began climbing again. He caught up with her at the top step, in front of the tall double doors. "There are dozens of miles of pipe in this tower, of every gauge and purpose. Not to mention the boiler rooms, the engines . . . Going through the logs alone will take days. Isn't there something more immediate I can do?"

"You could talk to them," Ms. Kevarian said, and pointed to the sea of people through which their carriage had come.

Behind him, a deep-voiced man somewhere within the crowd cried shouted: "God is dead!" A few among the group took up his chant. Ms. Kevarian didn't appear to notice.

Abelard swallowed hard, and envisioned himself preaching to their wrath. What words would he use? What could he say to bring the people of Alt Coulumb back to themselves, to remind them of the glory of Kos? In his vision, he shouted into a whirlwind of rage, and his own breath returned to choke him. "I'll check the generators."

"You'd best get started, in that case." Lady Kevarian flicked a finger at the front gate, which flew open with a resounding gong.

198 ■ *Max Gladstone* ■

She strode into the tower's gullet, eyes front and ready for battle.

Abelard straightened his robe and followed her. As he entered the shadows of the worship hall, she gestured again and the doors slammed shut behind him, closing off the repeated cry of triumph or lamentation: "God is dead! God is dead!"

A blanket of clouds muffled the declining sun. The sky should have caught fire. Instead, the light began to die. Tara and Cat rode through its death throes in a driverless carriage, and watched the city.

"Is it always so cloudy here?"

"No," Cat said, "though you wouldn't know it from the last few days. Our autumns are usually clear, because of the trade winds." Color had returned to her face, and mirth to her voice. Her hands lay still in her lap, and she smiled, if weakly. Tara watched her body fight its way free of the Blacksuit, and knew better than to mention the change.

"You sail?" she asked instead.

"No. I just hear sailors talking."

They found the Infirmary of Justice much as they had left it: white institutional walls, too-bright floors, and a reassuring smell of antiseptic. Reassuring at least to Tara, because the smell signaled that the people running this infirmary knew about antiseptic. It was surprising how much people didn't know once you left the cities of the Deathless Kings. A young man in one of the caravans she joined after first leaving Edgemont had claimed in all earnestness that alcohol made people drunk because demons liked its taste, crept within the bottles, and slept there, invisible and intangible. When you drank the alcohol, you drank the demons. Different demons liked different kinds of booze, which was why a man belligerently drunk on whiskey would sleep after a glass of vodka or laugh after drinking beer.

The other girls in the caravan had found this theory fascinating, but to Tara its parsimony left something to be desired.

"What do you need to see here?" Cat asked, drawing ahead of her in the hallway.

"The kid with no face. The witness in Cabot's murder."

"Yeah." She nodded. "We still don't have any leads on the face, by the way. We're scouring local Craft suppliers, but the equipment for stealing a face isn't all that specialized, it turns out."

"I'm sorry to hear that." Some poor Craftswoman was having a rough day dealing with Blacksuits in her shop, but better her than Tara. She reviewed the last several hours she had spent with Cat, trying to figure out when the woman could have received a report from the other Blacksuits. "Did you check in while I was arguing in court?"

"Justice told me when I put the suit on back at the library." Cat wiggled the fingers of one hand in the vicinity of her temple.

"All this information comes and goes from your head, without your permission. Gods." Tara wasn't given to swearing or to mentioning deities in general, but both seemed appropriate.

"What's so weird about that?"

"How can you let something into your mind? Justice could tie you in knots if she wanted."

"She wouldn't."

"You know what I mean." Her voice grew sharp, and Cat froze in midstride. Tara made to brush past her, but the other woman seized her arm. She tried to shrug Cat off, but her grip was strong. "Let me go."

"Is there something you need to get off your chest?"

Tara pulled again, harder this time, with no more success. "I don't like it when people mess with my head. I can't understand how you'd volunteer for the experience."

"Justice isn't a person." Cat was cold and immobile. "I wouldn't allow this if she was."

"Like you'd have a choice."

"What's that supposed to mean?"

"You need your fix."

Cat's eyes narrowed. "I have a job to do. I keep this city safe."

Tara didn't reply.

The sudden surge of anger passed, and Cat's shoulders sagged. "Gods, look, if you want to talk . . ."

"No. Thanks." She nearly spat the second word.

Cat let go, and Tara stormed down the hall. On the third step she realized she didn't know where she was going.

"Do you know where the witness is?" she called over her shoulder.

"I do."

"Well?"

"I'm not going to tell you." Deep within the infirmary, an unseen doctor chose that moment to set a broken bone or pull a tooth. The patient's scream echoed in the empty hall, and Tara and Cat winced at the same time. Apparently these doctors were more familiar with antiseptic than anesthetic.

"What do you want?" Tara said.

"You've trusted me less since you learned I was a Blacksuit than when you thought I was a simple junkie. Tell me what I've done, what Justice has done to earn your contempt."

"It's not contempt."

"The hells it isn't. Will you be straight with me?"

Tara considered Cat: her hands on her hips, her firm, generous mouth, the steel behind the green lake of her eyes, the scars at her throat, the emblem of Justice that hung beneath her shirt. She thought about her own fall from the schools, about Shale resting faceless in a white-walled, black-curtained room. She thought, too, of another room in this same building, where Raz Pelham lay sleeping. He could not have returned to his ship. Suntan or no suntan, the walk would have fried him.

"Fine," Tara said. "I'll tell you on the way."

Daily maintenance reports were kept on the Sanctum's eighth floor, in the windowless Efficiency Office at the heart of the tower. Despite its location, the office was well ventilated; turbines in the massive boiler room beneath sucked air through the chamber to regulate the boilers' temperature. In winter, the office remained ten degrees warmer than the rest of the building thanks to its proximity to the generators, and in summer ten degrees cooler, thanks to the air flow.

Ingenious.

Abelard first visited the Efficiency Office at the age of twelve, on a field trip for introductory theology. He had stared about himself in awe as a Novice Theologian, who seemed so mature to Abelard at the time and had been at most twenty-six, used the second law of thermodynamics as a metaphor for original sin. Upon leaving the office, twelve-year-old Abelard promptly forgot the color of its walls (red), its dimensions (forty feet across and ten high, with a ladder in the center leading down into the boilers), and even its shape (round), not to mention the theologian's argument. He remembered the ventilation system. It was the first complex machine he understood, and its union of physical law with man's creative spark filled him with joy and love for God.

Now Kos was gone, but the system remained.

He sat at one of the four curved metal desks in the circular room, overshadowed by a pile of papers and plans and schedules. First he browsed through the energy output records and found nothing unexpected. Draw on the generators peaked at evening and midday, bottoming out between midnight and dawn, and again between three in the afternoon and twilight. The logs showed no major repairs, and hardly any tinkering since the coolant system's upgrade months before. Materials and parts consumption normal. But the service records for the last few days . . .

He raised one hand. A few seconds and a rustling of robes later, he heard a woman's voice. "Yes, Brother?"

He looked up from the records to see the almond eyes and wizened face of Sister Miriel, who had ruled the Efficiency Office and kept its archives for longer than most Cardinals could remember. Sister Miriel was the reason no young novice had ever successfully pranked the maintenance department. She was disarmingly sweet but viciously clever, and detected each planted gas bomb, every swapped document and mislabeled pot of glue in time to turn the jokes against their plotters.

"Sister," he said, "you've logged twice as many maintenance shifts as usual in the last three days, but made no repairs."

"We'd have made repairs if we found what we needed to repair, wouldn't we?" she answered ruefully.

"I'd expect so."

"Well, there you are." She leaned forward, skimming the

plans and timesheets. "We're tracking a bug in the works. Though truth be told, it's less a bug and more a monkey."

"Monkey?" That was a new term on Abelard.

"Bugs nest in one place and stay there. A monkey roams."

He waved at the paperwork. "I don't see any service outages."

"Because you're thinking of the problem wrong," she said with the kindness of a grandmother offering candy. "Our generators are redundant, so you wouldn't see a drop in output. Look here."

"The coolant system is operating under capacity."

Sister Miriel's head bobbed, and Abelard felt as if he were back in school.

"Which means . . ." He chewed the words before saying them. "The exhaust isn't as hot as it should be. Heat must escape before exhaust reaches the coolant system."

"Our reasoning exactly, but we found no leak, even though we tore the system apart."

"That would have taken weeks, not just three days of double shifts."

"It did take weeks." She pointed to the schedule. "If you look at the older maintenance logs, you'll see that our crews have been pulling extra hours for months. The problem first showed up in spring, though back then it was predictable—every night, between one and four in the morning. In the last few days the drain became chaotic. Yesterday there was a peak just before dawn, and one or two small surges during the days before that. Nothing for the last twenty-four hours, though. There's no pattern we can see."

Between one and four in the morning, as he knelt before an altar, waiting in vain for God to answer his prayers. "It changed three days ago?"

"A few before that, actually, but the early morning draw stopped three days ago. We wondered if our current theological"— she paused out of propriety—"troubles were at fault, but the problem isn't worse, only less predictable. We've waited all day for a repeat incident with no luck."

Abelard turned to another page of schematics, and tried not to think about the "current theological troubles." The crowd's cries echoed in his mind. He could collapse, or keep working. The choice was obvious, but it was not easy.

"Brother," Miriel said after a quiet interval. "I hear you are accompanying the Godless ones."

"I am."

"What are they like?"

Those two lengths of pipe didn't match up on the schematic. Were these really maps of the same subsection? "The younger one . . . she wants to be strong. The older, I don't know what to say about her."

"Will they help us?"

He was about to quibble over the definitions of help, but that was not what Sister Miriel wanted to hear. "I think so." He rolled up the blueprints and slid them back into their cases.

"You're done with the schematics?"

"No," he said, and glanced down the ladder into the humid darkness of the boiler room. "Can I borrow a lantern?"

"I first realized I had an aptitude for the Craft," Tara said, "when I was maybe five or six." Her heels tapped down the hallway in perfect rhythm. "More importantly, I liked it. Liked using it, working it around me. It was almost a religious feeling. I wanted to make a life out of the Craft, so I had to leave Edgemont. Which was fine, because I wanted to do that anyway."

She waited for Cat to speak, but she didn't. Their footsteps were in time. Tara could have been walking alone, had she not been able to see the other woman by her side.

Good. This was hard enough without interruption.

"I took a job on the next merchant's caravan that came through town, and wandered with them for a few years, learning everything I could from their lesser Craftsmen, fighting Raiders, keeping the scorpionkind at bay. One night after the campfire died, I sat naked on the sand, soaking in the starlight I would need for the next day's Craft, and I looked up and saw the Hidden

Schools: towers rising out of midair and plummeting into empty space, castles with parapets on both ends, hovering globes of glass and crystal the size of the Third Court of Craft.

"I was terrified. I had been calling the schools to me for months, as any young Craftswoman who wants to study there will do, but they never answered before.

"I'd tell you about the rainbow bridge that descended from the twelve-spired Elder Hall, a building so old it became new again, to offer me entrance; I'd tell you about the challenges I faced as I climbed that rainbow, of might and Craft and cunning; I'd tell you about being welcomed into the Hidden Schools as they cloaked themselves in clouds that were not clouds. But none of these things are important to my story.

"I had a room, for the first time in years, rather than a wagon bed, and a roommate, which took more getting used to. Her name was Daphne, and her family had been Craftsmen as far back as you could go, and Theologians before that. What I didn't know about the Craftswoman's world, she helped me learn. She was one of those people you hate a little on first meeting, until you realize their generous act isn't an act at all."

Tara let the pause drag out. She breathed in, and heard a faint inhalation beside her. Cat turned left. Tara followed.

"She introduced me to Professor Denovo. He was the most famous teacher on the faculty if not the best-loved, and she brought me to a dinner he threw for his advanced students. Denovo had come from the bottom, like me. His family had been well off, watchmakers, but ignorant of Craft until their son showed himself a prodigy. Before long Daphne and I began to work in his lab. There, I found camaraderie, acceptance, common purpose. You've felt the same, I'm sure. Your bond with Justice is probably similar to the bond between Denovo and his students, and no small wonder. It was Denovo that broke Seril's corpse open and stitched it back together into Justice, forty years ago.

"Few people realize how blind human beings are to change. At the beginning I spent one hour a day at his lab; a few weeks later, six. The lab became my life, and its rhythms determined mine. I dreamed of work, and it seemed completely natural, as natural as you falling in step with me now. My strength dwindled, bit by bit. After weeks of this, I struggled to light a candle on my own outside the laboratory walls. Conversations with Denovo sparked with wit and life, and the rest of the world went dark by comparison, and I didn't notice.

"I didn't notice when Daphne stopped laughing, though one day I realized I couldn't remember the last time she smiled, and that I couldn't remember the last time I smiled, either. I examined the two of us, and the others who worked in our lab. My head felt stuffed with cotton, but after days I could trace the web of subtle Craft Denovo had woven through our souls. In the service of his will, we worked as a massive organism. Separate from his purpose we were half ourselves, or less.

"I confronted him about it. He laughed. 'We do good work,' he said. 'Better than any Craftsmen or Craftswomen in history. Together, we achieve greatness.'

" 'Not of ourselves,' I said, 'or for ourselves. We achieve greatness for you.'

" 'Someone has to direct our studies,' he replied. He invited me to go to the leaders of the schools and unmask him. I did."

Another turn. Stairs. A nurse wheeled a small cart laden with bloody knives past them.

"Denovo's lab, they said, was one of the greatest centers of learning in the world. The lab advanced the knowledge of all Craftsmen everywhere. They questioned my judgment, questioned my priorities, as he sucked his students dry and grew fat on the power he stole from them. I tried to quit, but he didn't let me. Tried to strike him down, but with his lab behind him, he was too strong. Daphne fell asleep in her room one day after a week of work with no rest, and didn't wake up. Her parents came to take her home. I never saw her again.

"Late one night, after the students left, I snuck into Denovo's lab and burned it. That place was the focus of the web he had spun through us all. As it burned I felt his grip on my soul burn, too. Power returned to me. My Craft was mine again.

"I didn't announce what I had done, but I made no secret of it, either. Discovering my rebellion, Denovo had me dragged before the Disciplinary Board. He wanted to kill me, but there was no punishment on the books allowing a student to be put to death. They graduated me instead, because no rule states that when you graduate the school has to put you down somewhere you can survive. I confronted the entire faculty, and laughed as they threw me down over the Crack of the World, not far, I suppose, from where Seril died.

"I survived."

Cat stopped at a bare wooden door with a brass number riveted onto it. No sound emerged from beyond, not even breathing. Tara felt the tingle of her own Craft within. This was the place.

She set a hand upon Cat's shoulder and squeezed, hard. Her nails dimpled skin through cotton, but Cat didn't start or draw away. The other signs, when she checked them, were all correct. Slightly dilated pupils, breathing in time with Tara's own. When she closed her eyes she saw the tiny threads that now connected Cat's mind to hers.

In three states is the mind most vulnerable, Professor Denovo had once told her: in love, in sleep, and in rapt attention to a story. Cat hated gargoyles. She would not have understood Tara's protection of Shale, nor would she believe he was innocent. Even if, by some miracle, Cat did believe, Justice would not, and Cat was too much in her dark Lady's thrall to resist wearing her Blacksuit for long. As Tara searched the other woman's dark, uncomprehending eyes, she felt a moment of intense self-loathing for what she had done, and was about to do.

"Cat?"

A slow "yes" followed a second later, as if Cat had forgotten how to use her own voice.

"I'm going to review the witness. Look for evidence Justice may have missed."

This time, a more ready answer. "Yes."

"I can do this alone. I'll be safe. I want you to be sure Captain Pelham is safe, too. If he's hurt, we'll lose our best lead in the case."

"Should I check on him?"

That was how Denovo's trick worked, at its subtlest. The target didn't lose her will, but became malleable, grateful for guidance. "Yes. I think you should make sure he's well."

Cat's footsteps sounded heavier than usual as she retreated down the long white hallway.

There was a Hell, and there were demons in it. Tara had visited, on school vacation. Nobody knew much about the demons' society or motives, and there was considerable argument as to whether they captured dead souls or merely copied them before they went elsewhere. The demons themselves were coy on the subject.

But if, in Hell, wicked souls were tortured for their sins, Tara expected she was bound there.

She opened the door into Shale's room and stepped inside.

14

Abelard swung from the last rung of the ladder to an overhanging pipe and dropped into the red-flushed dark of the boiler room, landing lightly on his feet. Steam and coolant lines tangled about and above him like jungle vines, and beyond them squatted the boilers, huge and round and warm. Humid air condensed into a slick sheen on his skin, mingling with new sweat. The heat was familiar and oppressive as the memories of an unpleasant childhood.

But the part of his childhood Abelard spent in the shadow of these giant clanking machines had not been unpleasant. Complicated, rather, full of adventure, of hide-and-seek and narrow escapes. The tiny crannies grownup engineers resented as side effects of poor design gleamed to a child's eyes like silver roads to freedom. Mastering this sweaty, benighted labyrinth, learning every path and obstacle, had been an ordeal of fascination and obsession. Abelard and his friends approached the garden of metal as if they were the first people in the world, consumed by its every facet, creating in the act of discovery.

The boiler room was not a safe place to play, and children were injured every season in their games. Abelard boasted a half-moon scar on his abdomen where, at thirteen, a falling girder tore through his leather work apron and robes to embed itself in his side. That afternoon he first felt the healing touch of his God, the holy fire that seared his skin, blackening and purifying.

He bore himself away from the boilers and up, sliding and swinging from pipe to girder to scaffold until the plummeting temperature made the steam that rose from his skin crackle and grow sharp. The Sanctum's generators were a closed system, though imperfect. Water flowed into the massive boilers, where

it became steam that drove the turbines that powered Alt Coulumb's trains and lights and lifts and the endless smaller mechanisms by which four million people lived in close quarters
without strangling on their own filth.

Superheated steam raced along a series of exhaust pipes to the
fourteenth floor, where the coolant system wrapped its icy tendrils
about Kos's hot iron veins. The coolant system was more dangerous by far than the steam pipes. Those would scald and burn, but
these would grip one's flesh with the strength of ice, and not all
the hot water in the world could thaw skin so frozen. When the
principles behind the generators were explained to him, Abelard
had envisioned the coolant system as a ravenous monster, devouring heat and life. His childhood nightmare was not far from the
truth.

He ducked under a pair of dangling chains and approached
the thick net of coolant coils, slick and shining with frost. Each
coil curled thrice about an exhaust pipe before bearing the heat
thus drained back to the coolant system's core, which waited like
a hungry maw in the darkness above. He climbed toward it.

Once, Sister Miriel liked to tell, there had been no coolant system. Once, Seril granted Her touch of moonlight and ice and cold
stone to the pipes, calling Her element back to itself: rushing, cool-
flowing water. When Seril died, the Church desperately sought
another solution.

Seril. The dead Goddess had loomed large in Abelard's life in
the last two days. As he climbed through the monstrous tangle of
the coolant system, he wondered how life in Alt Coulumb had dif-
fered while She lived. What were those nights like, lit by a watchful eye, guarded by creatures powerful, imperfect and passionate,
fierce as they were relentless? Had the moon shone brighter on
that city? Had its fullness caused the blood to leap for joy? Had
Kos, too, been different?

Such thoughts verged on blasphemy, but climbing this scaf-
folding, smoldering cigarette jutting from the corner of his mouth,
with no one near and with his God lying dead in starlight beyond
the realm of man, Abelard allowed himself to wonder.

What had Kos been like, when Seril lived? God withheld the

full force of his love these days, the old monks said, for fear He might burn the world to a cinder. Abelard had felt Lord Kos's flame lap gently against his own mortal soul, but had He kept a part of Himself back even then? Could Seril's presence have let Kos draw even closer to His people? If She still lived, would He have died?

The narrow cleft Abelard had been climbing opened; he stepped from the scaffold onto a vast plane of black rock, the ceiling of an entire clerical floor below, and found himself swaddled in darkness profound as the abyss. The air was chill as winter night, and there were no lamps. Light was heat, and this room was sacred to the deadly cold.

The chamber was three stories tall and nearly as broad as the Sanctum itself. Pylons thick and thin bridged the gap from floor to ceiling: staircases, people movers, large lifts for freight or groups of supplicants, all swaddled in layers of insulation to keep warm outside air from polluting the chill emptiness.

Abelard swept the narrow beam of his bull's-eye lantern through the black.

Suspended from the vaulted ceiling and the rough stone walls by thick chains hung the immense, entwined double toroid of the central coolant tank. Black slick metal, it drank the beam of his lantern.

He wished he had Tara's sensitivity to the Craft, for the central coolant tank was not a product of mortal engineering. Its inner workings were a mystery to even the most diligent and faithful of Kos's priests. They knew the black box consumed heat and fed it to Justice by an unseen mechanism, powering Blacksuits throughout the city. That was all. It lay like an open wound in the center of Abelard's mind, an affront to the laws of the universe.

He sat down on the stone, and closed his lantern.

Darkness rushed in, blacker than any night he had ever known, child of cities that he was. The tip of his cigarette burned against cold shadows.

He closed his eyes and traced in his memory the paths of the four hundred seventy-two threadlike coolant lines that wound over cold stone and through empty air to the central tank. They glowed in his mind's eye, precise and exact.

He inhaled, and his breath froze in his chest.

They glowed not only in his mind's eye, but in the black beyond his eyelids.

He opened his eyes, and saw nothing. Closed them, and the coolant pipes glimmered silver and cold in empty space. The silver lines seemed painted on the backs of his eyelids, or rather his eyelids seemed to have become filters that only this light could penetrate.

To his closed eyes, the coolant tank was a tangle of clockwork outlined in silver. Its innards spun and turned and wound, and in places silver light tangled about invisible, physical gears, pistons, camshafts. Power flowed down the chains that suspended the tank in midair, and proceeded through hidden paths across town to the Temple of Justice.

He inhaled smoke and exhaled it. The light gleamed more brightly. He opened his eyes, and the silver visions vanished.

"What is this?" he asked the empty space and the machines.

They didn't answer, but something within him whispered, *look further.*

He closed his eyes again. Lines of spider silk filled the black, but not all of them were silver. In their midst, one ran a burgeoning red and gold along the floor to disappear into the rock. That line was darker than the others, barely shedding light. Dormant. It was not tied to the coolant system, he reasoned, and thus lacked the coolant system's pale, hungry hue.

He opened his eyes and the cover of his lantern, shedding a narrow beam of light along the path of the anomalous pipe, fixed to the stone by iron bolts. It was less corroded than the surrounding coolant lines, but indistinguishable from them in gauge and make. Someone had intended this pipe to blend with the coolant system. Without his newfound vision, Abelard would never have seen the difference. No wonder the maintenance crews discovered nothing.

Returning to the scaffold, he traced the pipe back down into the boiler room's sauna heat. His quarry wound about the primary steam exhaust pipe like ivy around the trunk of an ancient dying tree. It fed on the heat, draining it—slowly now, but he suspected it could drain faster, and indeed pull enough heat to steal power from Justice herself. This was no doubt the cause of the coolant fluctuations Sister Miriel had observed.

Back he climbed through the dark, guided sometimes by lantern light, sometimes by the vision that hung before his closed eyes.

Returning to the coolant system's chamber, he traced the errant pipe until it plunged into the floor near a stairwell. By comparing the pattern of ventilation ducts and power conduits with the Sanctum's floor plan, etched in his memory, Abelard identified the rooms below. Offices mostly, a scriptorium, a meeting hall. He knew the Sanctum better than his own body, but he did not know where this pipe led.

He paused to light another cigarette from the embers of his last. Breathing in, he closed his eyes.

Three steps to his left, beside the red ribbon of the fake coolant pipe, a red square burned in outline on the floor, a few feet on each side. At one edge of the square, the strange dull light illuminated a depression in the rock, invisible when Abelard examined the same space with his lantern.

A handle, concealed.

He placed his fingers into the depression and felt them wrap around a metal D-ring. When he pulled, the entire square of rock shifted up on an invisible hinge. Abelard expected the stone to be heavy, but it rose easily in his grip.

Below the hidden door, a tunnel dropped into darkness that Abelard's new second sight could not pierce. A ladder was riveted to the tunnel's round wall.

He glanced about, thinking that he should go for help. But access to the boiler room was limited to priests and monks and the occasional, heavily supervised consultant. Building such a complex project as this, with secret doors and tunnels and pipes, required time and power, or numbers, or both. An outsider could not have accomplished it without help from within the Church.

He thought back to Sister Miriel's calm assurance, to her

bafflement at the coolant problem. Sincere? Or secure, knowing he could not find what she and her comrades had hidden?

Perhaps Tara had made him paranoid, but Abelard did not feel like trusting anyone.

He set one foot on the ladder and descended alone.

Ms. Kevarian did not find Cardinal Gustave in his office, nor in the library. An aide said he had gone to the rooftop to meditate. She sought him there.

Cresting the stairs she found the Cardinal leaning on his staff near the edge of the roof. Ordinarily from this vantage point Alt Coulumb stretched from horizon to horizon, but today clouds wadded about the Sanctum like thick wool. The world ended in a blank expanse beyond the tower, as if some god had forgotten to draw the rest of the image on the page, or having drawn it, frowned, and reached for the eraser. The noise of the crowd below was barely audible, an undifferentiated mash of sound in the misty depths.

"Your people are angry," she said without preamble.

"Their faith is weak."

"They want someone to explain the situation. Assuage their fears."

He did not respond. Wind whipped his robes about him, but did not touch her.

"I wanted to talk to you about Kos's resurrection."

"Talk."

"We need a strategy for rebuilding Kos, and the first step is for me to understand what the Church wants. What you want."

"I want." He did not say those words often, she thought. "I want my Lord back. The way He was."

"Kos as you knew him is gone, Cardinal. We can resurrect him, but we can't save everything. I need to know your priorities."

"Our priority," the old man said, "is to defeat Alexander Denovo."

Ms. Kevarian joined him at the tower's edge. She remembered that tension in his voice from his brief talk with Denovo at court. "This isn't an adversarial process. We win to the extent we get what we want. Denovo loses to the extent he does not get what his clients want." Wind filled the silence. Through the mist she heard the mechanical rush of a passing train. "Unless you know something I don't."

"I remember when you were not much older than your apprentice is now," the Cardinal said. "And I was younger."

"You were."

"It doesn't seem fair, that all the things of this world pass— that Gods pass—and not you."

"I'll take that as a compliment."

"I don't mean you in particular. Your people. Craftsmen. Craftswomen. Lingering on, untouchable."

His words died somewhere in the depths of the cloud.

"Hardly untouchable," she said.

"Denovo looks even less aged than you."

"He drinks the life of those who come too close to him. Steals their youth. Also," she said after a pause, "he moisturizes."

She intended that as a joke, but the Cardinal did not laugh.

"Cardinal, I need you to tell me if you're hiding anything about your relationship with Denovo."

No response. Far below, she heard raised voices.

"When you met him at court, you behaved as if he'd wounded you personally. That by itself means little, but this afternoon I visited several of your creditors, his clients. They told me he angled for this position. He's working virtually for free, and that's not his style. He wouldn't be here unless he thought he had something to gain, but your situation seems strong. Unless he knows something I don't."

Gustave turned away from the abyss, away from her. "You know the Technical Cardinal is responsible for maintaining Justice."

"Yes."

"For the last several months, Justice has felt a drain on her power in the early morning. The Blacksuits weaken on patrol, and Justice's thoughts grow sluggish. Our people determined this trouble was Craft-related, but they could not trace its source.

We sent word to Denovo, who was the chief architect of Justice. He came, advised me about our problem, and left."

"He didn't mention any of this when you met in the courtroom because . . ."

"We both felt it best his consultation remain secret. The Church did not want Justice to appear weak, and Denovo did not want anyone to know his greatest construct required maintenance."

A gust of wind billowed Ms. Kevarian's long coat behind her like a cape. She stuck her hands in her pockets. She heard, and he heard, the distant repeated cry: "God is dead! God is dead!"

"I think Denovo discovered something when he consulted for you," Ms. Kevarian said. "Something that made him think Kos was weaker than he seemed. Knowing that, he positioned himself to represent the creditors when Kos died."

Cardinal Gustave turned to face her. His expression was carefully blank. "Why? What could he gain from his position as counsel?"

"My question exactly."

Gustave considered this, and Ms. Kevarian, and the clouds around him, with a firm, fixed expression. Saying nothing, he walked to the stair that led back down into the Sanctum's depths.

"Where are you going?" she asked.

"Where else? I am going to speak with my people." His staff tapped out a slow, inevitable rhythm. "I will show them that Kos's truth endures, despite their weakness."

"Applied Theology won't work," she said, though he knew this already. "Kos's body may endure, but his soul is gone. He won't be able to help you direct his power."

"He appointed a little might for his priests' daily use. That will remain through the dark of the moon, like the generators and trains and all the rest."

"Without Kos, you can't shape and refine his power. If you tried to light a fire you'd end up destroying the fireplace."

"That," he said grimly as he descended into the shadows of the Sanctum tower, "will be enough."

Unseen within the gray erasure of the universe below, the crowd screamed on.

Tara stood in the hospital room, and caught her breath. Snaring Cat's mind had taken more strength than she expected. This cloud-covered city had so much light but so few stars. She needed to be more efficient to accomplish all she had planned for tonight. An interrogation lay before her, combat and pursuit, but at the end she would gain another piece to the many puzzles surrounding Kos's demise, and, if she was lucky, a weapon to use against Alexander Denovo.

In the process, she might even prove herself to Kelethras, Albrecht, and Ao, but that prospect seemed distant and barren to her now. It lacked the pleasant warmth that came when she thought of Denovo falling.

Shale lay in the bed, or at least his body did. The nurses had stripped him naked and plugged an intravenous drip into his arm. Risky at this low level of medicine, but there was no other way to feed him with his face gone. The folded bedsheets revealed the corded muscles of his chest, unsettling in their perfection, as if he had been built rather than grown. He was thinner, she thought, than yesterday. His freakishly swift metabolism was already cannibalizing fat and muscle. If Shale's incapacitation lasted much longer, his body would devour itself from the inside.

She set her shoulder bag on a table across from the bed, beside a vase of flowers. From within she produced her slender black book. Its silver trim glimmered in the dying sunlight. She took other items from the bag as well: a tiny gas burner the size of her clenched fist, a folded piece of black silk, a pen, a vial of ink the color of mercury, her small hammer, a pouch of silver nails, and a tiny silver knife.

Last chance to turn back, she told herself. *Even now you could probably apologize to Cat. Go farther, and you can rely on no one but yourself.*

She undid the latch on the black book. Sandwiched between the tenth and eleventh pages lay Shale's face. The cool skin twitched as her fingers feathered over its cheek.

Tara unfolded the face, set it features-down on the black silk, uncapped the ink, sterilized the silver knife with the gas flame, and began to work.

Cat arrived at the vampire's door, uncertain how she had come there. Her mind felt mulled, heated and seasoned. Need quickened in her breast.

She was tired. It had been a long and sober night, and a long day in plainclothes, relieved only by the brief ecstasy of the suit. The world felt empty, its colors garish and sharp without the flood of joy to cushion them.

In a moment's inattention she opened the door and stepped into the vampire's sickroom. She looked down at him, sleeping: lean and wiry, with black hair. His skin was marble-smooth, burned brown as old leather by exposure to sunlight. Slick, weak vampires like the one who had hustled her last night burst into flame in the sun, feared it like humans feared acid or spiders. This one had built up a tolerance, which took power, grit, and practice at enduring pain. He could sleep comfortably in a room with a window during the day, only blackout curtains separating him from death.

He could take her further down than she had ever been before.

His mouth had lolled open during his profound sleep, and she saw the tip of an ivory fang in the narrow gap between his lips.

The cuffs of her cotton shirt were too tight. She undid the buttons, rolled them up. Tiny blue veins pulsed beneath the pale skin of her forearm.

Outside, the sun kissed the edge of the horizon.

She walked toward the bed.

The darkness soon yielded to a dim blue glow. Abelard stepped off the ladder's last rung onto an unfinished rock floor, and turned to face the source of the light: three shining concentric circles set into the floor, graven round with runes. In their center stood a rough wooden altar, upon which lay a writhing pool of shadows impaled by a crystal dagger. A sharp stench of blood and ozone hung on the air. The fake coolant pipe descended from the low ceiling to merge with the altar. From the pipe's terminus spread eight cardinal lines of blue flame, which intersected the circles.

Someone had built this Craft at the heart of the Church, to drain Kos's heat from His own generators. Many questions burned in Abelard's mind, but three burned brightest: who, and why, and how could he stop them?

Abelard approached the altar. His skin tingled as he stepped over the first circle, careful not to touch the glowing lines. With another stride he crossed the second. A breath of hot air kissed his face and ruffled his robes. One left.

This, too, he crossed, but as his second foot touched down the world vanished. He was familiar with the sensation by now, and welcomed the nothingness and warmth, and the red edges to his vision as if a great light burned behind him. For the first time, he had the presence of mind to turn around and see what waited there.

Fire filled the void.

When he opened his eyes, he stood within the innermost circle. Before him lay the dilapidated altar, and the crystal dagger buried in its surface. Shadows writhed beneath the blade's tip.

No, not shadows. These were too coherent for shadows. An animated tangle of liquid black, like a catch of seaweed flowing with the tide.

When he closed his eyes, he saw the room mirrored in his newfound second sight. Innumerable silver threads drew heat from the pipe to the circle, then wove back up the altar to knot through the crystal blade. Whatever had been done here, that dagger was the keystone. Remove it, and the system might fall apart.

Or perhaps accelerate. Tara would know, or Lady Kevarian, but Abelard didn't want to risk leaving this chamber to find them. The conspirators wouldn't have made this intricate siphon of power so that disturbing it would damage the generators they hoped to use. Removing the dagger might break the Craft at work here, but there should be enough evidence left to find the people who had desecrated the holy places of Lord Kos.

Before he could talk himself out of it, he pulled the dagger free. It came loose easily, as if drawn from a sheath, and left a low ringing sound in the air.

The black tangle fell limp, but nothing else changed. The circles glowed with cold light. With eyes closed, Abelard saw the silver threads still knotted through the dagger. He opened his eyes again, and examined the weapon. Trapped within its crystal blade was a red fleck, the color of fresh blood.

When he lowered the dagger, he saw that the wooden altar was bare. There was no sign of the writhing shadow.

He heard a harsh rasp, like a chisel scraping over stone.

Was it his imagination, or had the chamber grown darker? Perhaps the light was fading.

No. The light had not changed, but the surrounding gloom was closer and more viscous, especially eight feet up the wall where a black pustule swelled, extending small tendrils to drink in the lesser shadows around it.

He backed out of the circle, gaze locked on that wriggling, growing darkness. Its limbs stretched out, some thick and others narrow, some soft, some hard, glittering like nightmares. As those tendrils moved over the stone, he heard the faint rasp again, and saw bits of rock dust fall.

Another step back. His breath was loud in his ears. Or was that only *his* breath?

His eyes burned. Without thinking, he blinked.

When he opened his eyes a fraction of a second later, the shadow on the wall was gone.

Above, he heard a thousand tiny chisels rake over bare stone.

He reached blindly behind himself and found the rungs of the ladder. His fingers shook; it took him two tries to jam his cigarette between his teeth. He turned around and began to climb.

He felt, rather than heard, a heavy diffuse collapse behind him, like a hundred pounds of dead insects falling from the ceiling. He surged up the ladder, granted strength and speed by fear. Scrabbling on stone below: the shadow creature, climbing. A few more feet and he would reach the main coolant chamber and its pitch darkness. With luck the shadow could not be behind and ahead of him at the same time.

The shadow skittered up the wall after Abelard, a herd of centipedes crossing a floor of night-black stone. Pain sliced through him—his leg caught by what felt like a circle of thorned rope. Abelard kicked, pulled. His robe tore, and his skin, too, but he was free, up, out, panting spread-eagled on the rock beneath the curved cold immensity of the coolant system. Darkness surrounded him, crisscrossed by pipes and tubes and vents and chains.

Below, behind, the shadow wound its first tendrils over the ladder's top rung.

Abelard forced his unwilling body to run.

Reattachment of a face was a simple process. Once Tara inscribed the geometric sigils and the ancient runes, only a few final cuts remained. Seven, for the seven apertures of the senses, on the reverse side of the face and on the blank flesh of Shale's head. Two cuts for the two eyes, two for the ears, one for each nostril, one for the mouth.

She found a spare bedsheet in a dresser drawer, ripped it to long thin shreds, and used the shreds to knot Shale to the bed frame. Then she matched the fresh wounds on face and head to one another and said the words that untied her bonds of Craft.

She kneaded the cheeks, pressed in at the temples, smoothed the eyes back into their sockets. Flesh knit to flesh, and the body welcomed its spirit's return. His features swelled and grew pink as blood rushed to them once more. Breath rattled in a throat that had not tasted air in more than a day. A pair of emerald eyes opened to regard the world. The lingering fog of Shale's exhaustion parted in a rush when Tara leaned close and whispered into his ear, "Time to wake up."

His sharp teeth snapped for her throat, but she had expected that and pulled back in advance.

"Not a good idea, Shale."

Steel-cord muscles strained against her improvised cloth ropes, but the knots held, and the strips of blanket were tight enough to deny him the leverage to tear free. He convulsed on his bed like a netted fish.

"I'd like you to answer my questions," she said.

"I'll kill you!" This time, Shale's voice was fierce, and passion-ate. Tara saw the gargoyle's eyes widen at the force of his re-claimed rage.

Which was all well and good, but if he didn't quiet down, he'd call the Blacksuits to them. "I gave you back your body as a show of good faith. I need your help."

"You imprisoned me."

"We've been over this," she said. "I got you off that roof with-out the Blacksuits seeing. Would you rather be in prison? Or dead? Everyone in Alt Coulumb seems to think Seril's Guardians are monsters. Would they give you a fair trial? You're an animal to them."

"Blasphemy." He spat the word at her.

"You know that's how they see you. You said as much your-self, yesterday. Let me help you prove them wrong."

"I don't know anything. I won't tell you anything."

"Those are two very different statements."

"My people will come for me."

"I've blocked their sense for you." Not true—how else had the gargoyles found her last night on the Xiltanda's roof?—and per-haps not even possible, but Shale was no Craftsman, and didn't know what she could and could not do. "I want to help them as much as I want to help you. Your leader, Aev, sent you to Judge Cabot's penthouse to receive a message. You pretended not to know more when last we spoke, but she wouldn't have sent you in blind."

"Aev said, talk to no one."

"A dark night is falling over this city, Shale. You can be with your people by moonrise if you tell me what I need to know."

Green eyes flicked from the window to the strips of cloth that held him. A bright instant of calculation flashed across his face. "I . . ." His voice dropped. He was weaker than he looked. "I was to receive something from Judge Cabot."

"Yes." She approached the bed, reeled in by his sinking voice. "What was it? And remember, I can tell if you lie." Also untrue, but he didn't know that.

"Don't know." He shook his head. "Just a courier."

"Why did you come into the city? Forty years with no

Guardians in Alt Coulumb, then this, putting your whole Flight at risk. What did Judge Cabot have for you?"

"He was going to help us. He'd been dream-talking with Aev for months. Everyone was excited."

"Why?"

"I don't know."

"You're lying."

"No." He was desperate, shaking his head.

"Yes. But we'll come back to that. Tell me what you saw when you reached Cabot's penthouse."

The setting sun's first shadow fell across Shale's face, and his body twitched. The knotted sheets held.

"Tell me."

"Blood," he said.

"And in the blood?"

His nostrils flared. "A face. Surrounded by bones."

"Cabot's face?"

"Cabot. His body broken. Flayed, but he could speak."

"What did he tell you?"

Shale looked away. She grabbed his chin, and forced him to face her. "Tell me. What did he say to you?"

Out of the corner of her eye, she saw his fingers flex. Silver-blue light crackled between them.

"What did he say, Shale?"

He opened his mouth. Something like a word came out. She leaned in to catch it.

But his mouth was not a human mouth anymore.

Cloth ripped and talons flashed. Beneath her was a creature ceasing to be human: skin now gray stone, muscles writhing and nerves rewiring themselves, whole being condensed in agony as wings unfurled from his back. His hooked beak spread to devour.

Tara fell back, screaming, and white light flashed between them.

Cat swam through a sea of need. She sat on the bed next to the vampire, who lay corpse-still beneath the sheets. Blood pounded through her veins, so much of it. She didn't need it all.

Captain Pelham—no, call him the vampire, that made it easier—lay lost in the predatory dreams of his kind, dreams of chase and capture, not the tremulous scavenger hallucinations of mortal man. Like all beings, his kind had sleeping reflexes. Bring blood to their lips, and they would suck.

There are more important matters at stake than your satisfaction, a tiny part of her protested, small and alone in a cave at the back of her mind. The vampire is in fine condition. No harm befell him during the day. Your mission is fulfilled. Go back to Tara. Do your duty.

Duty was a dry well, and the world a cold promontory. Light, life, and glory waited within his teeth.

She lowered her bare wrist, and slid it between his lips. The inside of his mouth was cold as peppermint, and his fangs pressed against her skin.

Small, and sharp.

She placed her free hand behind his head for support. His hair scratched her palm like a nest of wires.

Don't do it, that tiny part of her screamed. You're better than this.

She jammed her wrist onto the tips of his fangs.

15

Tara's scream did not stop Shale, but the shield of Craft she threw between them managed well enough. His talons raked across its translucent surface, once, twice, three times, scattering sparks that burned on tiles and furniture. She stumbled under the weight of his attack and fell, curling into a ball on the floor, but kept her hands and the shield between them.

Again he assailed her, and again her shield held. Tara gathered her legs deliberately beneath her and rose into a crouch. As she stood, she fixed Shale with the glare of a woman who could strangle gods on their thrones.

He froze for a fleeting moment, and through his eyes she traced the patterns of his thought. He had hoped to kill her quickly and flee to his people before the Blacksuits chased him down. Every wasted second reduced his chances of escape. Did his large ears detect the footfalls of Justice approaching their door?

Shale knew the steel inside her, and knew as well that he could not prevail against a Craftswoman and the Blacksuits together. He glanced over his shoulder toward the barred window. In that momentary pause, she drew her knife from the glyph above her heart.

There was no need to use it. He made the right choice, and leapt backward in a silver streak, somersaulting through the air to land facing the window. Tile cracked and splintered beneath his feet. One large hand ripped the metal bars free of their mooring, and another shattered the safety glass. Fluid as quicksilver, he leapt from the windowsill into space, teeth and claws naked and sharp, wings flared.

He landed with a thud on the fire escape of the building opposite, a God Wars–era pile of iron and red brick. Rusted metal creaked and bent under his weight but did not give. As Tara ran to the window he clamored up the metal frame, not bothering with the stairs. She marveled at him, swift, sure, strong.

But he wouldn't believe in such an easy escape.

The sunset paled and the hospital lights guttered as she drank in tiny flames of ghostlight and candle. She cloaked herself with darkness and power. Shadows trickled through her muscles and covered her body.

Ten feet from here to the next building over, she judged. Four stories of fall. The hole in the wall was not large enough for a running leap. She climbed onto the windowsill as Shale reached the seventh story of the building opposite. One more level and he would flee faster than she could follow.

Tara leapt.

Empty air yawned beneath her. Arms straight out in front, fingers outstretched. She must have let out a battle cry of some kind, for Shale turned and saw her, almost soaring though she lacked wings. Seven feet. Eight. Reach. You can make it.

The tips of her fingers curled about the iron railing, then let go.

She fell.

She slammed into the fire escape one floor down. Had she not shifted power from her muscles to the shadows that protected her, the impact would have broken her elbow. Wind whistled about her; an iron rail bounced off her ribs. Flailing, she grabbed hold of a banister for a second. The sudden jolt nearly dislocated her arms. Her grip broke, but at least she was falling slower.

The paving stones hit her like a god's hammer. Light exploded in her chest and behind her eyes. Through the haze that obscured the world, she saw Shale silhouetted against the clouds before he disappeared.

A flight of stone steps a few feet away led to the brick building's basement door. She crawled to those steps and worked her way down them until she found a shady corner. Crouching there, she drew darkness close as a blanket. Anyone examining the alley from above would see only shadows.

She leaned back against the rough brick wall, and with her

fingertips she tentatively explored the shelf of her ribs, her legs, her arms, the back of her skull. Her protective Craft had worked. She had a few bruises, one so deep it would surface slowly over the next several days, but no broken bones.

Her shoulder bag, with its needles and beakers and burners and silk and other implements of Craft, was a greater loss than any of her injuries, but there had been no other option. A savage assailant, hurried and carrying hostages, would not pause to collect their luggage. If the Blacksuits believed the gargoyle who stole their witness had taken her, too, they wouldn't seek her out, and she would be free to work. Besides, leaving her belongings should dispel any suspicion on Justice's part that Tara was kidnapper rather than kidnappee.

Still, she hoped she saw that bag again.

She waited, listening with shallow breath to the furor above as Blacksuits burst into Shale's room. It took them seconds to digest the chaos, and perhaps a minute to notice the fire escape opposite, bent and twisted where Shale hoisted himself up. The frame had not been designed to support a thousand pounds of gargoyle.

On cue, three black glass forms leapt from the infirmary window and clattered against the fire escape. Limbs surged like pistons as they climbed. Soon they reached the rooftops and vanished, continuing their hunt.

As a courier and Guardian of Seril, Shale knew how to evade pursuit. The Blacksuits sought a gargoyle carrying hostages. Shale, unburdened, could outpace and outmaneuver them.

So far, everything was going according to plan.

Tara smiled grotesquely, then winced at the pain in her side.

Abelard closed his eyes and ran, following the red glow of the coolant line. He tripped over a toolbox left by a maintenance monk and banged his knee against a sharp piece of unseen metal. If either metal or fall injured him, he couldn't feel it. The shadow creature's claws had torn holes in his leg, and numbness spread from them. With each heartbeat his feet grew heavier. Behind, he heard the shadow's limbs clatter over stone and metal, accelerating.

He could not rely on speed to escape, but in fifteen years of working in this boiler room, playing hide-and-seek and capture-the-wrench in its maze turns and dead ends, he had seldom re-lied on speed.

He leapt from the floor's edge onto a scaffold and climbed down a quick ten feet through a narrow gap between a wall and a water reservoir. Before reaching the boiler room he stepped off onto a side passage. His hands shook as he unclipped a wrench from his belt and threw it underhanded back into the gap. It clattered off the scaffold as it fell to the boiler room floor, sounding a great deal like a scared young man fleeing a predator. He retreated twenty feet into the side passage, where a ladder descended into another part of the boiler room. With one hand on that ladder's top rung, he crouched, turned, and set the bull's-eye lantern before him.

There had been no light in the hidden room save the glow of what he felt certain Tara would have called Craft. This thing grew in and fed on shadow. Real light might blind or injure it. Abelard had no reason to suspect his plan would work, but he needed to try something. He couldn't run forever.

He stilled his breath and readied his fingers on the lantern's cover. Calm. Careful. Wait.

Exhale.

Above, almost inaudible, tiny claws scraped across metal. Closer, descending the scaffold. A distinct inrush of air, amid the hundred metallic sounds of boiler and turbine and piston. Was the creature smelling for him? Could it see in the dark? How well? How smart was it? Why was it taking this long?

He tried to pray, without bothering to think who might answer.

Clicking, clattering, closer.

The hiss of foul breath deepened and grew louder. It had drawn even with the side passage.

He flicked open the lantern's lid, and hoped.

A beam of fiery light lanced through the cloying darkness. Narrow at the lantern's aperture, twenty feet out the beam was broad as the tunnel's mouth.

The shadow creature had grown. It nearly filled the eight-foot-tall passage, and longer, thinner thorn-limbs trailed beyond. Smoke rose from its body where the light touched. Jagged mandibles snapped open, and fanged mouths loosed a horrible, inhuman cry.

Don't be smart, Abelard whispered. Be fierce, be cruel, vindictive, but, please, Kos, don't let it be smart.

Scuttling on many sharp limbs the creature launched itself down the hall toward the lantern. Shadow-flesh shriveled as it moved. Light tore steaming gaps in its body.

Abelard breathed a silent prayer of thanks and descended the ladder as if in free fall.

The vampire's fangs pierced Cat's wrist, sharp as a bee sting. The pain was brief; his lips fastened reflexively on her wrist and euphoria spread from the wound as he began to suck. Pleasure tingled into her fingers, back up and around to her heart, from there to her entire body. Perfection enveloped the world. Knots within her soul untied, or else were sliced open by the sword of bliss.

Were her eyes open or shut? Was she still sitting up, or had she slumped against the vampire as the joy of him took hold? Was she even breathing?

Paltry, everyday concerns. Ecstasy ruled her soul.

She wasn't supposed to be here. She had a duty, someone to protect. A woman. A woman who had told her a story.

The red sun's bulk settled beneath the horizon, and the sky outside the window dimmed. Far away there came a crash of broken glass, followed by a cry Cat heard with spiritual ears: the cry of Justice, a summons to all Blacksuits to pursue a Stone Man who had abducted a witness and a Craftswoman.

Tara.

Tara had told Cat to check on the vampire. Here he was, unharmed, healthy, glorious. Hungry.

His eyes were open.

She saw satisfaction, confusion, and revulsion superimposed on his face. Roused from sleep, he found his teeth buried in a strange woman's wrist. He was hungry, and his will was weak.

He did not push her away. A beast within him woke, stretching and yawning in his red eyes. One clawed hand rose feebly from beneath the sheets and hesitated, uncertain whether to seize her or thrust her from him, unsure whether she was real or a predatory dream.

Cat tried to think through the rush. Why had she left Tara's side? Her orders had been to watch the Craftswoman. Cat's memory was hazy, but she recalled a story, a suggestion, a sudden desire.

Tara had done something to her. Twisted her.

The vampire's hand rose, curved, to grasp the back of her neck.

Pulling her wrist from his mouth was as hard as turning from the gates of paradise. She fell back off the bed and sat down hard on the tile floor. The vampire snarled and rose to a crouch, silhouetted by the last rays of the setting sun. Her blood stained his lips and his chin.

"What the hell were you doing?"

Cat's mouth fell open.

"What. I mean." He wiped the blood off his chin with his fingers and regarded it in fascination and disgust. "Seriously, woman. What is wrong with you? Haven't you ever heard of consent?"

She pressed her back against the wall and slowly stood. Blood pounded in her ears. The wound in her wrist had closed when his fangs left it, but it still hurt.

"I could have killed you," he said.

"I . . ." Words were hard, imprecise. Fog clouded her mind.

"Wait." Red eyes flicked from the crown of her head to the bottoms of her boots, and back. "I've seen you before."

"Before." She nodded. "When you spoke with . . . Tara." She spat the name.

His tongue flicked out, and the blood on his lips disappeared. He wiped his chin on his wrist, and licked that clean, too. "Where is she? Why are you here?"

Shaking her head did not clear her mind. "I'm . . . She made me come here."

"You're an addict," he said, with the distaste Cat reserved for words like "pusher" and "pimp." "You're an addict, but even an addict would know better than to give an unconscious vampire their blood. You've been . . . not drugged." His eyes narrowed. Vampires could see beyond the normal range of human sight, she knew. "Something's worked through your mind. Made you vulnerable."

"Tara did something to me. I wouldn't have left her alone otherwise."

How could you let someone into your mind, Tara had said with mock horror, before she bound Cat in chains forged from her own need. Gods and goddesses, that bite had felt so *good*.

"Alone? Where?"

Cat didn't answer. Justice depended on her, and she let herself trust Tara, let herself be betrayed. She shuffled unsteadily along the wall to the door, turned the handle, staggered out, and ran, lurching, down the hall. Justice railed in her mind for control, and she yearned to slip from the dead dry aftermath of the vampire's bite into her suit's cold embrace. If she did, though, Justice would know her sin. She could be dismissed for such a lapse, cut off from the the suit forever. She could not allow that.

"Wait!" The vampire—Captain Pelham—followed her out of the room. He wore boots and breeches already, and pulled a loose, unlaced shirt over his head as he jogged to keep pace. "I'm not staying in that bed one more minute. Something's happened, and I want to know what."

"That," she said, trying to ignore the clenching nausea of blood loss, "makes two of us."

Abelard heard a crash of broken glass above as the lantern shattered. Perhaps he had injured the shadow beast, perhaps not, but at least the light had slowed it. He needed every advantage he could seize. Sister Miriel kept the boiler room dimly lit so as not to damage the night vision of Technicians or maintenance crews bound for darker areas of the Sanctum. There were shadows enough here to nourish his pursuer.

He took his bearings, compression chambers to his left, yes, good, and the coal bins to his right, and ran. His cigarette he plucked from his mouth and gripped between two fingers. He needed fresh air in his lungs. Metal distended and tore behind him as the creature descended the ladder.

Winding through tubes and pipes, Abelard chose his escape path, clockwise through the compression chambers that ringed the boilers, and in through a narrow gap between a compressor and a stone wall. His heart lurched in fear as he imagined squeezing through a tight passage with the creature bearing down on him, but the next opening was three hundred feet farther along. Too far.

He turned a hard corner as a mass of shadow scrambled, slipped, and fell to the floor a few hundred yards behind him. Enough of a lead, he hoped.

He ran fifty feet. A legion of centipedes chased after, legs tickling rock and metal, the floor, the walls, the ceiling. A hundred feet, and the shadow's speed redoubled. It smelled him. Two hundred feet, made in a mad rush, cigarette in one hand and the crystal dagger stuck through his belt.

The dagger had pinned the shadow creature to the altar. Could it harm the thing again, hold it down? Abelard hoped he did not have a chance to learn the answer to that question.

Two hundred fifty feet. Breath hissed through numberless mouths, near, so near. There, the narrow gap. He leapt into it. Cobwebs parted before him. A spider landed on his hand and fell away.

The centipede army drew even with the narrow crack and stopped. Its bulk closed out the dusk-red light. Long, thin arms slid through the crack after Abelard.

Metal caught his robes and he pushed through; fabric ripped as he tumbled into the room beyond. Or, as his torso did.

Long hooks of shadow snared his legs, and pulled him back.

Screaming, he fell. In desperation he planted one foot on either side of the crack and resisted the creature's pull with all his strength. This only slowed his slide. He clawed for the dagger at his belt. His fingers closed around its hilt, and he stabbed at the tentacle gripping his left leg.

The crystal blade slid through the shadow and cut Abelard's shin. He cursed, but did not drop the dagger. The creature's strength grew as his faded. Nightmare mouths gaped above him, filled with nightmare teeth. Living shadow bubbled out through the passage, swelling in the vast dim space.

He was about to die.

In such moments, time expands. To Abelard's surprise he found the sensation almost pleasant. He was about to be eaten by a giant shadow beast, through no particular fault of his own, and there was nothing he could do.

As the night-mandibles reared to descend, he raised his cigarette to his mouth and inhaled.

Its tip flared.

Flared.

Light hurt this thing, enough at least to anger it. What would fire do?

As the mandibles struck, Abelard plucked the cigarette from his mouth, held it as if the ember were a blade, and stabbed blindly into the shadow.

A roar shook the boiler room. Abelard sprawled back, legs his own again, cigarette still clenched in his fingers. The creature convulsed, outlined in orange flame that chewed its slick sharp edges to crumpled ash. The fire died as it consumed, and Abelard doubted it would kill the shadow, but he didn't care. He was free, and safety near.

Lurching to his feet in a confusion of ripped robes and bloody limbs, he sprinted for the ladder to the maintenance office.

The sun set as Tara crouched in the basement stairwell. She imagined the chase above, Blacksuits swarming over rooftops in search of their winged quarry, who hid and ran, zigged and zagged, fast and brilliant. Night deepened and behind thick clouds the moon rose, granting Shale power and speed. The Blacksuits could not match him. When Professor Denovo defaced Seril's Guardians and rebuilt them for police work, he would have reduced their dependence on the moon for power—a sensible design decision that left the Blacksuits slower and weaker than their stone adversaries at night.

When enough time had elapsed, Tara touched a sigil on her wrist. It glowed with inner fire, and she saw in her mind's eye a map of the city from above, marked with a bloodred dot: the location of the tracking glyph she had cut into the back of Shale's face.

He would never have told her what she needed to know. Nor could she hope to follow him across the rooftops when even Blacksuits could not keep pace. Besides, she believed him when he claimed not to know where his Flight was hiding. They planned to seek him when night fell.

Night had fallen, and Shale moved within her mind, hunting his people. When he found them, Tara would find her answers. Judge Cabot, Kos, and the gargoyles were involved in some deep, secret Craft together, of that Tara had no doubt. Of those three, only the gargoyles survived. Their testimony could prove the Church was not responsible for Kos's weakness, and help Tara defeat Denovo. Tonight, she would convince the gargoyles to tell her what they knew. Or they would kill her. That was also a distinct possibility.

Tara stood, scaled the basement steps, and walked to the street. Carts and carriages rolled past on their private business. Across the rough cobblestones rose a soaring glass edifice bearing the red tau cross insignia of a Craft firm.

She squared her shoulders and lifted one hand.

A driverless carriage pulled to the curb. The horse eyed her ripped clothes and general disarray with suspicion as she climbed into the coachman's seat. "Don't give me that look," she said. "We're going to the waterfront. Now giddyup." The horse didn't budge. "I'll tell you where we're going when we get there," she said, exasperated. "Can you please move?"

With a toss of its mane, the horse surged forward, and the carriage shuddered into motion behind.

The unified chant of "God is dead!" had faded by the time Cardinal Gustave emerged from the small door set into the Sanctum's looming main gates. It was replaced, after the manner of mob cries, by a host of other slogans, which degenerated in their turn to meaningless roars. A few protesters regained their former ardor when they saw Gustave's priestly robes, but these were outnumbered by the ones who fell silent when he raised his head and looked upon them with his hard gray eyes.

"Citizens of Alt Coulumb," the Cardinal began. His voice suggested dark rooms and hidden mysteries.

"Citizens of Alt Coulumb," he repeated. "I should say, rather, children of Alt Coulumb. What right, you may ask, have I to come before you? My God, they say, is dead, and with Him my authority. I stand before a tower raised to a vanished ideal, and I wear the livery of an absent Lord."

These things were all true, yet when he said them the crowd beyond the cordon of Blacksuits did not scream their assent. Silence infected them, spread by those who stood near enough to feel firsthand the weight of the Cardinal's presence.

"Children of Alt Coulumb, ask yourself: what burns even now within your hearts? What fire dances through the pathways of your mind? When you look at me, do you feel the hot flame of righteous wrath that devours brush and brambles and soon gives way to soot and dust? Do you feel the sickly greenwood fire of treason or the slow coal-burn of contempt?"

The crowd was silent, yes, but their silence was dangerous. Cardinal Gustave had placed a shell of words around their anger, and their anger bucked and surged against it.

"Children of Alt Coulumb, that fire is your God!"

Cries rose from the audience, disbelief and half-formed epithets.

"You claim to know the mind of God, you claim to know His nature and His shape, His truth and His power. You claim He is dead when you yourselves are the proof of His glory. What citizens of any other nation would hear such news and come before me, to protest in the shadow of God's own temple?

"Children of Alt Coulumb, a fire burns within my voice. Within my mind. Within my heart. It is the fire of incense: a fire cultivated and refined through contemplation, strengthened through long practice and given proper fuel.

"That fire is Lord Kos's breath within me. It burns quietly, and its burning is a pleasure to the wise. Children of Alt Cou-

lumb, that fire is gentle. But *do not mistake me,*" he roared over
a tide of angry voices. "Do not mistake me, it still burns!"

Before him he thrust his staff. His brow furrowed, and he
drew in a measured breath.

A curtain of flame erupted from the staff's tip, red and orange
and yellow, and rose into the evening sky. It was the color of leaves
in autumn, but it was not autumn leaves. It was hot like the sun,
but it was not the sun. It was the fire of divinity. It eclipsed the
world, rippled over the reflective skin of immobile Blacksuits, and
cast the shadows of the mob upon the ground.

The frontmost protesters fell automatically to their knees,
from awe and to avoid the searing heat. Some near the back scrambled to escape.

Quickly as it came, the fire dissipated. The Cardinal lowered his staff. Its copper-shod tip settled with a clearly audible
tap against the Sanctum's basalt steps. His body swayed, but
within him, a thing that knew no age or weakness stood in-
domitable.

"Children of Alt Coulumb, your God slumbers within you. In
days to come, He will rise once more. Only your faith is weak."

The crowd remained bowed. Some, at the edges, slunk away.

Cardinal Gustave withdrew into the Sanctum shadows, and
closed the door behind him.

A Blacksuit guarded the door to the faceless witness's room, and
only let Cat and Captain Pelham pass when she flashed the badge
of Justice that hung around her neck. They found the room a
mess of broken and burned furniture. Tara's shoulder bag lay
open on the floor, the silver and crystal apparatus it once contained spilled out among splintered wood and shredded fabric.

"What happened here?" the Captain asked.

She had listened to Justice's mind on the walk over, gripping
her badge to hear as if through a layer of cotton the stream of de-
ductions and observations that resounded clear and bright within
her skull when she wore the Blacksuit. "A Stone Man burst in,
abducted Tara and the witness, and fled."

"Talon marks on the floor," Captain Pelham observed. "On the wall, here, and around the bed."

"The Blacksuits heard a scream, came running, found this." She paced. "Godsdammit."

"What? It makes sense, doesn't it? You saved Tara from the gargoyles last night, and this guy"—he pointed to the broken bed where the faceless man had lain—"witnessed their crime. They came to clean up."

"Tara invaded my mind to send me away. She must have had a reason."

"Maybe the gargoyle interrupted her while she was doing whatever it was."

"How?"

"Through the window." Captain Pelham pointed to the shattered casement.

"If so, where's the glass on the inside?" She knelt and swept her hand over the broken tiles, but discovered none. "See how these are bent?" She pointed to the bars. "Someone ripped the whole assembly out of the wall from this side."

"If you can see that, can't the other Blacksuits?"

"Not necessarily. They ran through, saw the Stone Man, and pursued. The examiners won't arrive for another quarter-hour at least." Her heartbeat quickened. If she found something Justice missed, she could use that to buy off her failure. She needed strong evidence, though. No mere guesswork would satisfy. "There was a Stone Man in this room. He didn't come in through the window, but he left that way. Could the witness have been a Stone Man all along? Pretending to be faceless?"

"Hard to pretend that, I think. Someone pretty much has to steal your face."

"Is there a way to break free of Craft that keeps you faceless, then?"

"Search me." Captain Pelham examined the bent bars, the shards of glass, the splintered windowsill. Dusk washed the outside world in weak shades of gray. "The Craft pays well, but I try to keep my distance. On the first job I took from a Craftswoman, I ended up with a hunger for blood and a bad sunlight allergy."

"Tara could have been in league with the Stone Men." Cat clutched her temples with one hand. She was missing something. The world blurred, shifted, solidified. Everything would be fine if she donned her suit. All the pieces would fall into place.

No. Not yet. She needed a real solution.

"If Tara was working with them," Captain Pelham asked, "why did they try to kill her last night?"

"I don't know!"

"Perhaps," he suggested, "you could ask her."

"What?"

He raised a finger to his lips and pointed out the window and down. She joined him at the sill and saw Tara in the alley below, brushing dirt off her sleeves and straightening her ripped skirt and checking her collar as she walked toward the street. Her clothes were a mess, as if she had just been in a fight.

Silent, they watched Tara reach the curb and summon a driverless carriage. "We need to follow her," Cat said.

"Follow her?"

Halfway out the window already, she paused, and swore.

"What?"

"She'll be gone before we can get down if I don't put on the Blacksuit, but if I do, Justice will know she controlled my mind and take me off the case."

"I'll catch you," Captain Pelham said.

She tried to stop him, but he flowed past her like mist and fell to the cobblestones below; the force of his landing barely bent his knees. He looked up to her in the gathering night and held out his arms.

Captain Pelham was a stranger, an outsider, a vampire. He didn't like her, and he had a rapport with Tara. If he dropped her, no one would ever know.

But he seemed like a good person, and if she didn't trust him, Tara would get away.

Cursing herself for a fool, she jumped. Her fall seemed to take longer than his.

He caught her, light as a bag of down.

Being held was nice, and being this close to his teeth was a terrible temptation. So strong. Old, too, and what mattered more, *original*. He had been made a vampire by Craft, firsthand, not by catching the condition from another.

In Cat's distraction she failed to notice Tara's carriage pull away from the curb, but Pelham's attention did not slip. He ran, the world blurring around them, and as her thoughts raced to catch up, he leapt.

Whipping wind, fluttering cloth, the street a surge of colors, and they landed—or rather he landed, with her still in his arms—stiff-legged atop the passenger compartment of an empty driverless carriage four cars behind Tara's. The horse reared and voiced a whinny of outrage, but when Pelham said, "Follow that cab and we'll pay you double," it gave no further complaint.

"You're insane," she said.

"At least I'm good at it."

"You can set me down now."

"Oh." He seemed to notice for the first time that he still held her cradled to his chest. "Sorry." With a flourish, he stood her on her feet. She almost lost her balance and fell into traffic, but caught herself and slid instead into the coachman's seat. "Occupational hazard. Pirate and all."

She glowered in response and offered him a hand down.

Abelard climbed three, four, five rungs at a time toward the Efficiency Office. Deterred but not destroyed, the shadow creature loped through the darkness after him. With a surge of terror-born strength he burst from the wet, warm air of the boiler room into light.

Scrambling off the ladder, he found himself surrounded by sound and fury. Alarms rang from all corners of the room— coolant alarms mostly, judging from the sonorous, *basso profundo* chorus of the Praise of Sacred Fuel—and Technicians rushed about checking chromed dials and pressure gauges and shouting to one another. Abelard's warning cries were lost amid the din.

Grasping a nearby table leg, he pulled himself to his feet. A startled hush fell over the room as the maintenance monks noticed his torn garments and the blood seeping from his legs.

"Something's down there! In the boiler room! Big." He sucked in breath. "Black, sharp . . ."

The astonished monks gave no sign they understood his words. They took him for mad, no doubt, another unfortunate cleric broken by the stress of the last few days. Two burly brothers approached, wearing fixed expressions of concern, to escort him out. Abelard pulled back. "Tell Sister Miriel!" Claws clicked on the ladder below. "It's coming! Get fire!"

Each monk grasped one of his arms and pulled, guiding Abelard toward the nearest door despite his squirming resistance. Others raised their heads from their work and blinked wide uncomprehending eyes, a clutch of tonsured seagulls. The creature would tear them apart before the light killed it. "It's coming!" Abelard lashed out with a wounded leg and kicked the back of one captor's knee. The man toppled and let go of Abelard's arm.

Free, he spun and pointed. "There! Look!"

Some of the monks listened, finally, and they did not return to their work.

A black, viscous thing bubbled up from the boiler room, thousand-eyed, probing with jagged limbs at the world. It thrashed and broke a nearby desk to splinters. Monks scattered. Opening many mouths, the creature let loose a terrifying hiss.

Religious men often think about death, and Abelard had given some thought to his last words. "I told you so" had not been on the list.

The creature roared, and lashed out with a claw of living darkness. Abelard ducked, and it skewered the monk who held his right arm. The man burst like an overripe fruit pricked with a needle. Abelard darted for the door.

He took five steps before he was brought up short. The air about him grew sharp, as before the onset of a thunderstorm.

Ms. Kevarian stood at the door of the Efficiency Office. The cant of her head and slant of her mouth reminded Abelard of a desert lizard he had seen once in a cabinet of curiosities. The

scholar who owned the cabinet introduced to his audience a spe-
cies of scorpion whose sting could kill a grown man in seconds,
then placed the scorpion in a glass tank with a flat-headed yellow
lizard. The lizard regarded the deadly insect in the same way Ms.
Kevarian regarded the shadow swelling and burning in the center of the room.

The scholar had explained, with a carnival barker's timing, that
this lizard's diet consisted chiefly of scorpions.

Ms. Kevarian's stillness broke into sudden motion. She
cupped the fingers of one hand as if scooping sand off a beach.
Behind Abelard, the shadow creature leapt toward this inter-
loper, barbed stingers tense to strike.

Ms. Kevarian raised her hand to the level of her eyes, and
with practiced deliberation closed her fingers into a fist.

A rush of wind from nowhere flattened Abelard's hair and
nearly plucked the burning cigarette from his lips. Lightning burst
within the chamber walls, but there was no light and no sound of
thunder, only a concussive wave. When he opened his eyes, the
creature hovered a few feet off the floor, revealed in full grotes-
querie and caught in a bubble made from solid air. Angry scrabbling talons glanced off curved transparent walls. Ms. Kevarian's
grip tightened, and the bubble began to shrink. Claws raked ineffectually; limbs buckled and bunched against one another like wet
towels pressed against a glass door. Still Ms. Kevarian squeezed
and still the invisible sphere tightened. Spider-arms melded into
thicker tentacles, and were crushed back into shadow. The creature's hisses were plaintive in the silence that accompanied
Ms. Kevarian's working of Craft.

The bubble crushed the creature into an undifferentiated black
mass. A small open space remained at the top, containing a pair
of desperately snapping mandibles. Still the bubble shrank, and
these too vanished, leaving a viscous sphere four feet, three feet,
two feet, one in diameter.

Ms. Kevarian strode into the room. Her heels tapped a funeral
beat against the stone floor. By the time she drew within arms'
length of the bubble of shadow, it was an inch and a half in diameter, vibrating softly. As she extended her free hand to pluck it

from the air it was an inch around. Holding it between thumb and forefinger, half an inch.

She opened her lips, put the pill of darkness inside her mouth, and swallowed.

A hint of pink tongue darted out to lick her upper lip. She turned to Abelard, who almost winced from the strength of her gaze. "Be glad," she said, "I came along when I did. Impressive alarms you have in this Sanctum."

He nodded, shivering. "What . . ." Vocal chords, like the rest of his muscles, were uncooperative. "What was that?"

"One of the gods' own rats," she said. "Rousted from hiding. Angry, hungry. Could have used salt. Where did you find it?"

"Be-below," he managed.

"You should get your temple cleaned more regularly." She crooked a finger at him. "Come. We have work to do."

Shale's red dot bounced like a child's ball around the map in Tara's mind. Every time she thought he reached a final hiding place he reversed course and veered again toward Midtown, darting through underground tunnels and sprinting down the tracks of elevated trains. Tara directed her carriage to wander side streets and keep away from main thoroughfares until at last, presumably after being found by his Flight, Shale came to rest at a warehouse three piers north of the *Kell's Bounty*'s mooring.

This was a dead and dangerous strip of city, where bleak talon-scarred buildings faced the night with shattered windows and broken doors. Dim streetlights illuminated loading docks strewn with rotted lumber and decayed canvas. In daylight, the warehouse would have looked like a health hazard. At night, it menaced from every approach.

Tara paid the horse and dismounted two blocks from her target. Navigating the dockside streets back to the warehouse proved less difficult than she feared. A gang of cutpurses tried to mug her, but they were no trouble. Thieves in this city fled from a little fire and the barest hint of death.

Her true quarry would not be so easily cowed.

No sentinels guarded the warehouse doors, nor could she see

anyone lurking on the rooftop. Not that she expected to. The Guardians knew Alt Coulumb in their blood, and blended into its shadows and murk like wolves into a deep forest. That bum sleeping under a ratty blanket, curled up near a streetlamp with a liquor bottle in one limp hand, might be one of them, or the doxy limping along the street, or the drunk pissing against a wall half a block down. Even in their true forms, any shadow could shelter them, any stone protrusion provide camouflage.

Five minutes were too many to waste outside an abandoned warehouse debating whether to enter. Raising her chin, Tara crossed the vacant lot and climbed the ramp to the loading dock. She picked her way through the detritus of economic endeavor to the doors, one of which still stood. The other, unhinged, had collapsed onto the rock floor within. She stepped over the threshold.

Decayed and long picked clean of valuables, the warehouse did not seem an ideal headquarters for a religious insurgency. One expected gargoyles to prefer the peaks of skyscrapers, where they could open their toothed maws to drink in the rising moon, not a place like this, a bare slab floor strewn with broken crates that had served as rats' nests before the cats moved in. High, broken windows admitted the streetlamps' yellow gas glow and the pale reflected light from the clouds above. At the far end of the warehouse, a long-abandoned foreman's office rose twenty feet above the ground on rotten wooden pillars.

Tara's mental map was accurate, but not precise. Shale was somewhere in this building, but she could not tell more. She had expected him to run until his people found him. Had he set an ambush instead?

Sudden movement seized Tara's attention. A shadow shifted behind a pile of broken crates, too big for a rodent or a cat.

Wary, she stepped forward. Her hand rose to her heart, and with a twist of her wrist she drew her knife, crackling and blue. It cast a pool of cool radiance at her feet. The noise and light gave away Tara's location and her skill with Craft to any hidden observer, but she lacked subtler weapons. She skirted to the right as she approached the pile of broken wood, to keep out of striking distance as she rounded the corner.

Behind the crate, Tara found only bare stone.

Had she imagined the movement? The night was dark and the building disturbing, but surely she was not so unnerved as to leap at shadows? Frustrated, she glanced about the warehouse for a potential cause: a swift scuttling lizard, an assailant trying to lure her into position, an urchin taking shelter from the night and the fierce dockside streets.

Nothing.

With an inward groan, she straightened, lowering her knife-hand to her side. Had Shale slipped her tracing charm? He would have needed to tear off his face and let it heal over. Did his powers of regeneration extend that far? Replacing a face was no simple affair of regrowing flesh. Sensory organs had to heal as well, and thousands upon thousands of nerve endings. The magnitude of power required, not to mention the pain . . .

As she contemplated the pain, the floor opened beneath her and she fell, arms flailing, into the abyss.

16

Blacksuits swarmed over the buildings and through the alleys of Alt Coulumb like ants at an abandoned picnic. One crouched at a roof's edge and glowered into the city with eyes that saw a broader range of light than the eyes of man. Another leapt from flagpole to flagpole, canvassing the Pleasure Quarters. A group of fifty cased the city one block at a time, moving with silent care down side streets.

The sight of them was enough to quell most of the sparks of civil unrest scattered throughout the city, and where mere sight was insufficient, they intervened in person. A middle-aged grocery-store owner struck a reedy young woman trying to steal food, and raised his hand to strike again; a rain of black fell over them, and when it lifted both were gone. A clutch of angry young men near the docks gathered to hear the protestations of a doom prophet, and twenty Blacksuits suddenly stood among the crowd where none had been before, watching and silent. The prophet's wrath broke as the eyeless stare of Justice settled upon him. Words of fear and hatred faltered on his tattooed lips.

But though the Blacksuits dealt with the criminals and madmen that lay within their path, they did not hunt humans tonight. They hunted men of stone.

A gargoyle had stolen a witness from Justice's infirmary, or perhaps had been disguised as that witness, or perhaps—Justice's many minds were divided on this issue, and the debate raged across the brains of a thousand active Blacksuits, dancing through their neurons and arguing about the tables of their cerebra. A Stone Man was on the run, that was certain, and there was no such thing as a lone Stone Man. Dead Seril's children moved in groups, or not at all.

Justice weighed the hearts of others, and did not spare much thought for her own. Had she examined her emotions, she might have recognized the petulant ire of the chess prodigy thwarted in mid-game. Mortals were meddling in Justice's sphere, and she was jealous of her sphere. She needed that Stone Man, and his brethren: parade them before the madding crowd, hang murder and blasphemy about their necks, and peace would return. Hate directed was easily controlled.

Blacksuits flocked in Alt Coulumb, a murder of silent crows with human bodies. Though the Stone Man had confused their scouts and their pursuers, for he was fast and could assume many shapes, he was mortal, limited, fallible. He played a smart game, but he would make a mistake, and the murder would descend.

Justice waited, sharpening her sword and polishing her scales.

"No Tara here either," Captain Pelham allowed as they sprinted out of the warehouse, night watchmen in hot pursuit.

Cat almost rolled her eyes, but that would have entailed taking them off the pavement, and in this part of town you never knew when a pothole or a mugger's tripwire might send you sprawling.

Captain Pelham had ordered their driverless carriage to stay as far back as possible without losing Tara as she wove into the waterfront district, then out, then in again, tracing a labyrinth of which only she knew the paths. Maybe it was a Craft thing, or maybe she was trying to throw off pursuit. On their most recent pass through the waterfront, they turned a corner and saw Tara's carriage pull away into obscurity, with Tara herself absent.

She must have abandoned the carriage to proceed on foot. Lacking a better option, they resorted to old-fashioned legwork, and had thus far eliminated a little more than half the warehouses in the area. Which meant, as Captain Pelham had reminded her with more good humor than she felt, that a little less than half remained.

It was hard to determine which warehouses were occupied and which abandoned. Near the docks, keeping one's property in good repair was a counterproductive endeavor. Clean, well-tended buildings hold valuable cargo. Dockside warehouse-keepers real-ized long ago that a few broken windows and vulgar scrawls of graffiti, fire scars on one wall and water damage on another, made it harder for the casual thieves abundant in this part of town to tell marks from firetraps.

Time ran short. They needed a new tactic.

"Let's try down this way," Cat said, pointing to a dark alley that led off the main street. "Shortcut."

"Sure you aren't luring me down here so you can force me to suck your blood?" He said the last bit with a heavy Old World ac-cent, and a fanged leer that disappeared when he saw the anger on her face. "I was joking," he said, lamely, as she strode past him.

"What kind of joke is that?"

"The kind where I make light of your nearly killing your-self."

"I knew what I was doing."

"So do most suicides."

Cat's mouth tightened. Her hands shook, and she stilled them. Not enough time in the suit today, which left her drawn and ir-ritable. Pelham's fangs, while glorious, were a poor substitute for Justice. She stalked down the alley, and he followed. "It's not like this is the first time I've been bit."

"You're a practiced user, then. Which is so much better."

"I'm not *using* you."

"Of course you are." He pointed to his mouth. "You need this. You use me, and people like me, to get it."

Shadows clustered around the trash bins ahead, and a rank stench rose from the open midden to their right. She turned on her heel to face him. "You get something from the deal, too."

"You think I need your blood? Shit, look, not every vampire is a wrinkled-leather leech like those kids you score off in the Plea-sure Quarters. Some of us have good relationships with the people we drink from. Some hunt. Some retrain, or drink off animals. Don't make assumptions to soothe your grungy little addict's ego."

Outrage widened her eyes, and words of rebuttal strangled one another in their rush to escape her throat. Fortunately for them both, the muggers Cat had noticed lurking in the alley before she left the main street chose that moment to attack. The first, a beefy young man with garlic on his breath, grasped Cat's neck from behind with massive hands, and was quite surprised when she grabbed him by the groin and used his own momentum to throw him into the midden. His three comrades had already jumped forward, blades out, and had no chance to flee.

Ten seconds later, Cat held one mugger in a painful arm lock, while Captain Pelham stood between the remaining two unkempt men, immobilizing both with the pressure of his hands on the back of their necks. Their swiftest comrade lay moaning in the filthy pit.

Cat's captive twisted in her grip until she cranked his arm, whereupon he let out a high-pitched whine and ceased struggling. She glanced him over: long, elf-locked hair, several days' stubble, three earrings in his right ear and one in his left. He wore a brown wool shirt that, somewhere in the mists of history, had once been yellow, and a pair of leather breeches more breach than leather.

He had been ill used recently, not just by Cat. Stripes of burned flesh raked across his face and chest, beneath sharp tears in his shirt. No natural fire had caused such damage. This had struck swiftly as a whip, not lingering long enough to catch his clothes aflame. "Hello, boys," she said. "We're looking for the young lady who gave you those scars. Dark skin, five-seven, curly black hair, curvy, freckles. Last seen surrounded by a halo of flame?"

"We dinn' see nuffink," Cat's captive gargled through the blood that gushed from his nose and mouth.

"Let's try again." Cat applied more torque to the mugger's arm, and something in his shoulder crinkled like crushed foil. "Tell us where our friend went, and we'll go away. Otherwise, we'll stay right here."

He looked over his shoulder at her. His eyes were wide, and scared.

She smiled. So did Raz.

As night deepened, the crowd beneath the Sanctum swelled. The original protesters were so diluted by the new arrivals that they vanished like drops of ink in a pool of clear water. Patient silence replaced the earlier fearful, angry cries. The Sanctum pointed like a confused compass needle into the clouds, and the people of Alt Coulumb stood or sat or knelt beyond the cordon of Blacksuits and watched the black tower's pinnacle in hope.

Following Ms. Kevarian down the Sanctum's front steps, Abelard recognized, or thought he recognized, a few faces within the crowd: a Crier they had passed that morning, a candy seller from his excursion into the Pleasure Quarters the previous night, a young woman from the Court of Craft. Even a few Northsiders had come in their suits and ties to watch, and wait. Before, the crowd was unified by anger. Now they stood as individuals, together.

He was mystified by their change, and when he realized this he felt ashamed. He should not have had so little faith in the city, or its people. They were passionate, yes, and powerful, but also wise.

Many in the crowd held candles, and the flickering flames cast their faces in shadow and light.

Ms. Kevarian's boots crushed the white gravel of the Sanctum's parking lot.

"There's a traitor within the Church," he said. After his rescue Abelard had breathlessly recounted his discoveries in the boiler room, but Ms. Kevarian only listened, and asked brief questions when his story was not clear. When he ran out of breath, she told him about her talk with the Cardinal, but did not comment on his tale. He tried again now to get some reaction from her, stating the problem as directly as he could. "A spy. A saboteur."

With a raised hand Ms. Kevarian summoned one of the carriages loitering near the Sanctum gates. The horse regarded crowd and Blacksuits alike with suspicion as it approached. "Indeed."

"They've been stealing power from Justice for months."

"It is a wonder," Ms. Kevarian replied, her voice dry.

"You expected this?"

As the carriage rolled toward them, she turned to Abelard. "It was a possibility. Your organization is large, and not especially secure. It would surprise me if the system had no leaks."

"Will that hurt our case?"

"Ordinarily, it might, but there are special circumstances at work."

"What do you mean?"

"I don't know enough to say. I need more information."

"Is that why we're in such a rush?"

The carriage pulled even with the foot of the stairs. Its rear doors opened, though no hand touched them. "We, dear Abelard, are in a rush for different reasons. You are in a rush because you need to find Ms. Abernathy." She produced a string of beads from a jacket pocket, the last of which was crudely carved in the shape of a woman. "The tracking rosary will lead you to her. Tell her everything. The secret room, the dagger, the monster, all of it. Relate my conversation with the Cardinal exactly as I told it to you. Be clear, precise, and do not exaggerate."

"What about you?"

She entered the carriage. "I go to a far worse fate. I have a date, my Novice, with a serpent who fears neither fire nor sword." She grimaced at Abelard's perplexed expression. "I have a business dinner. It would be impolitic for you to attend, which is just as well. Your search for Tara is more important. Do not fail to find her."

"Yes, ma'am."

"Take care." She closed the door and the carriage pulled away.

He stood statue-still, abandoned before the crowd. They watched him. Reflected candle flames shimmered in their expectant eyes.

The tracking rosary dangled from his fingers. "What," he said to it, "am I supposed to do with you?"

The string twitched, twirled in his grip, and came to rest extended taut in the direction of the waterfront.

Abelard looked about for another carriage.

Tara fell through shadow, slashing about with the flaring blade of her knife. By its glow she saw the basement floor moments before she hit. Ribs creaked and her head bounced off stone. The door through which she had fallen closed automatically above her, and she was trapped.

Trapped, and not alone. The click of talons and the rustle of stone wings echoed off nearby walls. The cellar smelled of dank earth and unfinished rock, of new-forged steel and burned silver. Gargoyles, looming figures in the dark, watched her with expectant emerald eyes.

If they wanted her dead, she would be dead. If they wanted to capture her, torture her, they would have moved already, rather than let her recover her balance. She eased into a crouch and stood, testing her bones. No bad breaks. A rib cracked, at most. Good.

What were they waiting for?

With a twirl of her fingers she absorbed the cold lightning of her knife back into her system. A gesture. I come in peace.

She was alone in the black. No lies would avail her. Once again she stood before the tribunal of the Hidden Schools, but this time she wasn't here for a fight.

"I want to help," she said.

Soft light bloomed around her, and she saw. This basement room had once been a dry cellar, perhaps thirty feet to a side, roofed by a lattice of pipes and rafters and copper wire. The remnants of decades-old cargo barrels, lay piled in corners. Broken hoops, rusty and sharp as wasps' stingers, jutted out from long-since rotted slats. A clean bedroll leaned against one wall, surrounded by bits of metal, religious effigies, and personal effects.

Tara stood in the center of the room. Gargoyles surrounded her, each one between eight and nine feet tall. Some were unearthly slender, some thickset, some heaped with muscle and others armored by protruding stomachs of hard rock. Strong stone arms hung from shoulders that could support the world. Hands terminated in hooked talons. Folded wings twitched. Five were male, five female, and all terrifying.

Least human were their faces, no two alike, features hideous and strangely noble, this one long-snouted and fanged like a wolf but with four eyes, that are bird-beaked and crested with a ridge of stone feathers, the next tusked like a boar and bearded like an aging scholar. Intelligence shone in their emerald eyes, sharp as a human's but bent differently. These creatures rejoiced in the hunt, not in the scavenger's heaven of boredom, satiety, and sleep.

Shale crouched against the wall, breathing hard. Charcoal blood leaked from a wound on his side. A young human man—or a gargoyle in human form—knelt next to him, keeping pressure on the wound with a dirty towel.

A great gray lady gargoyle stood before Tara, her countenance blunt and broad like a tiger's. She alone among them wore any form of decoration: a torque of silver that gleamed on her brow.

"What help can you offer us?" Tara remembered her earthquake voice from the Xiltanda's roof.

"I. Ah." Tara's mouth was dry. Ms. Kevarian's mouth wouldn't be dry if she were standing here. "I saved your messenger's life."

"By kidnapping him." Tara heard no rancor in the woman's words. Even, maybe, a touch of amusement. Tara hoped she was right. She remembered Abelard's story about the battle at the God Wars' end, and remembered too the scarred stones of Alt Coulumb. *Have you ever seen a gargoyle enraged?*

She needed this. The gargoyles could prove that the Church of Kos was not responsible for the fire-god's weakness. With their evidence she would send Denovo running back to his lab. Her weapon was here, if she survived long enough to find it.

"Justice believes your messenger killed Judge Cabot. Your attack on me last night didn't help your case."

Some of the gargoyles bared their teeth as she spoke. She heard snarls behind her. The stone woman raised one hand, and silence reclaimed the hidden chamber. Clearly she was their leader. Shale had called her Aev.

"What do you think?" Aev asked.

"Shale didn't kill the Judge. He lacks even the rudiments of Craft needed to bind Cabot's soul. I couldn't have stolen his face otherwise. Besides, why kill Cabot when he was working for you?" Tara met her own gaze reflected in the gargoyle's gemlike eyes. "Or, working to help you on Kos's behalf. Months ago, the fire-god asked him for help transferring an immense amount of soul-stuff without the Church's knowledge. Kos loves his Church. Why would he do such a thing? Unless he wished to help the Church's sworn enemy, a group this city exiled more than four decades ago, but toward which he still feels indebted: the Guardians of Seril."

No reply.

"I may be the only person in this city who believes you're innocent, but I need your help to prove it. I need to know why you sent Shale to Judge Cabot's penthouse yesterday morning."

Aev cocked her head to one side. Tara prepared to fight, and, most likely, to die.

"The story," Aev said at last, "is not all mine to tell."

Tara tried not to look relieved. There would be ample chances tonight to get herself killed. "Whose is it?"

The young human had divided his attention between the conversation and Shale's wound. Aev indicated him with a sweep of a massive arm. "Its beginning belongs to David Cabot, late-come to our Flight."

David stood, shoulders slumped and expression apprehensive. His features, now that Tara saw them straight on, were a younger, less fleshy (and less bloodstained) imitation of his father's. He waved sheepishly. "Hi."

The coach let Ms. Kevarian off at the Xiltanda's gates. A queue stretched down the block, rank upon rank of pleasant young flesh revealingly clad to excite the club members' appetites for sex or blood or human spirit. These confections of leather and black lace and pale makeup knew their city's God was dead, their way of life doomed: Ms. Kevarian saw it in their too-broad smiles and too-loud laughs, in the self-congratulatory way they touched and kissed and pressed their bodies against one another, in the speed with which silver flasks moved from mouth to mouth within small circles of desperate friends. They knew, and they smiled and laughed and tempted and seduced and drank to fortify themselves against the coming storm.

She paid the coach and advanced on the rope line. She had wasted no time changing or applying makeup, but as she walked she called a modicum of Craft to herself. Her colors and outlines sharpened; the black of her suit lost its worn, professional three-dimensionality and assumed a uniform emptiness, as if she had clothed herself in a hole in space.

When she reached the entrance, the bouncers drew back without daring to check her membership. The club recognized her, and welcomed her return.

Entering, she spared an instant to appreciate the marble columns, the glowing sprites imprisoned in their crystal globes, the checkerboard stone pattern of the floor, and the intricate Old World tapestries that hung from the walls. Soft strains of smooth music in swing time floated through the bead curtain, and she followed them to their source.

As she swished toward the spiral staircase, she cut a wake through demons and skeletal Craftsmen, vampires and priests and technomancers and a deep purple, multi-tentacled horror it took her a moment to place as a client from a decade back. Voices familiar and strange enfolded her.

"Lady K! It's been an—"

"—thought I'd have been informed before you—"

"—this morning at the Court of Craft! I don't think you—"

"—will pay for your betrayal of the Seventh Circuit of Zataroth!"

"And would you care to join us for bridge someday soon?"

She excused herself from the conversation with a nod. The assassination attempt she thwarted according to club regulations, which politely but firmly requested members not damage the premises in their business dealings. She left her assailant, a vaguely familiar face from a cult she last remembered encountering in the Loan Crisis of the early eighties, a smear on the checkerboard floor. And she accepted the bridge date from the tentacled horror, with the proviso that her schedule would be inflexible for the next several weeks.

Up the staircase she climbed, escaping the party and the smooth jazz at once. Up through the *sturm und drang* of the dance floor, up through the pained screams of the dungeon level, where Craftsmen relished for a brief half hour the torments they inflicted on others during the workweek, gaining release upon the rack from whatever niggling sense of karmic inequity troubled their souls. Up, and up, and up, each level of private hell segmented neatly from the others. Nobody wanted to feel that his, or her, chosen medium of pleasure and punishment was anything less than a universal absolute.

At last she passed through a shell of darkness but did not emerge on the other side. She climbed through deep space, void of all light. Her suit fit right in.

Ten steps, she remembered, before the stairs drew even with the floor. Her mortal eyes were blind, but as she climbed she saw, with eyes of Craft, the clubgoers hovering in deprivation bubbles, and also the silver web that maintained the absolute darkness that settled around her as she stepped off the stairs onto a smooth tile floor.

She was not blind here, but close. This level had been designed for club members whose personal hell was the death of the senses. Since most clients were Craftsmen or Craftswomen, merely impeding mortal sight was insufficient. The club's owners spent months designing a system to deaden the eyes of the Craft. It was not perfect, and cost the Xiltanda a great deal, but the effect was chilling. Ms. Kevarian had to hold her eyes closed for a solid minute to detect even the dim outlines of Craft through the artificial darkness.

Footsteps approached from her left, and a rustle of stiff cloth. A woman's long fingers touched the sleeve of her coat. "Madam, your table has been set, and Professor Denovo is waiting."

"Thank you," she replied, and the hostess led Ms. Kevarian forward with a gentle grip about her upper arm. She heard nothing but her own breath and the breath of her guide, their intermingled footsteps and the tiny friction of fabric as they walked.

Twenty steps, twenty-five. The hostess stopped, and so did she. The pressure of fingertips left her upper arm and settled on her wrist, guiding her hand to the ridged back of a plush-cushioned chair. "Thank you," Ms. Kevarian repeated. With her free hand, she located the chair's padded velvet arms. It faced a table covered with smooth cotton. She sat, and leaned back into stiff, overstuffed cushions. "I'll have a vodka tonic."

"And the gentleman?"

She knew Alexander Denovo would be waiting for her, but

somehow it was still a surprise to hear his voice emerge from the subterranean darkness. "Whiskey and water," he said. "We'll have dinner after our drinks, please."

"Of course." Footsteps retreated from their table.

"I'm impressed," Ms. Kevarian said. "Those sound like very high heels to wear when you can't see where you're going."

"Practice," Alexander replied offhand. "Anyway, I think the club lets her see in the dark."

"Hardly sporting."

"What in life is?"

"Neither of us, certainly." After a pause to give him the opportunity of a rejoinder, she continued. "What are you here for, Alexander?"

"What did I ever do, Elayne, to make you hate me?"

She crossed her hands upon her lap, and schooled her voice. "You made me fall in love with you."

"Weak justification for such wrath."

"And. You took advantage of my trust to twine your will through my mind, drain my power, and leave me a shrunken wreck."

"Well," he said. "Fair enough."

The ensuing silence was broken by the tap of approaching heels: their hostess, bearing drinks.

"My father and I never agreed about much," David said, looking at the ground, at the ceiling, at anything but Tara. He stood outside the circle's perimeter, behind Aev's left shoulder. "He was happy the God Wars ended as they did, felt the gods should have given mortals control of their own affairs long ago. He knew the Craftsmen, and especially the Deathless Kings, were hurting the world, but he thought it was manageable. I thought he was wrong." He looked for approval in Tara's countenance, or in her body language, but she had none to spare.

"We fought. A lot. When I was old enough, I left, went to the Old World and tried to help there. It's amazing the damage Craftsmen can do if they're not careful. Miles of farmland reduced to desert in a day by a battle between a Deathless King and a pantheon of tribal gods. Of course the Craftsman doesn't care. He lives off starlight and bare earth. The people are left without water, without homes and the little protection their gods afforded them. 'Free,' the Craftsmen say." As would Tara, but she wasn't here to argue politics. "I wrote Dad letters, trying to explain, but he never answered, so I came back. There had to be something local I could do, to show him he wasn't always right. I didn't expect to meet Aev and her people." He placed a hand on the stone woman's arm, and she did not shrug him off.

"We found him," Aev said, "wandering in the deep forest with little food and less water. He said he believed we had been driven unfairly from the city. He was wrong. We fought Alt Coulumb because it betrayed our Goddess. But while David's facts were wrong, his heart was right."

Tara could not restrain herself. "Wait a second. What do you mean, the city betrayed your goddess? The people of Alt Coulumb salvaged as much of her as they could." No response. "They couldn't do anything more. Seril died in the war."

Aev bared her rear teeth, which was the closest Tara had seen her come to a smile. "Did She indeed?"

"It's not as though you didn't get your revenge," Denovo said after they sipped their drinks for a quiet interval. "When you discovered what I was doing, you escaped my clutches. Cut me off from Kelethras, Albrecht, and Ao. I don't know what rumors you spread, but for forty years I haven't been able to get another job at a Craft firm, and I loved private practice."

"I told the truth," she replied, between sips. "The firm agreed it was too risky to keep you on staff if you were going to subvert their employees. It's not like I cast you into a joyless, featureless limbo for all eternity. You parachuted comfortably into academia."

"Which is different how?" His tone sharpened, but kept its detached amusement. "I admit, the academy is more comfortable than I expected. To my surprise, the Hidden Schools were not so afraid of my . . . eccentricities as the great firms."

"Perhaps not so afraid as they should have been."

"If everyone thought like you, Elayne, no one would have seen the potential in *Das Thaumas* when it came out a hundred fifty years ago. We'd still be scratching at the edges of the gods' power with paltry Applied Theology, rather than wielding their might ourselves."

"If everyone thought like you, Alexander, we would never have realized the God Wars were killing this world in time to stop."

"There are other worlds."

"None we've been able to find that are suitable for human habitation."

"You think we'll still be human when we get there?" he asked with a gentle note of mockery. "Come, Elayne. If you think I'm satisfied with humanity's current form, you've missed the point of my work. I've been developing networks capable of distributed action, directed by a single will. You saw what happened at the Court of Craft this morning. Tara's brilliant, but had it not been for that information dump, I would have broken her mind wide open. There's no question my way is better."

"Still, she beat you."

"She does have a singular facility at that," he admitted.

"It's one reason I hired her. Any young woman so resourceful deserves better than to be blacklisted because she avenged her friends against an unethical professor."

"Unethical? If you asked most of my, ah, students, they'd claim they are quite happy with my methods."

"Because you don't allow them to be unhappy."

"It's a fulfilling experience, being devoted to a cause."

"I didn't feel fulfilled, as I remember."

"Your experience was a prototype. An early model. I've ironed out most of the kinks."

She took a sip of her vodka tonic, relishing the sharp, burning flavor and the bubbles on her tongue. "I've read your papers, Alexander."

"All of them?"

"Your vision is compelling. But you insist on a proposition I don't think you can support."

Ice clinked against the side of his glass. "Indeed?"

"You claim your collective action networks are most efficient when a single node directs the whole."

"That's what my experiments suggest."

"I recommend you re-evaluate your assumptions."

"You think I'm corrupting my own data?"

"I think you're only happy with a philosophical framework that allows you to be a god."

The smell of roast meat washed out of the darkness, and once more she heard footsteps.

"Dinner," he said, "is apparently served."

"Can't we go faster?" Abelard asked the horse, who whinnied something that, though Abelard had never learned to interpret Horse, likely translated to, "Perhaps if you got out and pushed."

The tracking rosary had led him through Alt Coulumb with the constancy of a compass. The closer he drew to the waterfront, the more insistent the beads became, yanking at his arm. He kept a firm grip on them. This was not a good neighborhood in which to dismount in pursuit of an errant necklace.

He had to find Tara. Not because Lady Kevarian required it, but because he needed someone he could trust. The Church itself harbored a traitor, who not only stole from Kos, but set His resurrection at risk.

Two days ago, Abelard would have called such blasphemy impossible. He wasn't sure what he believed anymore—save in Lord Kos, and He was gone.

As they rattled down uneven cobblestones, urgency and desire warred in Abelard's heart. The shakes were back, severe as the day after Kos's death. Cigarettes barely helped; he had stopped in the Pleasure Quarters to refresh his supply. He had not slept straight through a night in three days, but whatever exhaustion he felt was buried under adrenaline and fear.

"Look, I'll pay double if you pick up the pace."

He had made this offer once before, and the horse accepted it again, surging into a slow trot down the narrow sea-rank streets of the waterfront.

"Seril died in the war," Tara said automatically. "She fought the King in Red and fell."

Growls rose around her, stone grinding on stone, but these didn't move her as much as Aev's slow shake of the head.

"Her power was spent," Tara protested. "There wasn't enough left to sustain her."

"Sustain? No. Not as She was."

"Consciousness is one of the first things to go when a goddess loses power."

"Not," Aev cut in, "if consciousness is all that is required."

Tara's eyes narrowed as dormant wheels in the difference engine of her brain began to rotate. She remembered Abelard saying that Seril created the gargoyles directly. If that was true, an immense amount of her soulstuff was bound inside them. They were obliged to her for their very existence, and she to them for their worship. How much of Seril's power had been at her own disposal after all, and how much anchored in the bodies of these magnificent monsters? Could the King in Red have killed Seril completely, while her Guardians remained? "You're saying you kept Seril alive, pared down. An echo of the goddess she used to be."

"Not an echo. Still that Goddess, only less." The gargoyles lowered their massive heads in reverence. Wings drooped. "She died by the Crack in the World, but as the King in Red struck the killing blow, our need, the need of Her true faithful, caught at Her. She fled into our hearts."

Translating from the religious jargon, Tara watched the confrontation play out inside her mind. "A part of her died in battle, but another part, the part bound up with you and your people, survived. The power she invested in the Guardians, and the hooks of your faith in her, pulled her back from the brink, but the process ripped her in half. To her devotees in Alt Coulumb she perished, and to you she lived, or a part of her did. But," Tara objected, "even if you could support her by faith alone, she would be an invalid as goddesses go. Powerless. She couldn't help you."

"We did not require Her help."

"Why bring her back, then? Why not let her die?"

"Because She loves us."

260 Max Gladstone

Tara paced the confines of the circle, uncomprehending, heedless of the several tons of violent stone that surrounded her. "You kept the rituals, worshiped her, sacrificed to her, to keep her alive. Even though she could do nothing for you, whatsoever, other than love you and be loved by you."

"Is that strange?" Aev asked.

"Yes," she said. "It makes you the most stupid, single-minded collection of religious fanatics I've ever come across. I mean," she amended as growls rose about her and green eyes narrowed, "I could not imagine ever doing something like that, but it's terribly sweet."

"We did not expect Seril's half-death to last. When we returned Her to the city, we saw the Church of Kos cooperating with outsiders, godless Craftsmen. We appealed to the Church, but our appeals were rebuffed."

"Really?" Tara was eager to move the conversation away from the evils of godless Craftsmen. "I haven't heard anything about this."

"After Seril's death, heretics within the Church of Kos claimed their Fiery Lord should reign unopposed by our Lady. They contrived that Kos should not know Seril survived, and they kept us from the city."

Tara saw, as if from above, the binding circle of white gravel laid into the green grass of the Holy Precinct. It had not, after all, been intended to keep Kos locked within the City—no mortal Craft could do such a thing—but it was more than strong enough to keep a barely living echo of a theologically problematic goddess out. Black hells.

"You fought them."

"Our brothers in Alt Coulumb lost their minds when the Lady died, for they were far away and could not feel that She lived. They fought like wild things. When we returned, we were barred from our own city, as our enemies desecrated our Lady's body to create an enslaved mockery of Her. What would you have done?"

Burn the city to the ground. "Abelard said that you fled when the Blacksuits joined the battle."

"Justice is an echo of the Lady we love. We could not fight her then. Today, we would not be so selective."

"You ran to the woods."

"Yes. We hid among the weak, wet, stinking trees." Aev made no effort to hide her disgust. "Far from our home. We lived there for years, until David came. And Kos."

"Divinity," Alexander said between bites, "was always the point, wasn't it? Remember the first sentence of *Das Thaumas*. 'Societies characterized by the relationship between the divine and the mortal'—all societies, when Gerhardt was writing—'appear as an "immense accumulation of power."' It's the energy that matters, not the nature of the participants in that relationship. Gods and men only differ in how they accumulate and apply power."

Ms. Kevarian had barely touched her salmon steak. "Don't take Gerhardt out of context. His next sentence was, 'To improve these societies, we must understand the dynamics of power.' He was trying to help civilization, human and divine."

"Sure, and as soon as we began to apply his writings the gods tried to kill us all."

He couldn't see her roll her eyes, so she made her derision evident in the tone of her voice. "They were scared. Gerhardt's first experiments created half the desert we call the Northern Gleb. Twenty years later, Belladonna Albrecht made the Crack in the World."

"It was a war," he said with an audible shrug.

"We fought for our freedom. For the human race's freedom, so we could live with or without gods as we chose. The course of action for which you argue in your papers, not to mention your private life, would make Craftsmen and Craftswomen no better than the tyrant deities we overthrew in that damn war."

"Language, Elayne."

"My apologies," she said after another sip of vodka. "One gets carried away when one feels one's dinner companion has made an inexcusable moral error."

262 ■ *Max Gladstone* ■

"How did Kos get into this?" Tara asked.

"The Everburning Lord," David said in the tones of the un-questioning devout, "sees all. This is a lot to sort through, how-ever. Occasionally His attention must be drawn to particular issues."

"We thought Kos turned against our Lady with his priests," Aev supplied. "Not so."

David continued. "I hoped to find the Guardians in the forest and record their stories, document their practices. For posterity. I, ah." Suddenly nervous, he glanced left and right. "I thought the Seril tradition was about to die out. I didn't expect to find a live culture, and a live Goddess, too. I returned to the city for supplies, prayed for guidance, and, well, I received an unprecedented an-swer. God was confused."

He broke off, and Aev took over the story. "It was soon after that," she began, "that my dreams of fire started. They spread through the pack. Flame overshadowed our souls, seeking truth within us. The next month, as we danced in the sky at the dark of the moon, we sang to the Goddess about the fire-dreams, and She shivered in anticipation." The rapture on Aev's face twisted in Tara's gut. She had never looked at anything that way.

"Kos learned that Seril was still alive," Tara said, fitting the pieces together. "But he couldn't break the binding circle and communicate with her directly without his clergy knowing. He didn't want to confront his priests; maybe he was afraid of what he would learn if he did, afraid of what his faithful had done, or might have done. He wanted to help Seril in secret. And you"— she turned to David—"suggested he work through your father."

"I tried to tell Dad myself," David stammered. "He didn't understand, at first. But he was a faithful man, and when Kos spoke to him in a dream, he listened."

"These dreams of fire came in the middle of the night?" Tara asked. "Between one and four in the morning." She remembered Abelard's pain when he spoke of his lack of faith. His faith had not been weak. God's attention was simply elsewhere. He was so caught up in stealing power from himself that he couldn't bother to comfort a poor, distraught cleric. Typical. "Kos couldn't risk the clergy tracking you down, so he bought a couple Concerns with Cabot's aid and combined them into one, a shell that could hold his power and transfer it to Seril." She raised one finger. "The last step was to give her part control over that Concern, so she could use his power. Which was supposed to happen yesterday morning, I imagine." David stared at her, stunned. She ignored him. "Shale found the Judge dead, and tried to run." No sense dancing around the truth. "Neither he nor the Judge's body contained any Craft that I could see, though. No Concern."

"The murderer must have taken the Concern," Aev supplied. "Now, with your help, we will claim the power that rightfully belongs to our Lady."

Tara chose her next words with care. The gargoyles waited. Their patience made her silence deeper. "Without that Concern, there's nothing to prove your claim on Kos."

"We will testify. David will testify. Surely that will be enough."

"That might help prove Shale's innocence of the murder, but it won't give you a claim to Kos's body." And if they had no solid claim, then the evidence that Kos was responsible for his own weakness was suspect. Professor Denovo would shred her story and flay her arguments. The Guardians had to have something incontrovertible, some documentation they weren't telling her about. "You're interested parties with little corroborating evidence, and no contract in hand. You'd rank below every one of Denovo's clients on the creditor's committee."

Aev bared her teeth. "That man robbed us of our birthright and mutilated our Goddess. We shall not crawl to him in supplication!"

"I'm not suggesting you do. When we take this before a Judge, though, she'll say your tale could be a big fabrication."

"You accuse us of lying?"

"No." She held out her hands against their threatening growls. "I'm saying that we need proof. So far I haven't even seen evidence that Seril is still alive."

"What do you think is lighting this room?"

No candles or lamps were set into the rough stone walls about them. A broken lantern lay in one corner, but it was not the source of the faint radiance. Unconsciously, Tara had assumed the light was a form of Craft, but when she closed her eyes she saw no mortal thaumaturgy. After a moment of darkness, a swirling vortex appeared at the edge of her vision, interwoven lines and overlaid patterns, an echo of the aura that shrouded Alt Coulumb when seen from the sea.

When she opened her eyes, the Guardians glowed with moonlight.

"If you do not believe," Aev said, voice deep as surf, "we will show you."

Light rolled in on Tara like the tide, and on that tide she heard a voice.

Information from the erstwhile muggers narrowed Cat and Captain Pelham's options to three warehouses on the same row, two well-defended and the third dilapidated. It was an easy choice.

"We shouldn't have let them go," Cat whispered as they approached the broken door. "They were criminals."

"Eh." Raz waved dismissively.

"What if they hurt someone else? It will be our fault."

"I don't think those four will take any more purses for a while. Muggers are as superstitious as fishermen, and much less stubborn. Two unfortunate encounters in one night would cause the heartiest to reconsider his choice of career."

"You don't know that."

"What should we have done, exactly?"

"Tied them up, and called the Blacksuits." It would have been so easy to summon them, if only Cat let Justice take over. No. Not yet.

"With broken arms and legs they still would have wriggled free before the Blacksuits got here. Don't you think those kids have suffered enough for one night?"

"Kids? If we hadn't kicked their asses, they'd probably have killed us."

"If we hadn't been able to kick their asses, we wouldn't have been in the back streets of the waterfront after dark." Captain Pelham stepped over the rotted threshold into the warehouse. He laid a finger to his lips, and she clapped her mouth shut. As if she needed to be told when to keep silent.

Shadows everywhere. Cat and the Captain spread out, communicating with hand signals across the empty space. Five minutes later, they determined the warehouse clear of any watch or rear guard, and met in the center of the room.

"I haven't found anything," Pelham breathed into her ear.

"Neither have I." She kicked the bare stone floor in frustration.

The bare stone floor.

"Wait," she said.

"What?"

"No tracks in the dust on the floor."

"Of course not. There's no dust on the floor."

She didn't say anything. He pulled back from her. Understanding dawned slowly on his face.

"Well," Captain Pelham said, "curse me for a seagoing idiot."

"A trapdoor."

"Yes."

Not one trapdoor, but four, they discovered in short order, one in each corner of the warehouse. Designed to store valuables, equipment or foodstuffs or shipments of magesterium wood that might otherwise walk off the premises in the pockets or lunch pails of warehouse staff, these doors were once marked with yellow paint, but someone had painstakingly removed that paint with a sharp chisel (or talon, Cat thought). Only tiny cracks around their concealed edges remained.

None of which would have mattered had tracks on the warehouse floor indicated the direction of foot traffic. Whoever was using this warehouse must have scoured the floors for the first time in decades, ridding them of dust and foul refuse, all in vain. That very cleanliness had caused Cat to look further.

Her hand rose to the level of her neck, but she forced it down.

There were many reasons to hide a door, and Justice would not forgive her failure with Tara if all she offered in penance were a paltry smuggler's cache.

The first three trapdoors were unoccupied. They heard no sound within them, and no light leaked from the crack between door and doorjamb after Cat worked the dirt packed there free with her pocketknife.

She and Raz knelt beside the fourth trapdoor and pressed their ears to the stone. Cat heard distant chants, and an oceanic roar. She cleared away some gravel near a hidden hinge, and peered inside.

She pulled back out of reflex, vision stung by unexpected light. Once more she lowered her head.

Through the narrow aperture she saw the enemy, giant, chanting. Stone Men. A young human stood near the gathered Flight—a captive, perhaps, or a traitor. Cat glossed over him. She recognized the smallest Stone Man as Cabot's killer. Through her badge she had gleaned a few hazy images of the creature that broke out of the faceless witness's window, and the small gargoyle matched those, too. No Stone Man could have entered the hospital undetected. He must have been there already—must have been the witness all along, somehow. It was the only explanation that made sense. But how had he removed his own face?

Cat's gaze slid from the killer to the other familiar figure in that basement room. Tara hovered in the center of the Stone Men, lost in a flood of silver radiance, an astonished smile on her lips.

Hard to fake being faceless, Raz had said. Someone has to steal your face. Tara could have done that, easily, back at Cabot's penthouse.

A crystal of ice formed in Cat's brain, freezing as it spread. Even though Tara had warped her mind and betrayed her to a vampire's embrace, Cat wanted to like the woman. At least, she wanted to believe Tara was a human being, loyal to her own kind. Tara didn't trust Justice. Maybe when the murderer changed back to his true form and fled, she decided to track him down herself.

But why send Cat away, unless she had something to hide?

And what could she have to hide, save that she knew the witness was a Stone Man? If she knew, why keep that knowledge from Justice? Why would Tara shelter a killer, unless she was on his side? Unless she had helped him hide from the Blacksuits since the very beginning?

No wonder she hid from Justice and fled across town. No wonder she regarded Cat with suspicion, grilling Abelard about her behind her back. No wonder she violated Cat's mind, and forced her to betray herself and her city. She had been working with the Stone Men all along.

All this was conjecture. Suspicion, hearsay. Cat leaped from conclusion to conclusion. She wanted Tara to be guilty. Her brain pulsed against the limits of her skull. The world was muddy, absurd, unreal. She needed clarity. She needed logic greater than her fragile mind could bear. She needed Justice.

Her whole body shook at the thought, and sharp tears sliced her eyes. Gods and hells, she needed Justice.

The Stone Men were below her. This had to be enough to buy back her cold Lady's love.

The ice reached the nape of Cat's neck and crept down to her rapidly cooling heart.

She waved for Captain Pelham to approach. He knelt next to her and mouthed, "What?"

Cat pointed to the tiny hole. He bent close, and when his attention was engrossed by the view beyond the peephole, she reached beneath her shirt and gripped the badge on its chain around her neck.

The Blacksuit overcame her in an instant, sensing her need and shattering her mind's shell. Captain Pelham glanced over his shoulder.

No eye could follow the speed of the Blacksuit's motion.

The soft crack of breaking bone burst the inflated silence of the warehouse. Below the layers of diamond that enclosed Cat's mind, she remembered the strength of his arms as he caught her, falling.

He was Tara's friend. He would have tried to prevent Cat from fulfilling her duty.

Anyway, it was not her fault. She was a servant of Justice. Her mind was ice and her body black glass. She did not tremble. She did not feel pain, or guilt.

She called the other Blacksuits to her.

17

A thousand ebon statues scattered across the city turned toward a single spot on the waterfront. At first slowly, then faster, like a drummer intoxicated with a new and rapid beat, they began to run.

Tara rode the surf of a silver ocean in moonlight. Or perhaps she was the surf, floating atop the water and one with it at once. When she lay with a lover and woke slowly the next morning, not knowing of or caring for the world beyond her skin, or time beyond her joyous heart's slow beat, she felt like this, but now her skin was the endless ocean, and her heart beat in measured rhythm against unknown sands. No thought of gargoyles or Craft or murder could command her. She lay free and glowing on the waters.

Cool light bathed her. She opened eyes she had not known were closed, looked up, and saw herself, arched in the sky above as she lay curved upon the sea. Up there, she was full and round, glowing with love and serenity. The night was her flesh. Stars clustered in the hollows of her hips and at the base of her neck.

She felt as a tiger cub must feel looking at her mother, who gives her milk, licks her clean with a rough tongue, and nuzzles her when she tries and fails to walk, her mother who stretches three sinewy meters from nose to tail tip, her mother whose piercing claws and beating engine of a heart no Craftsman would have dared to shape.

Was that truly her, in the sky? She blinked, and saw Ma Abernathy, smiling. Again, and it seemed to be Ms. Kevarian. Again, and she saw all of them, and none of them, and more, a power her mind desperately sought to fix in a familiar shape though it overflowed them all.

She was looking at a Goddess. Not a fragmentary divine spirit like the ones she had dissected at school, nor a corpse bereft of life, but a Goddess old as history, Seril Green-Eyed, Seril Undying of Alt Coulumb, Great Lady of Green and Silver.

Her eyes were open, huge as moons. Reflected in them, Tara saw an endless ocean where Seril lay as fully one with the water as she was with the sky. There was no difference between Seril of the water and Seril of the night.

Tara was not looking at a Goddess.

She was *one* with a Goddess.

She drew a ragged breath of cool air.

In the darkness of the Xiltanda, Alexander Denovo laid down his fork. Wood raked across polished tile as he pushed his chair back from the table.

"What is it?" Ms. Kevarian asked.

"Your assistant is in trouble."

"Indeed?" She felt strangely calm as she ate another forkful of salmon. "How do you know that?"

"I remain in contact with Justice," he said at last, and, when she did not react, "You're not surprised?"

"On the contrary, I am quite concerned with Ms. Abernathy's fate. I wonder what you intend to accomplish by rushing out in the middle of dinner."

"The Stone Men are inside Alt Coulumb," he said, as if this were something she did not know.

"Justice is searching for them."

"Tara found them, and Justice discovered her in their company. She'll be held as an accessory to Cabot's murder."

Ms. Kevarian set down her fork as well.

"Come with me to the Temple of Justice," he said. "We'll sort this out. Get Tara back."

She stood, the consternation on her features unseen in the darkness. "Yes," she echoed, her voice soft. "We must sort this out."

As they moved through the dark room to the stairs, she knew, somehow, that Alexander Denovo was smiling.

Cat, who was also Justice, waited as hundreds of her brothers and sisters descended on the warehouse. The Stone Men's ceremony continued below, silver waves receding to break again on Tara's body. Justice's vast thoughts still debated the facts, but Cat had her own theory: Tara saved the Stone Men's assassin in exchange for their performance of this ritual, which flooded her precise soul with pleasure. Tara was as much an addict as Cat herself.

On the floor, the vampire twisted in pain as his regenerative system struggled to repair his spine. His mouth worked, his eyes stared, and little mewling noises escaped his ruined throat. He lacked the motor control to turn them into words.

She raised her foot over his back. Perhaps he was innocent, but she could not let him warn Tara. He would heal.

Her foot struck his neck above the flare of the latissimus. Bones splintered.

The noise was louder than she expected. Below, the chanting ceased. At the same time, she heard a chorus of dull collisions above as more of her brethren landed on the roof. Louder than landings or breaking bone, though, was the rust scream of the door behind her opening.

Who would be so stupid as to open the closed door into an abandoned warehouse when its mate lay unhinged on the floor beside it?

She turned and saw Abelard.

He looked from her, to the vampire on the floor, and back. Few could recognize a man or woman covered by the Blacksuit, but Abelard saw through the layer of her office to the person beneath, and was stunned or foolish enough to call out her name. "Cat!"

The trapdoor behind her exploded. Fortunately, the Blacksuits chose that exact moment to abandon subtlety and burst in through the roof.

Lost beyond herself, Tara heard a voice, her mother's voice almost but deeper. In her left ear it whispered: "Something is wrong." In her right: "Permit me—"

The world cracked open, and Seril's voice dissolved into a mess of sea-foam sound. Tara felt as if she had been torn from her body, then realized she was actually being forced back into it. Her flesh felt tight about her soul, like a dress shrunken in the wash.

The Guardians would not have interrupted the ceremony. They must have been disturbed.

Attacked.

Tara needed to help them. To help Her.

She realized with a tremor of fear that she was thinking of Seril in capital letters.

As the rosary guided Abelard to the waterfront, he had noticed that every Blacksuit in the city was going his way. They flitted from shadow to shadow down side streets, or leapt across the rooftops, featherlight footfalls filling the night with a sound like rapid beating wings.

When his carriage arrived at the broken warehouse, Blacksuits writhing on its roof like maggots upon old meat, he swallowed hard, threw the horse its pay, and ran toward the abandoned loading dock. He expected imminent arrest, but either Justice's attention was elsewhere or the Blacksuits deemed his arrival part of a larger plan. Great birds of shadow bristling the buildings above, they watched him stumble and fall, panting, through the warehouse's one standing door, just as Cat broke Captain Pelham's neck.

Unthinking, Abelard cried out her name, but his voice was lost amid the crack of shattered stone as gargoyles erupted from the floor.

Talons out and wings flared, the great beasts leapt for Cat, but Blacksuits rained through the ceiling to repulse them. Battle was joined. Within it Cat darted and struck, locked in combat with a giant tiger-headed gargoyle who wore a torque of glimmering silver.

Abelard's tracking rosary pointed straight ahead. Fear quickened in his stomach and caught in his lungs, or perhaps that was cigarette smoke.

He could hide, watch, and wait for this to pass. The Blacksuits would take care of everything. That was their purpose: to protect and defend. But in the last two days, he had spent too long hiding, watching, and waiting.

He remembered the dry, wooden snap of Raz Pelham's breaking, spine and a strange thought rose from the chaos of his mind: who were the Blacksuits protecting, and from what?

Tara was somewhere inside that maelstrom.

He ran in after her.

Pressure and confinement ushered Tara back to consciousness. She found herself in the warehouse basement, cradled in a male Blacksuit's unyielding arms. Before she could object, he bent his legs and leapt twenty feet into the air.

She struggled in his iron grip as they reached the apex of their flight. About her and below the Guardians were locked in battle, gray blurs afflicted with parasites of black. Seril's children were losing. Blacksuits grabbed their wings, locked their arms, and pulled them to the slab floor.

Tara was weak, denied starlight by this damned cloud cover, but she had tricks at her disposal, especially against enemies like these who seldom fought a Craftswoman. As her captor prepared to land, she twisted her right arm around, and grazed with her palm the sculpted precision of his external obliques. The Blacksuit was divine in origin, thus too tightly woven to easily dismantle, but divine Craft was still Craft. She drank it in.

She could draw only a miniscule amount of power, but that was enough. The Blacksuit's enhanced leg muscles went slack. Instead of landing he collapsed, and Tara pitched from his arms, falling unceremoniously on her face.

As she rose to a crouch a flailing gargoyle shook a Blacksuit off his arm, hurtling the servant of Justice toward her. Dodging, she careened into a downed Guardian who bucked and clawed as six Blacksuits bent a thick, flexible band of iron around his wings. She scrabbled away on hands and feet like a crab, breathing hard. Near the battle's edge, her fingers touched something soft and cold behind her, wrapped in cloth. A human body.

Turning, she saw Captain Pelham, splintered bone protruding from the skin of his neck. His mouth worked without sound, but his red eyes recognized her.

"Shit," she said, her first word since wakening. Glancing about, ready to duck or dodge, Tara squatted over Raz's shoulders, worked her left hand beneath his throat, and peeled free the skin wedged between the flagstones. She placed her right hand over his broken spine, then pressed down with her full weight and pulled up at the same time. Raz's body flopped like a landed fish, but she heard the cheerful pop of bone settling, more or less, into its proper position. Close enough for his own formidable powers to heal the rest.

A hand fell on her shoulder. Swinging around she saw first the Blacksuit, then the woman within. Cat, wrapped in Justice's embrace.

Tara's second word after awakening was the same as her first.

You will surrender, the suit said in a voice scarcely like Cat's own. *You are accused of collaboration and conspiracy to commit murder.* Around them gargoyles fell, wrestled to the ground by superior numbers. Iron bonds were fitted and locked around wings and arms and legs. Tight clamps held fanged mouths closed. Tara smelled burnt flesh and stone.

"They're innocent!" She pulled ineffectually against Cat's grip. "They haven't committed any crime but hiding from you."

The Stone Men are accused of conspiracy to commit murder. They will be tried. Cat leaned close to Tara's face. *As will you.*

Tara called upon the Craft and prepared to fight, to free herself whatever the consequences, but the opportunity never came.

Abelard crashed into Cat from behind in a flare of orange and brown robes, ripping her hand from Tara's arm. Tara saw him frozen in time, eyes wide, cigarette clenched between his bared teeth. A tracking rosary dangled from his fist.

A Blacksuit tackled him. Tara leapt to his defense, blind with fury and adrenaline, her knife out and her power drawn about her.

Cat's fist struck her in the cheek.

The force of impact lifted Tara off the floor. A host of fireflies obscured her vision, and scattered when she hit the ground shoulders first.

Breath left her in a rush. Cat settled like a sack of wet sand on her chest, threading an iron band around Tara's arms and beneath her back as she thrashed, a netted wild thing. She heard a click and the metal tightened, pressing against her skin until her bones creaked.

Tara saw the last of the gargoyles fall. Blacksuits wrestled Aev and David to the floor bare feet from one another, and bound them. Groans of pain and the muffled expletive aftermath of combat mingled with the Blacksuits' calm, scraping voices as they recounted to each captive the crimes of which they were accused.

Cat gathered Tara in her arms and stood. Other Blacksuits lifted Abelard, squirming and likewise restrained, and Captain Pelham, who hung limp though his neck was mostly healed.

"Where are you taking us?" Tara asked.

To judgment.

"My Lord." Cardinal Gustave's assistant hesitated, uncertain whether to continue. "We have news from Justice."

The Cardinal sat regarding a page of scripture, his flame-red hood drawn back. "Indeed."

"The Blacksuits have apprehended a small coven of Stone Men within the city, and believe them guilty of Alphonse Cabot's murder. You asked to be informed if progress was made on the case."

"Yes." Cardinal Gustave closed his book. "Thank you, Theofric."

"Sir."

The Cardinal raised one eyebrow at his assistant's hesitation. "There's more?"

"Sir, Justice has also arrested Novice Technician Abelard, and Ms. Abernathy, Lady Kevarian's assistant. I understand Lady Kevarian and her opposing counsel, Professor Denovo, are aware of this development, and are on their way to Justice's Temple. Justice believes they will object to the arrest." Theofric waited for a reaction, but saw none. The Cardinal hefted the scripture, weighing the prayers and admonitions within. At last he set the book atop a short stack of papers.

"My Lord?"

Gustave stood, leaning too much on his desk. Moving with heavy steps, he retrieved his staff of office from where it rested against the wall. "Inform Justice that I may attend the hearing, though I am feeling unwell."

"The faithful are still outside our front door, sir. They are no longer chanting, but their numbers have grown, and they could become dangerous. Should I summon an escort for your carriage?"

"No, Theofric." He strode to the door. "I must contemplate the throne of our Lord. Find me there if you have need."

Alexander Denovo led Ms. Kevarian through the dancing mass; she followed as if through a fog. It was hard to concentrate. Tara had found the gargoyles. Good. But Justice had found Tara, too. Less good.

They reached the street and raised their arms to call for a cab at the same time. He opened the door, and she stepped in. The carriage shuddered them on their way, the clatter of wheels and hooves over cobblestones rhythmic, hypnotizing.

She folded her hands on the lap of her skirt.

"This is fun, isn't it," Alexander said with a manic grin. "You and me? Off once more, on a mad mission to save everything we hold dear? We make a good team, don't we?"

"We're not teammates. I told you forty years ago." She wanted to put more rancor into her words, but she felt so tired. "I want nothing more to do with you. You manipulate. You abuse. You're not trustworthy."

There should have been more punch in that last sentence. Instead, it hung lame on the air between them, too insubstantial to resist when Alexander leaned forward and kissed her.

At first, she thought she pulled away, slapped him, called upon her Craft and burned him to ash. Then she realized she had done none of these things.

Her stomach turned. His beard prickled and scratched at the flesh of her cheeks and chin. His lips were cold, passionless. Mocking.

She could not bite him, could not strike him, could not stab him or burn him or crucify him with lightning. Only one option was left: she exhaled Craft and shadow into his open mouth along with air. He fell back, stunned, wearing an impish smile.

"What was that?" he said, rubbing his lips. "You shouldn't be able to do anything at all. You're incredibly resourceful."

"What have you done to me?" She tried to scream but it came out as a dull question.

"Elayne," he said with gentle reproof, "if you know you're dealing with a man who can twist your own will against you, perhaps you should be careful how much you let him talk?"

The Blacksuits carried Tara, Abelard, and the other captives to black wagons waiting on the street outside. Tara and Abelard were only bound about their arms, while the gargoyles were swaddled in iron. Some tried to shift into human form and escape, but the bonds adjusted to fit the prisoner, immobilizing no matter what perversion of human or animal shape Seril's children assumed.

Tara and Abelard were placed alone in the second wagon with David, who had been knocked unconscious during the fight. Blacksuits latched the three captives' bonds into bolts in the wagon walls. Cat frisked them herself. She left Abelard's priestly work belt untouched, but she wrested a crystal dagger from his pocket despite his protests.

After the wagon doors were closed, Abelard examined their restraints, but had no leverage to free himself or the others.

"Abelard," Tara said. She still couldn't believe his presence here, much less his attack on Cat. Was he some kind of hallucination?

"Hi." His sheepish smile dispelled her doubts. No figment of her imagination could have seemed so earnest. "How have you been keeping yourself?"

"What are you doing here?"

"I saw Cat kill Captain Pelham," he said. "She'd never do something like that. Nor would Justice. There has to be something wrong with them."

"I don't mean why did you try to save me. Why were you at the warehouse at all? Aren't you supposed to be with Ms. Kevarian?"

278 ■ *Max Gladstone* ■

"Ms. Kevarian went to dinner with Professor Denovo. She sent me to find you. She wants you to know what we've learned."

A chill ran up Tara's arms and the backs of her legs. "Tell me everything."

David groaned, head lolling from side to side as the wagon jerked along. A purpling bruise discolored his mouth and jaw, and a strand of blood stained his pale cheek beneath the new-growth forest of stubble.

Abelard started to talk.

Cardinal Gustave stood before the pale metal Altar of the Defiant, upon which bloomed the gold wire cage where his God once sat, judge and friend to the people of Alt Coulumb. Wooden bas relief carvings lined the Sanctum walls around him, readouts disguised as decorations. The position of the sun over that ancient battlefield indicated steam pressure levels in the primary valves, while the racing elephants on the opposite wall displayed the power output of various turbines. Though Kos was gone, all readouts remained nominal. God's covenant with his people would last until the death of the moon.

Provided nothing untoward happened.

Provided.

"I won't let what happened to Seril happen to Kos," Elayne Kevarian had said. Cardinal Gustave would not let such a disaster come to pass either.

"Lord," he said, praying to a God no longer there to hear, "my life's work has been to glorify You." Lantern light cast his face in shadow and flickering flame. "I will set matters right."

He walked from the altar to the floor-to-ceiling window. As he passed the bas-relief carvings, he tapped a carved monkey's head on the ear, twisted a soaring falcon twenty degrees counterclockwise, raised a trio of frolicking fish a few inches within their wooden pond, and pulled a lever disguised as a lamp stand. Gears clanked behind metal walls and the window rose, jerkily at first, from its moorings. A rush of wind caught the Cardinal's thin hair in a silver tangle.

The air rising off the Holy Precinct smelled of fresh-cut grass and urban excess. Far below, the gathered crowd with their lit candles watched the Sanctum and waited for their God to present Himself. They sang old hymns half-remembered from childhood, but even in youth their faith had been weak, and they only remembered traces of the holy words. When the songs could not sustain them they turned to chanting, and occasionally to curses shouted at the black tower. They wanted guidance, and He would guide them, later. At the moment, more important matters commanded His attention.

Northward, an elevated train wound serpentine through the crystal towers of the Deathless Kings. Amid those pinnacles, the Cardinal saw the black pyramid of the Third Court of Craft, and beside it, an edifice of white marble. The Temple of Justice.

Kos might be dead, but His power lived on.

Cardinal Gustave breathed in deep and stepped out of the open window.

Wind buoyed him up, whipping the red robes of his office about his frail form. Divine power sang in his aged veins. A wish could whirl him to far continents, a whim could raise him to the stars and a fancy sink him to the depths of the earth. He laughed, and Kos's majesty bore him north, away from the Holy Precinct and the desperate crowd.

The window closed behind him. A half hour later, when Theofric sought his Cardinal in the Sanctum Sanctorum, he found only an empty room.

18

As night deepened, the Business District died. Its workers bled out in a dual current, west to the residential neighborhoods and east to the Pleasure Quarters. Their beds received them, or else the welcoming embrace of pub doors and back-alley dancers; they rested their heads on pillows or the flesh of lovers or the slick countertops of mostly clean, almost well-lighted diners that never closed, even when the night-shift waitress drowsed off at two in the morning and left the patrons to serve themselves from the pot of bitter, bad coffee warming on the slow burner.

Those who sought solace in the city that night found it wanting. Uncertainty took root and flourished even in minds and hearts ignorant of Kos's death. When tired people sought their lovers or clients, their usual hungry and desperate companions, they found them unable to reassure, cherish, or comfort. They whispered broken sentences to one another, or fought and slept angrily apart, or drank and laughed in the dark, or wandered to the Holy Precinct and joined the candlelit crowd.

A few stragglers remained in their skyscraper offices near the Temple of Justice, sludging toward an illusory finish line. Work weighed them down and tied them to their desks. None rose to look out their windows, so none saw the line of black wagons pull up to the curb beneath the blind, accusatory gaze of the statue of Justice with her sword and scales.

They labored on in ignorance, while around them the world began to change.

Some Blacksuits jogged beside the wagons as they rolled through the vacant streets, while others rode atop them, guarding against escape or rescue. Arriving at their destination, Justice's servants cordoned off the street, creating a gauntlet that led up the broad white steps and into the Temple's inner chambers.

A Blacksuit detachment escorted the prisoners from the wagons. Most of the gargoyles went limp from protest, forcing Justice's servants to carry their thousand pounds of weight. Tara and Abelard gave their captors no trouble, and were allowed to walk under their own power.

Tara looked at the imposing white marble Temple, fronted with columns and statuary, but did not see it. Her mind raced, reviewing all Abelard had told her on the ride over, about Denovo's desire to work on this case and his consultation with Cardinal Gustave; about the shadow creature, about the circle of Craft inside the Sanctum, about a crystal dagger with a drop of blood at its heart—the same dagger Cat had taken from him. As Tara weighed these facts against the gargoyles' story, she felt like a mosaic artist with a box of colored tiles and no plan.

"You can get us out of this, right?" Abelard said around his cigarette.

"I don't know."

"That's encouraging."

She shook her head. "I can show the gargoyles are innocent, but that tips my hand to Professor Denovo. He'll have time to prepare a response, and that will hurt the Church's case."

"Will a strong case do us any good if we're in prison?"

"Ms. Kevarian can bail us out."

"If Justice lets her."

"I know." She forced the words out through her clenched teeth. "I'm trying to think."

They crested the stairs and passed around Justice's statue, Abelard to the right and Tara to the left. Together, they continued down the gauntlet of Blacksuits through the open Temple doors into shadow.

The main corridor was long and straight. Lanterns hung unlit from iron mounts on polished marble walls. Every few feet stood iron tripods upon which iron braziers rested, their incense fires ebbed to embers. Thin strings of fragrant smoke rose from the piles of ash. The hall ended in a large wooden door, open to reveal a broad chamber and a gigantic statue within. Tara did not deviate from her path or slow, and soon she and Abelard entered the Inner Sanctum of Justice.

She closed her eyes and saw.

Justice was a goddess remade in the image of man. Craft wound through her Sanctum, a great silver web of mind connecting thousands of Blacksuits across Alt Coulumb, but the web was not Justice. She swelled within it unseen, a colossal distortion at the heart of coarse human Craft. Tara saw her in outline, a face pressed against, or trapped beneath, a shroud of silk. She was immense, she was beautiful, and she had no eyes.

Tara opened her own eyes and looked upon the chamber as Abelard did. A glass dome arched forty feet above the unfinished marble floor. At the hall's far end stood a polished obsidian statue whose head nearly touched that glass; Justice, robed as outside the Temple gates, with her blindfold removed. Her empty eye sockets were pits of broken, glittering stone.

Tiered steps were carved into the chamber's sloping walls, and on each tier a row of Blacksuits stood single file, heads thrown back to contemplate the statue of their maimed Lady. The enormity of the scene pressed against Tara's skin, against her soul. Great and terrible work had been accomplished here. She imagined Professor Denovo climbing that statue, chisel in hand, to pry the goddess's eyes from her face. Her stomach turned, and she tried not to vomit.

When the Guardians saw the statue, they surged against their bonds, raging. Blacksuits struck them and forced them to their knees. Aev fell last.

The doors swung shut behind Tara.

The statue spoke.

"I will destroy you," Elayne Kevarian said.

"Not in the near future, obviously," Alexander replied, crossing and uncrossing his legs. "You know they don't let you smoke indoors at the schools these days? I had to quit. Wish I had a cigarette now."

"You've been trying to kill us all along."

"Have not."

"Liar." His grip on her mind blocked the course of her fiercest emotions, and denied her the mental clarity required to work Craft, but she could speak, if she remained civil. He had not made a move against her body after that first kiss, intended as a mere demonstration of his control. This did not make her comfortable with the situation. "You wanted me out of the way."

"Hardly."

He peeked out of the coach's curtains, and Elayne seized on his momentary distraction to test the limits of his control. What she found did not please her. Denovo's technique had grown subtle down the decades. She could adjust her posture, even gesture in conversation, but dramatic movements were denied her. Standing up, striking him, throwing herself from the carriage, all felt pointless, tiring. Why fight? Her heartbeat quickened.

"Elayne, if I wanted to kill you, you would be dead already."

She inclined her head, neither agreeing with nor denying his assertion.

"I have not moved against you or your assistant. You simply had the misfortune to wander into my experiment."

"Your experiment." She found she could still express scorn. "What is its object, pray tell?"

"What else?" Denovo asked rhetorically. "Immortality, and the benefits customarily thought to accrue to it. Feel this." Leaning forward, he cupped her cheek in his hand. His fingers were deathly cold, as was proper for a Craftsman of his age. She knew her face felt the same, two statues of ice touching. With a shake of his head he released her and drew back. "Was this what Gerhardt wanted, do you think, when he published *Das Thaumas*? To stretch into eternity, until life becomes nothing but the search for more life? Or did he dream of something greater?"

Elayne, who had never found such questions worthy of meditation, did not reply.

Their carriage drew to a halt amid a jangle of tack and bit and a creaking of wheels. Denovo opened the carriage door, and

Elayne saw the marble columns and blind statuary of the Temple of Justice. Leaping to the pavement, he offered her a hand, which she accepted.

"Shall we?"

The accused stand before us, said a voice several octaves too deep and too high at once to be human. Reverberating from the skin of the eyeless statue and the flesh of the rapt Blacksuits alike, it nearly bore Tara to the ground. The gargoyles, whose hearing was more acute than her own, quaked where they knelt.

The accused stand before us, charged with abetting the murder of a Judge of Alt Coulumb.

The air about struggling Shale glowed with corpse-light, casting him in sickly green.

This one is charged with murder. Above the prisoners, shining motes of dust danced and rearranged themselves into a picture, three-dimensional and vivid: Judge Cabot's rooftop garden picked out in neon, rotating in empty space. The Judge lay as Tara had found him, dismembered in a pool of his own blood. David let out a choked sound, sobbing or retching. Shale reared over Cabot's body, blood slick on his stone hands and talons and chest. Tara saw pain in his snarl, but to someone burdened with years of hate, the gargoyle's expression would look like a roar of bestial triumph.

How do the defendants plead?

This was all wrong. There should be a chance for the accused to present evidence and consider the evidence presented against them before entering a plea. This was no trial. They were at the mercy of an arrogant, crippled goddess.

The bonds about Aev's mouth slackened. She rose to her feet. The sound of her weight settling on the stone floor echoed through the hall. She looked up at the holes where the statue's eyes should have been, and spat gravel and dust at its feet. The bonds tightened about her again, but she did not kneel.

The gargoyles would be executed, or worse, for murdering Cabot. Tara remembered Ms. Kevarian's words as they flew away from Edgemont: "We stay one step ahead of the mob." Justice might claim she was blind, but she saw through her Blacksuits. She was the mob, given a single voice.

But she believed she was fair. Tara could use that belief to save the gargoyles, and Abelard, and herself.

All she had to do in return was give up her advantage over Denovo. She had no illusions about her chances of defeating him if they were on an even footing. Denovo was the stronger and cannier Craftsman, even without his lab.

What was more important? Assuring her own victory, or protecting these people, whose city had betrayed them and cast them out? Whose own countrymen thought them monsters?

As the defendants have refused to enter a plea, they are subject to confinement—

"No."

It was a single word, but Tara put all her Craft into it. Justice fell silent. A vast mind settled its attention on her.

"What the hell are you doing?" Abelard hissed.

"Making things up as I go along," she replied in a harsh whisper. She stepped forward, summoning her composure and her technique and her reserves of voice. "Lady," she said to Justice, "I enter myself as counselor for the accused, and register a plea of not guilty."

Crimson robes flapped about Cardinal Gustave like a vulture's wings as he flew toward the Temple of Justice. The sky pressed against him, trying to force him back to earth. He thought of Lady Kevarian's assurances, and of the demon Denovo, encouraging, pricking, convincing with his teeth bared in mockery of a smile.

The lights of a passing train lit the Cardinal from below. An idle Crier paced the business district, singing listlessly to empty streets. The city had deserted him.

As it had deserted the Church.

Rounding a skyscraper, Cardinal Gustave saw the Doric and gleaming Temple of Justice. Beneath the glass dome of its inner Sanctum, tiny figures moved at the blind goddess's feet. Even from this height, Gustave could identify Abelard among them, and Lady Kevarian's apprentice.

He descended, watching.

Tara advanced between bowed figures and Abelard followed. As she neared the statue of Justice, a Blacksuit barred her path. Tara recognized Cat, and the crystal dagger in her grip.

Justice spoke again. *What do you intend to prove, Counselor?*

"Lady, the accused did not murder Alphonse Cabot. The Judge was assassinated by a third party, who wished to prevent him from serving the god who until three days ago watched over this city and its people. Nor was Judge Cabot the sole victim of assassination in Alt Coulumb this week. There has been one other.

"Kos Everburning."

Cat watched, astonished, from within her Blacksuit as Tara spoke. A silent war waged through Justice's mind over whether to recognize the Craftswoman's right to argue her case. Some parts of Justice were intrigued; others felt this was not Tara's city, nor her affair. Strike her down, they said, and proceed with the trial.

Tara indicated with one hand Raz Pelham's body on the floor nearby.

"Three days ago, a trap was sprung against the nation of Iskar. A mercenary armada attacked the Iskari treasure fleet. Iskar used Kos's power to defend itself, and Kos died as he honored his obligation to them. But the defense contract was clear and carefully wrought: Iskar could not have drawn enough power through it to kill Kos, unless he was far weaker than his Church knew."

How did you learn of these attacks?

"I have eyewitness testimony," Tara said. No backing out now. "If Raz Pelham will rise?"

Raz did not twitch. His wounds had long since healed, bones fused, skin and flesh knit together, but he remained still, no doubt hoping to preserve the element of surprise. Calling him as a witness played one of Tara's few hole cards, but if Justice didn't believe her argument, the gargoyles wouldn't survive long enough to benefit from any other scheme.

"Raz," she said, softly. "Please get up."

A Blacksuit approached the Captain's body, but Raz stood on his own, brushing grime off the front of his shirt. Shadows flowed on the face of the Justice statue as it fixed him with its broken stare.

Identify yourself.

"Captain Rasophilius Pelham," Raz said, "of the *Kell's Bounty*."

A pirate.

"An entrepreneur and occasional mercenary. I was hired to attack the Iskari treasure fleet. I vouch that everything Tara has said is true."

Who hired you?

"I can't give you that information."

You must.

He raised his chin and bared his teeth. "With all due respect"—though his tone did not imply much—"I am willing to identify my employer, but unable to do so. My employer destroyed my memories of his—or her"—with a nod to Tara—"identity after I fulfilled my contract."

Half of Justice objected in a voice that issued from the Blacksuits to the hall's right. *Tara Abernathy strays from the question before Us. Are the accused guilty of murder?* A second later, other Blacksuits echoed and emphasized the theme. *How is an attack on Iskar connected to the death of a Judge in Alt Coulumb?*

Tara's throat was dry, her chest tight, her muscles sore, but she'd be damned if she let herself look weak. "The Judge's death fits into a larger story in which the accused appear as victims, not aggressors."

Reach the point. Kos died when He should not have. The battles in Iskar were a factor in Kos's demise, but could not have been so had He been at full power. We accept this for the comment.

Tara waited as the eyes of Blacksuits and chained gargoyles turned to her. She heard tobacco burning at the tip of Abelard's cigarette. Steepling her fingers, she began to pace.

"Kos was not at full strength that evening because for the last several months he had worked in secret with Judge Cabot to transfer much of his own power out of the Church's control without its knowledge. Proof of this is on file at the Third Court of Craft.

"Kos contacted Judge Cabot because he learned, through the prayers of the Judge's son"—she pointed to David, who blanched at being singled out—"that Seril Green-Eyed, Seril Undying, survived the God Wars. Broken, nearly powerless, but alive, preserved by the fervent belief of these few Guardians and others like them. From David, Kos learned that some of his own priests had kept Seril's survival from him."

Abelard could no longer restrain himself. "That can't be true."

Tara had anticipated his interruption, and turned on him with a rejoinder. "You said the Priests of Kos mistrusted Seril and Her Guardians. Is it difficult to imagine some welcomed Her death? Welcomed it enough to prevent Kos from knowing that a part of Her survived?"

The world lurched from side to side. He realized he was shaking his head. "How could they do something like that, even if they wanted to? Men can't blind gods."

He said it without thinking, and should have anticipated her slight, pleased smile. "Gods are not almighty. The Craft can circumscribe their powers. The white gravel paths of the Holy Precinct trace a binding circle strong enough to prevent a weakened Seril from contacting Kos. It worked, too, until David Cabot found Seril, and brought news of Her survival back to the City."

"It's true," David said to the watching Blacksuits and to Abelard. "I prayed when I returned to Alt Coulumb. Lord Kos visited my dreams at night, and saw my soul. I led Him to the Guardians, and He began to visit their dreams as well."

Abelard's chest clenched around the smoke in his lungs. He sucked air through his cigarette. Which was more improbable: that Tara was lying, or that she was telling the truth? There were traitors within the Church. To bind Kos, to blind Him even in part, was hubris beyond hubris. But someone had blinded Justice, once.

Tara nodded. "How long ago was this, David?"

"Four months. A little more."

"And after Kos learned Seril was still alive, he sought out your father, didn't he?"

"Yes."

"Why?"

David's brow furrowed. "Seril was weak. Lord Kos wanted to help Her by giving Her some of His own power, but He couldn't do it Himself, because the Church would know. He worked with my father to set something up. I don't know the details."

"Wouldn't Kos's Church have noticed their god plotting behind their back?"

"They worked late at night, when nobody would notice."

"By late at night, you mean . . ."

"After midnight, and before dawn."

"Abelard." He recoiled a step as Tara turned back to him. "You told me you had problems contacting Kos during your watch, between one and four in the morning. How long ago did those problems begin?"

"Four months ago," he replied when he found his voice.

"Four months ago," she repeated. "Four months ago, the Blacksuits also started to experience a drain on their power, also between one and four in the morning. Isn't that the case?"

The chamber's silence weighed on Abelard. He struggled to breathe, and to answer her question. "That's what Cardinal Gustave told Lady Kevarian, and she told me."

"Justice is powered by excess heat from Alt Coulumb's generators, right?"

"Yes."

"So anything that made the generators run cooler could have caused the outage."

"That's right."

"And if Kos directed the bulk of his power outside the temple, to attend to matters he didn't want you, or any of his priests, to know about—that would make the generators run cooler, wouldn't it?"

Fire glared briefly at the tip of his cigarette, in his mouth, in his throat, in his stomach. His clothes felt too tight. His *body* felt too tight. "Yes. It's possible."

She broke eye contact with him and turned to the statue. Black curls swayed about her shoulders. "Four months ago Kos learned Seril was not dead. Four months ago Judge Cabot purchased a pair of Concerns and gave them secretly to Kos, who combined them into a single receptacle for his soulstuff. Kos moved a great deal of his power to this Concern in the small hours of the morning, when nobody but Abelard was watching. He intended to pass control of the Concern to Seril, restoring to his old lover a fraction of Her former glory. As he worked, his fire burned less fiercely in Alt Coulumb's generators, and Justice grew weak.

"You can find traces of all this at the Third Court of Craft. Cabot sealed most of the files connected with Kos, but everything's still there—except for Seril's name on the final contract of transfer. That name was erased from the sealed records by someone who could burn writing off a piece of paper without damaging the surrounding page. This person did not, however, erase the transfer's date. It was scheduled for yesterday morning.

"Craft is more than words in a ledger, though. A schedule does not guarantee a transfer: a piece of the Concern had to pass from one party to the other. A key. Yesterday Shale was sent to receive this piece from Judge Cabot, and bring it to his Flight, and his Goddess."

She swung on Cat, the statue of ebony. "Tell me. What do you think happened yesterday morning in Judge Cabot's garden?"

Cat would have taken a step back had her feet not been rooted to the floor. Ordinarily, with the suit on, she felt neither fear nor remorse. She was an instrument of the Lady she served, and a pleasant haze of inevitability cushioned her every action. But Tara's eyes—

No, not her eyes. Or, not just her eyes. Tara's pupils, sharp and cold and black as space, were the twin points of a blade that was her entire self, a blade that pierced the Blacksuit and skewered Cat where she stood. For the first time in Cat's memory, she wanted to speak to someone while suited, not in her official capacity, but as a human being.

She wanted to say, "I'm sorry."

Tara didn't give her the chance.

"Describe the condition of Al Cabot's body."

The statue of Justice responded in a smooth chorus. *Cabot's body was—*

"Not you."

Gods are not used to being interrupted. Resurrected divine constructs have less experience overall, and as such are even less used to it.

Pardon me?

"You contain many elements, correct, Lady? Your mind works in many directions at once. One segment of you may conduct investigations, another direct patrols, and a third pass judgment."

Cat swallowed, and felt Justice as a pressure around her throat.

"I want to talk with the part of you that visited Cabot's penthouse."

I will speak for it, Cat said without meaning to.

Her flesh chilled. That had been her voice—Justice, talking through her, rather than with her. Never before had she felt so overshadowed, a passenger in her own mind.

"What summoned you to Judge Cabot's apartment?"

Several months ago, he requested security wards that would record an image at the instant of his death.

"Why did he have these wards installed?"

He believed his business dealings might place him in danger. He was too concerned for his own privacy to request a bodyguard, but he felt this system would protect him against violent death.

"He wasn't worried about poison? Or death by Craft?"

Cat's head tilted of its own volition. *As a Craftswoman, I expect you know how hard it is to poison someone who has spent his life as deep in darkness as the Judge. His wards would capture the impressions of any Craft used against him.*

So complete was Tara's poise that the bonds clamping her

arms to her sides seemed mere adornments. "Tell me about the Judge's body."

A flood of images poured through Cat's mind, too fast for her to comprehend, oceans of blood interrupted by islands of flesh and shoals of broken bone. *His body was opened along the spine and his vertebrae removed, thirteen of them then arranged around the corpse in a circle. His arms and legs were splayed, and his eyes plucked out. Craft kept Cabot's soul bound to his physical form until released by some trigger.* Out of the corner of her eye, Cat saw the young human prisoner—the man who claimed to be David Cabot—shake and sweat as if in the throes of a deep fever.

"Do you think one of these Guardians could have done that?"

You claim their mad goddess survives. Who knows what she might be capable of?

Snarls rose from the assembled gargoyles, and Cat felt eleven pairs of furious emerald eyes fix on her.

"Seril Undying," Tara said carefully, "is an echo of Her former self. But even if She had the strength to accomplish this, She would not have needed the aid of blood and bone. As I told your Blacksuits, Lady, the technique used on Cabot resembles Craft doctors use to preserve a patient until her body recovers. Only a rank amateur would need so powerful a focus as the patient's spine to produce this effect.

"But there are amateurs in the world. Stranger than the use of the spine was the corpse's pristine condition. Human Craft takes power from the world around it. Touch it to dead flesh and that flesh decays. Yet Cabot's body was unspoiled. The power used to bind his soul did not come from a mortal Craftsman or Craftswoman."

You accuse a God? A priest?

"A god wouldn't need the spine any more than I do. A priest working miracles with Applied Theology would not need it either. He would tell his god what needed to be done, and the god would do the difficult bits for him. Without a god, an Applied Theologian lacks the control to bind a soul, or to burn a name off a contract without harming the rest of the book. But there are ways to steal divine power, siphon it, and use it to fuel your own Craft. Today

Abelard found a circle built for this purpose within the Sanctum of Kos, in an area only the clergy could access." She glanced over her shoulder at Abelard, who nodded by way of confirmation.

"This circle works by draining heat from the generators' exhaust before Justice consumes it. When used, the circle weakens the Blacksuits, the same way they were weakened when Kos made Alt Coulumb's generators run cool. If I'm right, Justice had several brown-outs yesterday, one of which began about an hour before Cabot died."

Justice did not reply. Cat wanted to assent, but she was trapped within herself.

"The Judge was . . . dismantled . . . before Shale"—Tara pointed to the slender Stone Man—"set foot on his rooftop. Killed by a priest with a god's power but a student's skill—the same priest who used Kos's fire, finely controlled, to erase Seril's name from the records in the Third Court of Craft. He feared that if Seril gained access to Kos's body, She would destroy what was left of him, and do to his clergy what his clergy did to Hers.

"Shale found Judge Cabot lying in a pool of blood, and unwittingly broke the Craft that kept him alive, as the murderer expected. Cabot died, triggering his security wards. Shale had opportunity, but neither motive nor method. Our priest had all three."

Abelard clutched at Tara's arm. "Do you actually think a priest did this?"

"I do."

"We couldn't, I mean, nobody would have . . ." Both sentences withered to ash in his lungs. "Who?"

"I don't know," she answered. "But I have a suspicion."

Suspicion, Justice boomed, *is insufficient.*

The waiting Blacksuits leaned forward, birds of prey prepared to launch themselves at the accused. Justice looked on, merciless.

Time ran down like an unwound clock, and was shattered by a deep, familiar voice. "I have evidence to introduce in Ms. Abernathy's support."

Many heads turned in the Temple of Justice, but none so fast as Tara's. The ground beneath her feet shook, and rage sped her beating heart.

Through the doors of the grand hall, thumbs thrust into his belt loops, black eyes blazing and chin held high, strode Alexander Denovo. Elayne Kevarian followed him.

19

"Professor," Tara said coldly as he advanced. "Why are you here?"

"Tara." He saluted her. His smile was wide and white as a deep wound. "I'd like you to remember this in the future. Me riding in out of the night to save your ass."

"I'm doing fine."

"If it hadn't sounded like Justice was about to confine you to her deepest, darkest dungeons, I would not have stepped in to help."

Ms. Kevarian said nothing. Perhaps she supported Professor Denovo, though it was outlandish to think so. Or—was her step more wooden than usual, her expression more stiff? Tara blinked and looked on the world with a Craftswoman's eyes, but the hall was too crowded with interlacing weaves to identify the cobweb strands that would have bound Ms. Kevarian's mind to the Professor's, had he suborned her. Tara thought back frantically. Had her boss been in step with Denovo as they entered the chamber?

"Well?" the Professor asked. "No 'Thank you, Professor'? Fortunate for you that I'm a generous man." He addressed the goddess he had blinded. "I can prove the truth of Tara's allegations. A senior official within Kos's Church hired me four months ago to investigate a power failure. In my research, I learned of the god's desire to aid our stone companions." The nearest gargoyle lunged for his legs; a blinding flash erupted from the floor, and when Tara blinked the spots from her eyes, the Guardian lay in a fetal position, clutching his smoldering abdomen and surrounded by chips of broken stone. Denovo had not looked away from Justice, nor allowed the attack to interrupt the flow of his speech. Tara felt his voice more than heard it, familiar as a bad habit and every bit as compelling.

"A rift between god and clergy is dangerous at the best of

times, and, Lady, these are not the best of times. Knowing my services as a specialist in deific reconstruction might be required, I sought a position as counselor to Kos's creditors, having a personal inclination to represent their side in such engagements. I first learned of Judge Cabot's death this afternoon, and was understandably horrified."

Denovo raised one finger. "Thus far my testimony consists of my word against the Church, but I can prove that Shale," pointing with his full hand, "did not kill Judge Cabot. In fact, he has nearly completed his mission unawares."

"He doesn't have any part of the Concern," Tara objected. "I would have seen it."

"Would you indeed, if it had been camouflaged by a paranoid god and a Judge made wise by decades of service?" Denovo raised one eyebrow. "I have a great deal of experience with such things. I can see. As can Lady Kevarian."

"It's true," Tara's boss said, voice steady and sharp. "I can see it within him." No sign of stress, but she agreed so readily. Had she and the Professor inhaled at the same time? The hair on the back of Tara's neck rose. Against either of them, she was outmatched. Against both, she would be a child set against an avalanche.

"Constructs of Craft," Denovo said, "cannot be taken from a person without his consent. An untrained individual may be tortured, or tricked, into relinquishing one, but Judge Cabot spent too long in the shadows to be fooled, or swayed by torture. Pain was just one more sensation for him." Revolving on his heels, he took three measured steps and came to rest in front of Shale, immobilized in iron. "Shale does not know what he carries. There was time only for the Judge to pass on his burden, not explain it. Allow me to produce this evidence for the court."

Shale was tense with terror. He shook his head, but could not protest through his iron gag.

"He is," the Professor noted, "distracted and fearful, thus uncooperative. But if he does not know how to help himself, I will have to take on the burden of assisting him."

Denovo extended one hand, fingers splayed, and closed his eyes. Every light in the grand hall flickered and grew dim. Denovo shook with tension. A silver mist rose from the slick stone of Shale's body and hung around him like a halo. The gargoyle began to scream.

Tara closed her eyes, too. The Professor was a spider of thorn and wire, limbs innumerable and barbed. His claws struck into the tangle of Shale's soul and began to pry.

He pierced knots of empathy and love and compassion, and seized something beneath them, a core of absence in Shale's heart, a tightly wound ball of invisible threads. Opening her eyes, Tara saw the mist tinged with reddish gold. Denovo's face was a sweat-slick mask, his lips peeled to bare white teeth. He was not enjoying his work. However Kos and the dead Judge had protected the key to their Concern, Denovo was straining even to see, let alone to extract, it.

He stood vulnerable before her. Her fingers flexed, preparing to summon her knife. She could strike him down, and be slain by Blacksuits. Who would subsequently consider her case a fabric of lies, and find the gargoyles guilty. The Church would never benefit from her discoveries. Abelard would lose his god. But she would have her revenge.

Was that enough?

She forced her fingers to relax.

Besides, Blacksuits were fast. She might not be able to kill him in time.

Torn free of Shale's body, the mist rose and coalesced into a rotating sphere made from interlocking rings of fire and ruby-orange light. The cold hall felt suddenly warm, its immensity confining.

Denovo smiled in cold triumph. He looked as she remembered him on the day he threw her from the Hidden Schools. Reflected in his eyes, that fiery sphere was every horror in the world. He reached out to grasp it.

With a silent apology to Abelard, Tara clenched her hand into a fist and gathered her power to strike. She undid her bonds with a charm and a whispered word. Iron slipped from her, and unburdened, she raised her knife.

Then the skylight shattered, and shards of glass and fire rained down.

Roiling flame scored the rough marble floor, and a column of coherent fire engulfed Alexander Denovo. Crying out, the bound gargoyles rolled back from the blast, their iron restraints clattering on stone. Tara threw up her arm and hardened the air above her into a dome to block falling shards. Ms. Kevarian did not duck, did not call upon her power, did not betray any sign of shock. Which settled the question for Tara: Denovo must have gotten to her somehow.

Bastard.

A wave of fire scattered Blacksuits and prisoners both. Raz fell, screaming, and rolled to extinguish the flames caught on his jacket.

The sphere of ruby-orange light revolved in midair, unperturbed by the chaos.

A robed figure descended through the broken skylight.

A deep bass rumble shook the hall, and the pillar of fire about Denovo broke like morning mist to reveal him, scorched but shimmering with protective Craft. His right hand rose to the glyph above his heart, and a knife of lightning flashed in his grip, ascending through the mystic and deadly curve of Kethek Loes, blade bearing shadow and swift death.

Before he could complete the motion, flame struck again, surgically precise. Denovo's shield muted the heat of the blow, but its impact tossed him across the hall like a twig in a tornado. He slammed into the floor twenty feet back and skidded.

The figure hovered above the marble and debris, wreathed in fire. Its robe was brilliant crimson, its hood pulled back. The face thus revealed, contorted in the throes of righteous anger, belonged to Cardinal Gustave.

Abelard took cover beneath his robe when the skylight caved in. The clustered stone bodies of the Guardians shielded him from the fire. Heat seared his face, scalded his nostrils. His clothes were burning. His cigarette, at least, remained undamaged, and with hasty handwork he preserved it as he rolled over broken glass to extinguish the smoldering rest of him.

Recovering, he glanced about himself, and took stock. Denovo stood pinioned by a spear of flame, unharmed but immobile, forearms crossed before his face. The arrayed Blacksuits did not move; the Guardians struggled in futility against their chains to rise, to fight. Captain Pelham flailed, but could not extinguish the flames devouring his flesh and his clothing. Tara stood near Denovo, alert and ready to ward off attack. Abelard's gaze rose to the figure in midair.

"Father!" he cried, but his voice did not carry.

Professor Denovo's, on the other hand, overruled all other sound. "Cardinal," he said, sly and stable, betraying no sign of strain. "Pleasure as always. Have you joined us for some evening conversation? A spot of theological discourse perhaps?"

Rage filled Gustave's face and form. "You have poisoned this assembly with your lies."

"What lies? You must have heard Tara as you lurked up there: Judge Cabot was killed by a cleric of Kos, with the god's own stolen power. I wonder if you can help us compile a list of suspects. We're looking for someone who can fly and call upon the fire of a dead god. About your height and build, I'd say."

"Traitor!" Gustave cried. A second line of flame struck Denovo with the force of divine judgment. Smoke rose from the Professor's jacket. His defenses trembled, but held. "I name you traitor, Alexander Denovo. You gave me this blasphemous power to ward against a greater blasphemy. I will use your own gift to destroy you."

"You're not improving your predicament, my Lord Cardinal," Denovo replied. "What do you hope to gain by attacking a man in the presence of Justice herself?"

Gustave's lips twisted in a sneer. "Justice cannot move while I press the attack. My every strike against you drains her. My God will be avenged."

Abelard smelled smoke. Was his robe still burning? Glancing over his shoulder, he jumped to see Ms. Kevarian five feet behind him, apparently unperturbed, though her skin and suit had been torn by falling glass, and her black jacket was on fire. She betrayed no sign of pain.

Her lips moved. He could not hear her words. Abelard looked from her to the Cardinal and back. Flares of color surrounded the man as if he were a saint in stained glass, lit from behind by a setting sun.

Abelard encircled Ms. Kevarian in his cloak and bore her to the ground. She lay unresisting amid the debris as he smothered the flames under heavy folds of cloth. Blinking, she seemed to recognize him. When he laid the back of his hand on her forehead, he found it cold and damp, like a stone wall after a long night—feverish compared to the ice of her earlier touch.

"Lady Kevarian," he shouted over the clash. "Are you okay?"

Her body was stiff, almost lifeless, but her mouth moved. The same movements, over and over again. A single word.

"Lady?" He bent forward. "I can't hear you." He lowered his ear to her lips, and understood.

"Dagger," she repeated, over and over.

He turned, not to Professor Denovo, nor to Cardinal Gustave, nor to the Guardians nor Tara, but to Cat, wrapped, trapped, in her Blacksuit. She held the crystal knife Abelard had discovered in the Sanctum's boiler room.

The drop of blood within its transparent blade glowed more brilliantly with every blast that issued from Cardinal Gustave.

Abelard had forced himself to accept the thought of a priest as traitor, but the Cardinal? There had to be some reason, some explanation.

Abelard shot a worried glance at Ms. Kevarian. Dread command glinted in her eye.

Striking against Gustave was tantamount to heresy. Could stopping a murderer be heretical?

You may have to choose between the city you believe you inhabit, and Alt Coulumb as it exists in truth.

With an urgency born of fear, he left Ms. Kevarian and sprinted toward Cat. Behind him, the embers of the Craftswoman's jacket burgeoned again into flame.

Tara heard Raz Pelham scream, and with a wave of her hand she quenched the fire that consumed him. He slumped, unconscious, but mostly intact. As her mind extinguished the flames, she felt within them inhuman power melded to malevolent human will.

This fire was not born of mortal Craft. Subtle, divine workings gave form and strength to Gustave's rage: millions of strands of spider silk vibrating like bowed violin strings, their friction creating insatiable flames.

You gave me this power, Cardinal Gustave had said. Of course. Who else would Gustave have asked to build the Craft circle, other than the man he trusted to maintain Justice? What other Craftsman would have done such a thing, in violation of all professional ethics?

"Help me, Tara!" Sweat slicked Denovo's pale skin and wet the curls of his beard. His arms shook as he blunted Gustave's attack with power stolen from students and teachers and distant gods. When Tara saw him with closed eyes, he glowed like a neon prayer wheel. She could not have resisted the Cardinal's fury for more than a few seconds. For all Denovo's power, he could barely manage it. "He murdered Judge Cabot."

Yes, Tara thought. *With tools you gave him.* This would be a neat revenge, and all she had to do was watch.

"I do not murder." Gustave's voice was low and dangerous, a hiss of snow in a mountain pass, the omen of an avalanche. "I am an agent of my Lord's wrath."

Looking at Gustave was like staring into the heart of the sun. One instant he possessed all colors, the next none, fading to a bruised gray in Tara's vision.

She could sit back and observe the battle, but Gustave had not yet admitted to the Judge's murder. Justice was present, though she could not intervene. His confession would save the gargoyles, if any of them survived. "Cardinal," she shouted, "did you kill Judge Cabot?"

"I killed him. I would kill all who dare plot against Lord Kos."

Yes. Keep him talking. The more he said, the safer the gargoyles would be. "He wasn't plotting. He served your god!"

"Gods go mad, as do men. My Lord was sick at heart. When He recovered, He would have known my deeds for true faith. I prevented His desecration."

"Like you're doing now? Seizing his power this way—you've damaged his corpse more than Seril could have at Her greediest."

"Tara," Denovo cried. "Help me. We can defeat him together."

She ignored him. "Stop, Cardinal. Don't hurt Kos any more than you have already. He wanted peace between the city and the Guardians."

"They are vermin!" The word echoed like clashing thunder, but beneath a god's wrath she heard the weak and railing anger of a very old man. "Flying rats, lurking in the forgotten heights of our city. Should I let them sully my Lord with their claws?"

"You plotted Cabot's murder for months, ever since you learned what Kos asked him to do. Installing that Craft circle, learning the soul-binding technique. Did you ever ask your god for an explanation, in all that time?"

Tears glimmered in bright wet lines on Gustave's face. "Why would my Lord give so much to a pack of monsters?"

"He would have told you. You should have trusted him."

"He would have pitied me for not understanding! My Lord, my Master, my Friend would have pitied me for being unable to love *these*." He spat that word down on the Guardians.

"If you really feel that way," Tara shouted back, "maybe you never loved him in the first place."

Her heart froze as that sentence left her lips, and she realized it had been exactly the wrong thing to say. Gustave's ferocity turned upon her. She braced her legs and raised her arms. Fire struck her from on high, and she almost fell.

Almost.

Cat was lost. The cosmic high of union with Justice had ebbed, drawing her with it into depths where the world spun in contrary directions and no air reached her lungs when she breathed. Justice's song twisted her through itself, and she was a note tossed on its immensity like flotsam on a tidal wave. She lay beneath the surface, a drowned woman, and through the shifting black water she saw distorted Abelard approach, backlit by rosy flame.

"Cat!"

His voice fell on ears that did not belong to her, and though she tried to reply, a wall of stone closed up her mouth. Her body was not her own, lent away and the lessee absent.

His face was caught in the writhing shadows of the firefight. "Cat! The Cardinal's gone mad!"

She had heard, but memory was such a fragile thing, ephemeral and unreliable as breath.

"That dagger in your hand." His mouth wide, a gaping pit, yet his eyes were wider. "He draws power through it, from Kos."

What did he expect her to do? A Blacksuit's will belonged to Justice, and Justice was silent.

Which, she realized dreamily, was unusual.

Her attention drifted down, and she saw the dagger clutched in fingers that once belonged to her. Abelard wrapped his arm in his robe and struck the crystal blade, but it held and he fell back, a sharp red cut on his forearm where the dagger had sliced through his coarse robe.

"Are you going to let the Cardinal kill Tara? The Guardians? You think he'll let them live with what they've seen, what they know?" He gripped her shoulders, but she did not feel the pressure of his hands. "Help us, Cat."

Fire crisped and consumed Tara's world, endless, hungry, insensate. She had never fought a god before. If Kos Everburning raised himself against her, she would have perished in an instant. Flush with divine power, Cardinal Gustave still lacked a god's mastery of the energies he invoked. Even so, Tara buckled beneath the ferocity of his flames.

"Tara!" Denovo's voice was no longer smooth or collected. She heard fear at its edges. "We can throw him back if we work together." His mind skittered against the doors of her perception, cool, a refuge from the heat—an invitation to rejoin the link he shared with his lab, to give herself once more to him. "Please. Let me in."

Without his help, she was going to die. With his help, she would probably die anyway.

But why did Denovo need her? He fought in the God Wars.

He knew better than to match deities stroke for stroke. You dodged their power, twisted it against itself, stretched your divine Opponents thin. Cardinal Gustave should have been vulnerable to such tactics, but Denovo seemed desperate for her help, and her surrender.

Was that truly fear she heard in his voice, or the excitement of a con man who feels he has caught his mark?

Tara stood firm against the Cardinal's assault. As dead Kos's power pressed against her, she *shifted*.

Mind, soul, spirit, twisted out of reach. The fire sought her, found her not, and thrashed about, desperate for something to destroy.

As if releasing a bird from her hand, she offered it the seductive tendrils of Denovo's mind.

Blind, hungry, and mad, the fire accepted.

Elayne Kevarian followed the beacon of Alexander Denovo's pain through thick fog back into her body. Opening her eyes, she found herself prone on the unfinished marble floor of the Great Hall of Justice, beneath the gaze of a blind statue and surrounded by a thousand Blacksuits. She was wounded—deep gashes from fallen glass, myriad scrapes and bruises. And she was on fire.

Perfect.

She breathed in, and became cold. The flames caught on her suit flickered, flared, died. Ms. Kevarian felt their death, and their power flowed into her skin like warm sunlight on a summer morning.

A sword-slash smile played on her lips.

The Cardinal's features twisted in confusion as the fire he threw against Tara struck Denovo instead. The Craftsman's defenses did not break under this doubled assault. If anything, Denovo seemed less pressed than before. His shoulders squared, his arms steadied, and the stress cracks in his shield disappeared. Though Gustave was nearly blinded by God's brilliant flame, he saw Denovo shake his head.

"Tara," Denovo said, "you should have joined with me. It would have been more pleasant for us both."

Denovo shifted his defenses to his left arm, and reached out with his right, fingers clawed as if to grasp Gustave's throat. The claw tightened, and though Gustave was ignorant of all but the most fundamental tricks of Denovo's heathen Craft, he recognized breaking power in that gesture. He twitched in an involuntary spasm of fear.

But he felt nothing.

Tara saw victory on Denovo's face as he closed his hand. That gesture was a trigger, invoking a contract with a shred of nightmare, a rat in the walls of reality—the shadow creature in Gustave's Craft circle. Denovo must have planted the shadow when he made the circle, as insurance against the Cardinal's betrayal. He commanded it now to destroy the dagger through which Gustave drew his power. But Abelard had released the shadow creature hours ago, and Cat held the dagger.

When Denovo closed his hand, he expected the flame to die, and the old man to fall. Instead, Gustave redoubled his assault, and Denovo fell to his knees, betrayed by his own frustrated anticipation of success. Veins in his forehead bulged as he fought to regain control. Tara would have crowed in triumph, but a dozen new lances of flame descended on her from all directions as the Cardinal screamed, "Heretics! Blasphemers!"

"Help us."

It was the plea of a drowning man.

Cat knew what those sounded like. She had spent her entire life drowning.

Abelard needed her.

The world was a weight on her shoulders, so she let it bow her to the ground. Kneeling, she turned her wrist, as if it were the wrist of a marionette. Her arm was heavy. She aimed the point of the crystal dagger at the stone floor.

Her arm fell, and she leaned into it, exercising every scrap of her control over the Blacksuit. The dagger's point struck stone.

The crystal blade held. She sagged in despair.

It snapped.

There are as many different kinds of silence as of darkness. Some are so fragile a single breath will shatter them, but others are not so weak. The strongest silences deafen.

The flames of Kos died, and Cardinal Gustave fell screaming. He landed with a sound like a bundle of snapped twigs and lay gasping on the floor, red robes billowed out around him.

A small noise escaped Abelard, as though a mouse was being strangled in his throat. It was not a lament or a protest. It was too confused to be any of these things.

The nerves of limbs and stomach and heart moved him forward, though his brain remained transfixed by the sight of the Cardinal's twisted body. The ground shook as he approached the pool of red cloth and blood in which the old man lay.

Behind him, the world moved on. He heard raised voices—Tara's, the Professor's, sounds with no more meaning than the glass that broke like new spring ice beneath his boots. Even the heavy acid taste of smoke in his mouth felt distant. The gold-thread hem of the Cardinal's robe surrounded him like a mystic circle. Abelard crossed it, and fell to his knees.

The Cardinal still breathed. It was worse, almost, this way. Thin parched lips peeled back to reveal rows of bright teeth set in gums more scarlet than his robe. Air rattled in the cave of the old man's mouth, fast and shallow. His eyes were open. They sought Abelard's automatically, and the mouse in Abelard's throat cried out again.

Fifteen years ago, Abelard arrived at the Temple of Kos, eager to learn. Of all the priests and priestesses who taught him to glorify the Lord, this man had been, not the kindest, but the most worthy of admiration.

Fire, the Church taught, was life, energy's ever-changing dance upon a stage of decaying matter. Every priest and priestess, every citizen, had one duty before all else to their Lord: to recognize the glory of that transformation.

Abelard looked into the Cardinal's dying eyes, and saw within them no fire but that which consumes.

He inhaled. The tip of his cigarette flared orange.

Dying, Cardinal Gustave smiled.

Tara's senses were numb with exaltation at her survival, but there was no time to rejoice. Alexander Denovo staggered toward her, toward the bound gargoyles, toward the orange sphere that hovered above Shale's slumped form.

"I know what you're doing," she said, and blocked his path. Her legs threatened to collapse beneath her, but she steadied herself by main force of will.

"Do you indeed." Wisps of smoke rose from the brown curls of his hair, and scorch marks covered his clothes.

"You made that Craft circle. You gave Gustave power."

"He asked me for a weapon against heretics."

"And you gave him one."

"I sold him one, at a hefty price." Denovo shrugged. "You would have done the same. If you wouldn't, perhaps you should re-evaluate your line of work. The Craft isn't a charitable pursuit."

"If all you did was give him a weapon, then why did he try to kill you?"

"Because I was about to expose him. Honestly, Tara, what is the point of this?"

"Cardinal Gustave didn't attack because he was afraid for himself. He attacked because you were about to acquire something you should not have."

Denovo chuckled. "Gustave was mad. A murderer. He confessed as much."

"He confessed to killing Judge Cabot. He thought you were guilty of a greater crime."

He tried to skirt around her, but she stepped in front of him again.

"Four months ago, Gustave asked you to help him learn why Justice was losing power. You traced the dreams Kos sent into the forest, to Seril's children. You discovered that Kos was working with Cabot, and to what end."

Denovo shrugged, every bit the tired scholar.

"Was it you or the Cardinal, I wonder, who proposed killing the Judge?"

"I don't have to listen to this."

"For someone with your skills, persuading the Cardinal was easy. Cabot was a heretic, consorting with rebels and traitors. He deserved to die. You gave Gustave the means. You taught him how to bind Cabot's soul. You even told him which contracts to deface in the Third Court of Craft, and how to do it without being detected."

"Conjecture and foolishness."

"Cabot suspected you were onto him. That's why he installed security wards that could detect Craft. This isn't the West. The community of Craftsmen here is small and insular. The Judge had no enemies there. Hell, the locks on his apartment building wouldn't keep out a novice."

Denovo drew a step closer. Tara took a step back.

"You left Alt Coulumb several months ago, secretly as you had come, but you intended to return. You knew from court records when Cabot would pass the Concern to Seril. You had months to plan your attack."

"Here we go," he said, voice low and dangerous. "Accuse me."

"You organized the assault on the Iskari treasure fleet. You were the Craftsman who negotiated the Iskari defense contract, and you knew that it was the best weapon for your purposes. Your mercenaries attacked, and the Iskari drew on Kos's power to defend themselves, not knowing that Kos was already drained by his secret dealings. Kos couldn't stand the strain, and died. At your hand."

No flush of outrage came to Alexander Denovo's face. "Why, in this fantasy of yours, did I need Gustave to kill Cabot?"

"You wanted that Concern," she replied, cocking her head back in the direction of the rotating sphere. "Kos had more power than all your minions put together. You could feast for years on his corpse. But you couldn't get the Concern from Cabot by force, and if he died without passing it on, it would dissipate, no use to you or anyone.

"You could, however, force Cabot to give the Concern to someone weaker. You taught Gustave a way to kill the Judge without being detected, which also left his victim alive long enough to pass the Concern to someone else. You expected Cabot would give it to his butler, but the butler didn't find him first. Shale did, and he escaped. You must have been furious when you learned that bad timing had wrecked your plan. But the situation could still be salvaged. Shale, you reasoned, did not know what he carried. Cabot, by the time Shale found him, had no tongue, no throat, and was barely sane; he could not have explained the situation to a Guardian ignorant of Craft. Nor would Shale's people flee Alt Coulumb after Cabot's murder: they had staked too much on their deal with Kos to be so easily stymied. The Blacksuits would find Shale and his Flight eventually, and you would trick Justice into letting you claim the Concern, as you almost did a few minutes ago."

"What proof do you have?" Denovo said archly. "If you lack documentary evidence, at least call witnesses like a civilized person. Say, those mercenaries you *claim* I hired."

"You took their memories after the job was complete."

"Impossible."

"Not for the greatest Craftsman mentalist in the history of the Hidden Schools. You tried to wipe Captain Pelham's mind last night. You were hasty, obvious; you must have been terrified when you realized Ms. Kevarian had hired him to escort us to Alt Coulumb. You had to destroy him before he let something slip that would implicate you."

"I've been in the Skeld Archipelago all week. I only arrived this morning, on the ferry. Unless you think I could accomplish such delicate work from halfway around the world."

"You were in Alt Coulumb last night, not Skeld."

"A ferrymaster, and a hundred twenty passengers, will corroborate my story. Every one saw me arrive this morning."

"Where were you before the ferry?"

"My hotel in Skeld. Really, Tara, I don't understand the point you're trying to make."

"You weren't in Skeld yesterday evening. You were in Alt Coulumb. This morning you flew out and circled back around."

"The city is a no-fly zone."

"You could get around that."

"Circumvent a divine interdict? Perhaps you can tell me how to manage such a miracle."

"Simple. All you need is something built to be stronger than gods." Tara took another step back. She was not afraid, but if she was right—and she *was* right—she wanted space between herself and the Professor.

She was new to Alt Coulumb, but in the last two days she had stood upon its rooftops and crouched in its basements, visited its sick and swam in its oceans. She had walked the mind of its god and traced the paths of his wounds. In two days, she had not once seen the city's sky bare of clouds, yet never had its air seemed humid, nor had the clouds threatened to break into storm. Alt Coulumb was usually clear in the autumn, Cat had said, because of the trade winds.

Weather was difficult to control, subject to the earth's shifting in its orbit and to the whims of the moon. Craftsmen and Craftswomen tampered with rain and cloud only in extremity. But more than a hundred years ago, the builders of the first sky-cities had learned that floating buildings were difficult to defend, and easy to conceal.

The skin beneath the cleft of Tara's collarbone bore a tiny blue circle, the first glyph she had ever received: the Glyph of Acceptance that marked her as a student of the Hidden Schools, entitled to take refuge there in times of need. That privilege had not been revoked at her graduation. Even a prodigal daughter might one day return home.

Tara pressed the tattoo, and it glowed. A tiny gap appeared in the cloud cover beyond the broken skylight, dilating rapidly as a cat's pupil in darkness. An electric chill passed through her.

Starlight shone through the gap in the clouds. Far above, trapped between earth and heaven, hung the crystal towers and gothic arches and double-helix staircases of the Hidden Schools. Walkways of silver ribbon stretched from building to building, and scholars paced on the balconies. Atop one crenellated dormitory, a corpse-fire glowed, students no doubt clustered about it, drinking and telling stories and maybe making love.

No shimmering staircase of starlight descended from Elder Hall, no rainbow bridge to bear her home. The schools' Craft of Ingress fought Kos's interdict as machines fight, deadlocked in absolute certainty. The schools themselves were mightier than the interdict, but the Craft of Ingress had been designed to admit eager young scholars, not extract Craftswomen from the heart of a god's own territory.

Fortunately, Tara did not want to leave Alt Coulumb. The parting of the clouds was enough for her purposes. She inhaled shadow and starfire. Night adhered to her skin and flowed into her mind.

"You brought the schools here," she said, "and used their camouflage to obscure the stars and moon, weakening the Guardians and Craftswomen set against you. It was the schools' broader no-fly zone, not Alt Coulumb's, which interrupted Ms. Kevarian's flight yesterday and almost killed us both.

"The schools gave you an excellent alibi. It may be impossible to wipe a man's mind from a hundred miles away, but a thousand feet of altitude is no obstacle for a master like you. The Hidden Schools are broader than that from end to end, and you wove your commands through my classmates' minds and mine with no trouble."

Denovo's stern expression yielded to a childlike smile. "Tara." He stuck his hands in his pockets. "You amaze me."

"You killed Kos Everburning, Professor."

"What do you expect to accomplish with this posturing? If you want a fight, strike me and get it over with."

"Justice is watching," she said.

"Justice is blind. I blinded her myself, twenty years before you were born." He removed one hand from his pocket and examined the blunt tips of his fingers. "If you hope these automata will descend on me like a parliament of rooks on a bad storyteller"—he gestured to the motionless Blacksuits—"you've forgotten the first law of design. Never make anything that can be used to hurt you. They'll remain where they stand until I finish my business."

For the first time since Cardinal Gustave burst in the skylight, Tara truly looked at the Blacksuits. They did not twitch from their immobile rows. "You've done horrible things."

"Not as horrible as you, or your boss." He shook his head, tone still conversational. "You deserted our side long ago, as did a great many Craftsmen. You settled for a pleasant illusion, the facile lie that we could have peace with gods. You gave up on the dream."

"You're one of the most powerful Craftsmen in the world. What more do you want?"

"Well, for starters, I'm not a god yet."

Tara blinked. "What?"

"You said I wanted Kos's power. Clever but wrong. Power I have. It's godhood I want. Immortality and might, free of sickness and decay."

"Impossible."

"Hardly. It's a logical extension of the first principles of Craft. I struck on the idea while at school. Gods draw strength from faithful masses. Couldn't a Craftsman do the same? It took years to work out the ramifications of that insight. I took my first tender steps with Elayne four decades ago, winning her trust to tap her power for myself. She noticed, and defeated me, but I elaborated on my theory by creating the Blacksuits, believers tied to their god by sick need rather than mutual love."

He smiled nostalgically. "I built my lab and consumed the strength of my dear students and colleagues. I became the most powerful Craftsman on this continent. What then? Rot into a skeleton? Flee death from one decaying body to the next? Or take arms against a god, slay him, and become him? I can climb through that Concern into Kos's body and take his place at the center of Alt Coulumb's unassailable faith. I will make this such a city as has never been seen, a fiery flood sweeping across the globe. I could hardly believe when the opportunity fell within my grasp."

"A shame that it's slipping away." Tara's knife flickered into being in her hand, a twist of moonlight curved like a fang.

Denovo's grin didn't fade. He started to shake his head, but then he *moved*, fast as an uncoiling spring. The distance between them evaporated. Dark energy roiled around his fist.

The colors of the world inverted and Tara was not flying but falling, her protective shadows broken and struggling vainly to reform. There was a fist-sized hole in her blouse that had not existed a moment ago, and she was bleeding.

The floor struck her shoulders—or was it the other way around?—and a brown wave rolled in from the corners of her vision to engulf her.

Denovo rubbed his palms together like a baker flouring his hands, and surveyed the ruined hall. A pack of gargoyles lay chained upon the floor. Tara, his dangerously persistent student, landed fifteen feet away, unconscious, blood leaking from the wound he had left in her gut. Elayne was spread-eagled on the ground nearby, twitching but immobile. She fought his control of her motor neurons, but had only succeeded in turning a pathetic, rough circle on the floor. The skinny priest knelt by his dead master.

The Concern hovered over the inert body of the Stone Man who had so nearly completed his mission. Who would have succeeded, had he known what he carried.

Denovo straightened the cuffs of his tweed jacket, brushed a few specks of glass and dust off the lapels, and advanced on the sphere of Craft that was the key to his divinity.

As he walked, he shot a jaunty salute at the statue of Justice. "Sorry you can't see this, old girl. It's beautiful." A bound Stone Woman threw herself in his path; he kicked her out of his way with a broad sweep of Craft, and stepped beneath the sphere. It glowed ten feet overhead, out of reach.

The corners of his mouth cricked up into a smirk that did not reach his eyes. Inhaling, he constructed in his mind a framework of pulleys and wheels to lift him up. Exhaling, he called upon his students and colleagues in the Hidden Schools to convince Kos's troublesome interdict that rising a handful of feet above the earth's surface did not constitute flight.

On his second indrawn breath he rose a few inches, and on his exhale nearly a foot. His smile broadened. He reached out to grasp the revolving sphere, and felt for the first time in his life unmixed gratitude toward the universe.

Then one hundred forty pounds of bony, high-velocity Novice Technician hit him in the small of the back.

The dark waters about Cat parted when the Cardinal fell, but closed in again as love of Justice filled her mind, and with it, love of Denovo, Justice's creator, who hovered above the earth, reaching for a pearl of orange light. Cat loved this man though he mocked Justice to Her face. Though he had killed a god. She loved him, and knew not why. She hated him for very good reasons.

She had seen Abelard turn from the Cardinal's body and watch Tara confront Denovo. Abelard remained crouched, seemingly in mourning, waiting for the right moment. As Denovo rose toward his unearthly prize, the priest began to run.

He launched himself from the earth and struck the Craftsman from behind. They fell together, locked in combat. Abelard scrambled for a choke hold as they hit the ground, legs wrapped tight around the smaller man's torso, but Denovo was built broad and dense like a wrestler, and twisted out of his adversary's lock.

Cat struggled to break the bonds of love. Chemical passions warred in her breast. An addiction, like any other. Once more she pressed Raz Pelham's fangs to her wrist.

Denovo broke Abelard's hold. Lightning crackled about his clawed hand as he brought it down on the young priest's chest.

For an instant, Denovo was a figure of deepest black with shock-white hair, standing before an audience of alabaster statues. When light and time righted themselves, Abelard lay still on the rough marble, the stub of his cigarette smoking where it protruded from his lips. Denovo rose to his feet.

Abelard's chest did not move. Through the Blacksuit Cat could see further into the red and violet ranges than most humans, and she saw him grow cold.

Cat forgot love, forgot duty, forgot everything in the shock of that sight: Abelard, still as if sleeping. A taut piano string snapped within her chest. This pain was hers, and this grief. She was herself, Catherine Elle beneath the Blacksuit.

She remembered two things. First, she owned her body. Second, the Stone Men, chained on the floor, were innocent of the crime for which they had been charged. They should be freed.

Tara lay in a lake of silver, eyes half-closed, half-open in the dawn moment between sleep and waking. She felt arms around her, cool and comforting. She stared into deep green, endless eyes that were also her own. She remembered pain. She remembered Seril's voice. "Permit me—"

Permit what?

Permit me to come inside.

Returning to her body, she had felt as if her soul were too large to fit her skin.

Seril's were the eyes she opened in the Temple of Justice, and Seril's was the heart that beat within her chest.

She felt her stomach, and found blood there but no pain. A web of moonlight closed her wound. She was not alone inside her mind. Seril overlaid her, silver and ancient and beautiful.

She heard eleven manacles spring open, and a chorus of vengeful roars from throats of stone. Flame crackled and lightning snapped and nameless powers clashed like deep brass cymbals.

She stood. The stars and moon shone through a hole in the clouds above. She felt every grain in the stone beneath her feet.

Her Guardians were free, and dancing.

Their dance did not go well. Three sprawled upon the ground, wings broken and silver flesh splintered, one dead and two dying. Aev, high priestess, great lady, wheeled in the air to strike with both claws against the translucent dome that shielded Denovo. Three others pressed the assault with her. A pair lay writhing in pain, trapped in nets of fine red threads that burned body and soul. Two more struggled to restrain a third, her eyes glazed and her movements puppetlike. David, too, battered against Denovo's shield, but the Professor reserved his high and vengeful Craft for Guardians alone.

She saw every strike, every riposte, every counter, though faster than human eye could follow. Denovo moved like an orchestra conductor behind the electric mist of his shield.

She advanced upon the battle without walking; her feet hovered a few inches above the ground. Moonlight gave the Guardians' arms strength and their wings speed and their claws power to pierce and rend and tear. Lightning struck Guardians Jain and Rael, and they collapsed, but Her light pulled them from the brink of death; boar-tusked Gar fell into a pit of infinite depth, but Her love became a long thin silver cord to draw him back. Moonlight closed about Ashe's mind, and freed her from Denovo's control.

Denovo turned his attention to Tara. Though his face was fixed in an expression of intense effort, his smile did not falter.

"You know," he said through the roar and clash, "I nearly missed fighting in the God Wars. I was one of the youngest to join the battle."

He spun Craft toward the orange sphere above, but She arrested it with moonlight. Thorns of shadow caught Aev, but She dulled their piercing tips. Denovo's Craft lashed out at Tara as a bolt of flame, and She turned it aside.

Her thoughts came slowly now, and with effort.

"You're not the first goddess I've fought," he said, calm and cold. "You cannot abandon your faithful. I strike at what you love, and you protect it. When you're stretched to the limit of your power, I squeeze. Just . . . a . . . bit."

His eyes narrowed, and the thorns about Aev's body were sharper, the hole into which Gar fell deeper, darker, hungrier, the spear of flame pointed at Tara's heart more swift and sure.

With a sound like a ringing bell, the light of the world popped free from its perch in Tara's skull and hung revealed before her, a beautiful woman of frostlight and stone bound to those she could not abandon by cords of her own making.

Tara's wound reopened, and blood seeped through cracks in the cauterized flesh. Her mind was hollow, her own again, and the world not Seril's but hers. The Guardians' names she forgot, but she saw Cat curled in a fetal ball amid discarded iron restraints, trapped in a net of red wire. She had freed the Guardians. Good.

Ms. Kevarian lay on the ground, and next to her, Abelard. Unmoving.

"That's the trouble with ties," Denovo said. "They bind both ways."

Denovo reached out with a rope of flame to draw the sphere toward him.

Tara screamed, wove starfire into her own rope, and lassoed the sphere. Denovo was a supernova of Craft. He pulled and she pulled and Seril pulled and the gargoyles redoubled their attack, and still the sphere approached his outstretched hand. He grinned.

Tara blinked, and the darkness endured.

Tara reclined in a leather armchair beneath a glittering chandelier. Ms. Kevarian stood across from her, dressed in a businesswoman's black and in full control of herself.

Alexander Denovo sat in another chair to Tara's left, mouth slack with shock.

"What the hell?"

"We are between instants," Ms. Kevarian explained.

"How did you bring me here?"

"Ties bind both ways," she observed. "I thought I would give you an opportunity to surrender."

Denovo laughed outright. "Surrender? Apotheosis is within my grasp."

"Don't the odds trouble you?"

"I can hold out for the moments I require to assimilate Kos's power." He manifested a pipe out of dreamstuff and began to smoke it. "Then the opposition will fall."

"I can't guarantee your safety if you don't surrender now."

"When I am a god, Elayne, I will break you, body and soul."

Her eyes and her voice were made of diamond. "I'll take that as a no."

"Boss—" But the moment slipped, and Tara fell between earth and heaven.

Alexander Denovo whirled within his protective dome, and through electric distortion saw Elayne Kevarian, standing. He ordered her to sit, to surrender, to die, but his commands rolled off the ice of her mind. The young priest's body lay prone at her feet. A curving design, wet, red, and intricate, glimmered on the floor around them.

Breath caught in his throat.

Elayne Kevarian had lain prone under his control, twitching, pathetic, circling in place, bloody fingers grasping at pale stone. She had completed the circle. Drawn it in her own blood, worked it with sigils crude in their calligraphy but elegant in their architecture.

She stood within a resurrection circle, over a dead priest whose lips still clutched a smoldering cigarette. But this circle was not drawn for a man. It was drawn for a god.

Denovo called on all his Craft, releasing the gargoyles and their goddess and Tara, everything save for his hold on the fiery sphere. He threw doom and lightning against Elayne and rent the earth beneath her feet and cast her into the outer hells, or tried. Shadow seeped from her, devouring starlight and torchlight and his Craft alike. The blood circle blazed the myriad colors of pure white light.

Within the shadow, within the circle, the flame of a cigarette tip flared.

Abelard fell. It was a familiar sensation.

He fell farther, faster, and this time the fire did not merely linger at the edge of his vision and the borders of his mind. It burst upon him in a flood. It charred his soul and burnt his body to a cinder. It danced upon him the dance that destroyed and renewed. This fire was the heartbeat of the world. The fire was love. The fire was life.

The fire was his God.

A faint remnant of his logical mind remembered that for some reason, though he had smoked constantly since his Lord's death, in three days he had not once used a lighter or a match. Always he passed flame from one cigarette to the next.

He surrendered to God. Every breath of smoke lingering in his lungs, every trace of fire that calmed him in his hours of need, he gave them forth freely.

He was the size of a city, the size of the world, the size of the universe, smaller than the smallest atom. He was ash, and he burned eternal in a million suns.

Brilliant and new as a phoenix, Kos the Everburning rose from the ember at the tip of Abelard's cigarette.

There is a space beyond or beneath the world, where all that is not, which creates all that is, collects and congregates. Shadow dances and wars with light there. Life and mind play their eternal game of flight and pursuit.

That place looks like nothing the human mind can grasp, so think of it as a bar: polished wood, brass fixtures, dim lights, beer.

A woman sat alone, beautiful and lost and full of rage so old it had become a dull ache deadening every newborn sensation. She cradled a half-empty pint glass.

A man entered the bar from a door that had not been there before. He stood waiting for a thousand years as they measured time, but she did not acknowledge him.

He looked more lost than she, and more recently wounded. He opened his mouth to speak, but had no words in whatever tongue they used. He reached for her. Placed his hand on her shoulder.

For another millennium she did not respond to his touch.

She stared into the dregs of her glass. Her arm floated slowly upward, against the weight of history.

She closed her hand around his.

Tara heard Denovo scream, an ugly sound full of desire and thwarted ambition. Shadow rolled from Ms. Kevarian's circle to obscure the world. The air grew warm.

Fire broke reality.

She closed her eyes on reflex, and was nearly blinded in her second sight as webs of god-flame spun through Alt Coulumb with a speed beyond speed. The numberless threads that kept Kos's city running had hung slack; now they snapped taut as a spring-loaded trap. Across town, fire erupted on the altars of Kos's Sanctum. A beacon of holy light shone atop the Sanctum tower; a cry issued from the crowd below, wordless and exultant as the shadows vanished from their faces. Their candle flames leapt for joy.

Here in Justice's Hall, the Concern bloomed and fell like the folds of a bridal veil upon the silver shade that was Seril Green-Eyed. Denovo's defenses shriveled and snapped.

It was possible, Tara had said to Abelard, for a god to hide himself from obligations within the faith of his disciples, letting all but his consciousness die. It hurt more than death, and only the strongest deities could endure the pain for long. But it was possible. If you were powerful and your need was great—if, for example, this were the only way to save your long-lost love and avenge a grave crime, and if you knew that the fatal draw on your power would soon pass, leaving your body unharmed and ripe for rehabitation—you just might manage it.

Kos was awake once more, strong, and angry.

Seril vanished. Tara heard a great grinding of stone and looked up. The statue of Justice opened the pits of its eyes, and they blazed green.

Denovo hunched into a fighting crouch, knife out, nostrils flaring. The Guardians lurched out of striking range, but David was not so fast, and Denovo's knife slashed, sharp as thought.

Tara was faster. She reached David in a step, thrust him out of the way, and intercepted Denovo's knife with her own. The two blades met in arcs of light. Denovo's broke.

The Blacksuits moved.

Fifty fell upon Denovo, but Cat beat them all, grasping his neck as her colleagues wrapped arms of iron about his limbs and body. Craft struck him, too: the Craft of Elayne Kevarian.

His eyes rolled white, and he fell limp.

Tara stepped back.

Breath came heavy in her throat.

She turned from the unconscious professor to her boss. Ms.

Kevarian was covered in cuts and bruises, fingers bloody and clothing charred.

At her feet sat Novice Technician Abelard, rubbing his forehead. An extinguished cigarette dangled from his lips.

EPILOGUE

Sunset cast shadows of Alt Coulumb onto the soft waves of the turning tide. Along the docks, ropes creaked and boots tromped over wet planks; women swore and men strained against the weight of their burdens as the merchant fleet prepared to face the deep. Lookouts climbed webs of sheet and sail to nest in the rigging, and harpooners manned their posts warily, barbed and poisoned spears in hand. Serpents waited beyond the coastal shelf, and every sailor had sat vigil at least once for friends dragged screaming into the deep.

Raz Pelham emerged from his cabin onto the deck of the *Kell's Bounty*. The lingering sun burned his tanned skin. He had never felt more ready to sail. Twice he had visited this city at the bidding of Craftsmen, twice been brought to the edge of death and beyond. Affairs had fallen out better this time than forty years ago, but still he yearned for the water. Land lied to the feet, and to the soul. You stand, it whispered, upon unchanging ground. You build upon certainty, and your foundations will never crumble.

Ms. Kevarian had told him, on her first visit to Alt Coulumb four decades past, that beneath its solid shell the world was an ocean of molten rock and metal. Captain Pelham preferred the sea, which misled but seldom lied. The world flowed, the world changed, and many-mouthed terrors lurked beneath its surface.

According to the Church and the Crier's Guild, the city had reclaimed its usual equilibrium in the three weeks since Denovo's arrest. The College of Cardinals pronounced Kos's resurrection a miracle passing understanding, and Gustave a martyr to his Lord. This rhetoric did not persuade Alt Coulumb's people, who sensed the near passage of disaster and moved in its wake like sailors after a bitter storm. They did the work the world asked of them—bargained hard, loaded and unloaded cargo, paid their debts, and drank their wine—but beneath routine and ritual, Raz sensed a growing apprehension.

More had changed than they imagined. Pieces of the truth would surface in the coming months. Already moonlight shone mingled with fire in their dreams. Waves moved over and through Alt Coulumb, scouring its heart and tearing new channels in its soil.

The boatswain called to him from the hold. The last of their cargo loaded, the *Bounty* stood ready to depart on the evening tide for Iskar, bearing a cargo of luxury goods, textiles, and books. Harpooners stood ready, the windweaver sat cross-legged at the bow, and scarred and tattooed deckhands went about their disparate business.

Raz bared his fangs to the world as the sun fell below the horizon.

His smile faltered when he heard someone call his name from shore. Reluctantly, he approached the gangplank.

On the dock, dressed in loose slacks, a blue shirt, and a battered leather jacket, stood Catherine Elle. Her skin looked ruddier than he remembered from their last meeting, weeks before.

"Captain," she called out when he did not speak. "I wanted to drop by before you left." A pair of dockhands walked between them, wheeling a wagon piled with bales of wheat. "To apologize."

"For what?"

"For hitting you while your back was turned."

"Hit?" He shook his head. "You broke my neck."

"You got better." She bit down as if to catch the sentence's tail before it escaped her teeth. "And I wanted to apologize for what happened in the hospital."

"That wasn't your fault."

"Not entirely." She shifted her weight from one leg to the other, and ran a hand through her hair. "I don't think even Tara knew her suggestion would take me that far. I think I have a long road ahead of me."

She didn't say the next words, so he did. "But you're starting."

"I'm starting."

"I accept your apology."

A brief, bright smile crossed her face, but she stilled it. "Will you come back this way?"

"Sometime next month, I think."

"Maybe we'll see each other again."

"Maybe." Twenty feet down the dock, some ship's steward sprinted cursing through the crowd after a fleeing urchin who clutched a fat purse to his chest. "You have time? I can show you the *Bounty*."

"No, thanks," she replied. "I have work."

"See you around."

She nodded. "See you around." She turned from him and stepped back into the milling crowd. Two paces, three, he followed her retreating back before a spark of deep gray gleamed at her neck and flowed upward, out, over her clothes. She became a statue of quicksilver. Broad wings rose from her back, and spread. In a streak, she was gone.

He watched her go.

It was time to leave.

Tara found Ms. Kevarian packing at eight o'clock that evening. Her black valise stood open on her office desk, and as Tara watched, she placed into it five folded suits, six shirts, a black robe, ten thick tomes of theoretical Craft, a writing stand, three vials of ink (one silver, one red, one black), two cheap novels, seven pens (three for contracting, one for cancellation, two more for professional work, and one used exclusively in personal discourse), a silver bowl, a bell of cast iron, a box of bone chalk, and five blood candles.

"Only the essentials, boss?"

"Only the essentials, Ms. Abernathy," she said without turning. "But one must never be caught unprepared."

"Leaving already." Tara glanced around the room. The bed was made, its corners sharp and its covers turned down just as her own had been when they arrived in Alt Coulumb three weeks before. Not a speck of dust adhered to the bolsters, nor to the slick surface of her boss's desk.

"For the Archipelago. An infestation of sea-spirits has"—she searched for the appropriate word—"decimated a fishing Concern. They have need of our services."

Tara noted her use of the plural. "You've heard from Kelethras, Albrecht, and Ao, then? I'm not to be cast into the outer darkness?"

"Confirmation of your continued employment arrived two days ago. It did not seem worth mentioning. You know as well as I do that your performance has been exemplary. Though the particulars of the Church's case are not public, rumor does not always respect client confidentiality. The great firms know your name, and the quality of your work. Your escapades at the Hidden Schools will not be forgotten, but neither will your success here. Management would be fools to let you go, and though they may be risk-averse, they are not foolish."

Fighting an urge to smile, Tara ran her hand over the pristine surface of Ms. Kevarian's desk. "Sea-serpents, though. Seems simple, after everything we've been through in the last few weeks."

"Make no mistake." Ms. Kevarian closed her valise with a snap like the sealing of a coffin. "We've just begun our work. The reunification of Justice and Seril remains unstable. Seril's children are still unwelcome within Alt Coulumb, and the goddess's return is a secret, with good reason. Many blame her for abandoning the city to fight in the God Wars, and for the deaths her Guardians caused. That's not to mention the dubious status of Kos's contracts after his resurrection. We will return here again, soon."

"I wanted to talk to you about that." Tara's hand rose to her stomach. Beneath her shirt, the wound Denovo gave her was swaddled in thick bandages, still healing.

"About what?"

"About Kos," Tara said. Three weeks later, the afterimage of the god's rebirth still burned in bruised purple before her eyes. "And one or two related matters."

"What remains to be explained?"

She wanted to get to the point, but Ms. Kevarian's patient expression drained her courage. She had prepared for this moment, but it felt worse than she had expected. "When did you first know he was hiding in Abelard's cigarette?"

"When I met the boy in Gustave's office. I've seen hidden gods before, and recognized the signs. I caught a vanishing glimpse before Kos realized he was being observed and hid himself deeper than I could follow. He was almost dead in truth, comatose by human comparison. I reasoned that he must have mistrusted his clergy if he hid from them, so I kept Abelard away from other priests, in your company or in mine."

"You said he hid almost as soon as you saw him. It must have happened so fast. How did you know you weren't mistaken?"

"Simple." She leaned back against her desk. "I killed Abelard."

"What?"

"I pulled his life away, slowly. As I drew it from him, more poured in from another source: a fire beyond this world. I half-expected him to realize the truth then, but he was oblivious to Kos's presence, even as god-ash accumulated in his lungs. He began to see like a god or a Craftsman as he investigated the Sanctum's boiler room; he used the vision to good effect, but failed to realize its source. Didn't think anything of it when his so-called cigarette flame nearly killed that shadow-monster, either. Engineers: they spend so much time solving physical problems and obeying physical rules, they forget that nonphysical phenomena obey rules every bit as strict."

Tara imagined Ms. Kevarian casually snuffing out Abelard's life to test a theory. "You killed him when you took him to visit the ambassadors. Stand in their offices and look like a good little cleric, you said."

"I needed an opportunity to make the experiment, and to demonstrate to Denovo's clients that Kos still lived. They pulled their support from Alexander tacitly. Without that, he would have been more powerful when we faced him."

The stars beyond the window struggled against the light from Ms. Kevarian's desk lamp. "Very professional, boss."

"It was an intellectual challenge: how to draw our adversaries out without betraying our hand?" Satisfaction manifested in the curve of her lips, in the downward cast of her eyes and the sturdy line of her shoulders.

It did not last for long.

"That's what I thought. And it's why I wanted to talk to you."

Ms. Kevarian waited. When Tara did not continue, she said, "Yes?"

"You knew Kos was still alive, but you kept that knowledge from me, from Abelard, from everyone. You suspected Denovo was behind Kos's death, and maybe even Cabot's, all along; why else did you agree to meet with him in the dark room at Xiltanda, where you were functionally defenseless? You expected him to control your mind, because only when he had you at his mercy would he feel sure enough to lay all his cards on the table and begin the final phase of his plan. And you sent Abelard to me, knowing that, with his information and my own, I'd be able to piece together the truth, confront Denovo, and distract him long enough for you to get free. You guided my investigation so I would find whatever proof existed of Denovo's involvement. I'd ask why you didn't tell me your suspicions, but I already know: you thought I might confront him before you were prepared. You moved all of us like game pieces."

Those straight shoulders and that curved neck stiffened. "You're good, Tara. Without you, I could not have uncovered the gargoyles' role in events, let alone Seril's existence. Your work was invaluable."

"Thank you," she said. "I enjoyed that work, too. All of it. I was at least as manipulative as you. More so, in some ways: I stole Shale's face, I warped Cat's mind, while you barely used any Craft at all. But in the end I'm not sure either of us is any better than Denovo. He used other people because he wanted to become a god. We did the same because we wanted to win, wanted to be paid, wanted to see him fall. We're leaving behind us a broken city, and two resurrected gods. Alt Coulumb doesn't yet know the depth of the changes we have wrought upon it. And soon we'll be gone, because we've done our job."

Ms. Kevarian did not respond.

"My family left the east for Edgemont during the God Wars." Tara willed her voice not to shake. "They had good reasons, but they ran, and I think . . . I think somehow their running away became my running away. I ran from Edgemont for anywhere else, away from everything I knew. I think for once I shouldn't run. I know you've risked yourself to help me, to give me a chance at the firm. I'm more grateful than I can say. I enjoy working with you, and I owe you my life. But I don't want to leave. I want to stay here, and finish what we've started."

A terrible silence followed. Ms. Kevarian stood silhouetted by the moon, alone. Tara wanted to apologize, to say she hadn't meant anything by it, to fall in line. She did not. "What," said Ms. Kevarian after a time, "do you intend to do in Alt Coulumb if you remain?"

"The Church of Kos needs a Craftswoman on hand, someone who knows the city well enough to help them handle the aftershocks of Kos's resurrection and Seril's return. I can be that person. They need me. And I need to stop running away from everything I've done. I can't stay one step ahead of the mob forever."

"Remaining here might be another form of running."

"I know. But I think this is different."

Flickering lantern light cast Ms. Kevarian's shadow long on the carpet. Tara focused on the velvet sky, and waited. Ms. Kevarian raised her head.

"I understand."

"You do?"

"It's a silly idea, and it indicates a degree of immaturity on your part as a Craftswoman. But it's your idea. And you're young. There's plenty of time for you to grow." They exchanged a long glance, and Tara saw Ms. Kevarian as she must have been decades before, full and young and twenty-five, staring down a long dark path toward power. "Do it. These people need someone to keep them from killing one another."

"Thank you." The words sounded hollow, and the room seemed oddly empty.

"I'll swing back through Alt Coulumb when I'm done in the Archipelago a couple months from now," she said at last. "To see if you're ready to get back to work. You're a great talent, Ms. Abernathy. I will not lose you this easily."

"Thanks, boss."

Clergies do not accept change well as a rule. The struggle over who would succeed to the office of Technical Cardinal of the Church of Kos Everburning was fierce, pitting three distinct reform factions against two breeds of theological conservatives. Some of the priests praised Seril's return, and wished to admit Her to the liturgy. Others felt the gargoyles and their Goddess were best left alone. Seril Herself did not deign to address Her lover's clergy, which only fueled the debate.

Fortunately, the various prelates soon realized that whichever of them held the position of Technical Cardinal would be responsible for working with Elayne Kevarian and Tara Abernathy, and the brewing sectarian violence cooled to a simmer of backroom deals and machinations. Rival factions held long knives ready beneath their robes and waited for the Craftswomen to leave. In the meantime, Cardinal Gustave's old office remained empty.

With vacancy came uncertainty. None save Sister Miriel noticed when Novice Technician Abelard took advantage of this uncertainty to adjust a few time sheets and schedule his attendance upon God for the more reasonable interval between ten at night and one in the morning.

This was the only reward he claimed. In the preceding weeks, members of each faction had sought him out to promise promotion, elevation, sainthood in return for his support. Abelard had borne Lord Kos inside his heart (or in his cigarette—the difference didn't seem to matter). Whispers about his miracles resounded through Sanctum halls like echoes off flat rock, but Abelard did not heed them. He knew the truth. The prelates had not saved Alt Coulumb. Nor had Cardinal Gustave. Nor had he, for that matter.

All Abelard wanted was to think, and pray. The rest of the world could wait.

He knelt before the Altar of the Defiant, his back to the window beyond which spread Alt Coulumb's roads, its elevated trains, its towers and its palaces and the great globe of its sky, all shining like diamonds on black felt. Before him, the Rekindled Flame burned on its throne. Life beat on the drum of his heart.

"Glory to Thy Flame, Thou Ever-burning, Ever-transforming

Majesty," Abelard chanted, kneeling, before the glistening brass and chrome altar. He exhaled, and waited.

In the space between thoughts, he heard a voice.

Hello there, old friend, God said.

Deep below the Temple of Justice was a cell, well-apportioned but spare, walled on three sides by rock and on the fourth by a cold iron mesh. No sunlight reached there, nor starlight nor the light of the moon. A water clock on the room's sole desk told time, but it lost minutes on the hour and this effect had compounded itself over the last three weeks. The cell's only occupant thought the time was ten minutes before noon, rather than a quarter past one in the morning.

Alexander Denovo had just finished what he believed was lunch.

A heavy iron door swung open. Heels clicked on stone. He looked up, trying to place the stride, and succeeded a moment before Elayne Kevarian walked into view. She looked as one looks who has been contentedly busy for some time. He looked as one looks who has been idle and happy.

"Hello, Alexander," she said.

"Elayne." His nod was a parody of manners. "I would invite you to sit, but my jailers neglected to provide me with a receiving chair."

"You find your new quarters pleasant?"

"They are to my liking, for the moment. I have had time to read, to think, and to plan."

"Plan for what? You're here until the Blacksuits decide what to do with you. You have remained inviolate thus far only because they have not yet formulated a suitable punishment for deicide."

"I'm quite safe," he said with certainty. "Justice, possessed or not by your tame gargoyle-goddess, cannot harm me herself. Nor will Alt Coulumb extradite me to the Hidden Schools, or to the mercies of Iskar or Camlaan or even the Gleb; while Justice cannot harm me, neither can she countenance my release, and my crimes against Kos and Seril are not crimes in the lands of the Deathless Kings. So here I stay. Cocooned in iron below the earth."

"You sound suspiciously comfortable with that fact."

He shrugged. "I have many friends. They will loose me on the world again. Hell, you would do it yourself, if I asked."

Even in this cell, he had been able to draw some power to him, devouring the souls of rats and centipedes and deep earth-tunneling insects, feeding off the few taproots that extended so far beneath the city. He put that power into his voice, but Elayne batted it away with a blink of her eyes.

"Not likely."

"It was worth a shot."

"You're a bastard, Alexander."

"A brilliant bastard. I won't stay here forever. I've learned a great deal in the last few months. How to slay a deity in secret, and seize his power." He listed these things as if they were items on an invoice. "It's amazingly simple. I will achieve godhood one day. I'll find you, Elayne, and I'll do such beautiful things with you. Twist your soul into a pretzel and skewer your dignity with fishhooks. It'll be like it once was. You and me."

His tone was wistful and wicked, calculated for the shudder it invoked in her stomach. She stilled herself before it reached her shoulders.

He stood, and paced the confines of his cell. "There's nothing you can do. This cold iron grate? Woven with divine Craft. You could smite it with powers the . . . children . . . who populate this city have never imagined, and I'd sit here smiling. I'm snug as a chick in its egg, babe, until it's time for me to break this little world open and come hunting for you. And Tara of course. Sweet, stubborn girl. So proud." He assumed an airy, daydreaming tone of voice.

Her eyes closed, and so his did, too. He saw her as a python outlined in blue ice, filling the hallway. Her tongue flitted out to probe the iron lattice, found no gap in its protection, and retreated.

They opened their eyes at the same time. An irrational chill pricked up the hairs on the back of Denovo's neck. For no reason he could determine, Elayne was smiling.

"You're right," she said, with a perfunctory nod. "There's no possible way I can damage you through this cage."

He nodded, the lascivious gleam in his eye giving way to uncertainty.

"You worked it all out to perfection, Alexander. You planned Kos's murder and your own ascension, Cabot's assassination and Pelham's attack on Iskar. You anticipated the Church's asking me to represent them. You knew just how to slide back into control of my mind, and I expect you planned an alternative strategy if you failed at that. I do not doubt you have an escape plan, nor that if you continue down this path one day you will succeed, and make Ms. Abernathy and me grovel and scream and force us to commit all the other depravities you've dreamt of down your lonely, desperate, and angry life.

"But you made one crucial mistake."

"Oh?" He crossed his arms over his chest.

"You used a bound shadow to watch over Cardinal Gustave's dagger, in case he turned on you."

"Yes, and that god-benighted novice of yours let it loose. I am amazed he escaped alive." He nodded. "An error in judgment, I admit, but hardly crucial."

"Oh, you misunderstand me." Elayne shook her head. "Your use of the shadow wasn't a mistake. It was an efficient guardian, invisible to my own search of the Sanctum because its obedience to you was not ensured by direct Craft but by the terms under which you summoned it. You're right to be amazed at Abelard's survival. Your trap almost killed him, and several of his fellow priests, when he unwittingly set it free.

"I saved them. Ate your shadow, in fact, right in front of Abelard. You should have seen him, jaw slack and eyes bugged out." She laughed a little, and he laughed with her. "I took that darkness into me, but I did not destroy it. I made it mine."

He stopped laughing. Then he stopped smiling altogether.

"You made your one great mistake in the carriage between the Xiltanda and Justice's temple. You kissed me."

He thought back to that strange sensation as they kissed: a tingle of power and something else, like a worm slithering into his mouth. He remembered his surprise at her ingenuity. He had bound her Craft. She should not have been able to do anything to him.

She raised her hand, fingers crooked into a claw. He felt a sudden tightness in his chest. Something many-legged and sharp moved within his gullet.

"I did not employ the shadow against you in the Temple of Justice," she said, "because it was more poetic to use Kos. Besides, as Tara's mentor, I feel compelled to set a less bloodthirsty example. Call me a sentimentalist if you must."

"Elayne," he said, breath coming shallow and fast in his chest, "they'll know. Kill me here, and they'll know."

"You said it yourself. No Craft of mine can penetrate that iron mesh. I've given you no food, no water, no poison. Prisoners die of heart attacks all the time."

"Elayne."

Her tone remained cool. "You murdered one of the few gods in this world who never hurt a single Craftsman. You mutilated a goddess and perverted her teachings. You warped a priest into a weapon and taught him how to kill so his victims would persist in pain. You've broken countless people and bent them to your will, and you enjoyed breaking the women most of all."

"You bitch!" He leapt from his chair toward her, hands outstretched, mind consumed by rage. "You fucking—"

She closed her hand.

The world stopped without slowing.

He fell. Blood leaked from his mouth and pooled about him on the stone floor.

"Goodbye, Alexander," she said before she left.